The
Vampire
of Plainfield

The Vampire of Plainfield

Kristopher Rufty

SINISTER GRIN PRESS

MMXV

Austin, Texas

Sinister Grin Press

Austin, TX

www.sinistergrinpress.com

October 2015

"The Vampire of Plainfield" © 2015 Kristopher Rufty

This is a work of collected Fiction. All characters depicted in this book are fictitious, and any resemblance to actual events or persons, living or dead, is purely coincidental.

All rights reserved. No part of this book may be reproduced in whole or in part without the publisher's written consent, except for the purposes of review.

Cover Art by Jim Agpalza

Book Design by Frank Walls

Text Design by Travis Tarpley

ISBN 978-1-944044-05-3

For Malfi.

Acknowledgements

This book was a fun, yet difficult journey. Since I tried to be as respectful as possible, I needed some facts to make the story work. I thank Steve Golla for his input. Being a Plainfield native (and a great friend), his help and input for accuracy is very much appreciated. I also want to thank my wife, who always makes sure I have the opportunity to write my bizarre stories. Mega thanks goes to Paul Goblirsch and Tristan Thorne, for saying yes when I pitched this book—an idea that's been slogging around my head for a long time, with many false starts, probably would have never been written without their positivity. I also want to thank Ronald Malfi for his endless encouragement over the last several months. He's been this story's biggest fan from the get-go. And more thanks goes to my pre-reader, Tod Clark—the man who takes my jumbled first drafts and helps me fashion them into something coherent.

Author's Note

Make no mistake, Ed Gein was a *genuine* monster. There's no denying the terror and shame he inflicted on the small, family-oriented town of Plainfield, Wisconsin. This story is a complete work of fiction from the peculiar mind of a writer who enjoys ghost stories and tales of things that go bump in the night. This book is not meant to glorify Ed Gein, his sins, or his crimes. Some names have been altered. Many institutions, businesses, and street names from that time have also been changed. So, please, just take this book for what it is meant to be: a (with any luck) scary and thrilling story about a human monster that clashes with a supernatural monster and the drama of those stuck in the middle.

Plainfield is a real town; however, I would not recommend visiting for a Gein ghost walk. They do *not* take kindly to trespassing strangers, and would like—with good reason—for us to leave them be.

The Weirdees

Geiner:

*"There once was a man named Ed
Who wouldn't take a woman to bed.
When he wanted to diddle,
He cut out the middle,
And hung the rest in the shed."*

-1-

The shovel stabbed into the earth. The ground was hardened from the cold which made the noise as loud as a rifle blast in the silence of the night.

Ed winced.

Making enough racket to wake the dead.

Pausing, he peered down at the slanted headstone. In the moonlight, the old marker was a pale grin. The hair on his neck stiffened.

Don't get spooked.

Though Ed felt more at peace in them than almost anywhere else, graveyards could be creepy places. Sometimes he let his imagination get the best of him. Mama said it was one of his weaknesses.

And even in his forties, Ed had an imagination that sometimes went rampant.

Chuckling to himself, he shook his head. He should feel at home in this minute graveyard.

Nobody here to bother you.

He was with friends.

Nodding, Ed clapped his glove-covered hands together. He put the tip of the blade on the ground and stamped it in with the bottom of his boot. He hefted out a mound of compacted soil. Wisps of grass poked out like little green hairs. It was good seeing green again after so many months of harsh cold. Spring was near, and he was ready to welcome it.

He tossed the clump of hardened dirt aside, starting a pile that would be a minor hillock by the time he was done. There hadn't been a fresh fall of snow in nearly a week, but the strips of what still lingered had frozen into sparkling cement. The lantern, hanging from a tree limb, threw down an orange shimmer across the solid white crust. With the sickle moon sitting crooked above him like a toenail clipping and the lantern below, he had enough for light, but not so much he should worry about being spotted. This graveyard was small, tucked off the road in the woods. No caretaker to worry about unless he was here during daylight hours.

He was surprised he'd found it. He'd driven past the narrow path that etched through the woods many times. Never had any idea what was at the end of the trail until this morning.

Hadn't popped that tire, I still wouldn't know.

Probably the oldest graveyard around. And he'd found it by accident.

Did anybody else know it was back here?

Doubt it.

What had made him wander the trail, he couldn't say. Just a feeling inside had told him to start walking. He'd obliged, whistling as he'd strolled along with his hands in the pockets of his coat. Deep in the woods, the set of three graves sat on a small section of land that was devoid of grass. The olden headstones were blank, packed together and jutted from coffee dark soil the ice didn't cover. Even the trees surrounding the plot looked dead. Their frail, skeletal limbs looked ready to break apart. The trunks were hollowed out shells, what was inside melted away.

The graves were inside a fence. There were two gates: one in front, the other in back. Both were taller than him and bolted to the rusted iron enclosure. The front entry squeaked when Ed had opened it just enough to squeeze through. After one quick look around, Ed had decided then he would come back tonight and explore.

His tools were displayed on the flattened duffel bag in a row like a doctor's instruments—the pickax, another smaller shovel, and a woodsaw. He'd picked this grave because of the unnatural shape of the headstone. Narrowed at the top, it reminded him of a giant blade of rock stabbing up from the earth.

Ed took a break from digging. He backhanded the sweat off his brow. His gloves felt stiff and itchy on his damp skin.

He was down to his knees in the hole.

A rush of mild wind howled through the trees, shoving against his heavy coat and whipping his pants against his sore legs. Every muscle in his body ached. Even the marrow of his bones hurt. Wisconsin's bitter breezes always nipped with nasty teeth, but here in the graveyard, it felt as if it had fangs.

He tugged his checkered hunter's cap down. The wool did little to keep his head warm, but it was better than having nothing at all.

He resumed digging, letting his mind focus on the blade burrowing into the dirt. He flung the shovel to the side, launching the compacted soil. When it bespattered against the pile, he was able to count each clod that rolled down.

The next time he paused to check his progress, the hole reached his hips. The soil was mushy like clay, yet hard and cold. His arms were tired. How long had he been digging? Felt like forever. Even in this nasty cold, sweat streamed down his face. He wanted to rest. But this close to the treasure awaiting him, he didn't dare. And he knew there was a treasure below his feet, waiting.

He kept working.

With time, the hole developed into a tiny room with four walls of dirt that reached above his head. Any moment the tip of the shovel should strike something solid.

And it did within two minutes—a deep, firm *thump*.

Ed sighed with great relief.

Flipping the shovel around, he used its head to scrape away the powdery remains. Soon, an ancient toe-pincher coffin was unveiled. It looked pale and old under the gray moonlight. Built of wood, the top was wedge-shaped and narrowed as it reached the bottom. The cracked lid was coated in a slimy residue of mold and sludge.

A tingle of excitement coursed through him. Goosebumps hardened the skin of his arms.

Ed needed the lantern. Leaning the shovel against the dirt wall, he stepped across the coffin and reached up. His fingers gripped the hole's rim and held him as he climbed out.

Above ground, he brushed the dirt off his pants, then fetched the lantern from where it hung on the branch of a withered tree. Returning to the hole, he set the lantern close to the edge and carefully crawled back inside. Then he pulled the lantern down in with him.

He set the lantern at the foot of the coffin. The lantern's murky luster was like looking through a glass of piss. The smell of burning oil filled the tight space.

He sauntered to the bowed head of the casket, grabbed the shovel, and sank to a crouch. He lodged the narrowed blade under the lip of the lid. Gritting his teeth, he pulled up.

Strained.

Pressure bulged in his forehead, causing his eyes to throb.

The lid moved very little.

Stopping, he wiped away sweat. Took several deep breaths. And tried again.

The lid popped open with a splintered screech.

After taking a moment to catch his breath, he set the shovel off to his side. He gazed at the casket. The closure hung halfway open like the top of a lunchbox.

Ed waddled back into a narrow gutter of space beside the coffin. Crouched, he flung the lid high. Immediately, he was hit with an unbearable odor that gagged him. It felt like invisible dank hands had shoved their way down his throat, and squeezed his lungs.

"Ugh..." Ed coughed.

Trapped inside the casket with the corpse rot was another repugnant odor.

Garlic?

Brittle bulbs were spread inside the coffin. More were in piles pressed against the casket's inner walls. Though they were rotted and old and black, they were still intact and identifiable.

Elbows on his knees, Ed used his hand to fan away the fumes. He knuckled tears out of his eyes and stared back into the coffin.

The shriveled body of a woman lay amongst the garlic.

She had long hair the color of straw. Her eye sockets were hollow black chasms, her cheeks sunken back and cracking down to the jawline like mossy vines. Hints of cheek and jaw bones could be seen through the ragged gashes. Lips were gnarled back in a ghastly grin, exposing rotting teeth, and flaccid gums.

Two of her front teeth narrowed into points.

Like fangs.

Ed went tight and sick inside.

The pointed teeth weren't the only thing making his skin feel as if it were shrinking. Her head was in the wrong place. Instead of being the crown of her body, it was between her legs, pressed into the folds of the silky white gown she wore. The impressions of her scrawny thighs could be seen through the dirty garment. Where her head *should* be was a wrinkled nub between two boney shoulders.

Her head was chopped off!

A clean cut, by the looks of the neck. There was no tatty gradient, just a flat stump of old skin and bone.

The white gown bedecking the headless corpse was fancy and glossy, with noodle-thin straps over her leathery skin. The nails on her hands and toes had curled over the tops of each digit like talons.

He'd dug up many decrepit bodies. None had ever looked like this. Usually they withered down to nothing but some bedraggled clothes, and bones. She still had most of her skin, albeit decayed and shriveled. He could tell just by what was left of her that she had once been beautiful.

But the teeth...

He'd never seen teeth so sharp on a person. Looked like the teeth of a lion had been stuffed inside her rubbery mouth.

Ed removed his gloves, sitting them on her stomach. He inspected the rest of her. Her collarbone had started to show. He counted four visible ribs.

Touching the dress, the material felt smooth under his fingers. He moved his hand to her chest. She had two pruned lumps for breasts that felt hard as walnuts in his kneading hands.

The back of his head went numb. He rubbed drool from the corners of his mouth, then used a sleeve to dry the gelid sweat on his face.

Entwining his fingers in the bland, golden hair, he lifted the head. It was surprisingly light, like a small hollowed-out melon with hair. He held her face close to his own. She slowly swayed from one side to the other as if presenting herself to him. As if showing him her fangs that looked sharp enough to cut glass.

The head slowly swayed back, exhibiting the pantyhose-thin flesh of her cheek, her skull evident through the wispy flesh.

Shrink her. Hang her with the others.

Smiling, Ed stood. Holding the head by a hank of hair in one hand, he grabbed the shovel with the other. He used the tip of the blade to close the lid. Then he chucked the shovel over the top of the hole. He held the head up to look at her emaciated face one more time. His eyes returned to the fangs.

Were they real? He thought they looked it.

Didn't really matter to Ed. He'd found something special, he knew that much. And there were three more graves for him to play around in. Just not tonight. He'd spent too much on this one.

Ed tossed the head up top, then started to climb.

He'd be back soon to explore the rest.

-2-

"Why are we going this way, Timmy?"

Timmy Worden stopped pedaling his Schwinn Cruiser and looked over his shoulder. Peter was much farther back. His pudgy body struggled to stay upright as his legs spun with an astonishing speed. No matter how hard he worked, though, the bike still moved slower than a cow in mud. Even from where Timmy was, he could see the dark stains of sweat spreading down the sides of Peter's striped shirt.

"We're going to swing by Eddie's, see if he has any cold pop!"

Peter made a face, and Timmy knew it wasn't just caused by the struggle to pedal his bicycle, nor the unnatural hot day Plainfield was experiencing.

Peter was scared of Eddie Gein.

Scared of the Gein house, *is more like it.*

Most kids their age were, but not Timmy. He was one thirteen-year-old who didn't mind visiting the Gein house. Sure, it was a dump and Eddie seemed to collect his trash rather than dispose of it. And it probably hadn't been cleaned since Ms. Gein was still alive. These details didn't bother Timmy a bit. Besides, Eddie's odd decorations and magazines and books intrigued Timmy more than frightened him.

Peter, too, he knew, though his friend never wanted to admit it.

Some of it's a little weird, though.

"Hurry up, Peter!"

Peter moaned. "Can't we just go into town for pop? I bet Buck will give us a root beer float since it's so hot out."

"And what if he doesn't?"

"Then I'll *pay* for it!"

"Mine too?"

"Yes!"

That was a tempting offer, even though it stemmed from desperation, not kindness. Shaking his head, Timmy said, "Nah, we're a lot closer to Eddie's. It'll take us a long time to ride to Buck's."

"Yeah," said Peter, agreeing, though by his voice not willingly.

"We won't stay long," said Timmy.

Peter came to a wobbly halt beside Timmy. His hair, which he usually tried to style with a stiff wave like most kids in 1954, was plastered to his scalp with sweat. Panting, he leaned back on the seat, staring up at the cloudless blue sky.

"And its Saturday," said Timmy.

"So?"

"*So,* Eddie probably has some new stuff to look at."

Peter smiled. A dab of sweat hung from his bottom lip. Timmy watched it drip off. "Think so?"

"Doesn't he always?"

Peter shrugged. "I guess so. If Mama ever found out I read those magazines at Eddie's, she'd skin my ass."

"So would mine. Can't read *those* at Buck's, now can we?" Timmy tried not to smile as he watched his friend take the bait.

"Nope!"

"Let's head over there."

"What if he's not home?"

Timmy hadn't thought about that. Rarely was Eddie ever not at home, unless he was doing a job for somebody. He didn't work anything steady. Mama said it was because

Eddie lived off his inheritance, whatever that meant. But he still did odd jobs and favors around town—pumping gas for customers at the service station, repairing tractors, fixing roof leaks.

Mama called it busy work, another expression Timmy didn't quite understand.

"If he's not, I guess we'll head over to Buck's," Timmy said.

"Okay," said Peter. His eyebrows lifted. "Never know, Robin Hicks might be there."

Timmy fluttered inside. "At *Eddie's?*"

"No, dink. At Buck's."

It was possible. Just like everybody else, Robin liked going there. He'd seen her with her friends sitting at the bar, sipping a glass bottle of soda through a straw. He liked how her lips formed around the straw's tip, slightly puckering as the skin of her upper lip wrinkled. Her eyes drifted up as if she were reading something on the wall.

He could watch her without her knowing at Buck's. When she used to sit with him, he never dared to try. She'd catch him for sure.

Picturing her lips made Timmy feel squirmy inside. He was tempted to forget going to Eddie's, and pedal all the way back to Buck's just to see if she *was* there.

But they weren't far from the corner of Archer, where the Gein farm was. Might as well see if Eddie was home.

And get something cold to drink.

Eddie didn't have any power in the house, so he had no use for a refrigerator. But on Saturdays, he kept a tub filled with ice and the necks of glass bottles poking out like frosted weeds.

"Let's get going," said Timmy.

Peter took a deep, trembling breath. He still seemed overly winded from the ride. Timmy sometimes worried about his best friend's health. Peter maintained a fair complexion, even in the summer, though he was outside often. He never seemed to lose any of the fat that made his arms look like stems of dough sprouting from the short sleeves of his shirt. Timmy could tell Peter was on the verge of outgrowing the shirt he had on.

Though a lot of the other kids teased Peter for his weight, Timmy had never said anything about it. Sometimes he wondered if he should. Not to mock him, but to suggest he needed to do something about it.

"Why are you staring at me like that?"

"Huh?" said Timmy, blinking.

"You were staring at me like Eddie does."

"Oh, shut up. I was not."

"Catching the Weirdees?"

"The what?"

"The Weirdees. Ma says if I get too close to Eddie, I'll catch his *Weirdees*."

"Your ma's mean."

"That's like telling me the sky's blue. I *know*. I *live* with her."

Timmy laughed, then started pedaling. He kept his pace slow, so Peter could keep up. His friend huffed and grunted like a dog eating scraps as he rode next to Timmy.

The fields beside the road were already showing hints of green. Sunlight seemed to bounce off the fresh blades. It wasn't much past ten in the morning and it was already hot. It wouldn't last. By this evening, the temperatures would drop for a cold night. The weather never knew what it wanted to be in Plainfield.

Timmy pedaled without talking because Peter would hardly be able to hold a conversation through his wheezing. The chubby boy rode with his head down, his lips in a tight line as sweat streamed down his face.

Timmy forced his eyes forward. He didn't want to be accused of sharing Eddie's goofy staring problem again. *The*

Weirdees. Ms. Nelson was pretty lousy to most people, but she really seemed to despise Eddie more than others. She'd told Timmy's parents that Eddie made her feel uncomfortable because he always seemed to *watch* her.

"It's like he's trying to see through my clothes!" Timmy had heard her say to his father.

Dad had managed not to laugh until she had left their house. Mama had swatted him on the shoulder for making fun of Ms. Nelson.

"I'm not making fun of her," he'd said. "I only think she's...mistaken."

Timmy had watched from his bedroom doorway as his mother crossed her arms over her chest, making it look inflated. That was the first day he'd noticed how pretty she was, and it had caused him to feel uncomfortable and sad. "You're the deputy," she'd said. "And she came over here to tell you this because she thinks Ed Gein's strange."

"Everybody thinks Eddie's strange. He's harmless. Especially to women who look like her."

Mama had frowned at Dad, then walked to the kitchen, shaking her head.

Timmy knew why Dad had laughed off Ms. Nelson's worries. She was not a pretty woman—inside or out. She looked like an older version of Peter dressed in women's clothing. She wore too much make-up and always smelled like dying flowers because of her poignant perfume. The Nelson house was strangled in it. Which was one of the many reasons Timmy didn't like going over there.

The comely scenery around them swapped for a sicker looking landscape. The ground to the right was brown and gray, the trees naked and thin. Across from the field, off the road a bit, was the Gein farm.

Peter's pace slowed, and Timmy took the lead once again. He veered to the left, aiming the front balloon tire for

Gein's driveway. The rubber made crackling sounds as the tire rolled onto the dirt path.

More stalky trees bordered the driveway, their spindly branches reaching out. The fat tires ran them over. Timmy enjoyed the crunching sounds they made under his tires.

Though minutes ago the air had felt rough and hot, it now seemed much cooler. The shadows were heavy, though the trees had no leaves to block out the sun. Eddie's place always looked darker than others, even on beautiful days like this one.

The shadows seemed to love it here.

Timmy saw fragments of Eddie's house through the trees. It was a large, old home, three stories tall with an attached summer kitchen. In there, Eddie kept his tub of ice and pop. The ceiling of the house dipped slightly. The paint was flaking off and turning brown. The wood was dotted with holes, and needed many repairs.

Timmy cut through the deer path in the woods, heading for the summer kitchen. Just like the upper level of the house, Eddie didn't allow anybody inside. Timmy had asked what the big deal was more than once. Eddie's answer was always the same—those areas were private.

Peter once suggested they sneak inside to see what Eddie kept in there, but Timmy refused. It felt wrong and dishonest to break Eddie's rule.

He heard the wheels of Peter's bike chew through the dead grass behind him. Timmy was near the end of the path, so he pedaled harder to get the bike going faster. He loved his Cruiser. It was all he'd wanted for Christmas after seeing an advertisement for it in a magazine at the barbershop. He'd torn out the page and stuck it on the refrigerator, so his parents had to see it every day and would know it was what he wanted.

And now I have it.

Timmy shot out of the woods, leaving the trail—and Peter—behind him. He pedaled faster, enjoying the feel of the wind whipping his clothes against his body, his hair flapping back.

It was silly to think so, but he felt free on his Cruiser.

He leaned to the side, and swung the rear tire around. Dirt sprayed out in an arc. He came to a sudden stop and slapped his feet on the ground to keep from falling. His heart hammered in his throat, making light clucking sounds. It was hard for him to find his breath after it had been stolen by the rush of riding so fast.

Over a minute later, Peter rolled to a lethargic stop beside him. His shirt was nearly soaked through with sweat.

Timmy got off the bike, and walked it over to a thin tree. He leaned the bike against it. As he came back, Peter dismounted his bicycle. He let it drop to the ground with a crashing jangle.

Timmy winced. "You shouldn't just let it fall like that."

"Why not?"

"Might break it."

Peter swiped at the air, wrinkled his nose. "Then I could get a new one like you." He leaned forward slightly and spat. "I sure hope Eddie has some pop."

"Me too," said Timmy. His tongue felt swollen and limp.

Standing together, the boys looked around. There was no sign of Eddie. Any other time he'd have already come ambling up, twisting his checkered hunter's cap in his hands, grinning.

"I don't think he's home," said Peter.

"Of course he is," said Timmy. "His truck's parked right there." Timmy pointed at the corroded rattletrap with the dust-powdered windows.

Peter shrugged. "Maybe he's in the woods. Or at the creek." He grabbed the bottom of his shirt, and pulled it out, shaking it to fan his sweaty body.

"Maybe." Timmy looked around. He saw a cluster of leafless trees, branches sagging. He saw the field that led to the dense woods bordering the Gein property. The creek was deep in the woods.

There was no wind. No birds. Just complete silence.

Like at Aunt Agnes's funeral.

Though the church had been filled with relatives and friends, the hush in there had been insufferable. Each time Timmy had adjusted his position on the pew, the wood sounded like a growling beast in the quiet, hollow room.

Maybe Peter was right, and they'd come all the way out here for nothing.

A rustling sound came from behind the house. In the silence, it sounded like a large mouth chewing something crunchy. The boys turned their heads toward the rear corner.

A growling monster leaped out from behind the house, landing in a half squat.

In the fleeting glance Timmy managed to get of the hideous creature before fleeing for his Cruiser, he saw a gnarled face; he saw crooked, stretched lips; he saw wild black hair bouncing around limp ears and drooping eyelids.

The ugly beast shook a bone above its head. Something like a withered human head with blond hair dangled from the end, but smaller, the size of a baseball. Timmy glimpsed pointed teeth.

He was beginning to mount the Cruiser when he heard laughing. He realized he'd been screaming this whole time as the laughter grew louder.

Huh?

His screams tapered off to a soft whine in the back of his raw throat. He turned around. He saw Peter first, frozen in the spot where Timmy had left him. His mouth hung open as if he were screaming, though no sound came out. His body trembled, arms stiff at his sides, hands open.

Bent over, the beast's hands were on its knees. The bone pointed at the ground, the tiny head trembling from where it was knotted by its hair to the bone's tip.

The laughter came from the monster's weird crooked mouth. And the laughter was not menacing, not even a smudge frightening. Its tone was very familiar.

"Eddie?" Timmy asked.

Nodding, the monster raised its arm, pointing the shriveled head at Timmy. The skin on the tiny, hideous face reminded him of a rotten prune. Small hollow circles of blackness were where eyes had once been, and its mouth was a tight, bumpy line with two narrow points of teeth on each side.

"I think I shat myself!" said Peter, in a shrill voice.

This comment caused Eddie to laugh even harder, a deep throaty chortle that shot spit out of his mouth. Timmy also laughed, shaking his head.

Peter turned around, jutting his rump. "Do you see a stain?"

Timmy checked the seat of Peter's pants. "No."

"Thank Christ! I only farted!"

Eddie threw back his head, laughing. The skin hanging below the chin of the mask jiggled. The rest of the costume made raspy sounds as it shook against Ed's clothes.

What in the world is Eddie wearing?

In addition to the mask, Eddie had on a matching vest, held together in crudely stitched patterns. Some type of leathery gaiters had been strapped to the fronts of his legs. Gaps between the materials showed his pants behind them.

Timmy stepped beside Peter, and together they approached Eddie.

Timmy's legs felt a tad weak and stringy.

"Neat costume," said Peter, out of breath.

"Really like it?" asked Eddie. His voice was muffled behind the mask. He grabbed the flap of haggard skin at his neck and pulled the mask up, letting it rest on his head. It looked as if a face had sprouted from the top of his skull. Rough edges of skin hung around his face like a horrid hood. Eddie's face, the sallow expression and lazy eyes, were relieving to see.

"Not really," said Peter. "It's just...neat."

Eddie's smile flashed pride.

"Did you make it?" asked Timmy.

"Stitched it myself," he said.

"Wow," said Timmy. He reached out, rubbed the chest piece. It felt dry and gristly. There was a dark oval far to the side that looked like a nipple that had been split and sewn back together slightly off center, making one side a bit higher than the other. "What is this material?"

Eddie opened his mouth to answer.

Peter cut him off. "Get this stuff from your cousin in the South Seas?"

Eddie's cousin, Walter, was stationed across the world on a small, isolated military base. He always seemed to be sending Eddie some kind of strange artifact—shrunken heads like the one dangling from the tip of Eddie's bone, bowls that Eddie claimed were actually the caps of skulls, and various nasty decorations that Eddie kept on display inside his rundown home.

Eddie's mouth slowly shut. He seemed to think a moment before answering. Nodding, he said, "Yep. Walter sent it to me, but I stitched it up. It's *real* human skin."

Timmy snatched back his hand, putting it to his chest. The tips of his fingers felt dirty. "Bull."

That prideful smirk returned to Eddie's face. "It is so!"

Peter made a face as if he'd been eating the material. "How'd your cousin get *human skin*?"

"Remember those tribes I told you about?" Ed asked.

The cannibal tribes.

Eddie talked about them often. They were the subject of many articles in the magazines and old books Eddie liked to read. Some of them had *genuine* photographs of the tribes. Timmy liked to look at them because the women were always naked from the waist up. Their boobs just hung out. Most of the women had large nipples that looked as if they had melted then hardened again, some had tiny dots the size of freckles. He liked those better. All of them wore skirts made out of leaves or twigs, so he never saw them below the waist.

Some horror comics used such tribes as characters. Usually they featured a white woman in her underwear, tied to a stake and knee-deep in a pile of fire. The tribesmen wore weird masks with bones tacked through the nostrils and lips. Though Timmy would never admit it, the stories—and even the photographs—frightened him. He'd never understand why they fascinated Eddie so much.

Maybe he just likes weird things.

The Weirdees.

When Timmy's mind cleared, he realized he'd missed part of Eddie's and Peter's conversation. Eddie stroked the chest piece. His fingers made soft whispering sounds on the arid material. "…peel it off the bodies of their dead tribesmen. They wear it in battle."

Peter's nose wrinkled. "You mean they wear that stuff like army men wear green."

Eddie snapped his fingers. "Exactly!"

"Why?"

"The skin is like armor. It's thin and light, but it's hard for something sharp to go through." He thumbed the stomach of his vest. "See?"

Timmy felt strange, a little dizzy. He wanted to sit down. He wished Eddie would take the dumb costume off. Even if he didn't really believe it had come from a person, he was tired of looking at it. It made him feel like he was doing something wrong.

"Got any pop?" asked Timmy.

Eddie pulled the mask off, holding it by his side with his fingers slipped through the eyeholes. The hair looked bushy and wild, as if a critter had crawled up Eddie's leg. "In the summer kitchen. Just got the ice this morning, so they should be nice and cold by now."

"Great," said Peter. "We're thirsting to death."

"I'll go grab us some," said Eddie. He started for the house. As he walked, he talked over his shoulder. "You know thirsting someone is a form of torture. People use that method to get important information from somebody. They tie them to a chair, don't let them drink for days, then come in with one glass of ice water and put it on the table. If they tell them what they want to know they can have the water."

Eddie climbed the steps to the side door that led into the summer kitchen.

"I bet it works," said Peter. "I'd probably squeal all my secrets right now for some pop."

Laughing, Eddie opened the door. Gloomy darkness was on the other side. "Let me get my chair," he said. Then Eddie stepped through the doorway. The shadows inside swallowed him. His foot shot out of the gloom, and kicked the door shut.

Peter turned to Timmy, eyes wide. "What a weird costume, huh?"

"Yeah," said Timmy. He felt his face tighten into a wince. "I wouldn't want to wear it."

"You wouldn't? Couldn't you just imagine running around in that get-up? We'd scare the shit out of everybody for sure!"

"Why would you want to put somebody else's skin on you? That's just not right."

"I doubt it's *really* somebody's skin. Eddie was probably just fooling with us. I bet he really sent in for it from the back of a comic book."

"Maybe."

"Or those detective magazines. They have some strange things in those. Remember that advertisement for a plant that eats people? Weird!"

Timmy liked the advertisements, but would never actually send his money to one. Seemed he could toss his allowance into the creek and it would feel like less a waste of money.

The door to the summer kitchen swayed open, squeaking on its rusted hinges. Eddie stepped out with three glass bottles hanging from between the fingers of one hand.

No tiny head. No bone. No skin suit. Timmy was thankful Eddie left the stuff inside. Now, his awkward friend had on a gray T-shirt that was dark in spots from sweat and a pair of work pants. On his feet were the same old, worn-out work boots Eddie never took off.

Eddie pulled the door shut and trotted down the rickety steps.

"Want to go in the house?" he said.

"Got some new comics?" asked Peter.

"I do."

Timmy smiled. The icky sensation that had had his skin feeling cold and tight was starting to fade. "Awesome."

Eddie ushered them around the summer kitchen. "Let's head inside. It's a lot cooler in there, and we can sit down at the table in the kitchen."

-3-

Eddie's kitchen smelled like garbage and spoiled food. Dirty plates that Timmy doubted had been washed since Ms. Gein was alive were stacked across the counters and floor. A carpet of old newspapers had been tossed throughout the room, trails cutting through that led to the table, stove, and doorways.

Though there weren't any curtains over the windows, the room was heavy with murky shadows from the dark streaks on the glass. It looked as if Ed had painted them with motor oil. Just enough light pushed in for Timmy to see by, but it was like walking in the woods at sunset. He dodged boxes of junk, stepped over some pots lined with a dark crust, and kicked a path through trash and loose paper on his way to the table.

The table was buried under books, magazines, and comics. A paper bag was on top of the debris, and Timmy could tell it was stuffed.

Four chairs were spread around the table, and only three of them could be sat in. The fourth had a column of hardback books on its seat, stacked so high it was leaning slightly. Timmy glimpsed the word vampire in the title of the book on top.

Eddie sat at the head of the table as the boys each took their usual spots on either side. Using a tarnished bottle opener, Eddie popped the cap on his bottle. Cool vapor curled from the glassy mouth. He handed the opener to Timmy. When his bottle was open, he passed the opener over to Peter.

They gulped their sodas in silence. Timmy sighed as the pop spread a chilly flow through him. After he'd nearly drained his bottle, he set it on the table, and wiped his damp hand on his pants. He grabbed the paper bag from the top of a cluster of comics he'd already read. It was a little heavy and made rattling sounds as it drooped over his fingers. Looked like the same brand of paper bags Nana used at her store.

"Did you buy these at Nana's?" asked Timmy.

"A few of them," said Eddie. "Most of those came in the mail, and I just put them in there to keep them separated from the old ones for you guys. Can't get *all* the good stuff in town."

Timmy pulled out a stack. On top was a comic he'd never heard of. He looked at Eddie. *"The Vampire's Graveyard Kiss?"*

Eddie drank some pop, his eyes widening above the bottle.

"Ooh, let me see it," said Peter.

"Hang on," said Timmy.

Timmy looked back down at the cover. The setting was an old cemetery, with giant concrete statues of angels, weeping saints, and crosses that carried on in the background to become dark shapes on top of shadowy hills. The sky had been painted in heavy shades of purple and blue. A vampire was on the front, his cape gripped in his hand and spread wide around the body of a screaming blonde draped across his arm. The vampire resembled Bela Lugosi, but with less handsome features. Its pale face was animal-like, a snarling mouth with oversized fangs dripping blood. In the neck of the blonde woman, whose breasts were nearly spilling out of her sagging white gown, Timmy saw two large holes. Blood trickled from the wounds, dripping down to form the title. Underneath in very small print was the year of creation—1954.

"Take these," said Timmy, passing the rest of the stack to Peter.

"Come on," said Peter. "Let me see the vampire comic."

"In a minute," said Timmy.

Pouting, Peter began thumbing through the others.

Timmy turned his attention back to *The Vampire's Graveyard Kiss*. The table of contents showed him the comic was an anthology, a collection of five stories inside one comic. He flipped through the pages, surprised to find a lot of writing inside. Bubbles seemed to fill the spaces around the panels of mad horror. This pleased him. But he didn't attempt reading the stories in the meager lighting Eddie's kitchen provided. It'd give him a headache.

The artwork was fantastic. Some of the best Timmy had ever seen in a comic. He enjoyed the action books as well, but the drawing and colors were never as good as what the horror titles had. They somehow seemed...juicier. Wicked.

And naughty.

"You hit a homerun this time," said Peter.

"Got some good ones, huh?" said Eddie. He leaned back, propping his feet up on a box of junk.

Timmy glanced up from the vampire comic. Peter was smiling down at an opened magazine clutched tightly in his pudgy fingers. On the cover, a woman in some kind of short gown that made her legs look very bare was on a mattress. Her eyes were closed, mouth open. A wedge of tongue touched her plump bottom lip. Rope hung around her neck.

Detective Heroes.

Judging the cover, the heroes had been too late to save her.

Frowning, Timmy lowered his eyes to the comic. In the panels, the woman from the cover was lying on top of a slab of concrete in the graveyard. Her legs were spread, but the white dress draped between them. The vampire, on his knees, had an arm braced on the ground to keep him up.

Timmy turned the page and nearly gasped.

The vampire and woman were having sex on top of the slab.

Good God…

Timmy had never seen something so lurid in a comic. The scene was drawn to perfection—the woman moaning, the vampire thrusting. Her legs wrapped around his waist, ankles crossed behind his back. The dress was pulled down to expose a large breast and small turgid nipple.

In the next panel, the vampire's teeth sunk into the soft mound, the nipple vanishing inside his mouth.

Timmy felt his erection pushing against his jeans. He didn't dare adjust himself, though. Didn't want Eddie to know what he was doing. Most likely, Eddie had already read the comic. So he knew the scene was inside. If he saw Timmy squirming in his seat, he'd figure out which part he was at in the book.

He quickly turned the page.

The first panel showed the woman on all fours, the dress bunched up on her back. The vampire was on his knees behind her. The woman's head was tilted, mouth wide open in a pleasured moan.

Timmy closed the book.

He felt sweat on his brow, trickling into his eyebrows. His breathing had quickened, so he took measured breaths to slow it down.

He turned. Eddie stared at him. "Done already?"

"Huh? Oh, no…I…just can't see it so good. Too dark."

"Want me to light a lamp?"

"Oh, no, that's okay."

"Then take it home with you. I read it already. It's got some good stuff in there. Make sure you keep a light on, though. Read it by the lantern the other night and was mighty spooked by the time I was done."

"Yeah...I'll borrow it." Timmy saw the illustrated woman on her hands and knees, the vampire behind her. "Thanks."

Timmy expected Peter to ask to look at it next, but he was too intrigued by the magazine with the strangled woman on the front to care. "Can I take this one?" asked Peter.

"Your Ma would never let you have that," Timmy said.

"Like yours will let you keep the vampire comic."

"I'm going to hide it," said Timmy.

"Good idea," Eddie said. "Don't want the Sheriff Worden knocking down my door because of what I gave you."

Timmy said, "He wouldn't," but knew he just might bust Eddie's ass if he found out.

"I'll hide this one," said Peter, lowering the magazine. His eyes peered over the top of the pages. "Ma will never know."

Timmy rolled his eyes. "But your Ma searches your room all the time for cigarettes. She doesn't trust you at all. How are you going to keep that magazine hidden from *her*?"

Peter clucked his tongue. "She only thinks she knows everything about me." He raised the magazine and resumed reading.

The last comment bothered Timmy. He didn't know why.

"You boys can take whatever you want," said Eddie. "You know that."

The boys thanked him.

"Want something to eat?" Eddie asked. "I can throw on some pork and beans on the stove, or make some peanut butter sandwiches."

Timmy's stomach gave a sick gurgle at the idea of eating food cooked in those filthy pots. "No thanks."

"I'll take a peanut butter sandwich," said Peter. "Thanks!"

"What about you, Timmy?" Eddie asked. His eyes lifted, lips stuck out. "Just got a new jar from your nana's place yesterday. Hasn't even been opened and the bread's still fresh."

Timmy guessed a peanut butter sandwich would be okay. "Sure. I'll take one."

"Great," said Eddie. "And I'll grab us some more pop."

"Good man," said Peter.

Eddie scooted back the chair, and stood up with a groan. He walked to the counter across the room, pushing junk out of his way to clear off a spot. He opened the bread bag, then grabbed a knife from the sink. Some crusty clumps made ridges along the blade, probably peanut butter that had never been cleaned off. Timmy grimaced as he watched Eddie use the grimy knife to spread peanut butter on the bread.

Should've told Eddie no.

He wasn't going to eat that, no way.

Eddie returned to the table, a sandwich in each hand. "Here you are," he said.

Timmy took one, and, without looking up, Peter took the other. Before Timmy could warn him, Peter had already taken a bite. He nodded as if he approved of the taste.

"Thanks, Eddie," said Peter.

"You're welcome." He looked at Timmy, waiting.

Timmy held back his disgust as he took a bite. He smiled through the food in his mouth. "Thanks."

Eddie nodded, clapped his hands together. "Now I'll go get that pop! Be right back."

Eddie left the kitchen. The back door opened. Sunlight spread a wide path through the shadows in the hall. Timmy waited until the brightness went away and he heard the door bump shut before he spat out the wad of sandwich into his hand.

The Vampire of Plainfield

Looking around, he didn't see a trash can. But he spotted another box that didn't look quite as full as the others. He got up, hurried over to the box, and dropped the sandwich into it. He shook his hand to free the remaining soggy clumps of bread from his fingers. White dots splatted against a dark object inside the box. Timmy thought he saw something that looked like hair flutter when mushy bread hit it.

"What's that?" he muttered.

"Huh?" said Peter, his mouth full. He made gross smacking sounds as he chewed the sandwich. "Did you say something?"

Timmy ignored Peter as he looked at the box. He could see a lot of crinkled balls of paper, some torn newspaper pages, a hammer with a broken handle, some torn photographs, and a head.

"*Yah!*" Timmy jumped back. His feet scrambled out from under him, kicked the box, and dropped him hard on his rump.

"What's wrong?" Peter asked. The chair groaned across the floor. Then Timmy heard the heavy stomps of Peter running closer. "What happened?" Peter stood over Timmy, head moving back and forth.

"In the...box. I saw..."

"Saw what?" Frowning, Peter got down on his knees. His jeans made swishing sounds as his legs rubbed together.

"Stay away from it, Peter."

But Peter was already reaching into the box, nose wrinkled, and lips curled. "Is that what I think it is?" It sounded as if he'd asked himself more than Timmy.

"Yeah, it's..."

"A head!" Instead of recoiling as Timmy had, Peter laughed. "Neat!" Peter raised the decomposed head out of the box by a mane of raven-black hair. "Look at it! How *fake* does this look? Like something we'd see in the spookhouse at the carnival!"

Timmy stared at the porous face. What skin remained was putrefied and gray. A mound of skull showed on its forehead, a bulging socket of bone where the eye should be. Between its craggy lips, Timmy saw a grate of teeth. The upper row was bookended with fangs.

"The teeth," Timmy said.

"Huh?"

"Look. Just like the shrunken head Eddie had."

Peter turned his hand, making the head slowly spin toward him. Eyes narrowed, he leaned closer. Timmy expected the brittle jaws to suddenly pop open and bite off Peter's nose.

"Wow!" said Peter. "Fangs. Neat, huh!"

Timmy stared at the head. It slowly swayed back to peer at him with its eyeless hollows. "Put it back in the box," he said.

Peter acted as if he hadn't heard him. "I wonder where he got it. Think his cousin mailed it to him?" Before Timmy could think to respond, Peter said, "Nah. I bet Eddie made it. Looks like it, huh?" He rubbed its cheek with the tip of his thumb. "Feels like that fake volcano I made for a science project last year."

Timmy didn't care where it had come from. He wanted it back in the box, out of sight. He wished he could go back to moments ago, when he didn't know Eddie had a head in the kitchen.

Should've eaten the stupid sandwich.

"Put it back," Timmy said again.

Peter looked at him. "Why?"

Before Timmy could answer, Eddie said, "Found my head?"

Both boys jumped, but only Peter cried out. He dropped the head. It hit the side of the box, and tumbled onto the floor. Timmy watched it roll a few feet before stopping. Of course, on its side so the moldy face gazed right at him.

Eddie stood in the kitchen doorway, that customary goofy smirk twisting his face. He had three glass bottles hugged to his chest.

"Suh-suh-sorry, Eddie," said Peter. "We were just—I mean, Timmy saw the head...and I just wanted to—I mean, I touched it and..."

"Why are you acting so scared?" Eddie asked, smiling.

"I'm not *scared*," said Peter.

"You sure sound like it."

I am, Timmy thought.

An odd, almost hysterical laugh clattered out of Peter. "I don't mean to sound that way. I mean—wow! A head!"

"That's the third one," said Eddie. "You saw the first one earlier."

Timmy recalled the tiny head bouncing from the end of that large bone Eddie had been swinging all over. The one Peter had dropped was normal size, not a miniature duplicate.

"Why's it so big?" Timmy asked.

"What?" asked Eddie.

"The head. It's a lot bigger than the other."

"Oh." Eddie made a silly face, swept his hand through the air. "I just haven't shrunken it yet."

Peter laughed again, a shrill commotion that sounded like something wild. "He said shrunken it." Peter looked at Timmy. "You hear that? He said he shrunk it."

"You don't believe me?"

"Why-why-why wouldn't we believe you?" Peter asked. "Right, Timmy? We believe him, don't we?"

"It's real?" Timmy asked.

Eddie nodded. "Yes."

"Oh Jesus H." Peter's laugh turned to a wheeze. "Jesus H. I touched a dead woman's head."

"More stuff from your cousin?" Timmy asked.

Eddie sighed. Something about his appearance made Timmy think Eddie wanted to say more than he was. "Of course. Walter sent them. Usually they're already shrunken when I get them. But…uh, I learned how."

"To shrink them?" Timmy asked.

"Right."

"So he sent you normal heads?" Peter asked. Eddie nodded. "In the mail?"

Eddie nodded again.

Timmy bet Mr. Jasper, the mailman, would keel over if he knew he'd brought human heads to Eddie's house.

Is that even legal?

"There's nothing wrong with head shrinking," said Eddie. He spoke casually about it as if discussing the weather. "After my cousin sent me some, I got interested in it. Read about these practices from other countries where they shrink the heads of their enemies after killing them. Either in a battle or somebody who'd done them wrong. Then they'd hang the head outside their hut as a warning to others. And some would…"

"She was your enemy?" said Timmy.

"No. They're just heads. That's all. I don't *know* them."

"What's wrong with their teeth?"

Eddie smiled. "Maybe they're vampires."

A shiver wormed through Timmy's bowels. "Be serious, Eddie."

Laughing, Eddie said, "What I was about to say is shrunken heads are supposed to be for good luck, too. I was going to wait to give it to you, but…" Eddie walked over to the counter. Something small and bulbous rested in the windowsill. The sunlight behind it made the oval-shaped object a dark blot against the glass. Timmy hadn't noticed it before. "But since you found that one, I don't see why I can't go on and let you have it."

Eddie grabbed the object from the sill. It was the size of an apple, with a stringy tail hanging from the top of it. As Eddie neared, Timmy saw a different shrunken head balanced on his palm. The tail was actually braided hair dangling from the top of the pruned, skull-like face. The lips, like the first shrunken head, had been stitched shut. The white tips of sharp teeth barely peeked between them.

"It's yours," said Eddie. "Hang it somewhere in your room for good luck."

Timmy watched the head lower to him and was surprised to see his own hand rising to take it. Eddie placed it on the flat of his palm. It felt surprisingly light, no heavier than a peach. It rolled onto its side, the braided hair tickling his fingers.

"Thu-thanks..."

"Don't I get one?" asked Peter with a whine in his voice.

"Of course," said Eddie. He bent over, snatched the larger head by its hair, and stood. "I just have to make it first."

"Neat!"

Timmy figured the only reason why Peter no longer acted grossed out by the head was because Eddie had given him one and not Peter. He was like that. Always had to have what everybody else had or he'd throw a tantrum. Eddie probably hadn't intended to make one for Peter or he would've already done it.

Made one. A head! I'm holding a head in my hand!

But it didn't feel like one. And, really, it didn't look like one. Maybe Eddie was just fooling around. He liked to play pranks on them because they were so easy to trick. Timmy figured this was another one, just like the supposed skin suit he'd been wearing earlier. Probably nothing more than something he'd ordered from a catalog.

Yeah. That's probably it.

But Timmy didn't really believe that. No matter what, he would just pretend that was where this morbid decoration had come from.

Now, he just had to worry about hiding it from his parents.

-4-

Timmy wasn't surprised to see Eddie's truck parked at Nana's store when he pedaled up to the front of the building. He leaned his Cruiser against the porch railing and climbed the steps onto the porch. The eave shaded him, and it felt good to have the sun off his neck.

Worden's General Store was about the only place around anybody could find what they needed from food to motor oil. She also had a better selection of books and comics than the drugstore, though Timmy wouldn't tell his parents that. They might begin to suspect one of the reasons he came by so much was to gawp at the newest releases—which was what he planned to do now until Nana closed up. Plus, he needed some pencils and paper. He'd finished writing a story last weekend, and was ready to delve into another.

Eddie seemed to visit Nana's store more than anybody and, so far as Timmy could tell, Nana didn't mind. Other folks in town grew tired of Eddie's company rather quickly, but like Timmy, Nana enjoyed talking to the goofy loner. He made her laugh more than anybody Timmy had ever seen. Sometimes he wondered if they *liked* each other.

Nah. That's silly. Nana's as old as Eddie's Ma was.

But as Timmy approached the front door, he heard Nana unleash a boisterous laugh and he couldn't help but wonder.

"Oh, Eddie, you shouldn't!" she cried.

The deep clucking of Eddie's laughter was followed by a quiet mumbling that Timmy couldn't understand. Then Nana really let a guffaw go.

Timmy peeked through the display window. Dust made the glass look powdery, and the setting sun glinted off the window in a blinding gold shine. He made a visor with his hand and leaned close, pressing his face to the dusty glass. A nippy breeze drifted across his back, making the sweat under his shirt feel like ice on his skin. The wind was bringing a cold night to Plainfield.

Through the glass, he could see the counter across the room. Eddie, leaned over the top on his elbows, talked to Nana who stood behind the register with an arm braced on the lip of the counter. Both were smiling. Shaking his head, Timmy walked back to the door and opened it.

The bells jangled above the door, announcing his entrance.

Nana leaned to the side to see around Eddie's shoulder. Her face brightened even more when she saw Timmy. "If it isn't my favorite grandson!"

"I'm your only grandson."

"And my favorite," she said. "Come on in."

Eddie smiled as Timmy approached the counter. "Haven't seen you in a long time," he said, winking.

Timmy feigned a laugh. This was a normal banter for them.

"You went to Eddie's today?" Nana asked.

"Yeah. Peter and I rode over there earlier. He gave us some pop."

"And fed you lunch," said Eddie.

Timmy's stomach growled as if to dispute Eddie's claim. Peter had eaten the sandwich, but Timmy hadn't eaten anything since breakfast. Then he remembered the head in the box, and Eddie's gift—the shrunken head, which Timmy could feel in his pocket, pushing against his leg. He'd left the comic, rolled up, in his satchel on the Cruiser.

"Where's Peter now?" Nana asked.

"Had to get home for supper."

"Shouldn't *you* be getting home for supper?" Nana asked.

"Ma said I didn't have to come home until six."

"Ma? When'd you start calling her that?"

"I always have," said Timmy. He felt heat in his cheeks. He'd only started calling her that when talking about her to the guys at school after they began teasing him for still referring to her as *Mama*. Since they called their mothers *Ma,* Timmy decided it would work for him to.

"Does *she* know that?" Nana asked.

"Yeah," said Timmy, lying. He wasn't brave enough to try it on her yet.

"Well, I was just inviting Ed over for supper. Got a huge pot of vegetable soup that needs to be eaten by somebody."

"Did you make it with deer meat?" asked Timmy.

"Of course I did!" Nana laughed.

Timmy's mouth slavered. Mama liked to think she made the best vegetable soup around, but it couldn't compete with Nana's. Something about the spices and how she let it slowly cook all day made the difference. Mama rushed it in the evening, putting it together and hurrying it along.

"Can I come?" he asked.

"You sure can," said Nana. "But your *ma* might get upset."

"I don't think so," said Timmy. But he knew it would hurt her feelings. She seemed to take things like that as a personal attack.

"I'll call her and get her approval," Nana said.

Timmy smiled. If Nana called her, then Mama would say yes. Nobody argued with Bernice Worden. "Okay." He turned to Eddie. "You'll be there too?"

"Wish I could tonight," said Eddie.

"But he has *plans*," said Nana.

"You do?" Timmy hadn't meant to sound quite so shocked.

"I bet he's just planning to swing by Mary's place for a few beers."

Eddie's cheeks flushed.

Nana laughed. "I knew it. You'd rather spend your Saturday evening at the tavern than getting a full belly from my soup?"

"Oh, Nana," said Timmy. "Don't tease him about it."

"I'm not."

"Everybody goes to Mary's," said Timmy. "It's all there is to do around here."

"There's a movie theater not far away. Much better way to spend a night, if you ask me."

Timmy agreed. He saw in the paper that the theater was doing a triple-showing of *Dracula, Frankenstein,* and *The Wolf Man.* He'd seen them already, but that was two years ago. He'd love to see them again. Maybe tomorrow he could talk his dad into dropping him off there for the day.

Nana pointed at Timmy so quickly, he jumped. "I better not ever catch wind of you snooping around that scanty place, Timmy."

"Nana!"

"Well, I mean it!"

Nodding, Timmy took a few steps back. Eddie gave him a sympathetic look over his shoulder. Then he turned around to face Nana. "How much for the new handle?" He held up a small bar of wood.

Looked about the size for a hammer. Timmy remembered the broken hammer in the box.

With the head.

Timmy restrained a shiver as he made his way over to the book racks.

Scowling, Nana pecked some numbers on her cash register. Timmy was glad Eddie had distracted her before she could start lecturing him about Mary Hogan.

"Give me a dollar and we'll call it even for what you still owe me for the antifreeze."

"Yes, ma'am. You're breaking me, you know." Laughing, Eddie reached into his pocket and tugged out a crumpled dollar bill.

"I'm going to break you if you don't stop calling me 'ma'am'. I've told you a million times to call me Bernice. You're one of the few I don't mind doing so, and you'd better start."

It was odd to Timmy hearing anybody refer to his family by their proper name. He was eight before he'd even realized his parents had names other than *Mama* and *Papa.*

And Nana was right. She hated to be disrespected by folks and thought it showed manners if they said ma'am or sir. Apparently, Eddie had been exempted from that regulation.

"Sorry, ma...er—Bernice." Eddie smiled as if he'd just sampled something that tasted fine. "Bernice."

"Wasn't so hard, was it?"

She took the dollar and slid it into the drawer, then bumped it closed with her hip. "Let me write you out a receipt."

"Fine."

Timmy stood before the books that were crammed into the narrow shelves. As he usually did, he gazed at the myriad eye-catching paintings on the covers. He saw gothic horrors; castles cresting the jagged peaks of cliffs; lone gunmen westerns about revenge and cattle wars; and scantily-clad women on the mystery novels, dressed in some kind of bosom-revealing negligee and looking frightened by the ominous shadow-man approaching her.

He wasn't allowed to read any of them since they were geared towards adults. Sometimes Dad let him read the age-appropriate science fiction titles. Though he enjoyed space adventures, they weren't as fun to him as monster stories.

That might explain why Timmy had started writing his own. Whenever he saw creepily attractive covers on horror books, he imagined what they were about. Then he'd go home and start writing his own interpretations since he wasn't allowed to read the actual book. The course of creating his own imaginative versions of those books he dreamed to read, he'd learned something about himself—he loved writing stories.

Now, he wrote stories originating from ideas not influenced by books he couldn't read.

He saw the latest issue of *Weird Fantasy* on the rack and picked it up. His parents used to let him read *Tales from the Crypt* and *The Vault of Horror* but when they saw how bloody and gruesome the stories really were, they stopped allowing it.

"Hope your daddy doesn't walk in," said Nana.

Timmy returned it to the comic rack.

Nana laughed. "I was just teasing, Timmy. You know I don't mind if you flip through them."

"I know."

"Was that what brought you by?" she asked. She shook open a paper bag and dropped Eddie's hammer handle inside. She handed the bag to Eddie. "Wanted to peep at my newsstands?"

"No," said Timmy. He walked over to the stationary section which was just a small stand with paper, ink, pens, black greeting cards, sharpeners, and pencils. "Need to get some things."

"Ah," said Nana. "Some supplies, huh?"

"Yeah." He grabbed a pack of plain paper and a few pencils. Nana had a few kinds to choose from, but he liked the *Black Stallion* brand. A smooth-writing pencil, painted black. He carried them to the counter, and set them down.

"Starting another story?" Eddie asked.

"Yeah," said Timmy.

Nana slipped a paper bag off the top of the stack beside her register. "How many does that make now?"

"This will be number ten," he said.

"Wow," said Nana. "That's very impressive, Timmy."

"What's this one about?" asked Eddie.

Timmy was nervous to talk about his stories very much. Eddie seemed to like them, but when other adults learned what he liked to write about, they wouldn't shy away from letting him know how much they disapproved.

He cleared his throat. "Well…" His shirt suddenly felt too tight and he pulled at his collar. "It's about a dad bringing home an old radio. He sets it up in the living room. It only plays one mysterious broadcast over and over, and it sort of brainwashes the people in the town and makes them start killing each other."

"Neat!" said Eddie.

"My heavens," said Nana, dropping the paper and pencils into the bag. "It's no wonder you don't ever let anybody read them."

"I've read them," said Eddie. "I read a lot, and can honestly say they're really good. Timmy's talented."

Smiling, Timmy felt the back of his neck go hot and prickly.

"I don't doubt he's got talent," said Nana. "But if he'd write about something other than murderers, monsters, and goblins and things coming back from the grave, he might not have to keep his talent such a secret."

But Timmy didn't like writing about anything else. His dream was that he'd write something good enough to submit to EC Comics.

"Here," said Nana. She slid Timmy's bag across the counter. "You can work that off for me."

Timmy nodded. That was their arrangement. She paid him with items from her store for helping her.

"Well," said Eddie. He pushed himself away from the counter and pulled out his pocket watch. He opened the faceplate, looked at the time, and whistled. "Guess I better be on my way." Taking his bag with him, Eddie started walking for the door. He ruffled Timmy's hair as he passed by.

"You keep your senses out there, Ed," Nana said.

"Can't keep them, if I don't have them."

"Not funny, Ed." But Nana grinned. "Drive safe. I can tell by how it looks out there that warm weather we had today is on its way out. Keep warm."

"Yes, ma..." Eddie cleared his throat. "Bernice. Bye, Timmy."

"Bye, Eddie."

The bells rattled when Eddie opened the door. Then he walked out. Timmy watched him pass by the window, his shoulders slightly slouching and head down. He tugged at his plaid hunter's cap, pulling it low to his eyes as wind made his coat shudder.

"All right," said Bernice. "Now comes the hard part."

Timmy turned around. "The what?"

"The hardest part of my day."

"What's that?"

"When I tell your *Ma* that you'll be eating supper with me."

Timmy made a gulping sound that was partly fake, but mostly real.

Nana laughed, and headed over to a small desk behind the counter. Sitting down, she scooted the chair up to the desk. The legs made tooting sounds across the floor. She lifted the phone from the cradle, and began spinning the dial.

Timmy sat in one of the stools Nana kept at the counter for customers. As Nana started talking to Mama, he began to jot down notes for his new story.

-5-

Ed drove through town, an elbow hanging out the window. Chilly air rushed into the truck, caressing his cheek with an icy hand. He waved when he saw somebody out and about. Mostly, the town was empty. It was after six, most folks heading home for the night.

About to eat supper.

I could be eating supper with Bernice.

Eddie was tempted to put off the graveyard trip another night. Nothing like a night of Bernice's company and a belly full of warm food. Besides, Timmy would be there. And he liked the boy a lot.

But the grave...

He had one left to dig, and he wanted to see what was in it.

Ed forged ahead. He left the main strip of Plainfield behind, heading for Mary's Tavern. Bernice had been right. His plan was to waste some time there since it was still too early to visit the isolated graveyard.

The businesses were replaced by fields and farms on both sides of the road. He saw the tavern up ahead on the left. With the purple hues of the darkening sky behind it, the tavern was a dark block cresting a small hill.

Mary's Tavern, owned and operated solely by Mary Hogan, was a popular joint that served cold beer and stale nuts at cheap prices. Where you went to be loud, say whatever you wanted and ogle Mary's enormous tits. She had a pair as large as watermelons hefted high up on her chest, and liked to wear shirts that complimented their size. The rest of her was full and thick without being fat.

Meaty, as Mama used to call her type.

Ed knew Mary didn't mind letting men squeeze and fondle them if they were paying customers. If they bought two pitchers, they might even get squeezed back, more if they were willing to pay extra. Most Ed had gotten was a quick grab of a boob, and it had felt like kneading dough, yet jiggled like rubber.

He steered his truck onto the gravel parking lot, and parked at the far end. Killing the engine, he shouldered the door open. He climbed out, adjusted his cap, and started walking with his hands buried in the pockets of his coat.

The tavern was a humdrum, box-shaped structure, and Ed had to walk under the slanting roofed porch with his head tilted to get to the entrance. He passed customers standing on the porch, guzzling beer, and groping the rumps of the women they'd managed to persuade into joining them. Ed recognized none of them, so they must have traveled in from out of town.

Pushing open the tavern's door, Ed went inside. The stink of old beer and sweat rushed to greet him. There were masses of conversations coming from all directions. The loud volume was a little disorienting, mixed with the twangy music coming from the jukebox. He began to sweat as he shuffled his way through the crowd.

"Hey, Ed!" called Mary from behind the bar. Her voice was so loud and strident it muffled the others. "Was wondering if I'd see you tonight! Come have a seat. Take a load off."

He nodded. Though from the meek lighting, he doubted she saw it. Hanging from rungs along the ceiling were oil lanterns. The tavern had electricity and lightbulbs lining the ceiling, but other than the Christmas lights behind the bar, she rarely used them.

Ed fumbled his way around tables and wandering people to an empty stool at the bar.

Saving this seat for me?

Probably not, but the possibility made him a little squirmy. She *did* say she was wondering if she'd see him tonight. Maybe she was keeping this stool open just for him.

People liked to tease Ed that Mary had eyes for him, but whenever they did he always retorted back with: "She has eyes for everybody." It usually got a good laugh because it was true. She didn't mind taking a range of men to bed, and she also didn't care who knew about it.

Ed pulled the stool out from the bar and swung himself on top of it.

"Good evening, handsome," said Mary.

Her hair was down tonight. It looked good resting on her shoulders in cherry-colored waves. She wore a tight, silky shirt that looked too small for her chest. A pond of pale skin showed from the hollow of her neck to where her nipples should be. The shiny top just barely concealed them. Her breasts were bunched together, and the vale between them was tight and thin. Ruffles adorned her sleeves and torso. She looked like a barmaid from the old saloon days.

"Evening," Ed finally said back.

She knew he'd been staring and smiled coyly. "Want a beer?"

He nodded.

"Be right back."

She winked, then stepped down the bar to a row of levers. She reached underneath the bar and came back with an empty aluminum mug. She tugged the faucet in the middle towards her massive breasts with the mug underneath. It caught the frothy fluid as it sloshed out.

While Mary poured Ed's drink, he reached into his coat pocket and tugged out his tobacco pouch. He was packing some leaves into his pipe when Mary returned.

She sat the mug in front of him. "How has your day been, hun?" she asked, leaning forward with her arms on the bar.

Ed looked up to answer and was met by two constrained breasts behind her corset. "Fine," he muttered. "Yours?"

"Oh...it's been just a day as any other. I'm glad you came in tonight, Ed. Been gettin' a little boring in here. Why don't you do something crazy to liven it up?"

"I don't know what I could do for that."

She leaned closer, pushing her breasts forward. The lights threw writhing shadows across their milky slopes. He could smell the powdery fragrance of make-up on her face. "You could do a lot more than you realize."

"Mary!" called someone from down the bar.

Her smile dropped. *"What!"* The volume inside the tavern dipped.

"How about a refill, huh?"

"How about I refill your ass with my foot?"

The bar erupted with laughter and applause. Ed even snickered himself. Mary never held back what she wanted to say, a trait that some people admired about her. Mostly, it was what nearly everybody else in Plainfield despised. She wasn't ashamed of using her potty mouth.

"I'll be back in a few, Ed. Don't go anywhere."

"I'll be right here."

As Mary darted off to the darkened border of the bar, Ed raised the pipe to his mouth and clamped the stem between his teeth. He struck a match across the bar's lip. It flickered to a flame, dimly swilling his hand with orange light. He raised it to the bowl and put the fire on the leaves. Puffing on the stem, he pulled in smoke that tasted a little like acorns.

Before he could take a second puff, a hand clapped down on his shoulder. Peering up into the mirror between shelves of gleaming bottles on the other side of the bar, Ed found Deputy Worden standing behind him.

"Hey, Ed."

Ed choked on the smoke. Everything flashed, rolling through his mind like a movie: Black and white, bouncy, with hairs and noise dancing across the screen.

"Thought you could get away with it, did you?" asked Worden.

"Wuh-with what?"

"You took some things that don't belong to you. Things from our graveyards."

"I-I-I...just took some parts of the bodies! They won't miss 'em!"

"The jig is up, Gein. You're going to the big house..."

"Not the big house!" Ed flung himself off the stool, shoving Worden away. *"You'll never take me alive!"*

"Ed?"

Ed blinked his eyes. Everything was back to normal, and in color. When he looked at Deputy Worden again, he found him staring back with heavy concern on his face. He wasn't in his uniform, so that had to mean he wasn't here on business.

"Are you all right, Ed?"

"Yuh-yeah. I'm fine..." He grabbed his mug, straining to keep his hand from trembling as he took a swallow.

"Didn't mean to startle you."

Ed waved a hand. "No bother."

"What brings you out here tonight?" He sat his mug on the counter, and slid his way into the stool next to Ed just as somebody got up to leave. "Don't usually see you here unless something's on your mind."

Ed shrugged. "No reason...not really."

He wouldn't dare tell Worden that Bernice had been on his mind some. The deputy would probably drive him off somewhere and put a bullet in him as if he were a horse with a broken leg.

Worden frowned. He raised his own mug to his mouth and took three heavy gulps. When he pulled it away foam dotted the spiky hairs above his lip. He used the back of his hand to wipe it off. "Sorry if I was prying."

Deputy Worden looked how Ed figured Timmy would at forty. He had about two days worth of beard on his face. His wavy hair was combed and looked as if he'd put some oil in it to keep it under control.

"No apology needed. What brings you by?"

Worden sat his mug on the bar next to Ed's. "Just getting my usual three drafts for the night. Then I'm going to head home. Pot roast tonight." Deputy Worden pointed at Ed. It made his heart lurch in his throat. "Surprised you didn't eat with Mom tonight."

Ed shook his head, puffed his pipe. "I was invited. Vegetable soup."

Worden moaned. "With deer meat, I'm sure."

Another nod. "Yes, sir."

"I could sure go for a bowl of that myself."

Smiling around the stem of his pipe, Ed gave another nod. He puffed smoke into his lungs. "I think Timmy might have thought the same. I think he was going over there."

"Really? How do you know?"

"Was at the store before she closed up. Timmy was there, asking if he could."

Worden nodded. "That means I have a wife sitting home alone, probably wishing I was there to eat some of her pot roast."

Ed smiled. "Probably."

"Barb gets a little…worked up about all of us eating together. With Timmy at Mom's, she's probably a wreck thinking her food's no good." He looked around the room, eyes focused and narrowed.

Seeing Worden was doing it made Ed join him. Ed figured Worden was trying to spot Mary. All Ed saw were heavy shadows with hints of movement inside.

Worden spun back toward the bar. "I noticed you chatting with Mary earlier."

"Yeah..." He shrugged.

"A woman like that is trouble."

Ed knew this already. If Mama was still around to know he was here, she'd have left red stripes on his back with a belt.

Worden continued. "She's good for one thing, Ed, and one thing only. And I wouldn't normally say this to anybody, but I feel it might do you some good. Take what she's offering you, enjoy it, and send her on her way. Maybe when she offers it again, you take it then too, but just as long as that's *all* it is. Don't bring the likes of her home for good. Understand?"

Ed nodded.

"Good. Now if you'll excuse me, I'm going to sneak out of here and head home before Barbara..." Worden began to stand.

Mary appeared behind him. "You weren't leaving, were you Tom, dear?"

He dithered a moment, then shook his head.

Ed heard a smack come from behind Worden. The deputy jerked forward as if he'd just been popped. Ed assumed he had been, and on his ass by Mary's hand.

"I looked for you earlier," she said. "Thought you might've changed your mind again."

"I didn't," he said.

"Ready?" she asked.

Worden nodded again. Before following her away from the bar, he glanced at Ed from the lower regions of his eyes. Ed saw a flicker of shame in them.

Mary hooked her arm around Worden's arm and led him away. Ed continued watching until they reached a door on the right side of the bar. She opened it for Worden. He went inside first. Mary turned to Ed, gave a wicked devilish smile, and waved before following him in.

Then the door closed.

Some people at the tables began to clap.

"Getting him a piece..."

"Fucks her all the time..."

"Wonder if his wife has any idea..."

"Does your wife know you been sticking it in Mary, too?"

"Shut up!"

"Who cares? It's not our business anyway."

Ed puffed on his pipe. He was never one to keep up with the town's gossip, but he'd gathered enough information to know that Deputy Tom Worden had been fooling around with Mary for almost a year. It seemed everyone in Plainfield knew about it except for Barbara.

Maybe she did know, but chose to ignore it.

Did Bernice know?

How about Timmy?

Heat rushed up Ed's skin knowing Timmy's father was back there with Mary while his wife sat at home wondering where he was.

Worden probably had his face sandwiched between Mary's enormous breasts right now.

Ed had been in the back room before, not doing what Deputy Worden was, but fixing the drain in the sink. The front section of the back room was small, but opened on an alcove where she kept a stove for the rare occasions when Mary was offering cooked meals. And at the far back was a bed where people could sleep off their drunk. One thing Mary never allowed, was somebody to drive home if they'd had too many to drink.

Ed pictured Mary sitting at the edge of the mattress, her heavy breasts spilled out of her shirt. Her skirt was hiked up her meaty legs that were curved around Worden's head. Head arched back, mouth parted and moaning as Worden's tongue worked...

"He just can't get him enough of that woman, can he?"

Ed nearly gasped. He looked to where Worden had been sitting and found Burt Maxwell now occupying the stool. He'd sat down like a phantom without Ed's knowledge. He held a cigar between two fingers of his right hand, a mug of beer with his left. Burt had cut Ed's hair when he was younger and still did now. It was his shop where Ed used to sneak peeks in magazines Mama wouldn't let him read. Age hadn't been kind to Burt over the years. His cheeks sagged to meet the skin under his chin, pulling his nose down with it. His lips puckered out in a constant, hound dog pout.

"We don't know for sure what they're doing," Ed said.

Burt hocked a laugh. "Eddie, you know as well as I do what's going on in there."

"Even so. Ain't my business."

"Aren't you close with Bernice? And Timmy?"

It was like he'd been reading Ed's mind.

"Maybe you should say something to them," Burt added.

"I wouldn't know how..."

Burt's mouth twisted, eyebrows pointed up. "Maybe you'd better not. Might do more harm than good. After all, he *is* the law. Might make your life hell if you did."

Thinking about his graveyard carousing, Ed agreed. Probably a good idea to steer clear of Worden's bad side.

"So how have you been holding up, Eddie?" Squinting, he swiveled his head from side to side. "I see you're in need for a trim. Hair's getting scruffy over your ears and it's curling out in the back."

Ed blushed, embarrassed by his shabbiness.

"You've got straight hair, Eddie. If it's curling then that means it's long overdue for a snip." He thrust his cigar-pinching fingers in the air as if they were scissors and accidentally snapped his cigar in half. "Shit!"

The burning half fell onto the bar as the clumpy chewed tip dropped into Burt's lap. He brushed himself off, then picked up the burning half. After giving it a quick inspection, he plopped it back in his mouth.

"I'll try to get by soon," Ed said, though he had no intentions of doing so in the near future. He stuffed more tobacco in his pipe. His eyes made their way to the door again. He fought the images of what Mary and Worden were doing in there from surfacing.

Burt must have noticed. "I can't believe they aren't a little more discreet about it, you know?"

Ed nodded. He supposed being the deputy of a small town had its benefits, one of them being the only negative comments that were made about you were behind your back.

"How're you maintaining the house on your own?" asked Burt.

"Fine."

He nodded. Sipped from his mug. "It was a damn shame about your Ma, but at least she's not suffering anymore, right?"

He patted Ed's back. Though it had happened a few years ago, Burt spoke of Mama's death as if it were recent. That was okay with Ed, because it *felt* recent. Wasn't a day that didn't go by he didn't wish she was still in that big house with him. How it used to be, before her episodes began to slowly ravish her brain.

Burt looked around the room. "I think I'm going to head home. It's getting dead in here."

"Doing the same when I finish my beer."

"I hear you, Eddie." He stood up, his hand digging in the front pocket of his trousers. He pulled out a dollar bill and smacked it down on the bar. "That ought to cover it."

Ed glanced at the craggy piece of cash. If Burt had drank as much as Ed assumed he had, then a meager dollar was nowhere near enough to cover it.

"Oh, by the way," said Burt, turning. "Been meaning to ask you. What were you doing driving around at dawn last week?"

Ed's stomach gave a sickening lurch.

Burt continued as he buttoned up his coat. "I was driving back into town from visiting my sister and I saw your truck heading down seventy-three, didn't I?"

Ed remembered exactly where he was.

The old graveyard.

Ed cleared his throat, not trusting his voice. "Nope. Wasn't me."

Burt wrinkled his nose, baring his upper teeth. "Are you sure? I swear that was your truck. Coming back from the rural area? Nothing but woods that far out and I thought it was odd that you'd be back there. Hunting maybe?"

Ed shook his head. "Nope."

Burt stared at the floor as if he wasn't sure what it was. Then he shrugged. When he looked at Ed again, he was no longer frowning. "Oh, well, guess I made a mistake. I do that sometimes. Take care, Eddie. Get in the shop next week so we can take care of that wild nest on your head."

"Yes, sir."

Looking back at the door opposite the bar, Burt made a face. "Still not right." Then he spun around and walked away, vanishing into the tavern's darkness.

Ed sat at the bar, smoking his pipe and drinking his beer. When he finished what was left of the tobacco, he slid over an ash tray, and tapped the ashes from the pipe into it.

He blew into the stem to make sure nothing was clogged in there. It seemed fine.

Then he got up from the stool. He put down enough money to cover his tab. Then he added what he thought was sufficient to cover Burt's. He turned around and left the bar.

Ed made his way through the flock of drunken customers. It was a good thing they all feared Mary and wouldn't dare try stealing from her. How long she'd been in the back room with Worden, they could have robbed her blind.

Cold air dropped onto Ed when he exited the tavern.

In his truck, he drove along Highway 73.

The graveyard was waiting.

-6-

The graveyard was spooky in the pale glow of the moon. Flicking the head of a match with his thumbnail, a spark ignited, singeing the tip of his thumb. He ignored the minor burn as he lowered the sputtering flame into the lantern. The fire jumped onto the wick. Shaking out the match, he tossed it behind him.

Leaving the truck on the side of the road behind some brush, he'd hiked the narrow path back here. Now he stood just a few steps from the rusted gate, the lantern held out before him. It spread a soft golden shimmer in front of him.

Those other visits seemed forgotten, as if this was his first time gazing at the piercing contours of the wrought-iron gate. The tops of the fence narrowed to sharp tips that pointed at the sky, making Ed jittery inside. He could almost feel their cold sharpness punching into his flesh.

Time to get to work.

Tools clattered inside the duffel bag hanging behind his back as he adjusted the strap on his shoulder. But he didn't move.

He stared.

The headstones were inky shapes in the moonlight. Fog hovered above the stones, curling around the tops like cottony snakes.

Tonight felt different. It made his skin feel as if ants were skittering all over, made his head feel as if a cold ball was growing in his brain. His stomach buzzed and cramped. His heart sledged in his ears.

He took another deep breath to calm himself, then started walking up the short dirt path. Reaching the gate, he pushed it open, and entered.

Inside, he sunk to a crouch. He set the duffel bag on the ground, holding the lantern close to his face. He felt the heat drifting from the glass, smelled burning oil. Standing, he held the lantern up, and started walking alongside the headstones. The woods seemed to absorb all outside sounds, making his footsteps sound as if he were walking on newspaper.

Gold light flickered across the ragged markers jutting like the fingertips of a giant stone man reaching up from the earth. He examined the three he'd already dug up. They looked as if he'd done a good job recovering them. Nobody should be able to tell they'd been tampered with.

Unless they checked *inside* the caskets, then they'd realize the heads were missing.

He went to the tree with the low-hanging branches, sliding the lantern's hooped handle over a narrow, leafless branch. It bent slightly with the lantern's weight. He walked back to his duffel bag, and squatted.

Ed slid out the shovel, setting it on the ground beside him. Then he grabbed the pickax under its bowed blades and tugged it out. He didn't think he would need it tonight. Since there hadn't been snow in weeks, the ground wouldn't be hard.

Keep it close, just in case.

Ed twisted around. The lantern's orange spread tented the graveyard. The four headstones spread out in an arc, forming a grin of rock on the dead ground.

A hand clutching the shovel, Ed walked to the fourth grave—a lanky headstone that sat crooked in the ground. Fissures spread across the rock like webbing.

Putting the shovel's blade to the ground, he used the heel of his boot to stomp it in. The blade chomped into the dark earth. He pushed the handle down, tearing out a large clod of soil, and hefted it to the side. Dirt from the sides of the hole sprinkled down, as if trying to rebury itself. He shoveled out another clump, and added it to the small pile.

With the soil so loose, it took him longer to make his way down. One thing he preferred about digging in the winter months, the ground remained firm as he burrowed, keeping the dirt compacted and stiff. It was harder work and he needed to use the pickax more, but at least there wasn't the risk of the dirt collapsing and burying him alive.

That would be a horrible death—buried alive. Trying to breathe, but all you managed to inhale was old dirt. He wondered how long it would take somebody to die if they were planted like a seed.

Too long, he figured. Each second of life under a dirt blanket would be excruciating. Anybody would pray for their death at that point. Just begging God to kill them, though the suffering would last forever…

Thump!

The shovel came to a juddering halt and skidded out to the side. Looking around, Ed saw he was in the ground over his head. The hole was wide and long, the dirt wall sprinkling like an hourglass. It made soft trickling sounds around his feet.

He used the tip of the shovel to scrape what remained of the dirt away. The shovel bounced over something hard that seemed to jut under the dirt.

Crouching, Ed wiped with his hand. The glove worked as a duster that pushed the dirt away. The object began to take shape as he wiped and wiped.

A cross.

Carved of wood, the cross was attached to the top of the lid. He fingered the grooves, scraping away clinging dirt. The cross was part of the lid, as if whoever had carved it had whittled the religious symbol out of the lid. The craftsmanship was spectacular. Though Ed assumed the toe-pincher was as old as the others, he could be fooled into thinking it had been recently buried. Good wood and a talented builder had left this casket in great shape.

Finished with that, he stepped off to the side. He lowered the shovel's blade under the lip of the casket, and pushed it in as far as it would go. The wood creaked. He felt it rise slightly, then stop. The shovel slanted like an unbalanced teeter-totter. Using both hands, he gripped the handle and pushed down harder.

Sweat poured down from his cap. Nails screeched as they were forced to move. The lid began to rise. Thick dust swirled out from the gap, condensing into a putrid fog that floated upward. The stench hit Ed's nostrils, gagging him.

Turning away, his stomach heaved.

Mary's beer exploded from his mouth, spraying the wall beside him. The dirt turned gloppy as his frothy stomach stew coated it in stringy spatters.

Jesus H. Christ!

What a horrible smell! He'd unearthed enough caskets to know the death stench, and this one was the worst he'd ever smelled. Even worse than the preceding three, which had been packed with garlic. Sometimes cows dropped dead in the fields and it would be a long time before the farmers noticed, so they just lay there to rot. What had leaked from the casket was like a herd of dead cattle slow-baking in the summer sun for weeks.

Ed tried to take a breath, but his throat made a sound like a duck being skinned alive. He coughed up some more beer, spat it out, and wiped the tears from his eyes. When he was able to breathe again, he did so through his mouth to avoid smelling that abominable stink again.

"Oh...God..."

Ed closed his eyes, letting the cramping in his stomach subside. When he reopened them, he felt a little better.

He looked down at the casket. The blade of the shovel was halfway between the lid and casket wall. The rotten fog had cleared. But he knew once he got back to work, he'd just stir it up again. So he held his breath as he wiggled the shovel. He turned away as more fog was loosed. It filled the cramped space, making his eyes water. He blinked to clear them.

Pushing down on the shovel's handle, he felt the lid rise higher. The nails pried from the wood with a crunchy whine.

And the lid popped free.

Ed stumbled back. He made an involuntary reach and gripped the wall. His fingers slid across his vomit, coating the gloves in his stomach's warm contents.

"Ugh…" Ed muttered.

He shook his hand, flinging away vomit. He flexed his fingers a few times to keep the fabric from sticking together as he studied the casket. The lid sat crooked, showing a wide patch of darkness in the top right corner and lower left corner. Afraid of getting too close to the smell, he prodded the lid with the tip of the shovel. The lid bounced on the rim, lifted and dropped with a clatter. He got the blade underneath and threw the lid up. It tumbled sideways, falling against the dirt wall like a miniscule shelter.

Without the lid, the fog flowed out of the dark hollow of the casket. It seemed to fill the hole, taking shape as it drifted upward. In the dim lighting of the lantern and the moon, the smoke looked green as it shaped into a ball and two slants that narrowed to a wispy tail. Two empty holes like eyes appeared, a mouth parted into an oval.

And moaned.

Then it broke apart with a gust that blew Ed's cap off his head. His clothes flapped against his body as the wind tore through the hole. He fell back into the dirt wall, knocking some loose. Dirt poured down his shoulders, behind his collar. It felt itchy as it sprinkled down his shirt.

As quickly as the wind had started, it ended. Ed looked up, noticing the trees above swaying outward as the wind soared through.

Don't be a fool.

Wind didn't work that way.

But what was that moaning?

Ed shook his head, chalking it up as a trick of the light, and noises of the wind.

Wind that started at my feet.

"Horseshit," he muttered.

Shaking his head, he noticed it felt naked. The cool air seeped into his damp hair. He patted his head. His hat was gone. He spotted it inside the coffin, hanging at an odd angle.

Frowning, Ed reached inside, gripping the hat's bill. He lifted it.

And uncovered a half foot of protruding wood.

Confused, Ed fluffed the hat and put it on. He looked at the corpse inside.

His skin pulled taut against his bones. An army of spiders seemed to crawl up the nape of his neck and over his scalp. He couldn't make sense of what he was seeing.

This can't be right.

The deformed shape of the head, the large rounded ears that twisted outward to reveal deep canals that looked like rubber caverns. Its flattened face was tipped with a leaf-shaped nose and pinched jowls that showed large fangs in its frozen snarl. Two spikey teeth were bunched together in the center with longer hooked fangs on either side. Bushy hair hung around its face, connecting to a pair of sideburns that looked like half of a beard that ended before it reached the mouth. Cobwebs clung in the hair here and there.

Arms crossed on the stomach. Six fingers between its two hands, and all of them curled into claws. It wore a ruffled white shirt that was dark with stains under a black overcoat. Matching black pants shaped skinny legs, becoming tatters and strips around the talon-like feet with a third claw growing out from each heel like spears.

As horrifying and odd was the body, so was realizing what his hat had landed on—a chunk of wood jutting from its chest. The tip was mashed flat, as if it had been hammered into place. The edges looked as if they'd melted down into bulges.

A stake.

"Through the heart," Ed muttered.

Dread wormed through his bowels.

"Mary, mother of God…"

Knowing what he'd found, Ed felt a grin tugging the corners of his mouth.

He was staring at the corpse of a vampire.

-7-

Ed dropped on his ass. Sitting cross-legged, he stared at the vampire corpse. His eyes roamed the withered body, the flattened stake jutting from its heart.

A vampire.

And the other graves? The women?

Vampires!

He'd uncovered a vampire flock!

I'm going to be famous.

Ed saw himself shaking hands with the president before bowing his head so a medal could be slipped over his neck. It hung around his chest, round and gold. Flash bulbs popped as a tumult of questions were fired at him from the reporters there to get to the scoop.

I could take it on the road. A traveling show! Ed Gein and the Vampire Corpse. Charge two dollars to see it. Five to touch it.

Ed smiled. Maybe he could even joke around with the crowds, act as if he might pull the stake out.

Ed's eyes returned to the little rod. What would *happen* if he did pull the stake out?

People would want to know for sure. They'd tease me if I didn't pull the stake out. Nobody would believe it was a real vampire if I didn't prove it.

And what happened if people wanted to know how he'd found it? He couldn't say he just stumbled upon a vampire legion while digging up graves. That's what he had here, a legion of them. No doubt this one was the others' master. Just like in the horror books, just like Dracula.

Maybe he is Dracula...

Ed didn't think so. Dracula, though a creature of the night, was a handsome man. This *thing* was not handsome. It was vile, hideous.

A monster.

Maybe the books and movies lied all these years?

They didn't know. How could they?

But now Ed knew. He had a vampire master right here.

And nobody will believe it unless I can prove it to them.

What if he pulled the stake out on stage and nothing happened? People would laugh him out of the room, pointing and heckling, spouting hateful remarks. He wouldn't just be the laughing stock of Plainfield anymore. He'd be the world's biggest goober.

Pull the stake now. See what happens.

Ed shuddered. His stomach tried to force more beer up. He swallowed the acidic trail bubbling in the back of his throat, and got onto his knees. If he pulled the stake now, he could prove, at least to himself, that it was real.

Will this work?

Ed assumed it was like in every vampire story he'd read—the vampire would awaken if the stake was removed.

Ed trembled as he crawled beside the casket. Why would he want to wake up such a creature? Wouldn't it be thirsty after being dead for a long time? Nobody but Ed was around, so his blood would be needed to quench its centuries-old thirst.

He wasn't so sure he wanted to pull the stake now.

How will I know for sure?

Just stab the stake back into its heart before it awakened all the way!

Yes!

If it worked, he could repeat the performance for the crowds. Pull the stake, let the vampire move around some, maybe even flash its fangs, then hammer the stake back in and kill it again.

He heard the audience's whistles and cheers so vividly, they could have been in the woods with him. It made him smile. Filled his trembling muscles with strength and washed away the wariness.

First, pull the stake.

Once he knew whether the vampire was real or not, he'd whip up a story on how he came across it.

And the heads? He should have them in the show too. Nothing like showing off a vampire master *and* his brides.

But I shrunk them already.

Not all of them. There was one left. But he'd promised it to Peter.

Ed felt disappointment trying to ruin this moment. Then he snapped his fingers. It sounded like a muffled pop through the gloves.

Their bodies. I could take their bodies, attach other heads to them. Carve fangs out of the teeth...

Later. He'd figure it all out later.

First thing's first...

The stake.

Gulping, Ed peered at the stake. He felt cold and tight inside. No matter how he fantasized the outcome to be, he knew pulling the stake was the wrong thing to do.

If nothing happened, he failed.

But if something did happen...

Ed couldn't let himself dwell on that. It was a vampire, no confusion there. Who would go through so much trouble to bury this thing for a prank? The smell alone told him it wasn't fake.

He'd never be able to convince anybody else unless he knew for sure.

Without another thought, Ed's fingers gripped the jutting wood. He wrenched it out with a sound like crunched celery.

Holding the stake up, he gazed at the filed tip. It was darker than the exposed half. From its sharpness, he figured it shouldn't be hard to ram it back into the vampire if he needed to.

A moist crinkling sound came from the casket.

Ed felt his eyes widen. His body turned stodgy and stiff. The stake poised by his face, his eyes lowered to the corners so he could watch.

The body began to solidify.

Its bones moved like mechanics, resetting, pieces stretched, blood and veins reformed. A small lump inside the hole pulsated, growing with each lethargic beat. Arms and legs thickened with returning muscle. Its chest bulged and popped, like a bag being filled with water. The ruffled shirt expanded as a torso took shape beneath it.

The head twitched, snapped. Mouth yawning, tittering, the fangs twisted and extended. The eyeless sockets opened as a murky fluid deluged the chasms like milk spilled in a gopher hole. The fluid swelled to the brims, bubbling like rising dough. The surface hardened into a material that resembled glass. Crimson splashed inside, like cherry soda inside a bottle.

A shade like bruised peaches spilled over the decayed hues of the skin. Deep blue spread up its arms, its neck, as if painted with an invisible brush. Old skin flaked off, shedding in thin coils.

The hole above its heart sealed.

Stake it! Put the stake in!

Ed remained fixed in place, eyes glued on the dreadful image below him as popping sounds like burning logs filled the air. He wondered if he might be sleeping. Perhaps he'd fallen asleep while reading a horror story and any moment would wake up in his chair, coated in icy sweat.

I'm awake. God help me, I'm awake!

Ed wished he hadn't pulled out the stake.

The vampire's clothes stayed old and tattered as the body inside became fresh and strong. An arm moved, lifted, claws flexing as if trying to work out a cramp. The other arm shot into the air, hand open, turning so the dagger-like talons pointed at the sky, as if holding out its monstrous hand for a treat.

And Ed was the treat it wanted.

The creature's head whipped toward Ed. Its eyes flashed red.

The glowing crimson stare was like a slap that knocked Ed back. His feet kicked soil as he crab-walked in reverse until his back crashed against the dirt wall. Bits sprinkled down on his head, showering his face.

The vampire's blue maw dropped, the skin of its jowls stretching like melted rubber. Its face was demonic, yet surprisingly handsome behind the monstrous mutations and blue skin. Partly resembling something human, it seemed to be a combination of several evil monsters sculpted onto a man's body.

The protracted fangs were prominent and sharp, dripping saliva as a forked tongue slid across their glossy surfaces. It smacked its thin purple lips, relishing the taste of its soon-to-be meal.

Me...

"You're not getting me!" Ed shouted.

He hobbled on his knees toward the creature. Clawed hands pawed the air, arms stretching as if ready to embrace Ed.

The opened mouth unleashed a screech that ripped through Ed's ears, punched his brain, and split it into halves. He felt the roots of his teeth tremble inside his gums.

Wincing, he threw his arms up to block the fetid gust spurting from its lungs. In a quick, jarring glimpse, he noticed the vampire's legs weren't quite active yet. One was just starting to wiggle, but the other remained flaccid and useless.

But in a few seconds the monster would be completely healed.

Move, Ed!

Heeding his mental commands, Ed pushed through the force of the vampire's cry. He felt his hat try to fly away from his head and slapped a hand down to hold it there. Reaching the casket, he rose on his knees, tugged the cap down, lifted the stake, put both hands behind it, and drove it down.

The sharp point jerked to a halt just before the pointed tip pounded into its rejuvenated heart. Ed saw claws gripping his wrist. Felt frizzy hair sliding over his skin. The texture was like pig's skin—fuzzy and coarse.

Ed screamed.

The vampire gave another screech, pulled Ed down, and tilted its head to position its teeth above Ed's throat. Writhing on top of the rippling, crackling body, Ed fought to get his arms loose.

Ed heard the snap of teeth, felt the wind of a lashing bite as it just missed the exposed slant of his neck. The vampire tilted back its head, opened its mouth impossibly wide, and released a third screech that sounded more irritated.

Its jowls stretched like a snake's mouth about to swallow a rat whole.

Ed gazed at the creature's massive, sabretooth fangs. He squirmed, kicking his feet to bring his legs around. Now

Ed was splayed across the vampire's body as if he were a cub hunting for his mama's nipple. His arms, extended above him, gripped the stake with both hands as the vampire maintained its immovable hold of the sharp end. In this awkward position, Ed couldn't get the leverage he needed to shove the stake down.

So he scrambled up, digging his knees into the vampire's stomach.

The creature did not release Ed's forearms. Now Ed's wrists were crossed, making an X of his arms. Looking down, Ed saw the vampire turn its head to watch him. It unleashed another shriek that jiggled his flesh.

Must know what I'm trying to do.

What was he trying to do?

Ed wasn't even sure yet, but the vampire had figured it out.

Then he realized why he'd gotten in this position.

To drive his weight on top of the stake.

Ed twisted his knees, pushing them harder into the vampire's stomach. It felt hollow through the thin fabric of its shirt, like an empty sack. If Ed didn't get the stake back into its heart, his blood would be what sated its hungry belly.

Jerking his right leg forward, he planted his foot beside the creature's shoulder. He strained to pull his left foot out from under him. His ass pinned it down. It was hard work, but he finally got it out. Now he crouched above the creature, as if about to shit in the woods.

Ed bent low, felt his ass bump the vampire's legs, then hopped. The burden of his body came down on his arms. Drove the stake down. The vampire's arms flew apart as Ed landed on top of it. He felt the jolt of the stake when it punctured the vampire, heard the crunch of it being shoved through skin.

The vampire released its loudest and most agonizing wail yet.

The loose soil walls of the hole collapsed. Dirt poured from all around, quickly filling the bottom. Ed scurried off the vampire's body, only to be knocked down as more dirt fell.

The hole swallowed him.

Dirt pushed on his shoulders, forcing him lower. Earlier he'd wondered what being buried alive would feel like, and now he knew. It was even worse than he could have imagined. If he tried to breathe, it would be the end of him. His lungs would fill with grave dirt and strangle him.

Holding his breath, he kept his eyes closed as he tried to move. At first, the dirt felt tight around him, but he was able to get his elbows to slightly twist. Some dirt fell away, but more quickly replaced it, though much looser. Soon he was able to flap his arms like a duck. He felt some of the burden come off his back as dirt fell to fill to the warrens his elbows made. He felt his body moving up, his face pushing through dirt like gritty water.

Then his head burst through the top and he took in a heavy breath. Dust coated the inside of his mouth, but he didn't care. He was happy to be breathing again.

Buried to his shoulders, Ed waded through the loose soil. Realizing his shovel was at the bottom of this dirt trap, he felt a sense of loss. There were plenty more shovels at the house. Still, he hated to lose it.

But no matter how much he would miss his tool, he wasn't about to dig it out.

The vampire was down there.

I killed it.

Still, he didn't want to go near it. Knowing a creature was somewhere around his feet made Ed's heart feel as if it were being squeezed with icy hands. The tarn of dirt blinded him of the vampire's exact whereabouts, and that made it feel worse.

Reaching what was left of the nearest wall, Ed rested. He looked over his shoulder. Behind, him, the dirt piled down, forming a ridge that led up to the rim of the hole. It should be fairly easy to crawl out, but the dirt was probably still unstable.

He'd better be careful.

Ed pushed on the rim of the hole. He tried to lift himself.

Dirt exploded behind him.

Twisting his hips, Ed spotted the vampire thrashing out of the dirt a few feet behind him.

Throwing its arms wide, it leaned back, and shrieked. There was a *click* and wings burst out of its back, ripping through the overcoat and showering the tight area in dusty fog. Their span reached either side of the hole. Ed recognized a forearm, a thumb, long skinny fingers that curled down to the triangular tips of the wings. Between each appendage was a cape of thin flesh that rattled like a flag as the vampire trembled.

Giant damn bat wings!

Ed shook his head, unable to believe what he was seeing.

"I killed you!" shouted Ed.

The vampire bent forward, ruffled its wings, and shrieked again. Ed saw the torn patch of shirt over its heart. A blue patch of skin showed. No stake. Looking lower, he saw the stake jutting from low on its ribcage.

He'd missed the heart completely.

But he wasn't about to try again.

Screaming, Ed faced the slope that led out of the hole. He slapped his hands down, gripped, and pushed against the ground. The soil shifted around his hips as he clawed and pulled. Though he made the motions of a man wildly fleeing for his life, he remained in the same spot.

Stealing quick glimpses over his shoulder, he saw the vampire rip the stake out of its stomach. "Shit!" Ed cried, putting his back to the creature. He hopped and thrust, slapped and clawed. His hips came free of the dirt, knees following. He got his right knee on solid ground, and put his weight on it as he hoisted himself out. On his hands and knees, he looked behind him.

The vampire held the stake out—snapped it in half.

Ed's throat felt raw from another scream. He scrambled away from the dirt.

Dived.

His chest pounded the ground. Rolling, he moved away just as the creature's hand slapped down on solid ground. Its curved ears appeared above the edge, its eyes gleaming like embers from Hell.

Ed came to a stop on his stomach. Something twinkled in the gray glow of the moonlight.

The pickax!

Ed recognized its arched head, and gleefully hollered. Felt like seeing an old friend for the first time in years. A friend who's come to help him out of a dreadful situation.

Crawling, Ed made it over to the tool. His hands gripped the handle. Lifted. The heavy tool swayed low from the twin blades. They hadn't been fashioned from wood, but if he pounded one of the blades through the vampire's heart, he figured it would be enough to kill the damn thing again.

Screeching, the vampire shot into the sky with a burst of dirt and dust that showered the graveyard.

On his knees, Ed leaned far back, watching the vampire shrink as it went high. It flew in front of the moon, cutting a black flapping shape into the curve of white before vanishing.

It took Ed a few seconds to find it again. Small at first, it was quickly growing.

"Shit!"

It was coming back down.

Clutching the pickax, Ed scrambled to his feet. He gave another glance at the sky.

The creature was a little ways above the trees. The naked branches made crooked lines through the vampire's dark contour. He could hear the thin rattle of its flapping wings, loudening as it plunged.

Ed ran. He made a wide leap across the hole. On the other side, his feet slid on loose dirt around the edges. He threw back a hand to stop himself from tumbling back down into the hole. Getting up, he dashed for the gate, the pickax slung over his shoulder like a rifle.

A few steps from the gate, Ed turned back.

And spotted the vampire right behind him now, performing a downward swoop.

Maw yawning, tongue writhing, its teeth dripped gooey saliva. Ed smelled its horrible breath as the hungry mouth bore closer.

Ed shouldered through the gate. His feet tangled together. He crashed onto the ground. Rolling onto his back, he kicked the gate shut in the vampire's face and squirmed backwards.

The vampire smashed against the iron, throwing the gate wide.

Snapping off the turnstile in a rusted shriek, the gate rocketed over Ed. He heard trees snapping as it soared through the woods. Next, the vampire soared inches above him. Its long body blocked his view of the star-dotted sky on its way by.

Ed figured it had been traveling too fast to nab him.

Swerving high, the vampire shot into the sky, gliding in circles above the trees, wings lashing. It made motions like a fighter plane, tilting to fire its automatic guns.

Rolling over, Ed grabbed the pickax, and got to his feet. He spotted the path out of here, and smiled. So close. All he had to do was get to it, then to the road.

Then in his truck.

He'd be safe in there. Had to be.

Ed started moving, slower this time. His body ached with each step, shooting sharp tendrils of pain into his hips. He was sore, exhausted, and terrified.

A whoosh came from above, like a bomb being dropped from a passing plane.

Ed dared a glance up.

The vampire was plunging again, arms extended, hands open, mouth wide, fangs gleaming and sharp. It gave a triumphant wail, convinced it had won as the distance between them closed.

Ed waited until the vampire was right on top of him before he spun around with the pickax. The bowed blade punched into the vampire's stomach. He saw it shoot through its back, parting its wings. Its battle cry dwindled to a confused squeak.

Throwing himself out of the way, Ed avoided the vampire's frantic spiral. Its wings flapped, but couldn't lift it high enough to retreat. Crashing to the ground, it bounced and hopped before flying again. It spun around through the air, like a bird with a broken wing, only to fall again.

Ed leaned forward, hands on his knees. Panting, he watched the vampire skip across the ground, hover and drop, emanating injured yelps. It got a little ways up the dirt path before Ed breathed again.

It was hurt. Once the creature had tuckered itself out, Ed could finish it off.

Until then, he would rest. Catch his breath. Let his jumbled nerves settle.

The pickax landed on the road with a faint thump. A dusty cloud rose around it.

"Damn," he muttered.

With the pickax dislodged from its midriff, the vampire fluttered into the sky. Though its patterns were rocky and off-balance, it was able to fly without any more problems. He watched its dark form blend into the night sky.

Ed stared for several long moments before he turned around to study the graveyard. The turnstile was bent, the gate out of sight. Fog drifted through the ancient entryway, as if it had finally been set free.

"I'm a damned fool," said Ed.

A tight sick feeling spread through his aching muscles. There was no way he could fully comprehend the severity of his mistake. But he knew matters were going to become a lot worse.

Tears suddenly filled his eyes. He lowered his face into his glove-covered hands, and wept for the first time since Mama died.

-8-

Mary Hogan drove along the darkened stretch of Highway 73. Her front lights pushed a dim spread of light through the black in front of her. She was ready to get home and take a bath. She had six cocks' worth of seed stuffed inside of her, and a little swimming around her stomach.

She felt dirty, soiled.

It'd been a busy night.

Though she tried to regularly rinse herself at the tavern between men, she knew she wouldn't get all the goop cleaned out unless she soaked in a hot tub for a while.

Let the soap and water take care of the rest.

She glanced down at her purse, smiling. Close to two hundred dollars in there. Would be more if she'd charged Tom Worden. Because he was the law, he got his piece for free. Plus, she kind of liked him the most. She never got her own fix with other men, but Tom could do things with his tongue that sent her into a quivering fit every time.

Did his wife get that at home? Mary hoped not. She liked to pretend the tongue tricks were just for her. Sometimes when Mary allowed herself to think about Tom's home life, her skin turned hot, and she broke out in sweats.

Jealousy?

She didn't think so.

Resentment?

Most likely.

But it still wasn't fair to hold it against Tom. Mary was with multiple men a night while Tom only went home to one other woman—Barbara. Sure, she was a pretty bitch, after a lot of work. Sure, the esteemed Mrs. Worden had a good body, though nothing compared to Mary's.

Mary's tits got her more men than anything else. Men paid her good money just to fondle them. She didn't think Barbara had that specialty. Or if she did, she wouldn't know how to make it work in her favor. She was just a comely woman of the house. To somebody like Barbara, nothing existed outside those comforting walls.

But Mary had seen the world. She'd lived all over, traveled. Had had more men in the last few years than most would in two lifetimes. She'd even dabbled with women more than once, and had found them to be fun too. Sometimes she had multiple partners of both sexes at the same time. Those jaunts became a wild party that usually left her feeling emotionally drained, along with the shame, for days afterward. Those moments didn't last. But when they would come on, booze usually made her forget.

Mary knew what they said about her in Plainfield. She didn't care. Those prudes weren't getting rid of her. And if she got to fuck a stud like Tom Worden regularly, then being in Plainfield was even more worthwhile.

Keeping one hand on the wheel, Mary slapped at her purse. She pulled it closer, reaching inside. Her fingers brushed her cigarettes. The purse flaps wouldn't cooperate, and kept bending. Twisting her wrist painfully sideways, her fingers gripped the pack.

"Ah-ha!"

She tried to pull out the cigarettes. The purse moved with her hand, the flaps clutching her wrist.

"Damn it to hell."

Mary looked at her purse. It looked as if it had swallowed her hand. Shaking her arm, the purse didn't want to let go. She gave it a harder flick. Her hand came free, the cigarettes clutched in her fingers. "Got your little asses!"

The purse hit the seat, tumbling into the dark pool of the floorboard.

Laughing, Mary faced the road.

And screamed.

A face from a nightmare soared toward her, its red-glowing eyes wincing at the glare of her lights. It turned its blue face away, revealing a cavernous ear that curved on top through a thick shock of ruffling, black hair.

Mary glimpsed its mighty fangs, glowing in the bright light.

Her feet stomped the brakes.

The locked tires screamed louder than Mary as she was pitched forward. Her forehead bashed the whirling steering wheel. Jarred but still focused, she grabbed the helm with both hands. The giant bat-man-thing let out a screech that was cut short when it bounced over the hood of her car. The thing's back struck the windshield, caving it in with a crunch of splitting glass. Thick cracks shot outward on all sides.

The thing kept going, thumping above her as it toppled over the car.

Mary felt herself skidding to the right. Screaming, she fought with the wheel. It tried to pull the opposite way of her spin and, Mary knew if it succeeded, the car would flip. She'd been in an accident or two. Didn't take much for these machines to go ass over.

The car made a complete circle before coming to a rocky halt. Dust and smoke rose outside the windows, reflecting the lights' glow in shimmering waves.

The bat-thing smacked the ground several feet ahead of her. Other than slight twitching of its upstretched wings, it was motionless. After a moment, they crumpled down like paper.

Even with the car sitting still, Mary felt as if she were spiraling. She could still hear the squealing tires deep in her ears. Her hands felt glued to the steering wheel, and she had to pry them loose.

Holding out her hands, her fingers were bent, as if about to claw something.

What was that? Jesus! What the hell was that?

Parts of it seemed human, but others were...a bat?

A big damn man-bat-thing!

And its skin was blue!

Flying right at me!

Came at her car like a moth drawn by a candle flame.

Something trickled into her eye, making her blink. She reached up and rubbed the narrow runnel of stickiness that came down from her hairline. She held out her fingertips, and saw they were dabbed in blood.

Bonked my head good.

Seeing she was bleeding triggered a dull throb in her skull.

"Son of a bitch..."

Mary groaned. She felt around the door, found the handle, and pulled. The door clacked open. Climbing out, she held onto the top of the frame for balance. The cool air made her head sting.

"Bet my car's beaten to hell," she muttered.

Hands on the roof, she walked alongside the car, patting the metal so she wouldn't fall. The bat-thing had severely damaged her car.

Damaged me, too.

All that money she'd earned tonight probably wouldn't be enough to pay for it.

A glance at the front of her car made her moan. Besides the fractured windshield, a headlight had been smashed like a punctured eyeball. Bars hung from the wrecked grille as plumes of dark smoke curled out. The hood looked crumpled in the front like an old rug.

She hadn't been going *that* fast, but the destruction of her car was serious.

The *thing* must've been rocketing towards her.

And heavy as hell!

Mary turned around. The bat-thing hadn't moved. It lay in a folded heap a few feet away. Wings draped its back like a thin, tatty sheet.

Mary took a hesitant step forward. A gust of chilly wind blew at her from nowhere, stirring her hair. Her skirt flapped against her legs, molding around their thick curves. The ruffles of her shirt trembled, the exposed mounds of her breasts stippled with gooseflesh. She pulled her coat shut over them. Cold air licked the wound on her head. Wincing at the minor sting, the skin around her injury felt tight— probably from a forming welt.

"Damn it all," she muttered.

She might need to see a doctor. Mary hated doctor's offices, hated the sterile smell, how they put their hands on her. She walked along the verge of the road, slightly swaying. She must have bonked her noggin harder than she'd originally thought if she was this dizzy. Giving the forming lump another soft tap, she checked her finger again. There didn't seem to be as much blood this time.

Hopefully that was a good sign.

Eyes fixed on the limp form in the center of the road, Mary loomed closer. She stopped a couple inches from the frayed edges of its coat.

What is it?

Mary couldn't tell much from where she stood. Though folded at the waist, legs bent, she could tell it was tall and lanky and dressed in dark clothing. Sprouted through its coat, wings curled over its head and shoulders. Mary could see scraps of fabric writhing in the breeze around the wing's narrow stems.

Its back blocked her view of its arms and hands.

But its feet...

Good God!

Nowhere near human-like, its two toes were fuzzy and blue and tipped with talons. A single talon was where a heel should be.

Drive back to the tavern, phone Tom Worden at home and tell him to come see this.

That seemed like a good idea.

Mary was about to turn and leave when a thought stopped her.

He won't believe me.

And he'd probably reprimand her for calling his home. That was one of the few rules he had when it came to their liaisons. It happened at the tavern, and stayed there. No phone calls, no public interactions, other than at Mary's place of business, of course.

He'd probably accuse her of lying just to get him out of his bed and into hers.

Again.

But the body was proof she wasn't lying.

Mary could see it now. She'd get back to the tavern, get Tom over there. They'd come out here together and the damn carcass would be gone. Maybe somebody would drive by, see it lying there and pick it up. Maybe it'd go away on its own. Either way, she didn't want to risk anything by leaving it here.

Fine. I'll just drive this damn thing straight over to his house and dump it on his front lawn. He'll have to believe me then.

Mary felt herself smile. The dried blood on her cheeks made soft crinkling sounds.

That'd be a sight for sure. She pictured Barbara Worden standing in the front lawn in her robe, hair a mess. When she laid eyes on the thing, her pretty face would turn white. She'd scream. Probably faint too. Just drop flat on the dew-soaked grass.

Mary would pay money to see that.

As long as I can make it to Tom's.

She turned around and looked at her car. The one spherical light cut a slender tunnel through the dark. Dust swam through its beam like minute lightning bugs. She could hear the engine steadily pumping.

Seemed fine, though it didn't look it.

Mary looked down at the thing. She wondered if it was dead.

Has to be. Nobody could live through that.

Mary let out a deep breath that rattled her cheeks. Now she had to put it in her car.

Had to *touch* it.

Had to *carry* it to her car.

Had to put it in her trunk, if she planned to drive it over to Tom's house. No way was it riding inside with her.

Crouching, Mary's lower back and legs felt sore and tender from the crash. She reached out. Her hands skimmed the arid fabric of its overcoat.

The thing whipped around, hissing.

Screaming, Mary staggered back, dropping onto her rump. The landing jostled her, made her neck pop. A sharp pain stabbed her shoulders. Before she had a chance to react, the thing was crawling over her waist. Clawed hands ripped her top down the middle in a vicious swipe. Her giant breasts spilled out.

"No!"

Mary kicked out a foot, feeling the firm bash against the thing's face. Instead of it falling back like she'd hoped, the thing only shoved her leg aside, making a wide space between her thighs. A hand slapped down between her legs.

"Stop!"

Mary tried to roll over. She was pushed onto her back. Little bits of rock and debris scratched at her through her shirt. Some pecked the back of her head. Mary pounded her fists on the top of the thing's head as it crawled between her parted legs. She could've been hitting a slab of beef from the nil affect her resistance was having.

Looking up between the two hills of her bare breasts, she saw an elongated arm rise and swing down. Fabric ripped. Cold air washed over her groin. Her skirt and under garments had been torn away as easily as a spider-web.

Mary punched the hand pushing on her chest. It held on. She gripped a thick, fuzzy finger and tried to pry it back. The tip of its talons dug into the soft skin of her breasts. Blood flowed down the springy mounds in ribbons. The pain was like a dog bite that filled her with a paralyzing sensation. Her muscles locked, arms dropped to the ground and stayed there as if bound. All she could move were her eyes.

And she regretted this when she peered at the thing again.

It had lowered its pants. A dark blur of hair covered its scrawny legs. A tuft of fuzz rose under its stomach. Something like a flesh-colored slug sprouted, thickening as it pulsated and throbbed. A clear fluid dripped from the tip, burning her thighs like hot wax when it dribbled across her skin.

Mary tried to plead, to beg, but all she could produce were short coughing sounds.

On its knees, the thing hobbled closer, lowering its body onto hers. A forked tongue unfurled from its mouth, slithering across her breasts, coating them in stringy wetness. The serpentine tongue pressed her nipple between its cleft tips.

Mary watched with wide eyes as the thick, slimy member at the thing's crotch delved between her legs.

A hot log shoved into her, spreading her wide. The thing's thrusts filled her with fire. Mouth gaping, her groans were snagged in her throat and turned to retches. She felt as if she were melting inside, turning to liquid and sloshing out of her groin.

Mary told herself to move, to fight. Her body wouldn't obey the commands and only remained there in a dull paralysis. The creature sucked and shoved, pounding her into the hard road. The rough surface beneath her tore her clothes, scratched her back raw.

It went on for several minutes.

Then the hardness between her legs swelled. She felt something hard and oval-shaped shoot inside of her, turn runny, and spread a warming numbness throughout her body. What had once been pain turned to tingling prickles of pleasure. Each breath seemed to cause an orgasmic pull that turned her groans to moans.

Soon she was squealing.

And laughing.

The gooey seed buzzed under her skin.

In her mind, the old Mary dangled from a rocky ledge. Holding on by one hand, her legs kicked above an opened maw of darkness. This Mary knew what was happening to her. This Mary felt every jab and prod, felt the thing's hot scatter passing a sickness onto her. And when it was finished infecting her, the old Mary would no longer exist. A new Mary would take over, the old one never allowed back.

As she struggled to pull herself up from the ledge, boots that looked just like her own stomped her fingers.

She released her grip, and began to fall.

As she plunged, flapping her arms, she gave a fleeting glance at the edge. The new Mary stood above her, smirking as the old Mary vanished in the blank abyss.

In the middle of the road, Mary wore the same smirk on her bruised face. A newborn devotion had consumed her.

The Vampire of Plainfield

She knew the kind of creature she would serve now. And her heart only beat because the thing—*the vampire*—had allowed it. She would forever be indebted.

It needed to feed, and she would see that it got as much as it needed to regain its strength, to grow.

To live.

"I'll worship you forever," she gasped.

The thing gave a final thrust as the block inside her began to deflate like a slow-leaking balloon. The thing began to pull out of her and Mary quickly curled her thick legs around its skinny waist.

"Don't stop," she moaned. "Do it again…I want more."

And it gave her more.

A lot more.

The Vampire's Graveyard Kiss

Geiner:

Why did they have to keep the heat on in Ed Gein's house?
So the furniture wouldn't get goosebumps.

-9-

Ed opened the lunchbox. Though he already knew what was inside, he still sifted through what he'd packed. A couple small cans of beans, peanut butter sandwiches wrapped in paper, and a bottle of orange pop that was no longer cold. Same stuff that had been in there when he'd checked an hour ago.

Removing a can of beans, he slammed the lid on his lunchbox. The clap of the metal reverberated through the quiet woods. Birds chirped in the mild day. Other animals scampered, making soft rustling sounds in the distance.

This vigil was probably pointless. He'd been sitting on the ground in the woods since before sunrise. So far as Ed knew, the vampire hadn't come back to the graveyard since Ed accidentally let it go.

Hadn't come back the last few nights, but maybe tonight would be different. Ed planned to wait as long as he could stand it. If it didn't come back tonight, Ed doubted it was going to.

From where he sat, the graveyard looked almost untouched. The only evidence was the soil was a little trampled from where Ed had reburied the grave. But he doubted the creature had returned to its casket and somehow pulled the dirt back over itself.

Ed leaned forward, bringing his legs down and crossing them. He dug out his canoe knife from his pocket, folding out the blade. There was a click when it locked into place. Holding the can between his boots, he stabbed the blade into the top and began to saw around the lid. The sharp grating noises were awful and made Ed's teeth hurt. He stopped cutting when there was only a little section of tin left. Then he folded back the lid, letting it dangle upward like an opened mouth.

He dipped the knife into the chunky broth inside the can. He scooped out a soggy lump, and ate it. It was cold and slimy in his mouth, but tasted okay.

Since the other night, he'd begun reading all he could about vampires. He had plenty of material to search through at his house: comics, magazines, and books. What information he'd found so far had been mostly counterproductive. He'd expected it to make him feel better, or at least give him some kind of confidence. Instead, it just seemed to fill him with more dread.

Too many contradicting stories, not enough facts.

All he knew for sure was a stake through the heart had killed the vampire before. Removing it had awakened it.

And now the vampire was on the prowl. Ed had picked up a slim pattern in the newspapers. Just a couple short articles on the last page about a couple missing men, travelers making their way through central Wisconsin. Most wouldn't pay the articles any mind, but Ed had homed in on the connections right away.

The reports began a couple days ago. The men had been traveling alone, going from one town to another and the main avenue of Plainfield was most likely a path they'd taken. Somewhere before reaching their final destination, they'd vanished.

Dead cold.

Probably kibble for the vampire.

Ed just couldn't figure out where the vampire was resting during the day.

Not here.

He was convinced its sleeping place was the connection. The men must've somehow stumbled upon its territory.

Or were lured there.

Either way, Ed was clueless. He couldn't think of anything better to do than just park his ass in the woods, surveying the graveyard.

I'm trapped.

It was all on his shoulders, putting the vampire back down. When he did that, he'd think about the potentials that could follow later—the tour, the stage show, the fable on how he'd come to find the creature.

That can wait.

First, he had to kill it.

Ed leaned back against the tree, setting the can on his stomach. The bark felt bumpy and hard on the back his head. It snagged and plucked loose hairs whenever he moved his head.

Staring at the graveyard's busted gate, he used his knife to shovel beans into his mouth until he dozed off.

-10-

"Slow down, honey," said Mary. She gripped the hair at the back of the man's head and tugged him back. It was the only place he seemed to have any. Even the spaces behind his ears were bare, the horseshoe rounding the back of his skull didn't quite reach. "We have plenty of time. Save some for the bed."

There was a ruddy smear on the man's chin. His moustache looked mussed. "Come on, foxy, let me at 'em!"

He pushed his head back down to her breasts, digging his tongue into the valley between them. She heard gross slurping sounds as the inner sides of her breasts were coated with wetness. His tongue brushed the wounds, making her gasp. Her companion must have mistaken this as a signal of her approval, for he slammed against her. He pushed Mary back. She banged against the edge of the bar. It hurt. Putting her hands flat on his chest, she shoved him away.

"I said hold on!" she snapped.

The man, Jenkins she thought his name was, held up his hands. "Whoa, miss, I do apologize."

Mary adjusted the top of her dress. It was a red number, tight in the back, pulling against her breasts and lifting them like two globes on her chest. She'd powdered them so they would look even smoother than normal.

The man—*Jenkins?*—wasn't from Plainfield. He'd come into the tavern last night on his way to Doverton. She'd tried to convince him to stay the night, but he had something to do in the morning. So she'd worked out an arrangement to

The Vampire of Plainfield

meet him back here this afternoon. Though he'd seemed a little confused when she'd told him to park in the back, he was quick to agree to see her again.

"Don't want my husband to know," she'd said.

That had been enough to dissuade any suspicion. It'd worked on the others, so there had been no doubt it would trick Jenkins, either.

Mary stepped away from the bar. "Going to take off your clothes or what?" she asked.

"You told me to wait," he said. Giving her a goofy grin, Jenkins snapped his fingers. "But I'll have them off in a jiff." He started fidgeting with the belt of his trousers. It took some effort for him to get it undone. When it hung open, he pulled off his coat, tossed it onto a nearby table, and slid down his suspender straps.

His pants dropped. Holding out his hands as if presenting himself, he stepped out of the pants while kicking off his polished shoes.

A businessman, for sure.

Mary held in her laughter. He wore dark socks up to his knees, a garter band holding them up. There was a section of scrawny, milk-white legs before they vanished under the tails of his buttoned shirt. A red tie hung like a crooked tongue from his neck.

"How's this?" he asked.

"Get all of it off," she said. Then she tilted her head. "But leave the tie on."

"Oh?" An eyebrow raised, he started fumbling with the buttons of his shirt.

"I like it," she lied. Really, she just wanted something on him to grab. She supposed she could use his cock, but she preferred the tie.

Giving her that goofy smirk again, Jenkins flung his shirt wide. A white undershirt covered his chest. He wiggled out of the button shirt, then pulled the undershirt over his head. It got hung up on the tie, so he pulled harder to get it over his head. When he was done, he tossed the undershirt onto his pants.

"Better?" he asked.

"Almost." She pointed at his crotch.

Nodding, Jenkins slid his thumbs behind the bands of his shorts and pushed them down his legs. A paltry pecker pointed at her like a baby's finger. It was uncircumcised and moist, as if slicked in honey.

She'd seen cocks of all sizes and conditions, but this one had to be the lousiest.

It was hard to keep up her coquettish banter. "Come here, stud." Leaning against the bar, she motioned with her finger.

"About time, my love. I'm about to pop." He started walking.

"Can't have that, can we?"

"It's okay. I'll go again."

Mary resisted rolling her eyes. "A regular machine, huh?"

"Unstoppable," he said. Jenkins pressed against her. She felt a tiny nudge low on her belly from his pecker. She put her arms over his shoulders, hugging his neck. Pulled him close. And shoved her tongue into his mouth.

Moaning, Jenkins's eyes shot wide. She watched him panic as he tried to keep up with her darting tongue. Biting down on his lip, she pulled her head slightly back. Jenkins made a croaking sound as his lip stretched.

Without speaking, Mary hummed a tune that she hoped resembled *Follow me*.

Then she started walking backwards, tugging Jenkins.

Groaning, lip stuck between Mary's teeth, he followed her. His hands pawed and squeezed her breasts through her dress. She winced whenever he hit the sore spots on her breast.

Mary, having left her shoes at the bar, shuffled along the floor. Her feet made quick swishing sounds on the dusty wood. She guided him alongside the bar, dodging the stools, until she reached the end. She turned, bringing him forward until her back bumped against the door that led to her back room.

Pulling Jenkins close, she started kissing him again. She lifted her leg by his side. The dress fell away from her arched thigh. His hand gripped her under the thigh, fingers rubbing, climbing. She felt them dive between her legs. With nothing on under the dress, his fingers had the freedom to explore.

Moaning, Mary moved her weight to one foot and opened the space to give him more room. His fingers entered her, and this time it was Jenkins who moaned. She kind of enjoyed how he worked slowly, moving his fingers in and out.

Between kisses, Mary said, "Come back here with me."

Jenkins stepped back. Raising his arm to his mouth, Mary saw his fingers were wet. He used the side of his hand to wipe his mouth. Nodding, he said, "I'll follow you anywhere."

Some might have found the comment sweet, but Mary had heard it before from different lovers. Get them riled up, they'd say anything. She could probably convince him to marry her before he'd busted his nut.

Putting her back to Jenkins, she opened the door and threw it wide. The light was off, so the room was filled with dim darkness. It was colder in here, and caused her heated skin to harden with goosebumps.

"Come with me," she said, entering.

Mary passed the sink, the stove. She paused in the doorway to the little room where she kept a cot. Sometimes she slept on it, other times she let people from the bar who shouldn't be driving sleep off the booze.

Mostly she used it for her *special* customers.

Like Tom Worden.

Mary noticed Jenkins wasn't with her. She turned around. He was standing in the doorway, his tiny pecker now hanging flaccid. He stared at her.

"What's the matter, Lover?" she asked.

"Back there?"

Mary nodded. "What's wrong?"

"It's uh…"

"Too dark?"

She saw one of his shoulders bounce. "I don't know. Something's…off."

"Like it with the lights on, do you?"

"Not all of them, but some would help."

She supposed it might be a little too dark in here. There were no windows in this area, and she'd become used to the murkiness. There was a single bulb in the ceiling above the cot, but she wasn't going to turn it on and risk Jenkins seeing something too soon.

"I've got an idea," she said. Mary stepped over to the stove, running her hands across the cold smooth surface. She felt the box of matches. "Ah. Here they are." Shaking the box, the sticks rattled inside. She took out one, struck it against the wall. There was a crackling hiss as the flame sparked.

"There's an idea," said Jenkins.

"How about we set a mood?"

"Sounds good to me," he said.

Mary lowered the trembling flame to the candles on the shelf above the dials of the stove. There were three at different lengths. After she'd lighted all of them, the room was filled with yellow, guttering light. Shadows danced on the walls, slithering in shapeless forms.

Gripping the largest of the three sticks, she broke it from the base of melted candlewax. Facing Jenkins, she held the candle out, showering her pale skin in flickering light. She slid the dress down her shoulders, letting it fall to her ankles. Looking down at herself, she saw how her heavy breasts hung freely. Her large nipples pointed rigid. The tuft of hair between her legs was like a blotchy shadow. Her skin looked dusky in the candlelight, as if painted in gold.

Jenkins made a shivering breath. "Damn fine creation...but..."

"My butt's nice, too."

A corner of Jenkins's mouth curled. "I'm sure it is. The but I meant is..." He pointed at her chest.

Though she knew what he was talking about, she looked down as if confused. The marks of the vampire's claws had left two large dots on the upper slope of her breast. The wounds had hardened with scabbing, a spread of bruising connected them together. "Oh, these? They're nothing."

"They look painful."

"They were. But not anymore."

"Ah."

Smirking, Mary tilted her head. "Now will you come back here with me?"

Jenkins rushed in.

"Lover?" she said. Jenkins halted. "Shut the door?"

"Oh, right." Jenkins turned around, and pushed the door shut. Facing her, he held out his arms. His tiny pecker started to rise. "Better?"

"Much," she said, turning away from him. She entered the condensed room, walked over to the small table in the corner, and turned the candle sideways. Wax dribbled onto the table. There were blotches in the wood where wax had already left marks from other times. Fresh wax covered the table's old burns in gloppy goo. She stuck the candlestick into the puddle. When she took her hand away, the candle remained standing.

A guttering dimness filtered through the small room. She heard the bed hinges squeak and bounce. Heart pounding, Mary spun around.

Jenkins was on the bed, on his side. Head propped on his hand, he rubbed the mattress with the other, as if showing her she was meant to occupy that spot.

Not what she'd expected to find.

Damn. Thought he'd already jumped the gun...

Should've known better. Mary had to work them over a bit, get them ready.

"Coming to bed, Lover?" Jenkins asked.

Hearing him say 'lover' was almost enough to make Mary never use the frisky epithet again. Made it sound nasty coming from his mouth.

"Lay back and I will," she said.

Jenkins scooted upward, grinning like a child about to open presents on Christmas morning. He rested on the pillows, arms folded under his head. "Like this?"

Mary smiled. "Perfect."

Almost feel sorry for the shmuck.

Mary stepped to the edge of the bed. She gazed down at Jenkins. He was in the middle of the mattress, with equal amounts of space on either side. Usually she had to somehow chaperone them to the middle. Jenkins was making her work easier.

"See those metal bars on the head frame?"

Jenkins turned his head to look above him. "Yeah?"

"Grab them, please."

He looked at her. His eyes were round and eager. "Really? You're going to tie me up?"

"Why do you think I asked you to leave on the tie?"

Jenkins laughed. "Finally!" He did as she wanted. "I've wanted to be tied up ever since I read about it in a magazine at the cigar shop!"

"Your dream's coming true today, Lover."

"Hot damn!"

Mary climbed onto the mattress, crawling over Jenkins's excited legs. She could hear his animated squeaks as she made her way up. Straddling his stomach, she reached up and worked at the knot of his tie. When it was loose, she slid it out from under his neck. Then she fed the tie between the bars. First, she coiled it around one wrist, looped it between the bars, and tied the other wrist. When she was done, she leaned back.

"There you are," she said.

Jenkins tested the durability. Though the tie moved, his hands remained where they were. The knot was tight, and the tie was now too short for him to do anything.

"I'm all yours," he said.

"Yes," she said, smiling. "You are."

Jenkins's smile faltered. She saw something in his eyes that showed he realized he might have made a mistake. It went away when she reached behind her, found his pecker, and started stroking.

"Want this in my mouth?" she asked.

"Oh..." He nodded vigorously, moaned. "Please!"

"Want me to suck it?"

"PLEASE!"

Laughing, Mary gripped a nipple and twisted. Jenkins cried out in alarm, but it turned to moaning when Mary leaned over him, flicking his swelling nipple with her tongue. Her hand slid up the mattress, going under the pillow. Her fingers brushed the cold slickness she had hidden there.

Got it.

With Jenkins moaning, she pulled her hand out from under the pillow. She gave Jenkins a quick glance. His face pointed at the ceiling, eyes screwed shut and mouth wide.

Sitting up, Mary kept her right arm behind her as she moved back on her knees. Jenkins looked at her. Sweat dotted his brow. His moustache was wet with drool and fluttered as he panted.

"I'll make sure it's really good," she said. She rubbed the thin hairs on his stomach.

"I bet you will," he said in a winded voice.

Mary made her way back, getting on her stomach between his legs. Her face was a short distance from the pruned head of his pecker.

"It's the least I could do," she said.

"Huh?"

Mary sucked him inside. She felt his body stiffen as her mouth slid up and down the short length of his manhood. Jenkins's moans were nearly screams when her tongue licked the underside. She felt him quickly swell. She knew it was about to happen.

Mary brought the knife up to her face.

Jenkins burst in her mouth, shooting the back of her throat. Letting out a relieved moan, Jenkins's jerked and quaked. His feet dug into the mattress. Mary swallowed as he pumped. For such a small thing, it certainly was loaded.

Mary swallowed the last of it. Jenkins began to relax.

Then she used the knife to slice his pecker off.

Jenkins jerked and let out a quick grunt, but hardly noticed what had happened. Sitting up, Mary smiled as the spurting blood painted red stripes on her breasts and stomach. Jenkins turned, opened his eyes, and smiled.

The smile fell away when he saw her holding out his penis on the flat of her hand.

Jenkins screamed.

"Sorry, Lover," she said. She crawled backwards off the bed. Standing on the floor, she let his pecker drop into the materializing mist at her ankles. "I know it's awful, but it's not really that painful and I can't kill you right away. Made that mistake once already."

She'd used the knife on the first one's throat. He'd bled out before the vampire could feed. That night she'd learned the victims needed to be alive. Jenkins was number four, so she'd almost become an expert.

"You have to be bleeding," said Mary. "A lot. He's not quite strong enough to feed on his own, yet. And I have to make sure you don't *die* before he has a chance to get his fixings."

Screaming, Jenkins thrashed his head on the pillows. He jerked his arms, but the tie kept them above his head.

"I promised to make it good for you," she told Jenkins. "And I did. Think of it as your last hoorah before the end." She smiled as the smoke rose in front of her, making her view of Jenkins hazy.

Mary doubted Jenkins had heard anything she'd said. Blood squirted from the flat knob between his legs, coating his stomach and thighs in tacky crimson. But he wasn't even focused on that.

His eyes were glued to the swirling clouds filling the room.

They changed from gray to purple as plumes augmented from under the bed, swirling through the room. Though Jenkins hadn't stopped screaming, he watched the gaudy fog pull together, take shape.

Mary had witnessed this enactment a few times now, and it aroused her to see him awaken, to watch the thin haze solidify into tendons and tissue. The skin stretched, firming. She could tell its color had improved significantly since she'd brought him here. The blue was darker, healthier. Hair sprouted from its face. Its nose twitched, nostrils widening like knife slits, with sounds like crushed crackers. Two boils appeared on its back and grew, distending as wings developed inside the yolk-like bubbles. Soon the wings were too big for the translucent cocoons and burst through, spattering Mary's naked flesh in the warm goop.

As the vampire stalked toward the bed, she smeared the yolk over her skin with her hands, smothering her breasts in the warm slime. It left her nipples hard and tingly. She moaned as an orgasm shook her body and stole the strength in her legs. Dropping to her knees, she stared at the bed, still painting her body in the vampire's paste.

The vampire climbed up the edge of the bed, to the spurting nub that had been Jenkins's pecker. Its mouth stretched, dropping wide, flaunting its massive fangs. Then its mouth lowered over the hole, jaws clamping, teeth puncturing Jenkins's hairy mound.

Suckling sounds drowned out Jenkins's cries as the vampire fed like a calf on a teat.

-11-

Dorothy Clark peered out the car window. On the sidewalk, kids from her class spotted her, and stopped to stare. She gave them a haughty smile that she hoped told them how special she was. After all, *they* hadn't been asked to stay over and help Ms. Packer clean up the classroom. That was a treat only the most extraordinary students were given.

Besides, Dorothy knew she was Ms. Packer's favorite. None of the other kids came close.

"Aren't you going to wave at your friends?" asked Ms. Packer as she stopped at a crosswalk. Her brownish hair was pushed back by a hairband. The sun coming through the glass reflected off her pale face, making her red lipstick shine like fire. She was very pretty and Dorothy hoped she'd grow up to be just as pretty. Better yet, she hoped to grow up to look like her cousin, Robin. People told her she could pass for Robin's sister.

Dorothy saw herself in the mirror every day. She knew she was already pretty, and would probably get even prettier as she got older.

Dorothy watched a different pack of kids scurry across the road. Mr. Hollister, the crossing guard, ushered them along with his hand. He bit down on a whistle that twinkled in the bright light.

"Okay," Dorothy said. She threw her hand up and quickly shook it. Heads turned. Eyes narrowed. A couple kids stopped, leaned close, whispered.

Dorothy imagined what they were saying.

What's she doing in Ms. Packer's car?

She got to stay after and help?

She's so lucky!

I wish I was Dorothy Clark!

Smiling, Dorothy continued to wave. The kids kept watching until Mr. Hollister made them move. When they were across the road, Dorothy let her hand drop into her lap. Ms. Packer drove forward, giving the portly Mr. Hollister a quick wave by rolling her fingers. Dorothy liked how her teacher waved—fingers straight, wiggling them. Something about the gesture just seemed so grown up to Dorothy.

I should start waving at boys like that.

She felt a nervous flutter in her stomach.

Dorothy was the oldest in Ms. Packer's class, by a couple months. She was the first in the class to turn ten, so she was often granted more privileges and didn't mind bragging about it. Sometimes Ms. Packer called her a *Teacher's Assistant*, whatever that meant.

Though most of the kids didn't seem to really care, others were overly outraged and made it a point to voice their frustrations with name-calling.

Teacher's pet!

Brown-noser!

Bitch!

The last one had actually made her cry. Not in front of anybody, of course. She'd run off to the restroom to do it. Couldn't let them see how much their vicious teasing had hurt her.

"Thank you for staying after class," said Ms. Packer.

"You're welcome," said Dorothy.

"What a mess!" Ms. Packer chuckled. "Guess it's my fault for letting you all mess around with paint."

"*I* didn't make a mess," said Dorothy. She covered the paint stain on her dress with her hand, hiding the evidence that she'd made quite a mess herself. Hopefully Mama wouldn't be mad. "It was everybody else."

"Of course it was," said Ms. Packer, smiling. Something about her tone suggested she wasn't being serious. "But if I didn't have your help, I would still be there cleaning it up."

Dorothy felt heat in her cheeks from a blush. "Golly…"

"Are you sure your mama won't be upset that you're getting home a few minutes late?"

It was Tuesday, so Mama wouldn't be back from Grammy's yet. She wouldn't even *know* Dorothy had come home late. Grammy liked to have the adults over for lunch on Tuesdays and usually Mama stayed later to talk with Dorothy's aunts and uncles for a long time. Daddy made deliveries on Tuesdays, usually not getting home until late. They owned one of the biggest dairy farms around and it kept Daddy busy most of the time. He'd probably just get home in time for supper.

About time you got home, Mama would say. *Supper's nearly dead-cold!*

Sometimes Mama yelled at Daddy too much. When he wasn't around she sometimes said things about him that made Dorothy uncomfortable. Especially if Mama was mad at him. Dorothy mostly disagreed with Mama's sneering comments. To Dorothy, Daddy was great and she loved him very much.

Dorothy also understood Mama said a lot of things to hide how lonely she was when Daddy wasn't around.

From the corner of her eye, Dorothy noticed Ms. Packer give her a quick glance. She realized she hadn't answered the question. "No," she said. "Mama won't be mad."

"You're sure? You don't sound sure."

"I promise."

Dorothy turned, offering a smile she hoped would settle her teacher's unease. Ms. Packer gave her a quick smile back, then faced the road. She seemed fine with the answer.

As she drove, Ms. Packer talked about activities she'd planned for the remaining school year. All of them sounded fun. She asked Dorothy what she wanted to do over summer break. Dorothy told her about all the books she wanted to read. Some of them weren't at the library, so she'd have to beg her parents to order them for her.

"I have most of those," said Ms. Packer. "I'll bring them to school and you can keep them over the summer."

"Honest?" said Dorothy.

"Cross my heart," said Ms. Packer. "Just don't tell any of the other kids. They might not like it."

Dorothy's shoulders slumped. "Okay," she mumbled. Soon as Ms. Packer had made the offer, Dorothy was already planning how she would boast about it to everybody. Now she had to keep it to herself. If she crowed about the books, somebody would surely tell Ms. Packer. And Dorothy would no longer be the favorite.

Gazing out the window, Dorothy recognized the houses. She watched the spaces between them grow. Fields replaced yards. Patches of woods appeared, parting the fields into sections.

Dorothy spotted the black and white hair of her father's cows, grazing in the pastures. She felt the car slow down. When she faced forward, she saw the car was turning onto the dirt driveway that led to her house. The stretch of road continued beyond the house, to the barn and the stalls Daddy milked the cows in. Sometimes he asked her to help and she liked to do it whenever Mama allowed it.

Not a job for a little girl! Mama would say.

But she had fun working with Daddy.

Her house came into view, a three-story structure with a basement. The driveway was empty. The trees in the yard were thickening with green. Higher up, the limbs were still bare, as if skinny brown tails were reaching up from the green patches. She loved how the leaves coated the ground during the fall. Sometimes she'd play hide-and-seek with her cousins in the leaves, burying themselves under the dropped foliage while whoever was *It* counted to twenty.

Her eyes turned to the house. The windows were dark, reflecting the scenery on the glass like mirrors. Dorothy felt something stir inside of her. A noodle of coldness wiggled in her stomach, but she didn't know why.

The car thumped when it was put into Park. She heard shuffling sounds on the seat as Ms. Packer turned to face her.

"Are you feeling all right?" asked Ms. Packer.

"Huh?"

Dorothy turned. Ms. Packer frowned at her.

"You suddenly look pale," said Ms. Packer. "Feeling sick?"

"No." Dorothy shook her head. She noticed how it felt a little light and prickly. "No."

Ms. Packer's frown deepened. "If you're worried about your mama being mad..."

"I'm not," said Dorothy. "I promise."

"You sure you don't want me to come in and explain things to her?"

"No. It's fine."

Dorothy almost told her that Mama wasn't home. The carless driveway should have told Ms. Packer that. Maybe she thought Mama didn't drive and was inside waiting for Dorothy to come in.

If she confessed Mama was at Grammy's, then Ms. Packer might want to come in and wait with her until she came home. Dorothy was rarely left alone in the house, and she treasured each uncommon occasion as a blessing. It made her feel as if she were an adult in her own house, doing whatever she wanted.

"Fine," said Ms. Packer. "But if you get into any kind of trouble, tell me tomorrow, and I'll talk to her."

"I will."

"Promise?"

"I promise."

"All right. I'll see you tomorrow."

"Bye-bye!"

Dorothy groaned as she pushed the heavy car door open. She made sure it would stay that way before sticking out her legs. Too many times a car door had swung back and bashed her shins as she was climbing out.

Standing next to the car, Dorothy reached back in and picked up her school books from the floorboard. She hugged them to her chest.

"Have a good afternoon," said Ms. Packer.

"Okay. Bye!"

Dorothy walked around the door, leaned against it, and hobbled backwards. The door banged shut, jostling her. She nearly dropped her books.

She ran to the house, feeling her dress float out around her legs. She hurried up the steps, opened the door, and ran inside. She kicked the door shut behind her.

Two quick honks from Ms. Packer's horn made Dorothy jump. A little gasp escaped her. Walking back to the door, she pulled back the flimsy curtain over the narrow window beside it. She peeked out. The car was already turned around and heading down the driveway. Ms. Packer must have been telling her bye one last time. Dorothy watched until the car rounded the curve and trees blocked her view. She let the curtain fall back into place and turned around.

The Vampire of Plainfield

The short hallway before her was dark. Rectangles of pale light from the doorways on either side spilled on the floor, a wider splash at the end led into the kitchen. The stairs off to the side led up into a shelter of black.

It was very quiet, somehow quieter than normal. She could *feel* the silence, heavy and scary on her shoulders.

Dorothy shoved those feelings away. She wouldn't let this short stint of time be ruined. It would be another week before it happened again. And what if Mama decided to stay home next time? She didn't go to Grammy's *every* week.

Dorothy straightened her shoulders. She cradled her books in one arm, using the free hand to brush her dress. She took a deep breath and let it slowly out.

Better.

Nose in the air and smiling, she marched to the stairs and started up. She didn't let it bother her as it became darker the higher she got. She pretended not to notice her slight relaxing when she reached the second floor and the windows let in enough sunlight to kill every shadow.

Dorothy forged ahead to her bedroom. On her way in, she flipped on the light. Her room was empty, her bed made. Her dirty clothes were no longer on the floor.

Mama had cleaned up before she'd left this morning.

That meant Dorothy would get a stern talking-to when Mama got home. Maybe even a spanking. She'd told her last night to make sure she got her dirty clothes off the floor before school.

I forgot.

That wasn't an excuse Mama tolerated.

Dorothy tossed her books on the dresser. Her excitement of being home alone had been hampered by the dread she felt from knowing she was in trouble. Sighing, Dorothy crossed the room and sat down on the edge of her bed. She brought up a leg, turned slightly to the side, and put her foot on the mattress. She looked at the downy hairs on her shin as she started untying her saddle shoe. She hated the pale fuzz on her legs. Older girls didn't have them.

They get to use razors. Makes them smooth.

A couple months ago, she'd used Mama's razor on her own legs. She liked how they'd looked afterward, but was too scared to wear anything that showed them off. Mama would have known what she'd done. She'd promised herself she would never do it again until Mama told her she was finally *of the age.*

She couldn't wait until she was old enough to shave.

Gripping the heel of her shoe, Dorothy started to slip it off.

The floor in the hallway creaked softly.

Dorothy paused, a hand under her shoe, toes still inside. The wind blew outside, making the window in her room pop. She listened a few more seconds, and heard nothing else.

She looked down at her foot, about to pull off the shoe when the floor outside her room creaked again. She looked up.

And froze.

The shoe dangled from her toes, one leg propped up, her dress a curtain between her legs. Her first thought was Mama was coming in.

Then she quickly remembered Mama wasn't home.

A boy stood in her doorway. Though he looked vaguely familiar, she didn't think she knew him.

Dorothy's mouth slowly sagged. A breath of fear tickled the back of her throat, trying to form into a scream.

"Don't make a sound," he said in a high, shaky voice. Soaked in sweat, his striped shirt was glued to his front. The fabric was dark with wet stains. "Just keep your mouth *shut.*"

He entered her room and pushed the door. It closed with a *snick* that made Dorothy flinch. Though older than

The Vampire of Plainfield

Dorothy and *much* bigger, he wasn't a grown-up. His hair was flat and slick on his head. Wet, as if he'd been swimming.

Dorothy knew she should run, but couldn't. She felt stuck to the bed, stuck with her legs parted. His eyes flicked down there. The way he grinned made her feel sick inside. She started to lower her leg.

"Don't," he said. He sounded as if he'd been running for a long time. Out of breath, his throat made squeaky sounds. "I want to see...lift the dress. Let me...see." He took in a breath that made his chubby cheeks jiggle.

"No, please..."

"Do it."

Dorothy bit down on her bottom lip. She shook her head.

The boy's mouth pressed together. When he spoke again, it was through clenched teeth. "Now."

Dorothy didn't want to, but his tone told her she better listen. With a quick flick of her wrist, she flashed him her underwear. Then she pulled the dress taut between her legs and held it there.

The boy closed his eyes, sighing as if smelling something wonderful. "Good." He opened his eyes again. They looked glossy and dark. Fake. "Take off your dress."

"N...No." Dorothy shook her head. "I'm not going to."

"Do as I say. Take off your dress, take off everything...and lay back."

Dorothy looked down at her dress. Tears filled her eyes. "Please don't make me do that."

"Don't fight me and it'll be okay. I won't hurt you. *Don't want* to hurt you. So pretty. So, so pretty. Nice skin...looks so soft. I just want to touch it for a while, okay. Will that be okay? If I just touch it?"

"Nothing else?"

"Maybe not," he tried to smile but his lips wouldn't stop trembling long enough. "I want to touch you…in there." He pointed low on her body.

Dorothy looked down. Saw her dress gripped in her hand, pulled tight. She sniffled. Shook her head.

"Just undress, lay back."

"No." She stared at him. "You can't make me."

"Yes, I can." He reached behind his back with both hands. When he held them out, a knife was in one and some rope was in the other. The rope hung from his clenched fist like a long fuse on a stick of dynamite. It reminded Dorothy of cartoons she'd seen.

Oh, how she wished she were watching cartoons right now. She wished she was anywhere but here.

Her eyes locked on the knife. She recognized it from their kitchen.

She quickly looked around her room, trying to find a weapon of her own. She saw her school books resting on dolls and stuffed animals on her dresser. More stuffed animals piled up on the vanity mirror. There was nothing that could defend her from such a big person.

The boy's wide back showed in the reflective glass. There was a dark peak of wetness going up the middle of his shirt, as if trying to stab the back of his neck. She could also see herself on the bed. She looked so small and frightened. Weak. Her face was a wet mask of tears.

Another gust of wind outside made the window in her room thump. The boy jerked rigid, squeezing the knife tighter.

Dorothy threw her leg down, stomping. "Mama!" she called. "Mama, help!"

The boy rushed forward and pushed her chest. Her legs flew high, the loose shoe flying off her foot. It landed on the carpet with a soft bump. She bounced when she hit the mattress. Her headboard rocked against the wall.

"Shut up!" His breaths came like sharp wheezes. "She's not here! Nobody but us. She won't be home for two more hours and your daddy's out delivering."

Dorothy sobbed. How'd he know that? She had hoped calling for Mama would have sent him running.

As if he'd read her thoughts, he said, "I've been watching you for a couple weeks, Dorothy. I know all about you. I saw you at Buck's that morning, with your mama. You got a root beer float. You sat on the stool, your legs hanging off the front, ankles crossed. You were wearing a different dress, though. It was shorter than the one you have on. I just wanted to rub your legs a little." He tilted his head. Those dark, glassy eyes gazed at her. "Now I want to rub more."

Dorothy felt something like cold snakes squirming in her stomach. She wished she'd told Ms. Packer that Mama wasn't home. Ms. Packer would've come in the house, waited with her. This wouldn't be happening if she would have just told Ms. Packer the truth.

Ms. Packer! Please come back!

Maybe Ms. Packer would somehow hear Dorothy's pleas. If she thought hard enough, maybe Ms. Packer would suddenly sense that she was needed here.

Her teacher wasn't coming back. She was probably halfway home by now, feeling proud of Dorothy for how helpful she'd been today.

Dorothy felt hands grip her dress. Heard the fabric rip as it was torn from her body. She tried to hold on to her underwear, but it was useless. She felt them jerked away in a savage swipe. In nothing but her socks and one shoe, she tried to cover herself with her arms and hands. The air of the room felt cool and sickly on her bare skin.

The boy's breaths rose in pitch. She looked up at him. Though her eyes were blurry with tears, she could plainly see his evil leer. A cruel smile split his face.

Looking away, her eyes landed on the mirror. She saw herself laid back, an arm covering her chest, the other reaching down between her legs. The boy blocked her view of her legs. She saw him step forward.

The bed shook as he climbed up. His zipper made clicking sounds as it was lowered.

In the mirror, she saw his pants drop. His shirt hung down, covering half of his wide, pale rump as he bent over.

"Please don't," she said. Dorothy saw him push her legs apart. "Don't…"

Ignoring her, the boy lowered his heavy body onto hers.

Timmy, hands in his pockets, walked in front of the buildings. It was mostly warm outside, but a cool wind softly blew on his neck. He made a long step over a puddle. The water trembled in the wind. Leaning over, Timmy put his hands on his knees and studied the puddle. He liked how the water rippled.

Put it in a story.

Maybe an alien invasion tale with spaceships swooping down from the sky. The hero realizes something big is coming his way when he feels the wind, sees the puddles quivering as if the ground was shaking.

Yeah.

Timmy started walking again, nodding as the story made images in his head.

Then he looks up to the sky. Dark spheres are tearing through the clouds like hailstones, blasting everything in sight with lasers. The hero runs, ducks behind...

A bell jangled. A door flew at his face. Wood whacked his forehead. He was thrown aside. His back hit something solid, bringing him to a jarring halt. The dust on the ground made his shoes slide out from under him. He dropped at an angle. His shoulder pounded the ground.

"Timmy Worden! Golly!"

A girl's voice. Familiar. Lovely.

"What did I do?" the voice cried. "Oh, no. Oh, Golly no. Jeez..."

He heard the quick crunches of footfalls. Hands patted his chest, gripped his arm. Then he was pulled upright. Everything seemed slightly off balance and a little blurry. Timmy blinked a few times, but it hardly seemed to help his eyesight.

"Talk to me, Timmy? Are you okay?"

"Is he hurt?" A deeper voice said.

"I don't know, Mr. Vincent. He's not saying anything."

Mr. Vincent?

The drugstore?

The bells Timmy heard must've been the front door. Somebody opened it. He remembered seeing the door coming at him, the dark glass filling his vision before…

Timmy turned. He saw streaks of yellow swelling through a dusky canvas. Somebody leaned close to him, though he couldn't recognize who it was. A pleasing scent drifted toward him that reminded him of summer.

Blinking again finally cleared his vision. Robin Hicks's beautiful face came into focus. It was just inches from his. Gone was his dizziness. Now all he felt were fluttery sensations in his chest.

"Hi," he said. He felt a smile forming on his face.

Robin's full lips parted, showing the white of her teeth. "You're okay?"

Timmy started to nod, but stopped when he felt a dull jab in his head. He groaned. "Mostly okay."

"Need me to call your parents, Timmy?" said the deeper voice above him.

Timmy looked up and spotted Mr. Vincent standing over him. His hair was a stiff black mold on his head and the matching glasses, thick as pipes, made his face look overly small. He held a broom by the handle next to him as if it were his rifle.

"No…but thanks, Mr. Vincent."

"Are you sure?" he asked. "You took a nasty hit and had an even nastier fall."

"What?"

"Jeez," said Robin. She made a pained face that wrinkled her brow and lifted her cheeks. It somehow made her even more adorable. "My clumsy self." She shook her head. "I wasn't paying attention and just flung the door open and wailed you a good one, huh?"

"I'll be fine. Nothing a week or so in the hospital won't fix."

Robin laughed. Mr. Vincent made a harrumphing sound. The storeowner patted the ground with the bushy end of the broom before turning away.

"He's just as goofy as normal," said Mr. Vincent as he walked to the door. "He's fine." The bells jangled again when Mr. Vincent opened the door. He went inside.

Robin gave a glance at the store. "He's a nurturing soul, isn't he?"

"I'll say."

"Want me to help you up?" she asked.

Timmy didn't think he needed the help. But having Robin touch him sounded great. "Sure," he said.

"Okay. Hold this." She handed him a paper bag—her purchase from the drugstore, most likely. "I'm going to grab you here." She stuck her hand under his arm. Her fingers brushed his ribs. Her sweet-smelling hair tickled his cheek. "Okay?"

Timmy hardly had a voice when he said, "Yeah."

"On three. Ready?"

"Yeah."

She pulled at two, catching Timmy by surprise. He was jerked forward and quickly shuffled his feet under him and pushed up. Stumbling, Robin rubbed against his side, the hardness of her chest squishing against him. His nose brushed through her hair.

Robin staggered to the side, letting out a squeal. She caught herself and pushed back. Her arm remained tight on his back to hold him up.

"There we go," she said.

Timmy felt a little dizzy again, but mostly fine. "Thanks."

"You're welcome."

He realized she was still close, pressed against him. Being fifteen, she was slightly taller than him and Timmy had to look up to see her eyes. She gazed down at him, eyebrows raised and a slight smirk curling a corner of her mouth. "Better?"

Timmy nodded.

"Good."

She reached for his face. It felt warm on his cheek. Fingers tapped the tender spot on his head. Wincing, Timmy let out a hiss.

Frowning, Robin said, "You're not bleeding, but...it might leave a lump."

"It's fine."

Her hand slid down to his shoulder. Squeezed. Then she pulled away, stepped back, and held out her hand. Her chin lifted, turned, as she watched him.

At first, Timmy thought she wanted him to take her hand. Then he glanced down at his hands and saw her bag was still clutched in them. He held the bag close as if it were a purse. "Oh, right." He held out the bag. "Here."

Robin took the bag. "Thank you."

"So..." he said, not really knowing what to say now.

"So..." Robin squatted down, picked up her purse, and stood. She slid the paper bag under her arm. Timmy wondered what she'd needed from the drugstore. Probably best not to ask. Might seem like he was being nosey.

"What are you doing now?" he asked.

"Nothing really. Probably have to get home."

Timmy nodded. "Yeah. Me too."

"What were you doing out this way?"

"Went by Nan...my grandmother's store. Helped her out for an hour."

"Oh? That's neat. Does she pay you?"

"In supplies."

Robin laughed. "Pencils and paper?"

Timmy nodded. "My wage."

Smiling, Robin said, "Still writing those *scary* stories?"

"All the time."

"Wow. That's really neat. I'm glad you stuck with it. I liked reading them. When I'd be at your house?"

"You did?"

She swatted his shoulder. "Of course I did. Why do you think I always *asked* to read them?"

"Maybe you were just really bored?"

Robin jabbed his side with a finger. "Hey, mister. You never bored me. I always had fun with you. A lot."

Timmy did too. He missed her sitting with him for his parents. The last time was last summer, and she'd worn a nice yellow dress that showed more of her legs than he'd ever seen before. He remembered how shiny her skin had looked, the way the light had gleamed on the tawny shade of her shins.

"Want to walk with me?" she asked.

"Me?"

"No. The invisible guy standing beside you."

Timmy turned his head and immediately felt dumb. Robin laughed. He looked back at her. Her cheeks were flushed as she shook her head. He shrugged. "You never know," he said. "Might be an invisible person following me around."

"There's your story," she said, turning around. She started walking. "An invisible maniac!"

Timmy hurried to her side, then matched her speed. "It's been done before."

"Not like *The Invisible Man*. Do it differently. Something about an invisible *psycho*, you know? He could get you during the daylight."

Timmy nodded. "That's a good idea. You wouldn't be safe anywhere."

Robin winced. "That's scary, isn't it? What if you're in the bathroom? And he's in there?"

"Yeah," said Timmy.

"In the shower," she said.

Timmy pictured Robin standing under a shower's hot spray. The steam curled around her wet flesh as water sluiced down her naked body, plastering her yellow hair against her neck. He quickly shoved the image away. "Yeah."

"Ew, could you imagine? Getting out of the shower? *Naked?* And somebody's in there with you?"

Timmy pictured it. Again, it was Robin and not Timmy.

But maybe he was there.

Maybe *he* was the invisible maniac.

Not a maniac. Never.

No. He'd just be there to watch. Maybe he'd touch, not hurt her.

"Make it a woman," said Robin. "The psycho? She sneaks into bathrooms and watches cute boys bathe themselves."

Blushing, Timmy nodded. "Yeah. Neat."

Then an idea sparked from the tainted fantasy. This usually happened to him when he was thinking about a particular part to a story. Something would pop out of nowhere. He smiled. "And you see the steam from the shower parting around a solid shape, a man or woman's shape..."

Robin laughed. "Yeah!"

"Somebody's taking a bath, and they see the water tremble. Maybe they feel skin rub against theirs?"

"The invisible person's getting in the tub?"

"Yeah. The person *feels* somebody getting in the tub with her. Sees the water shaking, the dips of feet getting in..."

"Oh, stop!" Robin gasped. She shivered. "I could easily picture that!"

Timmy laughed. He couldn't help feeling a pang of pride knowing an idea of his had caused her reaction. It was a *fun* kind of disturbance Robin had. To Timmy, that was what horror was all about—the fun of being scared. He'd succeeded with Robin. Hers was not one of those repulsed, critical responses he was used to getting.

"Get any ideas from your dad?" she asked.

"My dad?"

"Yeah. Being the son of a deputy, you must hear stories."

"Not really. Seems kind of...dull."

Robin laughed softly. "Come on. Can't always be dull."

"Dull City."

Robin laughed. "At least he doesn't seem too strict."

"He can be."

"So can my old man. The worst."

Timmy knew her old man, and she wasn't exaggerating. He was a demanding tyrant most of the time. But Timmy figured when it came to Robin he was probably twice as harsh but also quick to give in. How could anybody say no to her?

"He doesn't let me do much anymore," she said. "I think it's because I'm getting older."

"Why do you say that? Shouldn't he be letting you do more?"

"Not *my* father," she said.

They reached the end of the walkway, paused. Robin looked both ways. Main Street cut through in front of them, the walkway starting again on the other side. A few people wandered about. A couple cars slowly rolled by.

What if he held Robin's hand as they crossed the street?

His stomach gave a sickening lurch.

He stuck his hand in his pocket.

Robin started across and Timmy walked with her. Their hands stayed where they had been.

"He used to be fine with me going to my friend's houses," said Robin, "or going to Buck's alone. Now he doesn't like it as much. Says that I don't know what people are thinking about when they see me. I know what they're thinking. It bothers me sometimes, but I can't stay cooped up in my room until I move out, can I?"

Probably thinking things along the line of what Timmy had been moments ago. "No," he said, "you can't stay cooped up."

"Right. And I tell him that. He eventually gives me permission, which is good. But if he didn't, I'd probably just sneak out anyway."

"You would?"

"Totally! Have you ever?"

"Snuck out?"

"Yeah."

"You have?"

"I asked you first."

Timmy sighed. "Never."

Robin's shoulders bopped up and down. "Oh, well. Bet that's too risky with your dad. I'm sure he'd be really mad, if he caught you."

If he did anything bad, Dad would skin his ass and hang it on the clothesline with the bedsheets and pillowcases.

The Vampire of Plainfield

Robin took a deep breath and kept talking. "I haven't ever snuck out, either. I could only imagine what my dad would do to *me* if he caught me. I've wanted to, though. Haven't you?"

From the corner of his eye, he saw her head turn toward him. He swallowed. It felt like a bubble of sharp air went down his throat. "Well...I guess I've never really had a reason to."

"I've been asked to," said Robin. "Some of my friends have wanted to sneak out a bunch of times. I don't know why. It's not like there's anything to do around here. Say we snuck out, then what?"

Last Halloween night, Timmy had gone with Peter to one of the graveyards to do some snooping around. But they'd gotten spooked and didn't stay very long. Peter thought he'd heard somebody digging. Timmy had listened, picking up the faint scraping sounds a shovel might make when it scooped out dirt. The noises had been enough to send them running back to Timmy's house.

But that had been close to ten o'clock, not the middle of the night. And their parents had known they were going to be out.

"Yeah," he said. "Wouldn't be much to do, except wander around."

Robin rolled her eyes. "I told my father I wanted to go to the movies Friday night. And he gave me his typical *'We'll see'* answer."

"What's playing?"

"*Phantom of the Rue Morgue.*"

"Rue Morgue? Like in the Poe story?"

"Who?"

Timmy ignored her lack of Poe knowledge. "It's playing around here?"

"Not too far away. You should go see it. I'm sure you'd *love* it."

"Sounds neat. But my dad's working this weekend and my ma would never take me to that. She hates scary stuff."

She also hated that Timmy loved it so much.

Robin laughed. "I see." He stole glances of her from the corner of his eye. She looked suddenly nervous, as if working up her nerve for something. "Why don't *we* go?"

"Together?"

Robin nodded. "Sure. They'd let you go with me, wouldn't they?"

Timmy didn't see why not. His parents had known Robin all her life. She sat with him for two years any night his parents wanted to go out together. It shouldn't matter that she was about to turn sixteen soon. They might appreciate her being there to keep an eye on him.

But his confidence quickly dissolved into dread. Robin had asked him to the movies. They would be there together. Alone. In a darkened theater. Sitting in those seats, close together, their elbows touching. Might even share popcorn. What if their hands touched when they both reached in at the same time?

"Is that a no?" he heard Robin say. She sounded far away.

"What?" Timmy shook his head. "No. I mean, that's not...a no."

Robin laughed. "So, no it's a no?"

"Right. It should be fine."

"Great. Want to meet at Buck's first? Get a milkshake, then we can head out there?"

Timmy wanted to shout his answer and spin in a circle with excitement. He held back, and only nodded. "Sounds fun to me."

"Maybe we can talk about the invisible maniac story some more, while we enjoy our shakes."

Timmy doubted he'd be able to enjoy anything. How jittery and cold his stomach felt now, he could only imagine the problems he'd have trying to drink his shake with Robin sitting across from him.

I'm going out with Robin Hicks!

Not that it was a date. But Timmy could pretend.

Robin started to say something when tires squealed off to the side of them.

Turning, Robin screamed and jumped back. Timmy saw the front end of a car heading straight for them. It made a sharp swerve and slid to a halt beside the sidewalk. He recognized the giant gold star on the door.

Dad?

The door flung open. Timmy's father hurried out. He looked at Robin, then Timmy, confusion showing for a moment before something more serious replaced it.

"Hey, Dad," said Timmy. "Everything okay?"

"Don't know just yet." He looked at Robin. "Sorry to scare you like this, but I spotted you walking and decided to stop."

Robin attempted a smile. "It's all right."

"I need to ask you something," Dad said.

Robin's eyebrows pushed together. "Me?"

"Yeah." He took a deep breath. "Have you seen Dorothy today?"

Robin's head made quick side-to-side movements. "No. Why? What's wrong?"

"Well..." Mouth tightening, Dad seemed hesitant at first. "Your aunt came home and Dorothy wasn't in the house. Her bed was a mess. Dresser drawers had been left open and ransacked. Dresses had been taken from the closet. Last person to see her was Ms. Packer from the school. She dropped her off and watched her go inside. That was over two hours ago."

"She's gone?" asked Robin. "Dorothy's gone?"

"Not gone. Just...we're having some trouble finding her."

Robin looked at Timmy, her face twisting with concern. She shook her head. "No. I haven't...I saw her yesterday, but not since."

"All right. The way I see it, she's only been...unaccounted for no longer than an hour. But she's not with any of her friends and the condition of her room brings up some concerns."

"Think she ran away?"

"Not saying just yet. But..." Dad shrugged.

Timmy couldn't begin to imagine how Robin felt. "Is there anything we can do, Dad?"

"Yeah. Hop in. Robin, I'm going to run you over to your aunt's house. Your mother is there, trying to help your aunt figure things out. She might feel better knowing where her own daughter is during this time. Then I'm taking you home, son."

Robin leaned against Timmy. Without thinking, he put his arm around her. When he looked at his Dad, he noticed the expression on his face was a combination of worry for Robin's cousin and pride that his son was with such a lovely girl.

-13-

Lying on his bed, Timmy gazed into the open pages of *The Vampire's Graveyard Kiss*. He'd reached the third story in the collection. It was about a young librarian who finds an ancient book in a secret room of the library she'd recently started working in. Reading the passages, she accidentally raises a vampire from the dead.

Timmy had already read it a few times. But he'd never noticed before how much the girl drawn in the story looked like Robin. They shared the same sunshine-colored hair that was kept away from their faces by a headband. Had the same bowed mouth with lipstick that was a dark, crimson shade. And both gals had a perfect dot above their upper lip.

He hadn't been able to turn the page. Seeing the girl in the comic had taken him back to this afternoon. The events replayed in his mind.

Feels like I dreamed it.

It *had been* a dream, a good one until Dad showed up. Robin had actually asked him to walk her home, and set a date for the movies on Friday. She'd even made hints about sneaking out in the middle of the night.

Then Dad showed up and ruined it.

Wasn't Dad's fault. He was just doing his job.

Poor Robin. He wondered if Dorothy had come home yet.

Don't think so. Dad isn't back.

If things had been wrapped up, Dad would have been home by now. He'd come home when Dorothy was safe at home or he was convinced she wasn't coming home.

A nervous feeling trickled through Timmy. He squirmed on the bed.

Hope she's okay.

Why wouldn't she be?

There was a soft quick tap outside his door.

"Yeah?"

"Timmy?" Mom's voice.

Timmy shot upright. He stuffed the comic book under his pillow. "Yeah?"

"Feel like company?"

Timmy sat up, pulled his legs close. "Um…?"

He couldn't remember the last time his mother had wanted to come into his room when they were home alone together. He might have been ten years old.

"I guess so," he said.

His mother said something in a soft voice that he couldn't understand. He was about to tell her he didn't hear her when—

"Thanks, Mrs. Worden!"

Peter.

Timmy could hear the floor pop as his mother walked away. The door knob turned with a quiet squeak and the door opened. Peter's bulky form filled the doorway, cutting a wide stretch of darkness into the light that spilled on the floor.

"Hey, Timmy."

"Peter."

Peter walked in, shutting the door. "Why are you sitting in the dark?"

Timmy looked around. His lamp was on, but other than the small glow of light it spread onto the bed, the room was black. "Uh…" He hadn't even realized how dark it had gotten outside. They hadn't even had dinner yet.

As if reading Timmy's thoughts, Peter said, "Your ma said the pot roast is almost done. Smells good too. Can I cut on the light?"

"Sure."

"Good. Being in a dark room feels strange, you know?"

"I guess so."

There was a thin click and the room exploded with brightness that made Timmy squint. He turned to Peter as the big boy came forward.

"Why's everybody so glum?" Peter asked.

Timmy swung his legs over the side of the bed, leaned forward. "What do you mean?"

"You're acting like your puppy died."

Peter seemed more chipper than normal, as if he'd just received wonderful news. He looked kind of goofy.

"Well," Timmy said, "why are you in such a good mood?"

Peter shrugged. He walked across the room to where Timmy's desk was. He pulled out the wooden chair, turned it so it faced the bed, and sat down. The wood popped and groaned under Peter's weight. "I'm not in a *good mood*," he said. "Just think it's kind of—I don't know—*neat* what's going on."

"Neat?" Peter nodded. "You heard about it?"

"It's all over town. A little girl disappears; of course people are going to know about it."

Nodding, Timmy turned sideways on the bed, bringing up a leg and hooking its foot under the other. "Yeah. I was walking with Robin when Dad came out of nowhere and told us about it. He took her to the Clark farmhouse and brought me home."

"I saw him driving around on my way over. I waved, but..." Peter shook his head. "Guess he didn't see me. Do they know anything yet?"

"I don't know."

Peter frowned, nodded. "Wonder what happened."

"Probably just out somewhere, you know?"

"What if there's a sicko running around?"

"Caught your ma's weirdees?"

Peter held up his hands. "Not my ma's. Eddie's."

Smiling, Timmy shook his head. He felt lousy for goofing around with Peter while Robin's cousin was missing.

Not missing. Just isn't home yet.

Peter snapped his fingers. "Maybe Eddie did it."

Timmy stood up. "Yeah, right! Eddie would never. You're a bum for even saying so."

"Might have her in that summer kitchen. Maybe that's why he never lets us in there. It's where he hides the bodies."

"You've been reading too many of Eddie's stupid crime magazines."

"Have not!"

Timmy laughed.

The phone rang. Timmy could hear the muffled jangle coming from the den. Timmy and Peter stared at each other. The floor groaned as Mama walked through the house. She answered it on the third ring.

Her high voice carried through the walls, though not enough to understand what she was saying. But Timmy could tell she was using that different voice of hers, the lighter one she saved just for the phone. As if she was trying to sound fancy.

"Who do you think it is?"

"Probably my dad."

Peter nodded. Gone was his smirk and eagerness. Now he looked like a kid about to enter the principal's office.

"Think it's your ma?" Timmy asked.

"I hope not. She'll make me come home and your ma asked me to stay for supper."

Timmy understood why Peter wouldn't be in a hurry to go home and eat supper at his house. His ma cooked up dishes that most people around Plainfield had never heard of. They smelled awful and tasted even worse.

The floor of the hallway made popping sounds as footsteps came closer. The sounds stopped outside Timmy's door.

"Telephone, Timmy!"

Peter looked relieved.

"Be right there!" said Timmy. "Who is it?"

"A girl."

Timmy felt a flutter in his stomach. "Thank you, Ma."

Peter's eyebrows rose, lips pursed. "A girl?"

"Ma?" said Mama. He heard her laughing as she walked away.

Peter leaned forward, resting his elbows on his knees. His fat pushed bulges into his shirt. "A girl?"

"I wonder who," said Timmy. But he already knew and when he saw Peter's face, figured he did as well.

"Come on, Timmy," said Peter. "You said you were with Robin. Who else would it be?"

"Yeah," said Timmy. "But why would she call me?"

"I have no idea, but you better tell me all about it when you get back."

Nodding, Timmy walked to the door on numb legs. It felt as if he was crossing a floor of cotton. He left the room, not closing his door.

In the hallway, he could smell Mama's pot roast. The house seemed to be filled with its wonderful scent.

Entering the den, he saw the chair and small table beside it. The handset was on the table, the mouthpiece and receiver in front of the base. The cord hung off the back of the table, twisted together. He sat in the chair, grabbed the handset, and put it against his ear. It felt cold against his skin. It smelled vaguely of Mama's perfume. Through the receiver, he could hear the static-drenched sounds of voices talking all at once.

"Huh-hello?"

"Hi, Timmy."

Robin.

"Hi," he said, louder than he'd wanted. "How...what's going on?"

"It's pretty bad over here," she said.

"I bet so. I'm sorry."

"It's not your fault." A brief pause. "I hope you don't mind my calling. I just...I don't know. I guess I needed to hear a friendly voice."

My voice.

"I don't mind," he said. "I'm glad you called."

He thought he heard her smile. "You are?"

"Yes."

"That's good. Thank you. In all this...madness, I really need a friend."

A friend.

Timmy felt himself slouch.

Better than nothing.

"Are you still there?" asked Robin.

Timmy blinked. "Yeah—yes! I'm here."

"They haven't found her yet."

Timmy felt a cold hardness in his bowels. "Still?"

"No. And now I'm getting *really* worried. This isn't like her."

"Nobody's seen her?"

"Not since Ms. Packer dropped her off."

"So she was definitely *in* the house."

"Yeah. Nobody knows anything after that."

Weird.

"But some of her clothes are missing. So is her suitcase she uses when she goes on sleepovers and some...undergarments. Aunt Carol noticed a knife was missing from the kitchen, but she couldn't say for sure it had been there this morning when she left. So for all she knows, it's been missing for months."

"Jeez," said Timmy. He knew it sounded dumb, but he didn't know what to say.

"Your dad's walking in right now."

Timmy recognized his father's deep tenor in the background. When he spoke, the other voices petered out, listening to what he had to say.

"Want me to hang up?" asked Timmy.

"No. Please don't."

"Okay."

Timmy couldn't stop the smile from coming. He knew Robin, along with the rest of her family, were going through a terrible crisis. But he was overjoyed to be on the phone with her. Even if the reasons behind it weren't good.

Listening, Timmy couldn't make out what his father was saying. The sympathetic quality suggested he wasn't delivering good news.

Livid voices cut him off.

"No news," she said. "Everybody's yelling at him."

Hearing how his father was being treated made Timmy angry. Dad was out there for them, when he should be home. He was trying to resolve this matter and they shouted at him for it? Sounded to Timmy like the snot had run away from home. Maybe Dad had told them the same thing.

"Something's not right," Robin said, her voice lower now. "I think somebody took her."

"*Took* her?"

"Yeah. You hear about it sometimes."

"Not here."

"Doesn't mean it *can't* happen."

Timmy tried to consider it. Couldn't. There was just no way she was *taken*.

"You don't think she ran away?" he asked.

There was a long pause and Timmy began to regret saying it.

"Sorry," he said. "I didn't mean to…"

"No," she said. "At first I thought so, but now I'm not so sure."

"Why not?"

Voices behind Robin continued to shout at Timmy's father. Though he enjoyed having Robin on the phone, he was getting tired of hearing her family treat his dad so terribly.

"I don't know why," she said. "But it doesn't make sense. Why would she run away and only take her dresses and underthings?"

"Well…" Timmy could hardly remember his own mindset at ten. Trying to delve into a ten-year-old girl's mind was impossible. And a little intimidating. "I don't know."

"She wouldn't," said Robin. "But everything here says that she did."

"The knife?"

"Who knows what happened to it, but…I don't know."

A woman's voice crackled with static behind Robin, close to the phone. There were brushing sounds of the phone being moved around.

"Robin?"

He could faintly hear Robin talking as the other voices carried on in subtle grumblings. There were more swishing sounds, and the noise seemed to clear.

"Okay," said Robin. "That was my mom. I have to go."

"Okay," he said. A sense of loss washed over him.

"Are we…still on for the movie?"

"Of course."

"Okay. I'll talk to you later. Bye."

She hung up before he could say it back. Timmy sat there with the dead phone to his ear, staring at the wall for several long moments. Then he leaned over the high arm of the chair, and put the phone on the cradle.

"Time to eat!" Mom called from the kitchen. "Hurry and wash up before it gets cold!"

The heavy clumps of Peter's footsteps pounded in the hallway. His round head peeked in. "There you are," he said.

"Yeah..."

"You look even worse than before. She dumped you already?"

Timmy shook his head. "No."

Peter rolled his eyes. "Time to eat, goofy! Come on. I'm starved. You still have to tell me what all you and Robin talked about today. Man, I wish I knew her like you do!"

Peter's cheeks jiggled when his head turned and vanished on the other side of the doorway. Timmy heard the heavy stomps as Peter padded down the hall.

"Smells good, Mrs. Worden!"

"Thank you, Peter. Wash your hands."

"Yes ma'am!"

Timmy took a deep breath. His stomach grumbled. Before, the rolling cramps had been caused by hunger, but now his stomach felt tight and bubbly, as if it were crinkling into a ball. Mama would make him eat his food no matter what. Hopefully he could keep it down.

He felt funny—a little shaken up from the fact Robin Hicks had called him. But mostly his chilly unease was from what she'd said.

Somebody took Dorothy?

Timmy never would've considered such a thought. Now it seemed to haunt his mind.

Standing up, Timmy wiped his cold, sweaty hands on his pants.

Then he started for the kitchen.

He wondered where Dorothy was right now.

-14-

The sun was gone, filling the woods in a deep blackness that brought cold temperatures with it. Lying on his stomach, Ed stared through the brush at the graveyard. Twiggy branches pressed closely together made a wall of shrubs that concealed him. He'd run back here this afternoon when he'd heard the voices in the distance.

He'd fallen asleep after eating another peanut butter sandwich and had been shocked awake by the gasping sounds of a girl. At first, he wasn't sure where he was, but he'd quickly remembered. Gathering up his food and weapons in a dash, he'd scurried behind some trees and ducked down behind a cluster of bushes.

Moments later, the pair had come into view, walking in from the old dirt road. The boy walked ahead of her, a bundled blanket under his arm, a small suitcase in one hand and tugging on a length of rope that led to the girl behind him with the other. The girl, staggering to keep up, had looked very young. Arms out, her wrists had been tied together. The girl had on a dress, but was barefoot. Even from behind the bushes, Ed had been able to tell she was crying.

The little girl was a prisoner.

Though she'd looked only vaguely familiar, the boy was somebody Ed knew very well.

Peter.

"Down," Peter snapped, jerking the rope.

The girl cried out as she was yanked. Stumbling forward, her stomach crashed onto the ground. Rolling onto her back, she moaned. Peter had already thrown down the blanket and suitcase. He wiped his mouth with the back of his hand. With the other hand, he fumbled with his belt. The girl had started crying when Peter pushed his pants down.

And Ed had watched what happened next with a sickened fascination. The girl on her back, legs wide as Peter, on top, shoved wildly. Through gritted teeth, the boy had made pig sounds. It had gone on and on, twisting Ed's stomach.

But he couldn't stop it.

Too many folks would wonder why he'd been out here. So he'd laid down on his front, folded his arms above him, and buried his face in the folds.

What was Eddie Gein doing at the old graveyard?
I didn't even know a graveyard was out there!
Yep! And Eddie Gein was there!
Good thing, or the girl could've been hurt worse.
But why was he there, anyway? What business did he have?
Why'd he have a lunchbox? Why'd he have old branches sharpened down into stakes?

He saw himself sitting in a chair, detectives walking circles around him. One would be nice, trying to make Ed comfortable, building his trust by giving him everything he wanted. The other, crustier flatfoot wouldn't care less about Ed's wishes as he tugged at his tie. A cigarette dangled from his mouth. His sleeves had been rolled up and on his knuckles were scars from previous interrogations.

No.

The risk of too many questions had prevented Ed from intervening.

Now, the girl was alone. Peter had left a while ago, whistling as he'd walked up the dirt path. Shortly after Peter vanished in the shaded pathway, Ed had heard the jingle of the boy's bicycle pedaling away.

Tied to the wrought-iron fence, hands behind her back, rope was looped around her stomach. The girl's mouth was muzzled with a rag. Ed could see the paleness of her body as flecks of moonlight bounced on her naked skin. She cried softly behind the gag. She'd had a blanket covering her, but it had fallen off at some point.

When Ed had first realized the sun was going down, he'd come up with a plan—sneak over to her when it was dark, untie the ropes, and let her go. If he stayed behind her, she couldn't see who was helping her. While she tried to figure out who'd freed her, he would have already fled through the woods.

Gotten to his truck.

And the hell away from here.

Just as he'd been about to do that very thing, another idea had come on.

Use her as bait.

And so he'd waited and still was. Surely, the creature would come along with this girl being offered to it. How could it resist? Ed would wait until it was about to take her, then he'd attack.

The vampire would once again be dead. The girl would be free. And she'd be able to tell what happened to her, who'd done those things to her.

And Ed would be left out of it entirely.

That was a better plan.

Ed rested his chin on his forearms. His coat made a nice pillow. He thought it might be comfortable enough to nap some more, but the soft sobs coming from the girl wouldn't allow it.

"Who's there?"

Ed jerked. His heart shot into his throat.

The girl had spoken.

"I heard you," she said between sniffles. "Please, help me."

But the gag?

Straining his eyes to see, Ed spotted the gagging hanging around her throat like a collar. Somehow, she'd wiggled her mouth free.

"Nobody's here," said Ed. He hadn't meant to say it aloud, only in his mind.

"Somebody *is* there!" The girl's sharp breaths turned squeaky. "Please! Help me. I'm tied up. This boy did...he's hurt me so bad. I'm bleeding."

Ed looked through the small gaps of space between the bush's thick branches. He could see the girl under a net of moonlight. Her head turned in all directions, trying to pinpoint where the voice had come from. Her hair flew out in a pale wave each time she looked. The ring of fabric from the gag bounced on her neck.

"Are you still there?" she asked. "Please?"

"I'm here," he said.

"Thank you, Jesus, thank you. Please. Help me."

"I...I can't."

The girl stopped moving. She looked in his direction now. Her face was smudged in shadows, her eyes deep black ovals that he could feel on his face.

"Wuh-why not?" she asked in a pitiful voice.

"Not yet," he said.

"He'll be back," she said. "He told me. He'll be back and he'll do it again. Please don't let him, please! Untie me!"

She squirmed against the ropes, pushing forward. The rope made dark indentions in her pale stomach. The fence made soft rattling sounds as she struggled. The fence would hold. The rope would hold. She wasn't going anywhere no matter how hard she tried. Peter had done a good job tying her up.

"Just stop," Ed said. "Okay? You can't get loose. You're going to hurt yourself even more."

The girl went slack, huffing. Her head hung low, pale hair draping her face. "I just want to go home, Mister. Please, let me go home."

Ed's vision turned blurry. He wiped the moisture from his eyes with a gloved finger. "I will. I promise. Just can't right now."

"*Why not?*"

Ed flinched at the loudness of her voice. He wished she'd be quiet. If Peter came back and heard her shouting like this, he'd know she was talking to somebody. And nobody could know Ed had been here. Nobody.

But she knows.

She knew *somebody* was here, but not that it was Ed.

Needs to stay that way.

"I'm setting a trap," Ed said.

"A...trap?"

"Yes. He'll come for you, I'm sure."

"He said he would."

Ed wasn't talking about Peter, but if she thought he was, then so be it. "I know," he said.

"And you'll pound him?"

"Yes. I'll pound him."

He heard the girl release a breath of relief. Her head leaned back against the bars, mouth open and pointed at the sky. Her chest rose and fell in rapid motions. "Thank you, Mister."

"You're welcome."

"I hoped he'd never come back. Now I want him to hurry up. So you can pound him."

Ed laughed.

He was glad to hear the girl did too.

"Will you pound him really hard?" she asked.

"Knock his block off."

"Clean off?"

"Right off his shoulders," said Ed. "It'll fly in the air."

"Sounds good to me."

"I'll even shrink it for you so you can hang it on your wall."

There was a long pause. Her mouth closed, lips pursed. She almost looked as if she were wincing. "What do you mean?" she asked.

"I use a special pot on my stove to do it. I mix up this broth and let the heads soak in it. After several days, the heads just get smaller and smaller. I turn them into trinkets."

"Wow, that's neat," she said.

"I could do that to Peter for you. Shrunken heads bring good luck. Nobody'll mess with you if you have that."

"Peter? That's his name?"

As always, Ed had said too much. Now she knew Ed knew the boy.

The girl shook her head. "Thought he looked familiar. I think my mama knows his mama. He said he'd seen me at Buck's."

"He likes to go there," said Ed.

Shut up, you fool! Quit talking so damn much!

"Me too," said the girl. "Do you like to go there?"

"No," said Ed. "Not really. I don't go to town much if I can help it."

"Are you ugly or something?"

Ed snorted. "Well..."

"Sorry. I mean, are you like the Hunchback? He never wanted to leave the bell tower because of his ugliness and the hump in his back."

"I'm not a hunchback," he said. "But that's a good story."

"Yeah," she said. "I like it too. I read a lot."

"So do I."

"What's your name?"

He couldn't tell her his name, not his real one. Unable to think of anything quickly, he said, "Theodore." His middle name.

"Hi, Theodore."

"Hi."

"I'm Dorothy."

"Nice to meet you."

He saw the white of her teeth as she smiled. "Thank you."

Ed nodded.

A few long moments of listening to crickets and frogs passed before Dorothy spoke again. "Promise you'll pound him?"

"Promise."

"Good. I'm tired and I'm cold. I want to go sleep. Do you promise not to…you know…do what Peter did? You're not weird, are you?"

"I won't."

"Swear?"

"I swear."

"Okay," she said. "Will you cover me up?"

Ed saw the dark blot of the blanket bunched on the ground next to her. As if to show how cold she was, her body shivered. He didn't want to leave her unprotected to the chilly night air, but he couldn't just walk out there and reveal himself to her. Though he couldn't recall where he knew her from, he was certain she'd recognize him. Everybody in Plainfield knew Ed Gein.

"Please, Theodore? I'm so cold and I can't cover myself."

"Look the other way," said Ed.

"Why?"

"I don't want you…to see who I am."

"Are you sure you aren't like the Hunchback?"

Smiling, Ed said "I'm sure. Just have to keep who I am a secret."

"Why?"

"Just do."

"Okay," she said in a disappointed tone. Her head turned, gazing toward the dark chasm of the pathway. "I'm not looking."

"Better not look when I get over there."

"Just keep your hands to yourself. Please? I don't...I'm not wearing any clothes."

"Well, I have to touch the blanket," he said.

"Just don't touch me like Peter did."

"I promised I wouldn't."

"Okay," she said.

Ed stood up, groaning as his joints popped. He'd been on the cold ground for a long time, and it felt good to stand. He stretched his back, rising onto the tips of his boots. Warmth flowed through him, tingling as his muscles loosened. With his earlier idea of freeing her, he'd mapped out his route to get to her without being seen. Only problem was, he hadn't considered needing to cover her up. With her hands behind her, he'd planned to come in through the other side of the graveyard, crouching behind the fence to work at the ropes.

To cover her, he'd have to move into the front.

She better not look.

Ed walked through woods. His movements sounded as if he was walking on an earth covered in dried oats. Dead leaves crackled and crunched with each step. Reaching the fence, he walked alongside it to reach her.

He saw her long legs, white in the moonlight, ankles crossed. Her knees were scraped raw. She had a few scratches on her thighs and something that looked like a purple button in the crease of her inner-thigh. Darker little indentions ringed the outside.

A bite?

"Is that you, Theodore?" she asked.

"Yes. Don't look."

"I'm not."

Keeping his eyes on the back of her head, Ed bent sideways, arm swinging in the air. His hand patted around, groping until his fingers bumped the blanket. It felt cool and thick and itchy. He picked it up and flapped it, spreading it out. It fluttered down, covering her body. Then he pulled the edges toward her chin, curling the corners over her shoulders.

"Better?" he asked.

"Yes, much better."

He saw her head starting to turn, so he spun around and dashed into the woods.

"Come back!" she called.

"No. I'm going back over here."

He knew if she'd gotten a glimpse of him, it was of his backside and probably too dark to tell much with the distance between them.

She promised! The dirty sneak!

Ed walked back to his spot behind the bushes and plopped down. He pulled his feet toward his crotch and crossed them. He looked through the space between the bushy limbs. Dorothy peered in his direction. The blanket still covered her.

"Thank you, Theodore," she said.

"Welcome."

"I'm going to close my eyes," she said through a yawn.

"Good night."

"Good night."

Ed watched Dorothy. The blanket made quick, fluttering movements. Her toes stuck out the bottom of the blanket, curling as her legs wiggled. Then her legs stopped moving. Soon the blanket lifted in a steady rhythm of her breaths.

She was asleep.

Ed hated being stuck in this predicament—unable to help her like she needed because he was afraid of being caught for what he'd done.

But if he hadn't freed the vampire, he wouldn't have been here waiting on it. And he wouldn't have met Dorothy. He didn't want to think about the things Peter might do to her next. Hard to believe the boy was capable of the things he'd seen so far.

Opening his lunchbox, Ed removed his last peanut butter sandwich. He thought about offering it to Dorothy, but decided to let her sleep.

Ed chewed softly, keeping his eyes on her.

He wanted to be done with all this so he could go back to digging up things in peace.

And he had a vampire tour to plan.

-15-

Peter coasted on his bicycle. Cold night air whipped his clothes against his body, making sounds like a sailboat. His hair flapped wildly, wagging in his eyes and across his forehead. He felt good and light, though his belly was full.

He'd *done it* three times today.

Once on Dorothy's bed and twice in the graveyard. The first time had felt the best, though it had been the quickest. That first burst had made him cry, it felt so good.

He was ready for another.

Should get home. Ma is probably waiting for me.

But he wanted to ride by the graveyard, have another go at Dorothy. In the morning, he'd bring her some food and water before school. After school, he'd ride back by the graveyard and have her again. He knew everybody was looking for her, but he doubted anybody would think to check the old graveyard. Probably most of the folks in town didn't even know it was there.

But Peter knew.

His daddy had taken him there when Peter was still little. They'd gone for a drive and Daddy had told ghost stories. He'd promised to show Peter something neat.

And neat it was.

Peter had gone back to the graveyard many times since then. He felt close to his daddy when he was there. Sometimes he even talked, as if Daddy were there to hear him. It looked a little different now. The gate had been broken. Peter wondered when the damage had happened. Could've been anytime, since he hadn't been out there in over a year.

It was safe though, he was certain.

Can't keep her there forever.

No. He'd have to move her. Probably tomorrow night. Where, he had no idea. He'd think of that later.

It was still hard for him to believe he'd finally done it. It was reading the garishly weird stories in crime magazines that had started his fantasies of doing *things* to girls. Usually they involved Robin Hicks, but the day he'd seen Dorothy in Buck's with Robin, his affection turned to her. She was a lot younger, but to Peter that made it even better.

He'd read stories about guys tying women up, cutting on them, smearing their blood over their skin, sticking their wieners in them. Sometimes there were pictures.

The magazines had taught Peter about sex, taught him how to force himself onto girls. He'd lie in bed at night, staring at his dark ceiling, dreaming of having his way with Dorothy. A rope and knife was all he'd needed.

He'd followed her around. Just a little here and there, to see what she liked to do, to see the places she liked to go. One night he'd tried to peek through her window and had been disappointed to discover her bedroom was on the upper floor.

Learning about Dorothy had been pretty easy, really. Because his Ma was friends with Dorothy's mother, he was able to find out the girl was home alone on Tuesday afternoons. So today when school let out, he'd pedaled his bicycle straight to her farmhouse. Then he'd hidden his bicycle in the woods and sneaked over to the house and in through the back door.

Expecting her to be home, he'd been surprised to find she wasn't. A few minutes later, she was dropped off by a car he didn't recognize. He'd almost run away. But he was grateful he'd stuck around, because the person hadn't come inside the house with Dorothy.

And now she was his for as long as he wanted her to be.

What was he going to do with her when he was finally finished?

Don't think about that. She's yours. Keep her for a long time.

First thing, he needed to pick a new place to hide her.

Maybe then he'd start cutting on her. He had the knife—taken from the Clark's house.

His heart pounded even harder than it already was, making him a little dizzy as he thought about rubbing a blade across her soft skin.

The knife was still at the graveyard. Before he'd left, he'd buried it. Maybe he'd use it a little tonight, just to see if he liked it.

Nah, not yet. Save it for when there's more time.

When Peter reached the intersection, he made a right instead of continuing straight to go to his house. As he pedaled away from home, he glanced back. He could see the porch light was on. Ma was probably pacing a gulley into the carpet, wondering where he was.

She's gonna beat my butt!

But it was worth it. Being with Dorothy one more time tonight was worth any spanking he'd get.

So long as Ma didn't ground him.

Please, no.

He doubted she would. She normally spanked him and left it at that.

Soon Peter left the neighborhood behind. He kept riding until he saw no more houses. Woods pushed deep shadows against him. The moon threw a blueish haze onto the road, making it a pale strip in the dark.

Thankfully he knew the road well enough to know the curve was up ahead. The trail to the graveyard was just past it. He'd have to cross the road to get to it.

He reached the bend and started across. Something in the woods caught his eye. He turned his head, steering the bike to the left, as he tried to see what it was.

The moon glinted off a windshield. He could make out the dark shape of a truck hidden in the woods.

Is that...Ed's?

Suddenly he was washed in a glaring brightness. The sound of an engine filled the night.

Peter turned and saw headlights boring down on him.

He screamed.

-16-

Mary saw the boy too late. All that had been in front of her was an empty road for miles. When she took the curve, the boy was suddenly there—gazing at the front of her car in wide-eyed fright through the thick fissures in her cracked windshield. She could hear his scream above the grumble of her engine.

A *bump* resounded from the front.

She slammed a foot on the brake while yanking the steering wheel to the right. The car skidded off the road. When the tires hit the grassy verge, she nearly lost control.

She managed to bring the car to a bumpy halt.

"Hot damn! What the hell was that?"

Twice now, Mary had been surprised by something in the road while driving this route. And twice she'd managed to plow it over with her car.

Mary jerked the gear to Park, turned in her seat, and stared out the back windshield.

Everything behind her was awash in the red of her taillights. She saw a bicycle in the center of the road, upturned, the bent wheel pointing at the sky. She saw the boy on the other side of the bicycle, on his side. His back faced her. She couldn't tell if he was breathing.

Dust hovered like a dirty fog.

"Oh, shit." Mary groaned. "What the hell am I going to do?"

The kid rolled onto his back. Now she could see the rapid motions his chest made as he breathed.

"Thank heavens for that."

She faced the front and saw her hand going for the gear again.

Am I really about to leave a hurt kid behind?

Mary turned again to look out the back. The kid hadn't moved. He still lay on his back, still panting. His arms were splayed out, but motionless.

What am I going to do with him?

The obvious choice was to take him to the hospital. She could drop him off up front. That way she wouldn't have to worry about talking to anybody. People in Plainfield find out she'd mowed down one of their kids, she'd have hell to pay.

Besides, she needed to get back to the tavern. She'd just finished dumping what was left of Jenkins's body and needed to get back to the master. She'd left the back room a mess after his feeding. It needed to be cleaned up, and she wanted...

The master!

Mary stared at the kid, a smile pulling at the corners of her mouth. She heard a wild laugh and wasn't surprised that it had come from her lungs.

Move, Mary, move!

Throwing open her door, Mary jumped out of the car. She ran around to the boy's wrecked bicycle, gave a quick look around, and crouched. She grabbed the front wheel and spun around. When she was facing the woods, she released the bicycle. It soared over the road, hit a barrier of limbs, and smashed through. It landed in the shadows with a rattling crash.

She gave another look both ways. The road was still clear.

Moaning, the boy tried to get onto his side, but couldn't do it. He rocked the other way, ending up on his back again. A big fellow. He'd probably strain her back when she lifted him. But she was a bigger woman and could throw freight better than most men, so she had little worry.

Mary shoved her arms underneath the boy and, using her legs, hoisted him up. She threw him over her shoulder like a sack of feed, and turned around. Keeping one arm straight out, she hobbled back to the car with her shoulder digging into the boy's stomach. Her other arm braced his rump to hold him in place. He made moaning sounds as if telling her he didn't want to go with her. Ignoring him, she made her way to the car.

She chucked him in. He landed on his side, nearly falling into the floorboard.

"Slide over," she said.

The boy held his stomach. She noticed scuff marks on his chin and forehead. His shirt was torn, as was a leg of his trousers. The skin showing through the rip was wet and dark.

He looked at her from over his shoulder with glassy eyes.

Mary slapped him on the rump. "I said slide over, damn it."

Crying, the boy scooted across the seat to the other side. His hands fumbled for the door latch. Leaning into the car, Mary grabbed his arm and shook him.

"Don't you dare," she snapped. "Stay still, you little bastard!"

Mary got into the car and pulled the door shut. She looked through the windshield, turned and checked behind her. Nobody was coming toward them. No headlights could be seen from either direction.

Smiling, Mary jerked the gear and drove away.

-17-

Mary flung the back room door open. From the dim glow flickering inside, she realized she'd forgotten to blow out the candle when she'd left.

Good way to burn the place down.

"What are you going to do to me?" the boy cried.

"Get in there," she said, shoving him.

The fat kid stumbled a few steps, and fell forward. He grabbed the edge of the sink to catch himself. On his knees, hands gripping the sink, he looked back at her. His nose wrinkled as he sniffed, grimacing as if he caught the scent of something terrible.

It smelled like rotted meat in here. Jenkins's leftovers had filled the room with a copper-like scent mixed with something like old meat.

"Get up," she said.

Nodding, the boy pulled himself upright with a groan. He had to be in some serious pain, but he seemed to be moving around just fine on his own, though a little sluggish.

Grabbing the collar of his coat, she pushed him, making him walk. The boy shuffled forward, feet tripping over each other, to the back of the room.

The boy saw the mess on the bed and screamed.

"Shut up," she said, slapping both hands on his back and shoving.

The boy flew forward. His knees hit the edge of the mattress. His legs shot out, throwing him onto the bed. He splashed in thick puddles of black blood.

Mary quickly scanned the room. Blood everywhere. It covered the floor like a gloppy rug, hung from the walls in thick gooey strings. "Got you somebody!" Mary called.

A retort of growls came from under the bed as the purple smoke eddied out in thick currents.

The boy froze. Turned his head sideways. And screamed.

He bucked against the mattress as he tried to get up, but kept slipping in the murky paste smothering the bed. His face dropped into a mushy pile of Jenkin's innards and he when he lifted his head, his screaming mouth was ringed with blood. A wet clump stuck to his bottom lip, reminding Mary of her grandfather when he chewed tobacco.

Now the fat kid really lashed, throwing his body up and down. He looked as if he was practicing how to swim by the way his arms and legs flapped and whirled. His skin was slick with dark blood.

A gnarled hand reached up from the edge of the bed, slapping three elongated spike-like claws down on the mattress. Seeing this made the boy shriek like an infant. He tried to pull his arm away in time.

But didn't.

The master's hand clenched a chubby wrist.

Then the boy was jerked from the bed, vanishing over the side. Feet kicking, it looked as if the boy had dropped something and was reaching down for it.

His feet shot out of sight as if he'd been sucked under the bed.

Mary stepped forward, fingers pressed to her mouth. She listened.

A heavy blanket of silence swathed the room.

Seconds that felt like hours passed by.

A juicy crunch made Mary jump. Blood spewed from under the bed as if from a hose. It showered the thick, oil-like puddles with fresh crimson, thinning them. The boy's screams covered the sounds of the master's feeding.

A calming tingle made her feel dizzy and weak. She walked out of the room and plopped in a chair at the small table in the kitchen area. She grabbed the box of matches, slid a cigarette from her pack, and struck flame to the match's tip with her fingernail. She raised the dancing flame to her cigarette, lighting it. Leaning back her head, she pulled in a deep drag of smoke, and gazed at the ceiling.

The suckling sounds stopped.

Mary turned her head, gazing into the room. "Master?"

Silence.

The master was never finished this quickly. Maybe because the boy was younger, it hadn't taken as long to feast.

Might not've been hungry.

Mary got to her feet. She shuffled toward the room on exhausted legs and was about to enter when a hole exploded in the mattress, sending metal springs, cotton, and bloody clods out in a cloud. Mary jumped back, screaming. The cigarette flew from her fingers.

The master appeared in the hole. The mattress covered him to his knees. Holding out his fuzzy-haired arms, elbows bent, it looked as if he was flexing. Head tilted back, his chin dropped, stretching its blue jowls like thin sheets of dough. Thin purple lips bared a row of spiked teeth that dripped blood. Tiny shreds of flesh clung between them. The master's eyes, which had been a faded orange when she'd met him, now blazed like an inferno inside the thrones of Hell.

A shriek ripped from the master's throat that vibrated the walls. Mary's breasts shook, her insides trembled. Other than his threadbare clothes, the master looked wonderful and healthy.

"Muh-master?" said Mary.

His large head slowly turned in her direction, the thick coal-colored hair shimmering as if wetted. His leaf-shaped nose was moist and flaring as he sniffed, the pink walls of his nostrils quivering with each inhale. The cavernous ears tilted this way and that. Gazing at her, the master ran his forked tongue across his mouth, leaving his lips dripping with moisture.

"You're...healed?" she asked.

"Reborn."

His voice touched her in places that made her quiver. The master held out his arm. His three, thick fingers curled upward. Walking to him, Mary was about to climb on the bed when the master held up his hand. Mary paused. "What?" she asked.

"We have...another."

His voice was deep and swished through her head like a faint spell. It nearly brought Mary to her knees.

"A son..." The master looked down. The hole he'd made in the mattress was a wide circle. Tattered sheets hung like old flags around his legs. He reached his other hand down and opened it.

Mary watched as a pale arm rose from the darkness of the hole. Its palsied hand slipped into the master's. The master lifted, pulling the boy up with him. The boy's clothes were sodden with blood and hung like wet blankets on his body. The boy's face wasn't recognizable under the red veneer and lumpy bits. Releasing the boy's hand, the master turned, allowing the boy to hug his waist.

He now has a son.

The master faced Mary. Opened his hand to her.

Mary climbed onto the bed and embraced them both.

-18-

"Theodore?"

Ed's eyes snapped open. He wasn't sure where he was—darkness all around, a cold hardness beneath his back that seeped freezing dampness through his clothes. Sitting up, Ed bonked his head on something hard. He dropped back, holding his head.

He groaned.

"Theodore?" The soft voice was concerned now. "Are you okay?"

"Who?" said Ed through a pain-filled moan.

"You," said the voice.

Theodore?

Ed stopped moving.

He remembered. He was at the graveyard. He'd told the girl his name was Theodore.

And he'd fallen asleep.

Great job, you dunce.

Ed winced at the dull throb that started in his hairline and pulsated through his skull. What'd he hit his head on? Turning slightly, he saw the wall of shrubs he'd been hiding behind. A gnarled, leafless branch twisted out from the thick leaves like a skeleton's deformed arm.

Guess I deserved it, for falling asleep.

What would he have done if the vampire had shown up while he was asleep? Or Peter?

Squat, that was what he'd have done.

"Theodore? I'm getting scared. Are you all right?"

"Huh?" said Ed. He cleared his throat. "Yeah, I'm all right."

"What happened?"

"Socked my noggin pretty good, that's what."

The softness of her laughter made him smile.

"Did it hurt?" she asked, snickering between the words.

"Not too much," he lied. He sat up. Groaned. "Very much. But it'll be okay."

"You're sure?"

"Yeah..."

"Wonder what time it is."

Ed wondered that as well. Reaching into his pocket, he dug out his watch. It was a copper-plated device that had belonged to his father. He pressed the button to open the cover, held the watch up, and tilted it into a blade of moonlight that stabbed through the trees.

"Nearly five in the morning," he said.

"Almost dawn," she said, yawning.

"I thought you'd sleep all night."

"Well...I woke up because I have to..."

Ed waited for her to finish, but she left the sentence hanging there. "You have to what?"

"I have to...tinkle..."

Ed sighed. He should have expected this at some point. "There's nothing I can really do about that, Dorothy."

"Untie me so I can go do it in the woods."

"I can't untie you," he said.

"Why not?"

"I told you before," he said.

"I'll come right back," she said. "And you don't even have to tie me back up. I'll just pretend to be tied."

"If Peter sees you're not tied..."

"He won't. I said I'll pretend."

"I don't know, Dorothy."

"Please!"

The hopeless desperation in Dorothy's voice made Ed flinch. She started to cry.

Ed knew he shouldn't untie her, but her pitiful sobs would soon make him nuts. "Okay," he said. "Be right there."

Sniffling, Dorothy muttered her thanks.

Ed took the same route he'd taken when covering her with the blanket to keep himself hidden, a bit slower this time since movement seemed to cause his head to ache even worse. At the rear of the graveyard, he gripped the tops of the fence under their sharp tips. Hoisting himself up, he threw his legs over, watching them narrowly evade being pricked, and dropped. His feet slapped the ground. Landing in a squat, Ed looked to the front. He could see the back of Dorothy's head. Her light hair was a shimmering pallor in the dark.

"Is that you?" she asked.

"It's me," he said, standing. He started walking.

She let out a relieved sigh. Reaching the other side of the graveyard, he crouched behind her. Her wrists stuck between the wrought-iron bars. A thick rope bound them together by a tight knot. Peter had done an immaculate job. Where'd a boy so young learn precision like this?

Ed started working to untie it, but his gloves made the task awkward and hard. Plus Ed had sausages for fingers. Holding nails was also a pain because his chubby fingers either dropped them, or would be bashed with the hammer because they stuck up so far above the rim of the nail head.

"Please hurry," said Dorothy, shaking. "I'm about to go."

"I've almost got it," said Ed.

The knot loosened more as Ed fidgeted with it. He pulled an end out of the loop, and the knot fell away. Now all that was left was to unwind it. He started twirling his arm, removing the rope piece by piece. Finally, it dropped from her wrists, though the marks it left on her skin made it look as if she were still tied.

Dorothy slumped forward, moaning. She pulled her arms forward, letting them hang in front of her.

"It hurts," she said. "Feels like needles…"

"Give them a minute to start working again," he said.

She started to turn around.

"Don't," he said.

"I can't see you?"

"No. I told you, you couldn't."

Dorothy sighed. "Fine."

"How're your arms now?"

"They *hurt*."

From the slow rolling of her shoulders, he figured she was rubbing the indentions on her skin. Probably felt raw and painful, like the worst carpet burn somebody could ever get. She'd probably have those bruises for a long time.

Dorothy leaned forward, putting her arms ahead of her. Her white rump rose on the other side of the bars. Ed quickly looked away. He heard Dorothy gasp and turned in time to watch her drop on her stomach. Her feet flew towards her back, heels bopping her buttocks.

Groaning, Dorothy lowered her head onto the ground and sobbed. "I can't walk," she said in a whiny voice. "They're numb. I can't move. I can't do *anything*. I hurt down there. My legs won't work right and my arms feel weird!"

Ed shushed her. "It's all right. Just got to give it a minute…"

"I can't! I'm about to pee!"

"Calm down," he said.

"Will you help me up?"

"I don't…can't…" Ed sighed. "You're not wearing anything."

"Please, Theodore. I need help."

Ed pressed his lips tightly together and huffed through his nose. He couldn't just leave her there. Wouldn't be right. But if he helped her get up, she'd see who he was. There was no way he could get her onto her feet without exposing his face to her.

"Fine," she said. "I'll do it myself."

"Hold on," he said.

Ed stood with a moan. His knees made cracking sounds as his legs straightened. He walked away from her, heading toward the front entrance. Since the vampire had broken the gate, he was able to walk straight through. He turned and started toward her.

Lying on her stomach, Dorothy's head turned to look at him. It tilted back. Her hair looked nearly bleached as it curtained her face. Moonlight showed her features in a soft glow.

Her eyes widened, mouth dropped. "I...know you..." she said, voice stammering.

"Thought you would."

"Ed Gein," she said.

He nodded.

"You said your name was Theodore."

"My middle name. Didn't want you to know who I was."

Keeping his eyes on hers, Ed sunk to a crouch beside her hip. He felt around the ground for the blanket. His fingers brushed a smooth, cold thigh. Gasping, Dorothy recoiled away. Before she'd known who he was, she hadn't seemed bothered that he could see her. Now that she knew he was Ed Gein, town goof, she acted frightened of him.

Feeling ashamed, he lowered his head. There was no reason for him to feel bad, but he couldn't stop it from happening. Should be used to this kind of reaction by now. Other than Timmy and Peter, most the kids looked at him as if he was from outer space. The adults treated him like a child trapped in a man's body.

Others pretended he didn't exist.

Of course Dorothy wouldn't be any different.

Ed found the blanket and pulled it over her.

"Ready?" he asked.

"I..." She looked around. "I think I can do it now."

"But you said you needed my help."

"It's okay," she said. "I think..."

Ed noticed the blanket move, her legs squirming underneath.

"Yeah," she said. "Thank you, but I think I can do it. Yeah. No problem."

Dorothy put her hands flat on the ground and pushed up. Gritting her teeth, she groaned as she made herself rise to her knees. The blanket dropped off her shoulders, unveiling her naked back. Ed glimpsed a patchwork of bruises before Dorothy made a frantic grab for the itchy wool, and pulled it around her. Her hand held it snugly closed in front.

Ed stood up, his tendons popping again with protest of the cold and his age. Dorothy looked up at him, fear making her eyes wide.

"Are you sure you don't need my help anymore?" he asked.

Dorothy shook her head. Wincing, she threw a leg in front of her, pushed off her foot and got upright. She swayed towards Ed and fell against him. He felt the coldness of her body through the blanket and his clothes as he held her up. Probably would come down with pneumonia before this ordeal was through.

He tried to help her find her balance, but she quickly pushed him back.

"I'm fine," she said.

"I really think you should..."

"Don't touch me, weirdo!"

Ed flinched. Dorothy stared at him with narrowed eyes, a corner of her lip curled, baring teeth. She studied him with restraint, as if she expected him to try and harm her.

"Fine," said Ed. "I'll wait here."

"So you can tie me up again?"

"You said you could fake it..."

"I'm not..." Dorothy stepped backward, shaking her head. "You just *want* me back here."

"What?"

"Bet you've *liked* watching me, haven't you? Mama said you like to watch people—that it's all you do. Did you like watching what Peter did to me?"

"No," said Ed, feeling sick at the memory. "No."

She jerked the blanket open, showing him her naked front. The pale skin was dotted in bruises. Above her small breast was a row of dents that might have been teeth marks.

Ed turned away.

"See me? Peter saw me! Bet you want to touch me too, don't you? Go ahead. Touch all you want! Might as well!"

"Dorothy, stop."

"Touch me in *there*," she cried. Her voice, high and cracking, sounded like a witch who'd gone mad. "Peter likes it in there! Bet you will too!"

"Stop it!"

He threw an arm out. He felt his hand lightly knock against the softness of Dorothy's stomach. She made a startled choking sound, and stopped her tantrum. Ed heard the blanket flap as it was pulled shut. Knowing it was safe to look, he turned, opening his mouth to apologize.

And Dorothy cut him off by slapping his cheek.

A stinging blast lit up the side of his face. His vision flashed with brightness. When it cleared, he saw Dorothy was hobbling away from him, making for the trail.

"No!" Ed shouted.

Dorothy limped and hopped, almost dragging her left foot behind her. The blanket fluttered out like a thick cape. Glancing over her shoulder, she saw him coming after her and loosed a frightened scream.

"Dorothy! Come back!" he cried.

"Stay away from me!"

Ed couldn't let her get away. She'd tell everybody he'd been here while Peter had hurt her. He'd have to confess about the vampire, what he'd done, and the graves he'd dug up.

Everybody would know what Ed Gein had been up to while they'd slept soundly in their beds.

No! They can't know!

"Dorothy, please!"

"Stay away!"

Ed was quickly gaining on her. She couldn't move nearly fast enough because of her condition. She gave a fleeting glance behind her, spotted Ed, and screamed louder. She turned forward and seemed to move a bit faster.

Ed heard a crack and Dorothy suddenly dropped with a painful screech.

The thud her body made on the ground was loud and firm in the night. On the ground, Dorothy screamed and cried, but she didn't stop trying to get away. Now she dragged herself along the ground, hands gripping the dirt like a ladder's rungs and tugging. Her right leg helped—knee digging into the ground and assisting with a push.

But the left one stayed straight and motionless.

And slowed her down like an anchor.

Ed noticed the flaccid foot was twisted to the side and jiggled with each movement. Below her toes, he saw a hump of root protruding from the ground.

It had snagged Dorothy's foot and made her fall.

Probably broke her ankle.

A cold knot formed in his gut. How could he explain *this?* A naked little girl, injuring herself just to get away from him.

Nobody would believe I wasn't involved with what had happened to her.

Everything had gone wrong so fast. All because he'd felt sorry for Dorothy.

The girl kept dragging herself over the ground, pulling her body out of the blanket. Naked, she wriggled up the path, leaving a flat gulley in the dirt.

She was moving so slowly now that Ed didn't need to run. He walked beside her, got above her head, and turned. He waited on her to reach his feet. Her fingers curled over the toes of his boots. Her jittering head leaned back. Yellow hair curtained her face, leaving her mouth in the open. Ed noticed her lips were trembling.

"I wasn't going to hurt you," he said.

Strings of spit clung to her lips and stretched as she cried. Tears dribbled down her cheeks, dripping off her jaw. She looked so...pitiful.

What was he going to do with her? She couldn't leave these woods.

Strangle her?

Ed's hands tingled at the thought. He flexed his fingers. Could he really do that to such a young girl? Could he do it to anybody?

No.

There had to be some other way to fix this.

"Please..." she said, breathless. "Don't..."

"I don't know what to do, Dorothy." Ed shrugged. "I'm out of ideas."

Dorothy closed her eyes, pushing out droplets of tears that streamed down her dirty cheeks.

Rising to her exposed neck, his hands made C shapes. He stopped just before they clasped her throat.

I can't.

He let his hands drop. "Okay…"

Panting and wincing, Dorothy watched him.

"Let's get you out of here," Ed said.

"Ruh-really?"

Nodding, Ed started to reach for her.

"Thanks for the help, Eddie." The voice had come from behind, and sounded like grating metal.

Ed's skin went tight and crawly.

Dorothy screamed.

Ed spun around.

Something that vaguely resembled Peter stood before him, with features that were deformed varieties of his former self. His brow now bulged and furrowed over eyes that had recessed into his skull and smoldered like liquid gold. His purple lips pulled back into a steely grin, presenting fangs where his teeth used to be. A black wedge of tongue reached out from the gulf of his mouth, tapping the fangs as if making sure Ed had noticed them. His filthy clothes, covered in dark muck, hung stiffly on his body. The skin that could be seen through the filth was insipid and reptilian in texture.

Jesus H. Christ, what happened to him?

The vampire must've gotten to him. Changed him.

How?

"I'll take care of our girl from here," Peter said.

Ed felt a mule-kick on his chest from Peter's swinging arm. Then Ed was soaring backwards, his arms and legs extended in front of him. As if the ground wanted Ed back, he was snatched from the air and pounded the earth. Air blasted from his lungs. He slid several feet before finally stopping.

Ed's lungs felt as if they were being twisted by cold hands. It hurt his chest to breathe. He didn't want to move. But Dorothy's screams made him roll to his side. Groaning and coughing, Ed looked toward the path and was shocked to see how far he'd been knocked. Dorothy was a small bucking shape on the tree-darkened path.

Peter was on top of her.

"*Help me!*" Dorothy's cry was like a knife in Ed's chest.

"*Help me!*" Peter mocked. *"Oh, Eddie, please help me, my hero!"*

Peter let out a wild cackle that Ed felt in the marrow of his bones. Ed pushed himself up on all fours, coughed, and nearly dropped back down. Trembling, Ed started crawling toward the bushes.

He'd left his bag over there.

Dorothy screamed from behind, high and shrill, like a banshee in the night. Ed pushed through the shrubs headfirst, closing his eyes against the slapping twigs. He felt stinging lashes on his mouth, cheeks, chin, and neck. He made it through to the other side. The skin of his face burned as if he'd recently shaved.

Spotting his bag, Ed quickly crawled to it. He sat back on his legs, jerked the sack onto his thighs, tugged it open, and reached in. He felt the sharp tip of a filed stake. He'd carved it himself from a fell branch he'd found in his yard. With the stake clenched in his fist, Ed stood.

He gazed toward the path from over the bushes. Dorothy no longer screamed. Peter no longer groaned or mocked. All Ed could hear was the soft rustling of leaves from a mild breeze and just underneath that a slurping sound, like somebody struggling to pull a chunk of milkshake through a thin straw.

Ed ran through the bushes, kneeing limbs out of his way. He reached the other side and kept running. Closing in, he began to make out Peter's dark form, slumped over, pale arcs on either side of his black hips.

Dorothy's legs.

The shadowy blob covered all of her but her splayed arms, spread legs, and tilted-back head. Her mouth was open wide, as if in a silent shriek while the black bubble of Peter's head jerked wildly at her neck. Blood spurted across her sweet, pallid face.

"Stop!" Ed shouted.

Peter's head shot up. Mouth wide and fangs flashing, he hissed. Blood smeared his lips and cheeks like sauce. Ed didn't give the boy the chance to react. He threw his foot out, the toe of his boot catching Peter under the chin. His jaw flew up, teeth clacked. He tumbled away from Dorothy's naked body.

Peter was already getting up when Ed pounced. He landed on the boy's pudgy stomach, sinking it inward under his weight. Peter hissed again. Blood spittle flew off his tongue. He gnashed his teeth. His attempted bites made hollow claps inches from Ed's arm as the stake raised into the air.

Ed brought the stake down. The tip banged Peter's chest above the heart.

And crumpled.

The sharp tip disintegrated into a cloud of chips and flakes. Sitting up, Ed examined the broken section he held in his hand. "Oh...damn..." he muttered.

Rotted wood.

Peter gave a short laugh. A hand shot out and clasped Ed's throat. Ed dropped the broken stake and used both hands to grab Peter's forearm midway between his wrist and elbow. He tried to pull the hand away from his throat to no avail.

Peter sat up, holding Ed in place with ease. Getting to his feet, Peter lifted Ed from the ground as he straightened. Ed rolled his eyes down. Below Peter's extended arm, Ed could see his kicking feet were above the ground.

Ed couldn't breathe. His lungs pulled for air that wasn't there to take. His chest felt as if it were swelling, fit to burst. He uselessly slapped and pounded Peter's arm.

The boy-creature took a few steps forward, ran his tongue across his lips.

"You released the master," Peter said in that dissonant voice.

Ed tried to speak but could only make quaking sounds.

Peter laughed in a tone like grinding stones. "He made me like this. Dorothy was to be my first feed. Now I'm whole. And now, Eddie, now you will be like me. You'll..." Peter gasped. His head shot towards the sky. His mouth stretched wide around the breathy hiss that gusted out. This one wasn't hungry and evil like the others. There was fear. "No," Peter cried, "no!"

Ed noticed a subtle change as everything seemed to fill with a pale glow that thinned the dark. At first he thought it was his eyeballs about to pop from their sockets. But he realized it was actually the sun giving its first peek through the clouds.

The pressure around Ed's throat went away. He dropped. His knees punched the ground. Though Peter had released his stranglehold, Ed's neck still felt as if it were being squeezed. Ed held his throat. The skin felt hot and itchy where Peter's hand had been. Looking up, he saw Peter was still focused on the brightening sky. His features were less monstrous now. Though he was milky white, he looked less like a thing and more like the Peter Ed had known.

Peter stepped back, head thrashing like a fox caught in a trap. His wild, feral eyes landed on Dorothy, then shot back to the sky. Peter's body sizzled as smoke began to drift from the sleeves of his T-shirt. "It burns!" he cried.

Peter, arm thrown over his face, ran toward Dorothy. Ed thought he meant to grab her, but instead, he snatched the blanket and spun it around his back and over his head like a shawl. Then he ran into the woods, the blanket flapping behind him, leaving a swirling trail of smoke in his retreat. It rose toward the thick branches above him, thinning until Ed could no longer see it at all.

Ed stayed on his knees for a long time—until the choking sensation in his throat went away. Until his knees could no longer take holding him up. Until the sun had burned away all evidence of the night.

He made himself get up, ignoring the aches he felt all through him. His heart still pounded his chest like a mallet. His breath still came in quick spurts.

Birds began to croon from all around; some chirped while others performed sweet melodies that seemed to carry on and on. Things scuttled and scampered, out of sight, making the leaves rustle and crunch.

A butterfly appeared in front of him, twirling and dipping low to the ground. Its paper-thin wings worked vigorously in yellow and black blurs. It was the first one Ed had seen this season. When the butterflies came out, that meant spring was here. And Ed could tell it would be a lovely day.

He watched the pretty insect flutter along the ground and perch on Dorothy's shoulder.

"Dorothy," Ed muttered.

In the bright sunlight, she looked painted white with a deep shading of blue. From where Ed stood, he could clearly see the dark holes in the side of her neck, an inch apart. Blood had left crimson rings around the holes and a thin line of red trickled down from each. Those looked dry as well.

The girl was dead.

Ed sighed. He felt zero remorse from her death, nor did he feel any real anger. It was the same kind of feeling he'd get when seeing somebody's pet on the side of the road, half trampled by tires. Was a sad thing to know how much her death was going to hurt somebody when they found out, but it didn't affect him at all.

He felt blank inside.

Ed walked through the undergrowth to his sack, leaned over, and grabbed it. He heaved it out from under the bushes. Grabbing the bottom of the sack, he flipped it over and dumped out the tools. They fell to the ground with a loud clatter that made him wince. He gave a quick look at Dorothy, expecting the racket to have awakened her.

She was still dead.

Ed turned the sack around and flapped it loose. He carried the empty sack over to Dorothy and dropped to his knees at her feet. Her broken ankle had turned a plum hue and hair-thin marks spread out from the bruise like cracks in glass. Keeping his eyes away from her upper body, he grabbed her feet and pulled her legs straight. Then he pushed her ankles together.

Opening the sack wide, he slipped one side under her feet, the other side *over* her toes and began to push the sack up like pants. Her rump stopped it. He moved around to her side, pushed her up by the hip, and pulled the sack through. He kept pulling it until Dorothy had been entirely swallowed.

Then he pulled the line taut to close the sack up.

Ed pulled the strap to his shoulder, slipped his arm through, and stood with a groan. Dorothy's weight pulled the sack against Ed's shoulder, but it wasn't so heavy that it made the chore impossible. He adjusted it the best he could, then walked to where he'd dumped his tools. Dorothy tugged at his shoulder, as if trying to hold him back.

He used his foot to lift the tools, one at a time, by their handles. When he had everything bunched together in his arms, he turned and started for the trail.

He checked around for Peter as he hiked toward the road. The woods were empty. He hadn't expected to see him anywhere. If the sunlight hadn't killed the boy, he was surely long gone by now.

At the end of the trail, Ed paused. He listened for sounds of automobiles. All he heard were the birds, singing happily as if nothing depraved had happened in their woods. He left the trail behind and walked to the spot where he'd hidden his truck. Not a bad spot at night, but during the daylight, it looked as if he'd just abandoned it on a small patch of flat land.

He threw his tools in the back. They made hollow clangs when they hit the metal walls of the bed. He left Dorothy in the sack and put her in the cab. He shoved her against the passenger door, then climbed inside the truck, and fired it up. He revved the gas until the exhaust chugging out the back was hardly noticeable. Then he drove off.

He was hungry. He decided on his way home he'd stop off at Buck's for a plate of food. A hot breakfast would make him feel better.

-19-

Timmy was surprised to spot his father standing in front of his police car when he walked down the front steps of the school. Dad had parked on the side of the road and stood with his arms crossed. Even from this distance, Timmy could tell he hadn't shaved recently. He also looked thinner.

Dad threw his hand in the air and waved. "Timmy!"

Nodding, Timmy waved back, then turned around and stared at the propped-open front doors of the school. From the brightness outside, looking into the school's hallways was like peering into a cave. Students hurried out in groups, some walked in pairs, and others were alone. They passed Timmy without noticing him.

Timmy gave another look at his father. The grim look on the man's face made his stomach turn ice cold.

"Come on, son," Dad called, waving a little more impatiently now.

"Okay," said Timmy. He gave another glance at the school. "Just a second!"

"Are you waiting on someone?" he heard shouted from behind him.

Heads of students turned to look at him as they walked by. Some giggled, others smiled. Some looked curious.

Timmy felt his cheeks warm. He nodded without turning around.

"Five minutes!" Dad said.

Timmy nodded again. His face felt like it was on fire. Everyone outside had heard their exchange and would probably tease him about it for weeks. At least Peter wasn't here. Peter would be holding his gut with laughter, his chubby face the color of an apple. But he'd missed school today. Maybe he was sick.

He was fine last night.

Not completely fine, now that Timmy thought about it. He'd been acting...

Timmy spotted the springy bop of a girl in the hall.

It's her!

His breath caught in his throat. The shadows of the hallway seemed to thin around her, as if she were a glowing light in a deep cave.

Robin.

Timmy couldn't look away as he watched her walk. Her hair, pulled firmly back, was held in place by a curved band. Her long ponytail swung behind her head like a golden pendulum. She hugged a few books to her chest. Her pink sweater was bundled on top and her chin rested on the fluffy fabric. Being a ninth grader, her locker was at the far side of the school. It had taken her longer to reach the front than Timmy.

Robin neared the doors. She saw him. Her cherry lips parted to show white. The mole over her lip rose with her smile. Timmy noticed guys had stopped to watch her walk by. When her back was to them, they turned to each other, their heads moving as rapidly as their mouths. Probably talking about how beautiful she was.

"Hi," she said. "This is a surprise. Waiting on me?"

Timmy gave a quick glance at his father and saw his eyes widen. A bit of a smile showed on his face.

Facing Robin again, Timmy said, "Hi. Yeah. I was...am. Yes." Timmy shook his head.

Way to go, bonehead.

Her nose wrinkled. "What's wrong? You look...flushed."

"Well, I wanted...but..." Timmy sighed.

"Came to walk me home?"

Timmy nodded, then shook his head. "My dad's here."

Her pleasant expression seemed to lessen. "I see." Frowning, she looked over Timmy's shoulder. "I wonder if something's wrong."

"I don't know."

"Hopefully nothing else has happened."

"Hope not."

Robin continued to frown, her eyes squinting from the bright sunlight. There were two small lines at the bridge of her nose. Puffy crescents underneath her eyes showed through her make-up to reveal how exhausted she truly was.

But she still looked as beautiful as always.

Perfect.

"Maybe he's come to tell me *good* news," he said.

Though Robin smiled, he could tell it was without merit. "Maybe," she said.

"I guess I can't walk you home today," he said.

Robin stuck out her lip into a cute pout. "I'm sorry. But my dad's car's over there." She pointed to the parking lot. There were a lot of cars out there. Timmy nodded as if he could see it. "I wouldn't have been able to walk with you," she added. "Daddy *insisted* he pick me up from school." She groaned. "Sometimes he just makes me so mad..."

"That's fine," Timmy said.

"It was a sweet gesture, though, Timmy. Honest. Means a lot."

Heat filled Timmy's cheeks. "No problem."

"You can walk me to Dad's car," she said. "If you want to."

Timmy smiled. "I'd love to."

"Great."

Robin shifted her books to one arm and curled her now free arm around his elbow. Timmy felt warm tendrils shoot through him.

"Let's get moving," she said.

Though he felt dizzy, he managed to keep himself together as they started down the steps. A soft breeze stirred his hair. It was slightly cool in the warm day. He gave Robin a glance from the corner of his eye and missed the bottom step. His knees folded, but Robin jerked his arm back before his knees bashed the concrete.

"Whoa!" she said. "Can't have you getting hurt *again* because of me."

Timmy leaned forward, putting his hands flat on his knees. He felt a mixture of embarrassment and anger. Tears made his eyes moist. He quickly blinked them away before Robin could notice. "Clumsy me," he said.

Robin laughed. "Falling head over heels for me?"

Timmy's stomach gave a sickening lurch. "Uh..."

Robin jabbed her elbow into his side. "Just teasing you."

Now disappointment trickled into the frenzy of emotions he already felt. "Bet everybody saw it."

"Not everybody. Just those who were here."

Timmy groaned. "Great."

Laughing, Robin tapped his shoulder. Timmy looked up at her. "Ready to try again?" she asked.

"I guess."

"Okay. Remember to put one foot in front of the other. Okay?"

"A laugh machine, we have here."

Robin giggled. "Come on." She gave his arm a gentle tug.

Timmy stood up straight. Nodded. "I'm ready."

"Good to hear."

Holding his arm, she guided him up the sidewalk.

The Vampire of Plainfield

"What time do you want to meet Friday?" he asked.

Robin shook her head. "Six?"

"Okay."

"Talked to your parents about it?" she asked.

"Not yet. I haven't seen my Dad to ask him. He hasn't been home long enough to..." Timmy stopped talking when he noticed the sadness in Robin's eyes. Then he realized what he was saying.

Another fine job, goober.

Complaining about Dad not being home to the cousin of the girl he's been out looking for.

"Maybe you can ask him today," Robin said. Something about her tone was odd. Almost sounded as if she no longer wanted to go with him on Friday. Trying not to show his concern, Timmy kept walking.

He glanced over his shoulder as they reached the end of the sidewalk and spotted his father. Now he stood on the sidewalk at the bottom of the school stairs. He watched Timmy, but said nothing. He didn't have to. Timmy understood if he walked any further, his dad was going to be mad.

"Guess this is as far as I can go," said Timmy.

Robin looked, saw Timmy's dad, and nodded. She waved at him. Dad gave a single wave in return.

"This is fine," she said. "Don't want your Dad getting mad. He might not let you go on Friday if he does."

"So you're really going to be there?"

He hadn't meant to ask. The question had already been on its way out before he'd realized it, and he wanted to kick himself. He supposed he needed to hear it one more time to make sure it was really going to happen. Last night, he'd lost a lot of sleep wondering if Robin had been pulling some kind of prank. He'd tried telling himself over and over that Robin wouldn't do that.

But still...the worry wouldn't go away.

Robin's mouth hung open. "You don't think I'll be there?"

"Well…" He huffed through his nose, nibbled his lip. "I…uh…"

Laughing, Robin bumped him with her hip. "You better stop that baloney. I'll be there. I would never stand you up, Timmy Worden. I asked *you*, remember?"

"Yeah. Sorry."

"Don't apologize. We'll have a good time."

"Yeah, we will."

"All right," said Robin. "Now that we've agreed, you'd better go." She turned, stepping in front of Timmy and blocking his father from his view. "Your old man might have a heart attack if he saw this."

"Saw wha…?"

Robin stepped forward and gave him a quick little kiss on his cheek. She pulled back, smiled, and said "Bye. See you later." Then she twirled around and hurried away, holding her books close. She didn't look in Dad's direction.

Timmy stared at her, watching her rump make the back of her skirt swish. The bottom floated around her calves, showing their smooth backs above the fluffy white of her socks. He could still feel her lips on his face, a phantom brush of softness. Reaching up, he rubbed his cheek and felt a greasy line from her lipstick.

She looked back at him from over her shoulder. "I didn't leave a mark." Before vanishing behind a truck, she added, "Stop acting so goofy or he'll know." Then she was gone.

Timmy had no idea how long he'd stared at the empty section of sidewalk before a hand slapped down on his shoulder. Timmy didn't even jump.

"Stop gawking, son. Just looks bad to stare like a creep." His father shook him softly. "Ready to go?"

Timmy thought he might have nodded.

The Vampire of Plainfield

"Good," said Dad. "I need to talk to you."

"Sure," said Timmy.

He felt as if he were walking on marshmallows while Dad guided him to the car. So far, so good. If Dad had noticed Robin had kissed him, he gave no signals. Dad opened the passenger door and Timmy plopped down in the seat. His legs felt heavy and weak when he pulled them into the car.

The door banging shut snapped Timmy out of the shock Robin's lips had left him in. Blinking, he looked around. He saw Dad's thermos on the seat between some wadded-up food wrappers. There was a stench hanging in the cab—a combination of cigarette smoke and coffee and maybe even body odor. Something about the smell made Timmy think his father had been in this car for a long time.

Though he shouldn't have told Robin, it was true he'd hardly seen his Dad since he dropped him off yesterday. He'd come home way past Timmy's bedtime, but he'd still been awake, thinking about the conversation with Robin and her subsequent phone call, when he'd heard the car pull up outside. Though his parents tried to be quiet, he'd been able to hear their voices through the wall. They'd been in the kitchen, probably sitting at the table and drinking coffee while Dad told Mama everything. It was hard to decipher every word Dad had said, but he'd understood a little.

There was nothing to go on. Dorothy might have vanished entirely.

Dad's door opened, startling Timmy. He turned to watch his father sit down. Dad leaned back, let out a small groan, and pulled the door shut. He turned to Timmy.

"Tired, Dad?"

Dad gave a slow nod. "So tired I can't see straight. But I better perk up, huh? The search parties start tonight."

"What's that?"

"Bunch of us from town are getting together. We're going to comb the countryside."

"What do you expect to find?"

"Answers."

Timmy nodded, then looked out the window. He stared at the kids outside, walking in groups, to cars parked all around. Seemed to be a lot more parents out here than normal.

Being safe.

The car rumbled to life, and pulled away.

"How's Robin doing?" Dad asked, steering them back onto the street.

"Okay, I guess."

"Yeah," Dad said. "Hard thing to handle. Other than Dorothy, Robin's the only kid in that whole family. Bet she has a lot of worry being thrown at her from all directions."

Dad was right, especially from her father.

They drove a little ways without any further conversation. Timmy gave his dad glances and could tell by the troubled look on his face that he was struggling to tell him something.

Finally, Dad said, "Peter came over last night." It wasn't a question. "Your mama said it was after six, maybe closer to seven, when he got there."

Timmy nodded. "Yeah. He ate supper with us."

Dad nodded. "Your mama said that too. Did Peter say where he was going after that?"

Timmy stared at Dad, wondering why he wanted to know. "I don't think so."

"Think, Tim. It's important. Did he say if he was going to go anywhere else? Anything like that, at all?"

"No. He didn't."

Dad held his breath a moment, then nodded. "All right."

The boys hadn't really talked about much after supper, except for Robin. Timmy had told Peter about the movies, how he'd walked with Robin until Dad had shown up.

The Vampire of Plainfield

Peter had tried to be interested, but Timmy could tell he was distracted by something. As if his thoughts were somewhere else.

Afraid he'd get Peter—and himself—in trouble, Timmy told Dad what he wanted to know, leaving out anything that had to do with Robin.

"Okay." Dad sighed. "Just as I thought."

"Is something wrong?"

Dad almost winced. He gave a single nod. "Yeah."

"What is it?"

"Peter never made it home last night."

Timmy suddenly felt tight and sick inside. "He didn't?"

Dad shook his head. "Far as I can tell, you're the last person to have seen him."

Though he was sweating, Timmy shivered. His hands trembled in his lap.

Peter was missing. He hadn't missed school because he was sick.

He was...gone.

Like Dorothy.

"So," Dad said, "now we have two kids...unaccounted for."

"Wow," said Timmy. It was hard to talk. His tongue felt numb, like it did after a trip to the dentist.

"Listen," said Dad. "I told you all of that because you're old enough to hear it. And you know I trust you. Something might be going on in our town. I wish I knew what, but I don't. Until we get to the bottom of things, you need to stay on high alert. Understand me?"

Nodding, Timmy gazed out his window, not seeing anything as it zipped by in a blur. He barely paid attention to where they were. His mind was blank, yet filled with a clutter of images and thoughts.

Peter was gone. Dorothy was gone. Both in the same day and nobody had seen anything.

Then he remembered what Robin had said. She thought Dorothy might have been taken by somebody. Would somebody want to take Peter too?

What's going on out there?

"New law of the house, Tim. No going out after dark, until this…business has been brought to an end. Too many questions and not enough answers makes it a possibly dangerous time out there."

"Come on, Dad. That's not fair."

"Tim. Two kids are missing. You're a kid. And your mother doesn't want you going out after dark until this has been handled. I agree with her. End of story."

"But Dad…"

"What? It better be important if you feel the need to keep talking back to me."

Timmy almost stopped right there. Maybe he should have. But he'd already started to say it and wanted to get his point out there. "Robin said she would take me to see a movie on Friday."

Dad was quiet a moment before he said, "Did she, now?"

Timmy nodded. "Yes. Sir."

Not a complete lie. Just a slight variation of the truth.

"And what movie?"

"*Phantom of the Rue Morgue.*"

"One of *those* movies, huh?" Dad shook his head. "I'll never understand what you like about those movies, Tim."

"They're just fun movies, Dad."

"And aren't you a little young to be going on a date with a ninth-grader?"

"It's not a date," Timmy quickly said.

"Uh-huh. Better hope your mama doesn't think so."

"Dad, I'm in the *seventh* grade. I'm a *kid,* you said so yourself. Why would a girl in the ninth grade want to go on a date with somebody like me, who's so much younger? Besides, she used to be my sitter."

Dad sighed. "Sometimes girls will surprise you by the things they really want. Things they keep to themselves. Find a guy willing to give them that..." Dad shook his head. "She'll *own* him. And Tim, there's nothing worse than a girl who knows she *owns* a man. They can control you, then. Make you do things you regret. A lot of things you regret."

Timmy wasn't sure what he meant by that. Probably an experience he'd had that he wouldn't elaborate on because he felt Timmy was too young to hear it. That happened more often than not with Dad. He'd share little hints of something bigger, but leave out the details that really mattered.

"So can I go?" Timmy asked.

Dad sighed even louder this time. "Tim...your mother..." He left the sentence hanging.

"Does Mama not like Robin?"

"Sure. She likes her."

Dad was lying. And Timmy realized he'd probably always known his mother didn't like Robin. There was a tone she had when it came to the ninth grader, a distrusting defiance.

"It's the age," Dad added. "She won't like the age difference."

"It's not a date, Dad."

"You keep saying that. But a guy and a girl going to a movie together sounds like a date to me. And it'll sound like one to your mama. Plus, you still have a bit of lipstick on your cheek from when she kissed you earlier."

Timmy slapped his cheek with his hand, vigorously rubbing. Dad laughed.

"Now I know for sure that was what she did when she leaned into you."

Checking his fingers, Timmy saw they were clean. There hadn't been any lipstick on his face. Dad tricked him. Sighing, Timmy let his hand fall into his lap.

"Want to tell me the truth?" Dad said.

Robin was right. I gave it away from how I acted.

"I told Robin about the movie, and that I really wanted to see it. She asked if you were going to take me and I told her I didn't think you could. So she said she would take me because it sounded like something she'd want to see too."

"Just the movies?" Dad asked.

"Well...I'm supposed to meet her at Buck's. Then we're going to the movies."

Dad's lips pressed together, then slowly separated. "I see. Dinner and a date to the show."

"It doesn't matter now, since I can't leave the house. She'll just go by herself and I'll just be a prisoner in my own room. I'll miss seeing *another* good movie and will have to hear about it from her next time I see her."

Dad chuckled softly. "Being a little theatrical, aren't you? It's not like we'd be boarding up your windows and sliding your meals under the door."

"Feels like it."

Dad patted Timmy's knee. "We'll see. How's that?" Dad laughed.

Timmy nearly bit his tongue to keep from arguing further. He knew his dad wouldn't let him go. At least, not until this business with Dorothy and Peter had been cleared up.

Remembering his best friend was missing made him feel lousy. He was sitting here debating he was old enough to go to a movie alone with a girl, when his friend was missing. There was good reason his parents didn't want him going out.

Robin's dad probably won't let her go, either. Not right now.

"So is it a deal?" Dad asked.

Timmy attempted a smile he hoped looked legitimate. "Deal."

"Good." Dad put both hands on the wheel. He yawned, then let out a low moan. "Your mother said she'd have supper done early tonight so I can actually eat with you two."

"Really? Good."

"Yeah."

"Know what she's making?"

"I think meatloaf, mashed potatoes, and something else. Said she'd make a chocolate pie for dessert."

Timmy's stomach rumbled, telling him that supper sounded just fine.

But behind the hunger, was a ping of sadness. His night with Robin had been put on hold.

He worried it might never happen at all.

-20-

Ed stood in the doorway of the summer kitchen. He leaned on the ax handle, the head on the floor bracing him up as he watched Dorothy. He'd placed her on an old door balanced on a pair of sawhorses, covered her with a blanket so she would no longer be naked, and wrapped a rope around her so many times, the little girl looked like a giant spool of thread that had sprouted a blond head.

He'd checked on her throughout the day. She hadn't moved. Once he'd touched her cheek with his fingertip. It felt cold and slimy. Dead. Just as dead as she had been when he'd crammed her in his tool sack.

But he figured if she was going to wake up again as they did in the stories, it would be after sundown.

The dwindling light outside was a dark purple hue. Inside the summer kitchen, Ed's lantern on his workbench spread a very dim flutter throughout the room. The corners were dark, as were the walls. The meager light seemed to hover around Dorothy.

He watched her. She remained still.

Still dead.

Would she wake up, thirsty for blood?

Ed raised the ax from the floor, letting it rest on his shoulder. The curve of the blade pointed up. If she did come back, Ed would be ready to lop off her head.

And if she stayed dead, he'd simply return her to the graveyard and bury her with the dead vampires.

He looked at her neck. The rims of the holes had dried into a crimson crust. Sure, he hated what happened to her, but when he thought back to the way she'd acted after realizing who he was, his remorse didn't feel as strong. Still wasn't right what Peter had done, and none of the mean words she'd said to Ed would make it right.

Ed stepped partway through the doorway, putting a foot on the top step. The sky was mostly dark with only a few spills of gaudy light showing behind the clouds. In a few minutes, the sky would be black. Stars already twinkled above like little sparkly dots, and the moon was a pale sliver among them.

He stood there, waiting until no more light remained. Once, he thought he heard Dorothy take a breath, but when he stared at her, he saw no sign she'd awakened.

The quiet whispery sound repeated. Ed jerked back, bringing the ax in front of him.

The lantern.

It was low on fuel. Whenever the supply got near the bottom, it would make soft hissing sounds like a gentle breeze rustling leaves.

Dorothy wasn't waking up.

And Ed had wasted a day preparing himself for it.

Lowering the ax, Ed let out a long breath. His chest hurt as if he'd been holding it in all day. His stomach relaxed.

And the crap he'd been squeezing back dropped, and suddenly became a need that had to be taken care of. Keeping his ass pinched a bit longer, he watched Dorothy. She remained a still, dark shape topped with a golden glow of hair. Her face looked very pale in the lantern's light. Unreal, like a cheap drugstore mask.

Nope. She's dead. She's not coming back.

Ed quickly walked to his workbench. He'd left the newspaper rolled up next to his tools and sewing supplies. He grabbed it, and started back for the door, giving Dorothy's motionless, creepy form another glance on his way.

The girl was dead.

Her hair looked artificial, like a doll's. Her skin looked painted in cruddy, white cream. Her lips were purple bends bearded in shadow. But her natural beauty still showed through the deadened features. She would have been a very nice woman to look at had she lived long enough to reach the age.

Ed turned away, and pulled the door shut. He tucked the newspaper under his arm, then hurried down the steps and around to the back of the house. One hand to his stomach, the other swung stiffly to his side. He made short, quick steps on his way to the outhouse. The grass made whispery lashing sounds against his pants.

The outhouse was a dark, emaciated structure of wooden planks that had warped and rotted with age. At the top, the wood curved out like the tips of thick streamers. The door hung partway open, a crescent moon carved out of the wood matched the curved slot in the sky. He stepped in, and pulled the door to him. It started to sway open, but he reached into a patch of shadow and found the thin, narrow hook. He slipped it through the eye in the frame to keep it shut.

He wanted to drop his trousers and sit right away, but it was too dark. The last time he'd tried to crap in total darkness, his bare ass had plopped down on a snake slithering around the rim of the seat. Luckily it hadn't been a poisonous one, since it had recoiled and stabbed its teeth into his right buttock. He'd run from the outhouse, screaming, with the snake dangling from his rump like a greasy tail.

He'd put a candle out here for night visits the next morning.

Using his thumbnail, he struck a match. He lowered it to the tip of the white candlestick on a small shelf. Dim light oozed around him, guttering against the tight walls in yellow waves. Ed shook the match out, turned sideways, and tossed it into the hole in the middle of the wooden bench he'd soon be sitting on. It made a faint sizzling sound when it landed inside.

The smell in here was rotten, but Ed had grown used to it. On his way to the seat, he unfastened his pants. They fell to his knees, so he shambled the rest of the way. Before sitting, he checked around the seat. No snakes. He turned so he faced the door and sat down.

He let his muscles relax, and nature handled the rest.

While things made heavy slopping sounds under him, he unfurled the newspaper. In order to read any of the words, he had to tilt the paper toward the candle. He skimmed through the short collection of articles until he reached the last page.

Another missing man—a traveling salesman from the Cradle Elk area. Ed frowned. How had nobody noticed the pattern? All of them had been traveling near or through Plainfield around the time of their disappearance. Surely somebody would have caught on to it by now.

Maybe they didn't know what to look for.

But there was something in Plainfield that linked them all together, other than the vampire. Somehow, they wound up here.

And dead.

The vampire was on a feeding spree. Ed had to stop it before somebody put the pieces together and evidence pointed the police his way.

Ed tore the last page of the newspaper and crumpled it into a ball. When it was good and compacted, he spread it back out. Then he crumpled it again, this time making sure he started from another direction. He did this a few more times until the paper felt fairly soft.

With the paper clasped in his fingers, he lowered it between his legs and wiped himself. Finished, he let it drop into the hole. It made no sound when it landed. Ed imagined it falling forever, as if a bottomless pit had opened up below him.

He checked his fingers to make sure nothing had gotten smeared on them. They were fine. He grabbed his pants by the waist and went to stand up.

Then the outhouse ceiling was torn away with an explosion of cracking wood.

Screaming, Ed looked up. Wind buffeted him. His hat was blown off his head. His graying hair danced around his forehead, lashing his eyes. He shook it away and gazed at the dark sky above him. Stars twinkled all over like glowing freckles.

Then he spotted it—a large dark shape floating above the edge of the now opened outhouse, clutching a chunk of the roof in its beefy blue hands.

"Shit almighty!" Ed screamed.

The vampire gazed down at him. Its gargantuan wings moved in a dynamic blur, emitting a high-pitched squealing sound that reminded Ed of an engine with a bad belt. The force of the wind was too much for Ed and threw him off the bench. He hit the wood floor with his bare knees, feeling the burn of his skin being scuffed up. Rolling onto his back, he slapped at his pants. His cock shook in the brutal gust, beating against his thighs. He managed to pull his pants up and cover himself.

The vampire tossed the jagged hunk of wood aside. It brought its right arm up, a long, claw-tipped finger extending toward Ed. *"You!"*

Ed thought he might have to shit again.

-21-

Ed was tossed at the summer kitchen. His body whammed the door, knocking it wide. He hit the floor and slid toward the makeshift table. He stopped just before his face collided with the leg of a sawhorse.

He felt pain all over, the back of his neck tight and sore from where the vampire had grabbed him. He'd been carried in the air like a kitten by its mother, his arms and legs dangling, for a short distance. Then the vampire had pitched him as effortlessly as the chunk of outhouse ceiling. Ed was grateful its aim was accurate and he hadn't smacked into the wall beside the door. The wall wouldn't have been so easy to give in.

Getting onto his back filled his body up with tiny bursts of pain. Ed gazed at the doorway. The vampire stood just outside, examining the uneven frame as if it had never seen one before. It looked at Ed.

"Invite me in," the vampire said. Its voice sounded like a clogged drain.

Ed tried to shake his head. Couldn't. So he said, "No..."

The vampire opened its mouth very wide, showing the array of fangs inside. Though still a faint blue, its skin was much smoother and healthier now. Had to be, from all the missing travelers it had sucked dry. *"Invite me in!"*

Ed took a deep breath and, louder, said, "NO!"

Apparently some of the vampire folklore he'd read was accurate—a vampire couldn't enter a house without an invite. And this was a frailty Ed greatly relished.

The vampire slammed its fist against the frame. It looked as if it was about to attempt entering regardless of the rules, but an arm appeared next to its shoulder, a *human* arm. The skin was smooth and pale, dotted with freckles. It rubbed the vampire's head, gingerly, as if to calm it down. Ed recognized the arm even before Mary revealed herself. She wore a blue dress that covered much of her, but it clung to her bulging shapes and curves.

"Let me, Master," she said.

"Master?" Ed said.

Mary turned to him, smiling. "Oh, yes, Eddie. He's my master..."

Something clicked in Ed's head. Things fell together and formed lucid patterns. The connecting piece all along had been Mary. "You helped him feed."

"That's right," she said. "Got him big and strong again."

Ed should have been shocked. He wasn't. Mary, of all people, would've been the type to help a creature like that. Somehow it made perfect sense. She'd lured the men straight to their deaths.

"And you know what else, Eddie-baby?"

Ed stared at her, saying nothing.

Her smile grew. "He hasn't changed *me.*" Mary crossed the threshold. "So I don't have to be invited to come inside."

"Damn..." Ed muttered.

"And you know what else?" She raised her arm, slowly extending the blade of a straight-razor. The lantern's flame glinted of the sharp block of metal. "I'm going to cut on you if you don't invite my master inside. I'll start with your fingers. Just slice them right off." Mary frowned. "But you know what? I'd probably get bored pretty quickly with those, plus the bone would make it a *lot* of work."

She loomed over him, gazing down. Her red hair hung around her face in a cherry hood, shadowing her facial expressions. But the wicked madness of her eyes gleamed through. "I'll probably just slice off your cock, piece by piece, instead, like cutting up a hot dog for a kid. Maybe start with your balls, since you've suddenly grown a pair. Take off the right one first, then the left. Then move onto your cock. Take off the head, then make my way down."

Mary crouched. She grabbed the waist of his pants and reached in.

"Duh-don't..." Ed said.

Her hand groped his cock, fingers curling around it. Though the situation was scary and intense and awfully humiliating, he felt his member growing in her hand.

Mary laughed. "I just have that effect on you, don't I, Eddie-baby?"

"Stop..." he said.

"I'll stop for a few minutes after the right nut comes off." She started pulling his privates through his pants.

"Please, Mary, don't do this!"

Mary laughed. Her arm moved forward. Ed felt cold metal against the thin skin of his scrotum. Mary would do it. She wasn't bluffing. She'd start cutting his privates until there was nothing left.

The blade pressed down.

"Okay!" Ed cried. He held his breath until the blade moved away. "It can come in..."

Mary laughed. "You have to invite him in, Eddie. Now, look at the master and ask him to come inside. It's not you he wants, anyway."

"It's...not?"

"No. You just have something he wants. Or should I say—someone?"

Ed leaned back his head. He could see the edge of the makeshift table Dorothy was lying on.

The vampire came for her.

But what would they do with *him* afterward?

"Eddie?" said Mary. Cold hardness touched the skin of his sack.

"Okay, okay!" Ed took a deep breath, then looked at the doorway. The vampire stood outside, bent slightly, its long arms reaching down to its knees. "Would you...please...?" Ed gulped. It tasted like sour copper. He must've bitten his tongue at some point and caused it to bleed. "Would you please come inside?"

The vampire let out a rapid-fire of guttural laughter. It entered the summer kitchen without a problem. Though it walked forward, its eyes never left Ed.

"You," it said. *"You are the one who awakened me from my slumber."*

"Yuh-yes..."

"For that, I owe you a debt. And that debt is your life. I will not kill you tonight, Edward Theodore Gein. And this deal will free me from any commitment to you. Are we in agreement?"

Ed couldn't find his voice. Mary squeezing his cock as if she wanted to squirt milk from it brought it back. "Yes!"

"Very well. This debt is no longer mine to keep after tonight."

The vampire's voice, though demonic and gruff, was strong with an accent that Ed had never heard before, ancient and proper, almost delicate in its burr.

"You may release him, sweet Mary. He will not be a threat to us tonight."

Smiling, Mary leaned close. She stroked Ed. "Want me to finish this for you?"

Gasping, Ed pushed her arm away. Scooting across the dusty floor on his back, he pulled his pants up. Mary cackled as she watched him squirm backwards. Ed didn't stop until his back hit the wall underneath his workbench. From this angle, he could see Dorothy on the table, the vampire creeping toward her, and Mary watching from the floor on her knees.

Ed fastened his pants. He brushed his hair out of his eyes. There were weapons all around him, but he wouldn't be able to get to them without being quickly stopped.

The vampire reached Dorothy. It stared at her for many long moments. *"Such a sweet child."*

"That boy did this," Mary said. "We shouldn't have let him run out last night. Shouldn't have let him out tonight. He's careless..."

"The boy did a fine job. Found me a daughter." Its black lips curled into something that might have been a grin. *"Yes. A beautiful daughter. A virtuous soul."* The vampire stroked her cheek, ran its long claws through her bright hair. *"I will wake her now."*

The vampire leaned over the table, putting a hand on either side of Dorothy. Its face lowered, delicately pressing its thin black lips against hers. Nothing happened right away. Then Ed noticed blue light spilling between the tight cracks of their connected mouths.

It's sucking out her soul!

The vampire didn't bring its lips away until the light no longer flowed between them. It stood up straight, loosing an orgasmic moan. *"So delicious!"*

Dorothy sat up in one quick motion that made Ed jerk against the wall. He pulled his legs to his chest and hugged them.

Unmoving, Dorothy stared ahead as if in a trance. Her eyes had turned into solid white, lifeless orbs. When she blinked, the white had faded to show dark dots inside.

"Now, my daughter. Go and feed."

Ed watched as Dorothy wiggled in the ropes, making them swell. They broke apart with a whipping snap. Pieces fell around her. Some fell to the floor. She swung her legs around and began to climb down from the table.

Ed closed his eyes, taking several deep breaths. When he reopened his eyes, Dorothy was gone.

Mary was gone.

He saw nobody in his summer kitchen. He began to think he had been left alone.

Then the vampire's face dropped down in front of Ed—its forehead at Ed's mouth, its mouth at Ed's forehead.

Ed screamed. Before he could do much else, hands gripped his shirt and yanked him out from under the workbench. When he was all the way out, the hands released him. Ed tumbled across the floor. Coming to a halt on his stomach, Ed raised his head.

Dust floated from the floor, creating a span of filthy fog. The vampire hung upside-down from the rafter by its talons, its head below the workbench.

Like a bat! A damned bat!

It dropped to the floor, landing in a crouch. Then it slowly stood.

"I have an arrangement to offer, Edward Gein."

Ed wanted to sit up, wanted to run. He wanted to get as far away from this creature as possible. He couldn't move.

The vampire moved forward. Its Y-shaped toes landed in fringed bits of rope that, until moments ago, had been coiled around Dorothy.

"You are a ghoul, Gein. And I can use a ghoul like you."

It passed by the wall where many of Ed's tools hung from nails, reached out, and took a shovel in an elegant movement that Ed hardly noticed. Then the shovel was flying toward Ed. He jerked back, throwing up his arms.

And caught the shovel before it could hit him.

"You start digging for me, and I will allow you to live."

"Dig...?" Speaking made Ed's chest hurt. Wincing, he had a hard time finding his breath. "Me?"

"Yes. You rob from the dead like the ghouls of my time. Taking what you want and leaving the rest to rot to dust. I need a ghoul to burrow the graves of this village for me. Unlike the ghouls of my time, you can voyage in the daylight."

Ed planted the shovel on the floor and, using the handle for support, made himself sit up. His body protested his movements with quick, achy jabs. "I can't just traipse the cemeteries and start digging up graves in broad daylight. I'll get caught!"

"Discretion, Edward. Move like the ghoul you are."

Ed supposed he could do it. He'd been digging up graves for years and nobody had become privy to it yet.

But at night. Somebody might catch him if he worked under the sun.

How does the vampire know?

It might have read his mind. *"You reek of the dead, Gein. Their putrid stench is in your skin. It flows through you and will never leave you. You have allowed yourself to become infected by the dead. And I want you to dig for me. Dig. Keep digging. Do not stop."*

"What am I digging *for?*"

"My existence."

Ed had no clue what that meant. "How will I know when I find it?"

"I will know."

"And you won't kill me?"

"Kill you?" The vampire gave a squeaky laugh that sounded like rusted hinges. *"We are in agreement. You will live."*

"When do I start?"

"Now."

"Now? I can't…"

"We are in agreement, Edward Gein. Do not break our bond. It will be your death."

The vampire held out its arms in a crucified pose. Wings snapped open with a loud slap. Tattered sails hung from the gaunt appendages. They began to flap, stirring up dust. Grits pinged Ed's eyes. He looked away, closing his stinging eyes as that broken-belt sound filled the cramped space. There was a loud whooshing gust that made his clothes shake, and the noise died.

When Ed was able to open his eyes, he saw the vampire was gone.

He looked down at the shovel in his hands.

-22-

Carol Clark sat up in bed with a gasp. A nightmare had shocked her awake, but its effects were already fading from her memory. Her nightgown clung to her sweaty body, the sheets uncomfortable and hot on her sleek skin.

She threw the covers off her. Russell grunted once from beside her, made a slight movement, then went still again. Carol looked down at her husband and the anger she felt inside cleared what remained of the groggy fog from her mind.

We should be out there looking for Dorothy right now.

The night howled outside. Trees limbs outside the window scratched at the glass. She saw the wriggling shadows they made through the moonlight seeping in.

Sheriff Worden had said it was supposed to storm tonight, the first big one of the spring. So he'd ended tonight's search early for cautionary measures. How raucous the wind was, it sounded like it might do something out there, but they could've handled some wind, if it meant the possibility of finding her daughter.

And Russell? She thought he would've agreed with her, but he'd sided with the sheriff.

"We need to be out there when the weather's working with us, not against us," he'd said.

Seemed to Carol that everybody was working against *her*. She stared at her sleeping husband. *Passed out husband.* A bottle of whiskey sat on the stand on his side of the bed, within easy reach. It had been glued to his hand all night.

She watched his facial expression, how his brow furrowed and his lips slightly puckered out.

Like Dorothy.

Carol liked to tell herself Dorothy had inherited her natural beauty from her, but really, it had come from Russell. Not that Carol was some kind of dog with sun-colored hair. Russell just had an effortless attraction that he did nothing to enhance. It was just there, like the hair on his head.

Which had probably been the reason they'd had sex tonight. With everything going on around them, they'd still felt it appropriate to fall into bed together. But what they'd done tonight hadn't been anything close to the kind of lovemaking she'd grown to enjoy with Russell over the years.

This had been *rutting*.

He'd nearly forced himself on her, and at first, Carol had wanted him to stop. Then she gave in and let him take her. And it had been good. Rough, but good. It was just what they'd needed in the moment, and it had ended with both of them satisfied and sleepy.

Moving her legs caused an ache where Russell had been jabbing deeply inside of her. She wished she could be mad at him for that. She'd needed it as much as him, she supposed. A distraction from the worry and stress.

Russell had fallen asleep naked. She'd at least managed to get her gown back on, though she was naked underneath.

And she needed to go to the bathroom.

That was going to be a painful chore.

Carol climbed out of bed, feeling soreness on many places of her body. The worst of it was between her legs. She didn't bother hunting for her slippers and hobbled barefooted to the doorway. The carpet felt soft and ticklish under her feet. Air drifted up her gown, caressing her with a gentle coolness that felt good on her heated skin.

Though she couldn't remember it, she figured the dream must have been a doozy. As she entered the hallway, she tried to recall what it had been about. No images would come. Maybe it was for the best.

Carol left the bathroom light off and the door open. The toilet was a faded shape in the dark, but familiar to find. She checked to make sure the lid was down, hiked the gown up to her hips, then dropped down. The cold porcelain made her tense up.

"Damn that's cold."

Though she'd whispered, it could've been a shout in the silent house. The wind howled and gusted outside in response, making the house pop in many places. After the shock of the frigid bite on her rump, Carol relaxed and let her bladder release.

Mommy.

Carol jerked. Her stream cut off as if it had been corked. She put a hand to her chest and felt her pounding heart through the cool silk of her gown. "Dor...Dorothy?"

A quiet house answered her.

Sitting on the toilet, Carol looked around. The tub was beside her, the curtain pulled shut. Had the voice come from there?

Sounded close.

But it also sounded far away.

How was that possible?

Carol looked at the dark sheet next to her. "Dorothy, sweetie? Are you in the tub?"

Soon as the question left her lips, she realized how dumb it had been to ask. Why would her daughter come home and hide in the bathtub?

Is she hurt?

Carol reached for the curtain, her arm a dark streak in the heavy murkiness of the bathroom. She saw the smudges of her fingers extended, felt them brush the curtain, heard it whisper with movement.

Carol took a deep, trembling breath.

Then jerked the curtain open. She leaned back, gasping.

The tub was empty.

Carol stared at the white walls, glimmering from a recent polishing. She should laugh at herself for acting so foolish, but couldn't find the humor in what she was going through.

"Stupid, Carol."

With a sigh, Carol allowed herself to finish what she'd come in here to do.

Out in the hallway, she felt wide-awake now and knew going back to sleep would be impossible. Maybe she should go downstairs, make some coffee, and sit in the quiet for a while.

The thought of being alone in this big house scared her.

Russell's here.

Passed out, though. Same as being alone.

Anything beat sitting in bed all night while her husband snored beside her.

On her way to the stairs, she paused at Dorothy's room. The door was shut. Tempted to look inside, she forced herself to leave it be. It was still a mess from Worden and the other officers rummaging through everything. Besides, she knew Dorothy wouldn't be in her bed.

The sense of loss she'd felt for a couple days now hit her all over again. Her throat tightened, and tears filled her eyes. Backhanding the moisture out of her eyes, she walked to the stairs.

Carol was halfway down when the front door clicked and swayed open. Bits of leaves and grit fluttered across the floor. The moonlight cut a bleached arc on the shadowy floor around the dark shape of a person's shadow.

Carol stopped, her hand gripping the rail.

The shape was noticeably human, but little, and seemed to have smaller, thinner shadows flapping around its head.

Long hair...

Carol recognized the dark silhouette easily. "Dorothy!"

Carol rushed down the stairs, nearly falling more than once. Reaching the floor without injuring herself, she ran to the door. Her bare feet slapped the floor. She felt hard things prick her skin from the debris that had blown inside. Her foot came down on some leaf shards and slipped out to the side. She tried to catch herself on the jutting doorknob but only managed to knock the door away from her.

Her hip whacked the floor. Not allowing herself to feel the pain her fall had caused, she scrambled to her hands and knees and crawled halfway through the doorway—her hands on the porch, her knees on the floor inside.

She gazed into the yard.

And spotted Dorothy, standing naked on the stone-lined dirt path that led from the driveway. The wind made her hair dance and lash around her head.

"Dorothy! It is you!"

Dorothy didn't move. Her arms hung limply at her sides, her feet slightly parted. She stared straight at Carol. "Mommy?" she said. Her voice was soft and hoarse. She sounded very parched.

"Oh, baby!" Tears dripping from her eyes, Carol got to her feet. Her hip throbbed with dull pain, but she didn't let it slow her down. She ran onto the porch, down the stairs, and onto the pathway in one quick burst. "Thank you, God!"

Carol scooped Dorothy into her arms, holding her close. Somehow she seemed much lighter now, as if she were hollow inside.

Stop it.

And her skin felt like ice. Carol tried to make her skimpy gown somehow stretch around her naked daughter. It wouldn't reach. She held Dorothy tightly, kissed her on the forehead. It was like kissing cold meat.

"What happened to your clothes, baby?" Carol asked.

"I'm thirsty, Mommy."

"Oh, baby. I'm sorry. I'm so sorry. Let's get you inside."

Carol charged up the steps, dashed inside. She elbowed the door, throwing it behind her. The wind, which was nearly screeching, sounded as if a giant hand had covered its mouth when the door closed.

"Russell!" Carol shouted in the foyer. "Get down here! I have Dorothy! Bring a blanket!"

Carol heard a loud thump upstairs followed by quick softer thumps that grew louder as they moved through the hallway. Russell appeared at the top of the stairs, naked, his hair a mess.

"Wha...?" he said. Then he quickly covered his crotch with both hands. "Dorothy!"

"Yes," said Carol. "She came home!"

"Oh my God! This isn't a dream!"

"No. Get a blanket, and damn it, get dressed!"

"Okay..."

As Russell turned away from the stairs for the bedroom, Carol ran into the living room. She dropped down on the couch, and clutched her daughter close.

"Daddy'll be back in a minute with a blanket."

"I'm cold, Mommy."

"I know. It's all right."

Need to call Worden. Get him over here. Then take Dorothy to the hospital.

"Hold me closer, Mommy."

"Of course, baby. Of course!"

Carol turned Dorothy so she faced her chest. She pulled her higher. Dorothy's long, skinny legs dangled over the arm of the couch. They looked so pale, the color of hospital bedsheets.

She felt Dorothy's face nuzzle against her neck. "So thirsty, Mommy..."

"I know. In a minute we'll..."

There's no breaths...

Carol gasped. Her daughter's mouth and nose were pressed against the side of her neck and she felt no warm breaths on her skin.

"Dorothy, what...?"

Her words stopped when she felt two sharp points sink into her neck. Her mouth opened, but nothing but choking sounds came out. She could feel her blood moving in a constant flowing motion in reverse as it was siphoned out.

Dorothy was sucking her blood.

Russell! Help!

Paralyzed, Carol was unable to resist as her daughter sucked her neck and made whispery cooing sounds in her ear. She felt warm trickles slide down her neck, under her gown, and onto her breasts.

A light clicked on in the foyer.

"Carol?"

In here!

If only she could have said it aloud. Instead, she only mouthed the words and hoped Russell would hear.

His feet pounded the floor. He appeared in the doorway, reached in, and felt for the switch. There was a click and light filled the room with a glare that hurt Carol's eyes. She was able to make them move toward her husband.

Russell, smiling, entered the living room. Bare to the waist, he'd put on pants. "Got her favorite blanket." His relieved demeanor melted away as he came closer. "Dorothy? What are you doing to your...?"

Dorothy's head whipped toward her father. Carol heard her hiss, saw her arms jerk up and hands curl like claws. Russell's eyes rounded. He jumped back, dropping the blanket. Then Dorothy sprang from Carol's lap like a cat and crashed into Russell. Her hands and feet slapped against him and drove him to the floor.

Carol slid down the couch, feeling her life draining away as the sounds of Dorothy attacking her father filled the room.

Edward Theodore Ghoul

Geiner:

*Why did Ed Gein's girlfriend stop going out with him?
Because he was such a cut-up.*

-23-

The sun felt like a hot, heavy hand pushing down on the back of Ed's neck. He stopped digging, leaving the shovel stuck in the dirt. He folded his hands on top of the rod, and rested his cheek on his gloves. The material was hot against his face. Reaching into his back pocket, he removed a kerchief. He pulled off his damp hat, using the kerchief to wipe the sweat from his brow. When he checked, he was surprised to find the thin towel was dry.

Ed had no more sweat left to shed. It had saturated his clothes, leaving them hanging like wet rags on his exhausted body. Something like warm sand pumped underneath his skin instead of blood.

He'd been digging through the night and the better part of the day. Deciding to start with the older graves, he'd worked all the way through the small graveyard behind the church. The plot was through a path and beyond a small cluster of trees, so he doubted anybody would notice the desecration right away. Good thing, since he'd been too tired to cover them back. Hopefully he could get back and finish the job before Reverend Carter noticed his cemetery had been disturbed.

Now he was in Plainfield's main cemetery, on the far south side near the trees. The sun had been starting to show above the clouds when he'd arrived. He was on his seventh grave, and so far, hadn't found anything that might interest the vampire in the previous six. Just a lot of bones and tattered clothing and ragged hair.

Ed stepped back from the shovel, his clothes making squelching sounds as he moved. His shirt was warm and soggy on his back. About to put back on his hat, movement to his right caught his eye.

Ed made a lethargic turn. Though he should be in heavy panic, he had no energy to properly react if somebody had caught him digging. He could only stare through his sweat-blinded eyes.

He didn't see anything right away, then a small dark shape hopped along the ground near the tree line. It went a couple feet in one direction, jumped around, and hopped back the way it had come. Black curves fluttered on either side of its narrow body.

What is that?

Wiping his face with his hat, he dried the sweat in his eyes. When he looked again, the sun seemed even brighter, so he squinted harder.

A vulture.

Its body was thick with dingy feathers. Fluffy white sprouted from the narrow neck that supported a scabrous, oval-shaped head and hooked beak. The head bopped this way and that, looking around. Its beady eyes landed on Ed and froze. The beak opened and a raspy, drawn-out hiss was released. Wings spread, stretching like a tattered kite.

Ed thought it meant to attack.

"I'm not dead yet," Ed said. "Get!"

The vulture loosed another long hiss, giving its wings a terse flap. An old, moldy odor drifted toward Ed.

"You're not eating me, pal. Now, get!"

The bird squawked.

"I said get!"

Ed threw his hat. It landed a foot or more in front of the bird. It hardly seemed to notice.

"Shit," said Ed.

He regretted throwing his hat at the vulture. It somewhat kept the sun off his face, and he'd rather have just a tittle of protection than none at all. At least with the hat, his face wouldn't feel as much like tight leather as the back of his neck did.

"See what you made me do?" he asked the vulture. Huffing, Ed planted his hands on the rim of the hole and jumped. He seemed much heavier now, his arms trembling as they struggled to support him. His legs kicked behind him until his knees pushed into the loose soil around the hole. He fell onto his side and squirmed away from the edge. Then he rolled over.

On his stomach, he stared at the vulture. It hadn't moved. It seemed to be…waiting.

Bastard bird.

Ed hoped it waited long enough for him to cave in its head with the shovel. Ed saw himself swinging the shovel down, the blade flattening the ugly bird's head. Then he could sit back and laugh while he watched the bird scamper around with its head shoved down into its chest.

Smiling, Ed wrenched the shovel from the hole. He brought it in front of him, throwing the blade over his shoulder. Chuckling to himself, he stalked toward the vulture. "Now you're going to get it, you bastard bird."

The vulture hissed, twitched its head. Flapped its wings. Seemed to Ed that it was daring him to make a move.

Ed planned to make a move, all right. The gloves made rubbery sounds as he gripped the handle. He began to lift the shovel off his shoulder. He stopped in front of the bird, bringing the shovel higher. The small, bumpy head tilted, black eyes blinked.

Ed brought the shovel down.

It panged when it hit the ground. The impact jolted his arms, sending a quivering burst into his chest. He quickly lifted the shovel and checked.

The Vampire of Plainfield

No flattened bird underneath.

A squawk resounded from off to his side. Ed spotted the bird at the woods, standing in a narrow gap between two large trees. The shade was heavy and dark, almost concealing the bird in its darkness. Wings rustled as if to mock Ed.

"You are a *bastard*, aren't you?"

The bird hissed as if admitting this characteristic.

"I'm going to pound you to bits, you little shit!"

The bird squawked, turned, and hurried into the woods. Ed chased after it, pausing long enough to snatch his hat off the ground. He ran into the woods, turning sideways to fit between the two trees.

A limb slapped his face. Another whacked his chest. Groaning, Ed stayed in pursuit. The bird was a few feet ahead, trotting forward with its wings held out. It hissed and squawked every few steps. Ed thought it might be laughing at him.

"Get back here, you bastard!"

The shovel blade caught the edge of a tree, making the handle slug his stomach. Grunting, Ed staggered sideways. His shoulder bashed another tree. He was thrown back to the right.

"Damn!" Ed shouted.

At least he'd stayed on his feet. But now he had fresh aches to add to those already abusing his poor body. Somewhere inside his worn-out mind, he understood how silly it was to be chasing after a bird. His anger and weariness exceeding his good sense, he picked up his speed.

And he just wanted to beat the vulture into a puddle of feathers and chunky bits.

Up ahead, the vulture made a quick right around a fat tree with low branches. Ed ducked his head and made the turn. When he came around the other side, he no longer saw the vulture.

Ed stopped running. Huffing, he looked this way and that. He held the shovel in both arms like a rifle. A breeze made the limbs tremble, rustling leaves. It brushed coolness across his face. Specks of sunlight danced on the trunks like the beams of flashlights.

But no vulture.

He'd lost it.

"Bastard," he muttered.

All that wasted energy. For nothing. A familiar feeling came upon Ed—he felt like a brainless nitwit. Disgusted with himself, Ed started to turn around.

Then he heard the vulture's raspy hiss from off in the distance.

Spinning around, Ed laughed. "Got you!"

He ran.

Ed burst through a section of brush, a wild laugh rattling his throat. When he saw the glowing fence of spikes before him, the laughter was choked off. His run slowed to a trot, which slowed to a wary stroll.

The enclosure formed a small area—once a circle, but now it was uneven from rods having sank into the ground. Other rods tipped forward, their sharp tops pointing at Ed. Though he could tell by the condition of the layout, the fencing was old, the rods themselves were in pristine shape. The skinny rods were the girth of cornstalks and shined even without the sunlight reaching them.

Silver?

Ed dropped the shovel, pulled off a glove, and rubbed a finger down the side of a rod. It felt smooth and polished, gleaming in the shadows.

Silver, all right.

He looked up. A wattle of intertwined tree limbs prevented any kind of light from reaching the area, giving a false impression of dusk. This probably explained why the vegetation looked dead and old. Brown vines curled through the spaces between the poles like thick spider webs. A carpet of dead leaves covered the ground beyond the barrier. The nearest trees were emaciated and leafless, the bark jagged and black.

And, Ed detected, the temperature was much cooler in this spot. Felt like late autumn in this dark area. He began to shiver, his teeth clacking.

The vulture's hiss brought his attention to the center of the small clearing the fence enclosed. The big bird was perched atop a small, gray nub protruding from the ground.

"How'd you get in there?" he asked.

The vulture's wings fluttered, sounding like an old flag in the wind. Its beak pointed to Ed's left. Ed followed the path of its gaze and spotted an old gate. It was closed, so that didn't explain how the bird had gotten inside.

Then he remembered it could fly and felt, once again, like a nitwit.

The bird had been showing Ed *his* way in.

Ed followed the fence to the gate. An old-fashioned lock held it shut, with an oddly shaped keyhole in the center. Ed had never seen a key that looked the type to fit this ancient latch. He grabbed the bars of the gate and tried to shake it.

The gate wouldn't budge.

Ed walked back to the shovel, grabbing it. Then he returned to the gate and wedged the tip of the blade in the small space between the gate and the silver frame. It didn't go in far, but Ed slowly wiggled the shovel back and forth. The gate made rusty, squeaky sounds as the shovel slowly moved deeper. The gate began to show some give.

"Come on..."

Gritting his teeth, Ed pulled the shovel toward him. The gate whined, bars groaned. He stopped pulling and switched to pushing. This time, the gate really began to bulge outward. He could feel the frame bending in the opposite direction.

Then, leaving the shovel sticking out of the frame, he stepped back. He threw his foot forward, kicking the handle. The wood snapped, causing him to stumble.

And the gate shot open with a screech. The other broken half of the shovel dropped to the ground.

Damn. Lost another one.

At least he'd gotten the gate open.

Ed entered.

The vulture waited for him, its knifelike talons curled over the tip of the nub. No grass grew around it, so it was easy to spot—a gray protrusion among a flatbed of dirt. To Ed, it looked like a headless neck made of stone.

"All right," Ed said, "you got me in here. Now what?"

The vulture hissed, then stepped back. Its talons scraped the top of the rock as it readjusted its position. Bending over, the vulture gave the top of the rock a few quick taps with its beak.

Ed understood.

This was where he should dig. As absurd as it was, this vulture had led him to where he needed to be. One ghoul helping out another. Somehow the vulture had just known what Ed was looking over, even if he didn't know himself.

Ed nodded his thanks. The vulture let out a quick squawk, then launched into the sky. The sounds of its wings flapping became fainter until Ed could no longer hear them at all.

Ed returned to the busted gate and picked up what was left of his shovel. The broken handle was the length of a hammer, and he held it like one as he returned to the rock. If Ed's assumptions were correct, the stone was what remained of an old grave marker. Since there wasn't enough room behind the stone because of the fence, he'd have to dig in front of it.

Getting on his knees, Ed leaned over and slammed the blade of the shovel into the ground. A sudden wind blew against him, dirt peppering his eyes. He used the shovel for a while, then switched to his hands, throwing handfuls of dirt aside like a dog that'd found a nest of rabbits.

When his hands ached, he returned to the shovel—stabbing, scooping and tossing.

This went on and on as the wind's force increased. The trees whispered and rattled, dropping leaves in a twirling rain outside the fence.

Ed paid it no mind. All that mattered was the task. He needed to reach what was buried in the earth. Had to open it up, had to free it.

For the master.

Ed smiled. How pleased the master was going to be with him. It filled Ed with virtuous delight that increased the fervor of his digging. Slogging dirt in every direction, Ed continued to sink as the hole deepened.

His movements came to a sudden halt when the shovel struck resistance.

Laughing, Ed flung the shovel over his shoulder. He held out his hands. One was covered with a glove, the other bloody and calloused and dirty from the dig. He couldn't remember how he'd lost the other glove, and this loosed another wild laugh. Then he began clawing at the dirt, flinging it between his legs in rapid swipes.

A casket began to appear like a hidden treasure.

It *was* a treasure, Ed knew. Thrusting his hands in the air, Ed howled. The master's existence was inside the casket.

Ed Gein had been the one to find it.

With a little help from another ghoul.

Ed looked up to the sky, saying a silent thanks to the vulture.

And spotted somebody peeking over the hole. From the person's position, Ed supposed he or she were on their hands and knees, gazing down at him. It was hard to make out any facial features through the mask of shadows hiding them.

Before he could say anything, he saw an arm raise. The broken half of the shovel was clutched in a fist. The sun behind it, the narrowed point of the blade gleamed.

Then it shot down at him fast. Ed heard a clang, felt a bam of pain, then darkness consumed him.

-24-

Water trickling down his face shocked Ed awake. Head throbbing, he started to sit up, but was pushed back down. He shook when he landed. Felt like a mattress under his back. Carefully, he moved his head. Comfort behind him—a pillow.

A bed...

He felt blankets covering him to his stomach. Opening his eyes, he saw wispy white curtains in front of a window. Dirty yellow light bled through the gauze-like fabric. The white walls were covered in old wallpaper.

Something cool and wet gently patted his forehead. More water trickled down into his brows, sliding down the sides of his face.

Turning his head, he saw Bernice leaning over him.

Bernice!

Gasping, his body turned rigid.

She'd been at the cemetery. She'd been at the spot in the woods while he'd...what?

Ed tried to recall. It was too hard, like using his hands to snatch a fish from a murky pond. His hand clasped a slippery fish, nearly lost it, but held on.

The memory returned.

Digging up a casket.

Ed moaned.

"Glad to see you can finally hold your eyes open longer than thirty seconds," Bernice said with coldness in her voice. It was the kind of tone she might use if she'd caught him fiddling with his pecker in public. Though she was above him, she somehow seemed shorter than usual. Then Ed realized she was sitting in a chair, acting as his nurse.

Ed opened his mouth to speak, but moaned again.

"I bet it does hurt, you fool."

"You...hit me."

"Yes sir, I did. Damn good thing I did, too."

He studied her, waiting for her to elaborate. She did not. Silent, she reached over to the table beside the bed, dipped a rag into a basin with flowery designs ringing the brim, and lifted it out. She squeezed the rag. Water squished out, pouring over her hand and making tapping sounds when it drizzled into the bowl.

She wore a dark blue dress that pushed out in the front from her massive breasts. Her curly hair was the color of a storm cloud, and a little mussed as if she'd been working in her garden all day.

"You're a mess," she said, rubbing the rag on his neck. "Such a mess." The rag moved under his collar, wiping the top of his chest.

Ed held his breath as she rubbed him. He liked how it felt until holding his breath caused his head to pound. He let it out in a long gust.

"I think it's too late to save your clothes with a simple wash. They look ruined. Probably have to throw them away."

Her tone remained flat and cold. Not quite anger. Instead she sounded incredibly disappointed, and that seemed worse to Ed than fuming anger.

"I went to your house earlier today."

Ed gulped. "Did you?"

"Mm-hmm." She held the rag up, rolled it around her hand. It unfurled and draped her fingers. "The door was open, so I walked right in. I tried the summer kitchen first, but it was locked."

Ed felt only minor relief knowing she hadn't seen inside the summer kitchen. She hadn't seen the body parts, casket pieces, headstone shards, and the many other items he'd robbed from the graves.

"Know what I found in your kitchen?" she asked.

"My heads?"

"Among other things. I understand the heads, Ed, believe it or not. They're supposed to ward off evil, but they don't. That's just stupid, ancient folklore. The shrunken heads invite it."

"How do you...?"

"Know what else I found?"

Ed tried to recall what all he had in the kitchen. Bowls made from skullcaps, mostly. The other stuff was in the living room. Bones he'd used to repair wobbly legs on furniture. The couch he'd been rebuilding with parts of the dead. But that was under a blanket for now. He doubted she'd checked under it.

"Your books," she said.

Gulping, Ed closed his eyes. "The ones on the table?"

He opened his eyes, and saw Bernice nod.

Her expression was sour. "What in the name of our Lord, Ed?" Before Ed could answer, she said, "All those vampire books."

"Yes."

"Why so many?"

"I've collected them."

"You're reading them?"

"Yes."

"Why, Ed?"

"Just wanted to."

Bernice closed her mouth, breathed through her nose. It made a long hiss. "That's the only reason?"

"Well...why else would I read them?" He made himself laugh. It sounded very loud in the heavy silence of the room, and made his head pulsate.

"You tell me, Ed."

Ed stared at Bernice. Though her face was smudged in shadow, he could see the soft gleam of her glasses. The lenses were like a reflective glass that concealed her eyes. But he could feel their gaze, heavy on his face.

"Have something to confess?" she said.

Ed hoped the blankets hid his shaking. His cheeks felt warm enough to burst into flames. "Well..." he said. He cleared his throat, held out his hand. "I just..."

Bernice suddenly unleashed a booming laugh. "Planning to hunt down some vampires?"

"Well, yes."

Bernice laughed even harder. "Ed Gein, Vampire Hunter."

Hearing Bernice's laughter was contagious. He joined her. "Yes," he said. "Going to track it down and put a stake in its heart!"

Bernice clapped her hands together. "You're a hoot!" She pitched back her head. He could see the white of her teeth inside the dark chasm of her mouth as she let out a deep guffaw. The rag shook in her hand as if hanging from the clothesline in the wind.

Ed took a deep breath and slowly let it out, puffing his cheeks. He was amazed by how much better he felt, sharing a laugh with Bernice.

Bernice's laughter petered out to something like a sniffling infant. She took a deep, trembling breath, coughing lightly. "Oh, Ed."

She slapped his face with the wet rag.

It made a sharp *smack* against his cheek that lit his face up with a flurry of stings. Crying out, Ed raised a hand to his face. "Why'd you...? Ow! That hurt!"

The Vampire of Plainfield

Bernice tossed the rag into the basin. Water splashed over the side. "It's loose."

Holding his cheek, Ed swallowed the knot in his throat. It made a wet popping sound. "What is?"

"Don't try to fool me, Ed. I remember where I found you today, what you were doing. And I've seen the grave. It's been disturbed. The gate had been thrown a clear hundred feet from the fence. *Something* tore out of there, something strong."

"I filled the grave myself. The dirt looked fine to me! How did you...?" Ed closed his eyes and groaned. He'd just said too much.

Seeing Bernice's smirk, he realized she'd hoped he would. "So you have been there. Thought so."

"How'd you know?"

"Oh, that's simple."

Bernice turned, reaching for the table. He heard her fingers tap something hard, a sound of scraping wood followed. Above him, she held something thick with a bulbous tip between her fingers. "I found this by the grave," she said.

Ed couldn't tell what it was right away. Bernice tilted it into the gloomy light.

My pipe.

Though he knew it wasn't there, he patted his pocket. It was flat against his leg, proving the one that Bernice held was his. It must've fallen out of his pocket during the fight with Peter.

Lowering his head, Ed sighed. He couldn't believe he hadn't noticed it was missing before now.

"Who was buried in the grave I found this at, Ed?"

"What do you mean?"

"You said you filled it in. Who'd you put in there?"

"Nobody. Was going to be Dorothy Clark, if she..." Ed stopped.

Bernice's lips pressed together. Another hiss came from her nostrils. "I knew it was her. Dorothy's parents were found dead in their home this morning."

Ed felt a pinch in his gut. "Dead?"

"Killed. The law—my son—thinks it was an animal attack from the condition of the bodies. Torn apart. A massacre."

"Good Lord."

Bernice nodded. "But we both know my son's belief is inaccurate, don't we?"

"The vampire?"

"Close. My guess is Dorothy went home to feed. Am I correct?"

Ed didn't know what to say.

Bernice stared at Ed a few more moments, sighed, then placed his pipe on the small table. "Suddenly you've forgotten your tongue." She shook her head. "Soon as I heard about the girl's disappearance, I got a strange feeling inside—something told me it was back. But I let it go. When I heard about Timmy's friend, I knew it wasn't a coincidence." Bernice's voice sounded thick and bubbly. "Why now? It's been so long since..." Bernice closed her eyes, mimed the shape of a cross over her chest. "Mary, mother of God, help us. It's loose and it got the girl..."

"No," Ed said. Bernice stopped talking and listened. "The vampire didn't get her. It kissed her...brought her back."

"Right. That's how it brings them back. Makes somebody one of his own."

"But it wasn't the one that...killed Dorothy."

"I don't understand, Ed."

There was plenty Ed didn't understand as well. How'd Bernice know about the vampire? How'd she know about the graveyard? How'd she know where to find him? How'd...?

How does she know so much?

His stress caused dull throbbing in his head. He closed his eyes. When he opened them, he said, "The vampire didn't get her. It was...Peter. He's a vampire, too."

Bernice made a face as if she were in pain. "Dear Christ, it's started already. He's building the family, preparing them for..." She looked at Ed, her eyes grim. "You have to tell me how much you know. Everything. Don't leave out any detail. Promise me you'll tell me *everything*."

"Everything?"

"Every-*damn*-thing."

Can't do that. Can't tell her everything. She'll tell Tom what I did. He'll take me to jail. She'll hate me. Timmy'll hate me. Everybody'll hate me.

D'you hear about Ol' Ed Gein? That weird fool was playing in the graveyards and accidentally set a vampire free.

Only an idiot would do that.

Well, you know Ed. He's the biggest idiot of them all.

Fingers snapping called Ed's attention. He looked up at Bernice. She had her hand close to his face, making her fingers snap. "Yoo-hoo, Ed."

He blinked his eyes. He pushed back his worrisome thoughts. Nodded. "Okay, Bernice."

She smiled. "You're learning. First time you've called me Bernice without me having to remind you."

Smiling, Ed gave his shoulder a small bump. "Yeah."

Bernice let out a heavy breath, almost whistling. "All right. Start talking."

Ed didn't think he could say anything at all, but when his mouth opened, words poured out. It surprised him how easily it was to tell her so much without giving any condemnatory details. Ed told her about Peter, how he'd watched the tubby kid assault Dorothy. Told her he'd taken Dorothy back to his house to see if she would wake up. Told her about the vampire coming to visit, how it awakened Dorothy. Told her about Mary. Told her the vampire, in exchange for allowing him to live, ordered him to start digging. At first, he hadn't known where to dig, but somehow he'd wound up at the right place and had been guided to the correct grave by a vulture.

He even confessed about his ridiculous plans to take the vampire on tour, to charge people a dollar to see it—three dollars a head to watch him pull the stake.

He'd expected Bernice to scold him for such foolish ideas, but she did not.

Of course, he didn't tell her *everything*. And he made some fibs.

Instead of admitting he'd dug up the vampire, he put that blame on Peter. Ed left in the part about blowing a tire and finding the trail that had led him to the graveyard. But he said he'd found the grave disturbed and Peter had already been there with Dorothy.

Bernice listened to everything without interrupting. Other than nodding at certain parts, she said nothing and didn't move. Her eyes were fixed on Ed as she listened intently.

When Ed was finished talking, he wanted to sleep.

"And Mary Hogan has the vampire?" she said when he was finished. "She's its keeper?"

"I guess so." His throat was dry and he wished he had something cold to drink.

"Makes sense. It always goes to the scum of the earth—weak-minded people it can seduce into doing its bidding. They're easy to manipulate with false promises of making them immortal. It might eventually turn her into one of its brood. Probably not, though. Just like a devil, it performs a devil's tricks. Plus, they need *people* to care after them while they sleep during the daylight. People willing to die to protect them."

Though Ed shouldn't, he felt bad for Mary. Like Ed, she'd been fooled into helping the creature. And Ed had put her in the position she hadn't been able to refuse.

"That's all?" asked Bernice.

"All I can remember for now."

Bernice nodded. "Okay." Taking a deep breath, she looked at Ed and slowly let it out. "That explains enough for now. Your truck is still parked in the woods near the Plainfield Cemetery. I'll drive you to your truck soon as I trust you'll be all right to move around on your own."

"I can now."

"No. First, we have to get some food and water in you. See if you can keep it down. Head injuries like that can be tricky to treat. Sorry I had to give you a solid knock like that, but you left me no other choice. You looked mad and were praising your master. Thought a good bonk would bring you to your senses."

"It did. Thank you."

"Don't thank me yet. Our work's just starting."

"Work?"

"Yep. After I take you to get your truck, we're going to your house to get you a change of clothes. Then we're stopping by the store."

"We are?"

"Yes."

"Why?"

"Supplies."

"Oh."

"And weapons."

Ed shot up in the bed. The blanket fell away from him. Though his head pounded from the sudden movement, it wasn't as bad as it had been minutes ago. *"Weapons?"*

"Yes, weapons. Jesus, Ed. Think we're going to go against vampires without some?"

"We're going to…" Ed felt his face scrunch up with his confusion. "Us?"

"We're going to pay a visit to Mary's Tavern. I figure since things have been happening around Plainfield, the vampire has to be close by. And if she's the vampire's daylight protector, I doubt she's hiding it at her house."

"Then what?"

"We kill it."

"And Mary?"

"Once the vampire is dead, the hold it has on her should be lifted."

"What about the kids?"

Bernice made a doleful face. "It's too late for them, which is very sad. We'll have to kill them too. A stake through their hearts, or lop off their heads."

Ed tried processing everything she'd told him. Seemed she had an answer for everything, and all it brought him were more questions. "Bernice?"

She was starting to stand when he spoke. Turning back to face him, she said, "Yes?"

"How do you know so much about the vampire?"

A corner of her mouth lifted into what might have been a grin, but there was no joy evident in her expression. "That's a story I'll tell you as we go along. Right now, you need to get up, use my bathroom. Clean yourself up a little. Mind the bandages on your hand, now."

Ed looked at his hand. The abraded fingers of his right had been bandaged, probably while he was out cold.

"We'll get you some water, we'll eat, then we'll hit the road."

-25-

Timmy, on his stomach at the foot of his bed, turned the comic book's page. Though he'd read the vampire comic enough times that he had each page, panel, and word memorized, the image he saw sent sickly warm tendrils through his stomach. The woman was on all fours, leaned over a headstone as the vampire pushed against her backside. Her white gown covered most of her, but the artist left a lot of flesh bare. The side of her rump, upper thigh, where it bent at the knee, and the vampire on his knees behind her.

Timmy leaned to the side, taking the pressure off his stiffening penis.

He felt odd and jittery as he looked at the panels. Each block of artwork depicted a different angle of her pleasure. The final, half-page square, featured the vampire pulling her toward his chest by her flowing yellow hair and biting her neck. Blood sprayed from the puncture wounds, showering the dialogue boxes in crimson.

The End.

Timmy let out the breath he'd been holding. He whistled. "Wow."

His voice sounded loud and a tad squeaky in the quiet room. The whole house was quiet tonight, which made it easier to hear the wind outside. Specks pelted his window, making soft tapping sounds whenever the wind gave a hard gust.

Like fingers...

Timmy's back felt as if ants were crawling up his spine. It didn't help matters that his dad wasn't home. He was out with the search parties. After Dorothy Clark's parents were discovered this morning, Dad had spent most of the day at their house. He'd come home long enough to eat a quick, early supper. Timmy had been made to leave the dining room after he'd finished eating, but he'd hung around the doorway and eavesdropped on what his parents talked about.

Dad suspected the Clarks had been killed by a wild animal. The teeth marks on the skin supported his idea. They'd probably gone looking for Dorothy during the night, against his warnings not to, and something followed them back to their house. Dad found claw markings on the floors, and body parts had been strewn all over. Before his parents had finished talking, Timmy snuck back to his room.

Dad left a while ago.

Timmy had tried to work on the invisible man story for Robin, but his mind had wandered too much for him to get anything done. He kept hoping she would call, but the telephone never made a sound. So he'd attempted to read a book. That hadn't worked, either. Then he'd brought the comic out of hiding from the shoebox in his closet and had been skimming through it ever since.

The house went completely silent an hour ago. Mom was in his parents' bedroom, alone again. He'd peeked out his door when she'd walked by and saw the dark bottle clasped in her hand by its neck. It was the bottle Dad sometimes drank from after a long day.

He hadn't seen a glass.

Timmy shut the comic and sat up. He swung his legs around, and put his feet on the floor. He stared down at his socks, wondering what to do. Should he try working on the story some more? Wash up and get ready for bed?

He didn't feel like doing either of those things. He really didn't know what he felt. A disorder of emotions pounded around inside his head. All of them seemed to fall away whenever he thought about Robin.

Tapping on his window made him jump.

Stupid wind.

But Timmy heard no heavy wind this time. Just a subtle swish that caused the leaves on the trees to softly rattle. The tapping continued, changing to a curious rhythm—two quick taps, followed by three, another two and one.

"Timmy!"

A voice. His mouth fell open.

Somebody was outside his window.

"Open up!"

Hard to tell who it was. The voice was a harsh whisper, loud and quiet at the same time.

"Who...? Who's there?"

Timmy's voice barely registered above the silence of his room.

More taps, another call of his name, and Timmy felt himself rise from the bed. He walked slow and wooden to the window.

He wanted to stop himself, to get his mom.

Instead, he stopped at the window.

Heart racing, he reached.

Gripped the curtains.

Pulled them back.

And jumped at the face mashed against the glass.

Staggering back, the curtain rod flew at him. He quickly jumped out of its way, eluding being pounded on its way down. Holding up his hand, he saw he still gripped the curtain. He'd accidentally pulled it down.

He brought his eyes up to the window. The bulb in his room threw yellow light across the window, enlightening the flattened grimace outside. It moved back and became Robin. Pale-yellow hair dangled around her pretty face in waves.

Robin's arms moved, hands gesturing for him to come to the window. Timmy let his arm drop by his side. The curtain slipped from his fingers. Feeling like an idiot, he walked to the window.

Can't believe I screamed like that.

In front of Robin.

What was she doing here?

Timmy saw the smile he loved make a white block in the darkness. He unlocked the window, then opened it. Crouching, he folded his arms on the sill.

Robin leaned inside. So close to her, he felt a little funny—nervous and excited at the same time.

"Sorry, Timmy. Didn't mean to scare you." She spoke in a loud whisper.

"It's fine. I wasn't scared. Just didn't…expect you."

Nibbling her lip, she gave a quick look around. "Think your mom heard that?"

Timmy had forgotten about this mother. He turned, looking at his shut bedroom door. Expecting it to fling open any moment, he began to relax when time passed without her coming in. Somehow, Mom hadn't heard his scream or the loud crash of the curtain rod.

Timmy leaned back onto the sill, inches from Robin's face. She smelled faintly of peaches and her breath had a scent that made his chest feel fizzy.

"What are you doing here?" he asked.

"I did it."

"Did what?"

"I *snuck* out."

"Jeez."

Robin nodded. "Can you believe it?"

He stared at her, not knowing what to say.

"I had to," she said. "I needed to see you."

Timmy couldn't believe it. "Me?"

"Yes. Your dad...I wanted..."

Right away Timmy knew why she was here. It had less to do with him and more to do with what his father knew. "You want to know about your aunt and uncle." It wasn't a question.

"Yes," she said. "Has he said anything at all about what happened?"

"I heard him talk to my ma about it."

"And?"

Timmy shrugged. He felt uncomfortable talking about this to her. "He believes that it's..."

"Don't say an *animal* attack."

Timmy gave another shrug. "Sorry."

Robin threw her hands in the air, put her back to him, and shook her head. Now he looked at her back. Her pink sweater hung past her rump. She had on a long, pale skirt that ended at the smooth bulges of her calves. A small section separated the end of the skirt from the puffy whites of her socks. Her hair was down and didn't look styled. He'd never seen it this way and really liked it.

"An animal," she said, turning around.

"That's what he thinks."

"What do *you* think?"

"Well, my dad's not a dummy."

"I didn't say he was. I know he's not. He's just...wrong. Why would he think an animal did that?"

"Something about..." Timmy swallowed hard. His throat felt a little scratchy. He didn't want to say more, but felt he should add this one last part. "I heard him say the bodies were pretty...chewed up."

"I heard. Don't you find that odd?"

"Well..."

"Dorothy vanishes. Peter vanishes. And now this?"

"I…" Frustrated, Timmy knew nothing he said would calm her down. "You're right. But I don't know what my dad can do about it."

"He's part of the law."

"I know."

"If he thinks it was an animal, he won't look for anything else."

Robin was right. If Dad veered his investigation in another direction, he might not be able to steer his way back. If it hadn't been an animal, the case would hit a wall, and whoever had actually done it would get away with it.

"I understand where you're coming from," said Timmy, "but what can we do?"

"They'd be at Goult's store, right?"

"Right. I think Dad said the medical examiner released them for burial preparation. So…"

"I want to see those bodies myself."

Timmy gripped the windowsill, leaning further out. Robin stood a few feet away in the yard, arms folded over her chest. "Are you nuts?" he asked.

"No. I believe I have the right to see them."

"Your parents won't let you do that."

"I know. I'm going without them."

"Old man Goult wouldn't let you, either."

R. A. Goult owned the combination furniture store and funeral home in Plainfield. He was a nice guy who told inappropriate, yet great jokes. But Timmy doubted even Robin could persuade him into letting her look at the dead bodies.

"I know that, Timmy. You're not catching on here."

Feeling dumb, Timmy looked down at his hands. His fingertips had turned white from gripping the sill. He let go.

"Sorry," said Robin. "I shouldn't have said that."

"It's fine."

"What I mean is—I'm heading over there right now."

"To Goult's?" Robin nodded. "He's closed!"

Robin's eyes widened as she shushed him. She gave a quick look around. "I don't think the whole street heard you."

"Don't give me that," he said. "You can't say something like that and not expect my voice to rise."

That was a phrase his ma had said to Timmy many times. It seemed to fit just fine here.

"Calm down, Timmy."

"I am *calm*."

"I'll be quick," she said. "Just a quick looksee and I'll be on my way."

"How are you going to get in? You know he locks the doors."

"That part's easy," she said. Smiling, she stepped off to the side, bent over, and picked up something. She held it up. "I'm going to jimmy the basement window open."

Timmy saw she held a prybar. Probably stolen from her father's tools. "Damn," he muttered.

"Everybody's out on the search, so Goult's should be deserted."

"Robin, this is…a bad idea."

"Remember what we talked about on the phone? What if somebody *did* do this? And what if they did it to Dorothy and Peter too?"

"Did you tell your parents about your ideas?"

Robin made a snorting sound. "Oh, sure. I tried to talk to my daddy about it."

"Didn't believe you?"

"Wouldn't even begin to try to." She threw her hand up, letting it fall and smack her thigh. Her skirt ruffled. "He said I didn't know what I was talking about. I wanted to go with them tonight, but my dad said I needed to stay home. The search party was *adult business*, not mine. I'm just a kid, he said."

Timmy nodded. He bet his dad would've said the same thing if Timmy had asked to go tonight.

"So I waited for them to leave and snuck out," Robin said. "Came here."

"Why?"

"I figured we could go together?"

Timmy's lips suddenly felt dry. He licked them, but his tongue felt dry too. "You want me to go?"

"What do you say? Want to sneak out with me? I'll let you carry the prybar." She held out the slender tool. It was pale and gleamed in the moonlight.

"Me?"

"No, your mom. She's standing behind you."

With a gasp, Timmy jerked his head around, an apology already heading for his tongue. His door was shut. He was alone in the room. He felt instant relief that turned to humiliation when he heard Robin snicker behind him. Slowly, he faced Robin again.

When she saw him, her laughter stopped. "I'm sorry. That was mean. I shouldn't have tricked you."

"It's...fine."

"No. I can be such a brat when I want to get my way. I shouldn't be like that to you. You're the only one who seems to understand me most of the time. That was wrong. I'm really sorry."

"It's..."

Robin cut him off by putting her lips against his. They were cool and slippery when they brushed his mouth. She gave him two quick, soft kisses before pulling away. Her fingers slipped into his hair at the back of his head and held him close. "Will you go with me tonight?" she asked.

Timmy didn't trust himself to speak, so he nodded.

"Great. Climb out and we'll get going."

Robin released his head and moved back a couple steps. Timmy stared at her, unable to move. A tingling current rushed through him. Tremors shook his shoulders, made him jittery. Robin grinned. There was no innocence to it. This time, he could tell she was glad to have caused his fleeting paralysis.

"Are you coming or staying?" she asked.

"I'm going with you."

"Then come on."

Nodding, Timmy managed to stand up. He felt hardness in his pants. Luckily his shirt covered it. He also felt he was in his socks. His shoes were by the front door, since Mama's main rule was to take off your shoes upon entering. Even his father had to abide by this regulation or there would be unpleasant consequences.

"Give me a minute," he said.

"I'll be right here."

Timmy walked backwards, keeping his eyes on Robin. He nearly tripped over his own feet a couple times.

"Watch where you're going," she said, smiling.

"Right."

Timmy turned around and nearly cried out when he almost collided with the door. Taking a moment to calm down, he tried to pretend he couldn't feel Robin's eyes on his back. He slowly turned the knob. It made a loud clicking sound when the tongue pulled back from the hole in the wall. There was no sound when he pulled the door toward him. He silently thanked his father for keeping the hinges oiled.

Timmy stepped into the dark hallway. A small spill of light to his right told him the dining room light had been left on. The living room was dark. To his left, the hallway was filled with oily blackness. He peered in the direction of his parents' room. He could faintly make out the pale shape of the closed door. No light showed at the bottom.

Quietly, Timmy crept to his parents' room. He stood outside the door, an ear pointed toward the room, listening. The rattle of his mother's snores were soft on the other side.

Smiling, Timmy turned around and hurried up the hall. His eyes had adjusted to the darkness, so it was easy to make his way to the front door without stumbling into a wall.

His shoes were on the mat beside the door. Picking them up, he gave a quick glance at his parents' room. The door remained shut. The only sounds he heard on this end of the house were the steady ticking of the clock in the dining room.

He carried his shoes back to his room and carefully shut the door. He leaned against it, breathing heavily. Sweating, his shirt was glued to his sides. Looking ahead, he saw his open window. The curtain lay on the floor in a heap, the rod stiff and crooked.

He'd fix it later.

Timmy dropped his shoes on the floor, slipped his feet in, and walked to the window. Putting his hands on the sill, he leaned out. Robin stood near the bushes, looking toward the road. She held the prybar down by her leg, the flattened tip aimed at the ground. The wind made her skirt flap below her knees, stirred her hair.

Take my jacket.

He leaned back into his room and walked to the closet. His jacket hung from a hanger amongst other clothes. Its candy red color and banana stripes were easy to spot. A Christmas present for his dad, it had been too small for him, so he'd given it to Timmy.

He pulled it down.

Putting it on, he started back for the window.

And stopped again.

He'd noticed the shoebox on the floor of his closet. In it were old school projects his mother hadn't wanted to throw away. But underneath had been the vampire comic and…

The shrunken head.

Ed said it was for good luck. At the time it had both repulsed and fascinated him. Now, he felt some kind of strange relief he had it. Timmy faced the closet again. He supposed they would need all the luck they could get tonight.

Returning to the closet, he crouched, and slid the box toward him. He flipped back the lid, and rummaged through the papers. His finger brushed something that felt dry and leathery. He jerked back his hand, holding his finger out as if something had stung it. Grimacing, he tried again. When his fingers brushed that gristly surface again, they gripped and pulled out the head. He stuffed it in the pocket of his jacket and stood up.

He turned around and nearly gasped when he saw Robin sitting on the windowsill, bent forward, so her head wouldn't bonk the window. "What was that you grabbed?" Her knees were glossy shapes that tapered into sleek shins before the fluffy rim of her socks. The toes of her saddle shoes touched the carpet of his floor.

Timmy buttoned his jacket. "Um...good luck charm."

Robin smiled. "Wish I had one."

Sure Ed would be glad to make one for you.

"All set?" she asked.

"I guess so."

"Then come on." Robin leaned back. She swung one leg outside. Straddling the sill, her skirt draped her thighs, forming the shapes of her legs. Then she pulled her other leg through, and dropped. He heard the slaps of her feet hitting the ground.

He walked to the window, ignoring the guilt that tried to talk him out of going.

If they got caught...

Don't think about it. If you think you'll get caught, you will. Just go.

Think about that kiss.

His mouth tingled from the memory. He ran his tongue between his lips. They felt dry and flaky.

Timmy climbed through the window, legs first. When his bottom was on the sill, he pushed with his hands and threw himself forward. His feet pounded the ground, knees bent. He moved his head away just before a knee rammed his chin. Before he could stand on his own, Robin was pulling him up.

"Are you okay?" Now she was whispering. "That was a hard landing."

"Yeah," said Timmy. "I'm fine."

"Good. Stop getting hurt around me."

"I'll do my best," said Timmy, stepping back to his window. He pulled it down close to the sill, but didn't close it. If somebody were to go by, they shouldn't notice the missing curtain and cracked-open window.

Fingers slid into his right hand. Robin gave him a couple gentle tugs, and led him around the side of the house. She paused at the corner. "Here," she said, offering him the prybar. "I promised."

"No thanks," he said.

Smiling, Robin started moving again. They passed his parents' window. No light showed inside. Mama was either asleep or had drank herself into a deep slumber. Whatever she'd done, it meant he was in the clear.

They made their way to the street and didn't stop walking. Robin guided him to the left.

Timmy wondered if it had ever been so quiet outside. The crunches of their shoes on the road made sounds like snapping tree branches. He wouldn't have been surprised if lights started clicking on all around them from curious people wondering if the sky was falling.

When the wind picked up, it beat against his jacket, making his hair thrash around. He and Robin turned their heads away from the gust to keep their eyes from being nicked by flakey debris.

But they forged ahead, making their way toward town. They passed clapboard houses, separated by wide patches of yard and bushes. Some had lights on through the windows, others were dark.

All were quiet.

No dogs barked. No cats mewed. Even the usual, perpetual moans of the myriad arrays of cattle couldn't be heard tonight. Seemed as if all of Plainfield held its breath, anticipating something.

Or they were all dead.

Don't start.

Timmy attempted a story once that began with a boy waking up one morning to find his town empty. It was as if everybody had simply moved on, and left him behind. He didn't get very far into the story before running out of ideas. However, the premise always stuck with him, terrified him. Sometimes it gave him nightmares.

The houses thinned as the patches of woods became larger. Soon there were no more houses, only trees smothered in darkness. Timmy couldn't see into the woods past the first couple of trees bordering the road.

"Where's the search party hunting tonight?" Robin asked.

Her sudden voice made Timmy jump.

Laughing softly, Robin said, "Sorry."

"It's fine." He pursed his lip, releasing his tensed breath, almost whistling. "Over by the farmlands, I think. They were supposed to last night, but it was supposed to storm…"

"Right. That's what I thought. We should be all right, then."

"I hope."

"Me too."

The road slanted upward, so they walked slightly leaned forward as they climbed the hill. Timmy's calves began to tighten, burning. Reaching the top, they paused.

The main strip of Plainfield was below them. The moon was nearly full on the expansive flatness of the sky and threw down a wide glow on the town. Timmy saw the dark shapes of the lifeless buildings on either side of the road. Nana's store was easy to spot on the corner, sitting at slight angle from the rest.

He saw Maxwell's Barbershop.

And next to it—the funeral home.

Timmy's throat tightened. He swallowed the cold dry lump.

We're going to see...dead bodies.

He'd seen the dead before. At funerals. After they'd been prepared, dressed, and readied for presentation. Seeing them in such a false representation of their former selves disturbed him. How would he handle bodies that were all messed up? Based on Dad's descriptions to Ma, Robin's aunt and uncle had been mangled beyond recognition.

I don't want to do this.

"Ready?" Robin asked. "We're almost there."

"Ready," he lied, trying to keep his voice from cracking.

"Let's go."

Robin moved first, and Timmy followed. Her hand felt warm and slippery in his. He wondered if it was his nervous sweat, hers, or a combination. Didn't matter. Though she'd put up a good front, Timmy figured she was just as scared as he was. Anybody in their position would have to be nearly terrified.

They were almost to Mr. Vincent's Drugstore when they heard the low chugging noise of an automobile.

"Shit on a toadstool!" Robin squealed. "Somebody's coming!"

Timmy's heart launched into his throat. Looking over his shoulder, he spotted headlights looming over the hill and starting down.

Oh, shit. Did somebody see us!

He pictured somebody looking out their window, spotting two kids walking by. Being meddlesome, the person left their house to go after them. Probably thought kids out after dark were up to no good.

And we're not!

Looked like a truck from how high up the lights sat. They made two, wide funnels through the darkness.

"Come on!" Robin squealed, yanking his arm forward.

Holding hands, they ran. Timmy stayed beside her, not knowing where she intended to go. When she started across the street, he figured it out. They were heading toward the barbershop, and would make their way to what was beside it.

Goult's.

"The alley!" she said, her voice shaky and breathless.

"Okay!"

The truck's lights raked across the road just as they made it across. In Timmy's jarring vision, he saw the alley between the two buildings like a drawbridge constructed of shadow. Robin went through a few steps before him, pulling his arm straight. The darkness swallowed her. It got Timmy's hand, then his arm. Soon, Timmy was engulfed by the black.

Robin jerked him to the right. His shoulder bumped the building's brick wall. He spun around to face the road.

The truck drove by without slowing.

"That's...Eddie's truck," said Timmy, huffing.

"Gein?"

"Yeah..."

The engines grumble began to fade, then suddenly steadied. Faintly, Timmy heard the squeaks of hinges of a door opening.

"He got out of the truck," Timmy said.

"Is he coming over here?"

"I...I don't think so. Sounds like he's at my grandmother's shop."

Listening, Timmy heard nothing but the truck's engine, chugging and sloughing. This went on for a few minutes before a door banged shut. The engine's tone shifted, then it drove away.

Within seconds, he couldn't hear it at all.

"You know him really well?" Robin's voice was dry and winded.

"Yeah..."

"What's...he doing out and about?"

"Not sure. Maybe he thought Nana would be at the store."

"Never mind," said Robin. "Come on."

He felt two quick yanks on his jacket. Turning around, Timmy saw the pale shape of Robin's backside dashing through the alley. From her swinging arms and flapping hair, it looked as if he were peering down at her as she drowned in a river of darkness.

He followed the swishing paleness of her hair to the other end of the alley.

When they stepped out, the moon gave them more illumination to see by. It was nearly bright compared to the dark-shrouded alley. They were behind the buildings now, walking across the gravel parking area. Rocks popped and crunched under their footsteps.

Robin made it to Goult's first. Ignoring the backdoor, she walked by the concrete steps, and squatted at the stone foundation. Timmy saw the faint, rectangle shape of a hopper window. It was maybe two feet long and three feet wide. A tight fit, but they should be able to wiggle through just fine.

I can't believe we're going to do this. We're going to break in!

Timmy Worden, son of Tom Worden was about to commit a crime.

His legs felt weak as shame washed over him. Dad's warnings replayed through his mind—about women controlling men, making them do things they normally wouldn't.

Now it made sense.

And within a day, Timmy had already disappointed his father without his knowing it.

Disappointed me, too.

Timmy jumped at the grating sound of metal scraping metal. Something clattered.

"Not so loud," he said.

"Sorry," Robin said in a strained voice. Sounded as if she were trying to lift something heavy. When the window popped open with a rusty snap, he realized she'd been struggling to break the lock. Robin let out a heavy breath that turned to laughter. "Got it."

Oh, God.

Though he hadn't realized it until now, he'd subconsciously hoped they wouldn't have been able to get inside. Maybe all along, he'd thought they really wouldn't have been able to, and he'd just gone along with it to make Robin feel better.

Now it was about to really happen.

"It's really dark in there," she said.

"That's good."

"How's it good? We won't be able to see."

"And anybody driving by won't be able to see a light moving around in there."

Robin was quiet a moment. "Makes sense. But we'll be in the basement, where Goult keeps the...bodies."

"Still, better not to risk it."

"You're right."

Robin remained squatting in front the window, her head ducked to see inside. Timmy figured she was trying to talk herself out of climbing through. Maybe he should try talking her out of it, too.

She'll think I'm a wimp.

Timmy stayed quiet.

Finally, Robin turned. "Let's get this over with."

-26-

Ed watched Bernice double-check the door to the store was locked. Then she stepped away, hurried down the steps, and jogged toward the truck. She was hugging a large satchel to her chest. Instead of getting in his truck, she bypassed the passenger door. Turning in his seat, he watched her through the back window. She dropped the large satchel in the back. It made a soft thump when it landed in the metal bed.

The door opened and Bernice climbed in. "Get moving, Ed."

Nodding, Ed pulled the gear and took off as Bernice slammed the door.

"Was that your...supplies?"

"It was."

"I see."

"How's your head feeling?"

"Good."

"Truth."

"Still hurts, but much better than it was."

"Good."

The hunter's cap made the pain worse than it probably would have been without it. But he didn't like going anywhere unless he had it on. He felt odd when without it, as if he'd left home without his pants. Nobody would probably recognize him if he wasn't sporting it.

Maybe I should take it off.

If somebody saw them tonight, he could say it wasn't him.

"Did they have a hat on?" he'd ask.

"Well, no..."

"Then it wasn't me."

Who'd see us?

Half the town was either asleep or out in the woods searching for kids they weren't going to find.

Unless they'd decided to feed on them.

Bernice said they wouldn't risk an attack tonight with so many people out.

"A silent takeover," she'd said. "Like a plague that wipes out a village one-by-one."

They'd been sitting at her table, eating a tasty meal of meatloaf and mashed potatoes. Ed was on his second plate and fourth glass of water.

"Why are they here?" he'd asked.

"They've always been here."

"How do you *know* that?"

"My family's been involved with this vampire for a long time, Ed. A long time."

"Did your husband know?"

"No, he did not. I kept it from him. This was passed down to me from my father's side of the family. My dear husband was just a clueless schmuck when it came to this, God rest his soul."

"And Tom?"

Bernice shook her head. "No. He doesn't know, either. I had hoped to tell him about it someday, but he..." She looked off to the side, nose wrinkling. "He took after his daddy a little too much. He's sensitive. And so is Timmy to a degree, but my grandson has something in him that shows an open mind and strong heart. Probably gets that from his mother. She's a tough one, if I ever saw one."

"Gets it from you, too," Ed said.

Bernice waved off the compliment, then reached under the table. Soft scraping sounds could be heard as her arm fidgeted. "I'll show you this first," she'd said, sliding a folded piece of paper, browned with time, across the table. "Lay that out for me."

Nodding, Eddie took the paper square. Afraid that he'd tear it, he carefully unfolded it piece by piece. He moved his plate and glass to make room. By the time he'd finished, it covered a large chunk of the table.

A map. A very old one that looked hand-drawn, not at all like the kind Bernice sold at her store. Inked at the top of the page in a thick black scrawl was *Plainfield.*

"That's a map of our town," Bernice had said. "Long before roads plowed through the fields and our forests were cut down for more houses and businesses. See these, Ed?" She leaned forward, tapping lines on the paper. "These were the old wagon trails. See where they intersect right here?"

"I do," said Eddie.

Coming from multiple directions, they joined in a particular spot to form a cross.

"That's the old graveyard."

"Where the vampire was?"

"Right," she'd said. "That's where my granddaddy put it back down when I was just a little girl. He killed the vampire and its damn undead-women slaves. He left my daddy in charge to watch over the graveyard when he got ill, and when it came time for my daddy to pass on, he bestowed that duty onto me. One day, I'd planned to give it to Timmy."

Ed nodded.

"I really failed, huh?" she'd said. "The vampire's awake and killing again. He'll keep turning people into his minions as he tries to take over the town one person at a time. And he'll do it too." Bernice had looked sad, the dim light of the room twinkling in her wet eyes. "I really didn't think there was anything left to worry about. It's been so long since my granddaddy had slain the vampire, I thought we were safe. I got lazy, content. I stopped going out there as much. I stopped preparing for the possibility of the vampire's return a long time ago."

"Why was I digging?" Ed had asked the question without even realizing he wanted to. He flinched at the sound of his voice.

"It wants to find its bride. And to bring her back."

"Bride...? The vampire said I was looking for its existence."

"To that creature, she is its existence. It can't seem to function without her. And until you found where she was buried, it hadn't known where she was."

"It knows now?"

Bernice nodded. "Oh, yes. It knows. But it does the vampire no good just to know. It needs *you* to bring her out of the grave. It can't get to her. That fence?"

Ed nodded.

"It's made out of silver. The silver had been brought over here with intentions to use it to build the town. Instead, the fence was made to keep the vampire out, and the bride *in*."

"Those graves at the small graveyard, those weren't its brides?"

"Hardly. Just women it turned to help with its quest. Women from town it wanted for their family. One of them was my aunt. The others were just wives who'd been brainwashed into joining the vampire legion."

"Was his bride somebody from Plainfield?"

"Not our Plainfield. They were joined together long before. My daddy explained it to me like this—and his information was scarce to none. We both know Plainfield was founded in 1849, but what we didn't know was that Elijah Waterman was a member of the first group that slayed the vampires. Plainfield used to be a vampire village in the old times and our ancestors, well, not yours, since you're not from Plainfield, were their slaves. From the little that I know, these vampires were together for as long as anybody can tell. I don't know if one changed the other, or if they'd been bonded in their blood-thirst. But back in 1849, the vampires were defeated. The bride was killed first, and buried in secret. A cage of silver was erected around her to keep her there if she were to wake up. The vampire had no knowledge where she was buried. He was slain before he could learn. Soon after, Plainfield was founded as a new village, free of the vampires' power.

"Somehow, when I was a little girl, it was awakened. The town was, again, held captive in the vampire's clutch. Nobody other than my granddaddy knew where the bride had been buried, and the vampire went mad trying to find her. And my granddaddy, the last living relative of the original slayers, and a few others, were able to kill it and its three minions. They were buried in the old graveyard. Silver wasn't rightfully available then to build another protective fence, so iron was used. It appears the iron was utterly useless. And the consecration the priest put on the land was broken the moment the grave was defiled."

Ed hadn't realized he'd been holding his breath until his lungs felt about to burst. He'd let out a long gust of air before speaking. "So the vampire was forcing me to dig up every grave in Plainfield until I found her?"

"More than likely."

"Why didn't it have Mary do it?"

"It needs her protection while it sleeps. It can't be left alone when it's so vulnerable."

Bernice guzzled what was left of her water. She gently set the empty glass on the table. "Augusta never told you any of this?"

Minutes passed before Ed had been able to speak again. "My mama? How did she know anything about the vampires? Was she involved?"

"She wasn't necessarily *involved,* but when I first met her all those years ago, I knew straightaway Augusta knew the Bible better than any preacher I'd ever met. I sat her down one day and told her everything. To my surprise, she believed all of it without question. She said she'd felt God calling her to move to Plainfield for His mission for a long time before she finally obeyed Him. With her assistance, I felt that if the vampire did return, her religious knowledge would come in handy. She'd made a vow to me she'd start preparing you and your brother, Henry, for the moment, should it happen. But after Henry's accident, she...well, things were different then. And I guess when she got sick, I just decided to stop trying myself."

Ed had been hit by a flutter of memories—his mother's consistent warnings, her preaching's of evil things lurking in the dark places nobody could see. He'd chalked it up as the paranoid ramblings of a mother trying to control her sons with punishments of doom and hellfire.

Instead, she'd been trying to teach him.

And when Henry died, Mama lost all hope.

Then her episodes, as the doctor had called it, her strokes, handled the rest.

That means...

In the truck, Ed came to the same conclusion he had back at Bernice's table. Ed Gein had been destined to fight this vampire from the beginning.

Gripping the steering wheel, his breaths came in short bursts.

"Are you all right?" Bernice asked.

Ed nodded. "Just thinking about things."

"Well, it's time you stop letting your mind strike you down with fear." She pointed out the windshield.

Ed saw where her finger was aimed. Mary's Tavern was up ahead on the left.

Cold ruptured in his stomach, squirming through his bowels like icy worms.

We're almost there.

-27-

Though he was reluctant, Timmy volunteered to climb through the window first. Getting on his stomach, he went in feet first. His waist bent over the edge as he kicked air. Finally, his foot tapped something sturdy. He brought his other foot down. It felt durable enough to hold him up.

He dropped. His fall was short. Abruptly landing on his feet, his eyes were level with the window. He figured he was probably standing on a desk or a short bookcase.

"Okay," he said. "Your turn."

Robin nodded, then repeated Timmy's motions. Feet first, she wiggled her legs through the window. The skirt hiked high up on her legs, leaving her legs very bare. Each time her thighs parted, Timmy glimpsed the white band of her underwear between her legs. Averting his eyes, he focused on her calves.

Reaching up, he caught a kicking leg in each hand. Her skin felt soft and velvety in his hold. He braced her legs as she wiggled through the window, legs sliding through his hands. Shins first. Then her knees.

Then her thighs. His knuckles brushed the silky material of her underwear.

Then she dropped down. The hard soles of her shoes made a solid whacking sound when she landed. Robin let out a long sigh of relief. "Made it without breaking our necks." Though she whispered, her voice still sounded loud in the heavy quiet.

"We're not down yet."

"Where are we?"

"The basement."

"I mean, *where* in the basement?"

Timmy looked around. All he saw was darkness. The floor seemed nonexistent below them. As if they were to jump, they'd never touch bottom.

"I don't know," he said.

"Look."

Timmy couldn't tell where she was pointing. "What?"

"A lamp."

"I don't see it."

"Wait here," she said.

"No, Robin, I..."

"I'll be just a minute."

"But the light, somebody might see."

"We need it, Timmy. It's too dark."

Timmy stopped arguing. He felt Robin turn beside him, press against him. Her lips kissed the side of his mouth. She'd probably been aiming for the front, and missed.

"Give me a minute," she said, turning away from him. She crouched slightly. Then jumped down. She let out a soft squeal when her feet smacked the floor. At least, Timmy figured it was the floor. Sounded like concrete. "That was unexpected."

"Are you okay?" he asked.

"Yeah. Just wasn't expecting to land so soon." Her shoes made scuffling sounds on the floor as she moved away from him.

Her footsteps stopped.

Timmy waited. Silence fell over the room like a heavy blanket.

"Robin?"

No response.

"Robin?"

A hissing flame suddenly burst in the dark, washing Robin's features in a fluttering glow. He saw her squint against the flame's dim brightness. The flame lowered, vanished, then reappeared even dimmer.

She was lighting the oil lamp.

"There you are," he said.

"Yeah," she said, leaning over a small desk. She pulled the match out of the lamp, shaking it out. "Sorry. It took longer to find the matches."

The flame inside the lantern grew, filling the corner Robin stood in with light. There was a bulletin board of some kind hanging on the wall. Stacks of paperwork had been tacked to it.

Though the light made Timmy nervous, he was glad they had it.

"Much better," she said. Turning to face Timmy, she smiled. It slowly drooped into a confused grimace before changing into repulsion. "Oh, God, Timmy…"

The look on her face made Timmy's insides squirm. "What's wrong?"

"Look…" She pointed at him. "You're standing on…"

Slowly, Timmy looked down. A flat sheet of wood was under his feet. Turning his head, he noticed how the wood seemed to narrow when it reached the end. He looked at the other end. It was broader, a flat top and jutting corners.

"Is that…?" Timmy started to say. "Oh, God. It's a coffin!"

Timmy leaped from the top. He landed in a squat, sprang to his feet, and dashed over to where Robin stood. Elbows touching, they stared at the coffin. On top of a table, the lid was closed.

Timmy felt sorry, and a little sick, knowing he'd been standing on something designed to house a dead person.

Over to the left, he saw another coffin, partially completed. On the far side of the room, the wall was lined with overstocked shelves: Books, tools, jars and bottles. Beside the half-finished coffin Timmy saw two slabs. On top of each were white sheets that draped the slab and hung over the edges. Shapes showed beneath, body shapes. Distinct forms of featureless heads, shoulders, and torsos. Poking out the bottoms of each sheet were bare feet. The larger set was smooth and gray, the smaller, petite pair had dark, clean scratches on the bottom. Both looked as if they'd been sleeping and accidentally kicked the sheet off their feet.

"Oh, God," he muttered.

"That's them," said Robin.

"Yuh-yeah...it is."

In shock, Timmy stared at the white shapes.

That's people under there.

Not just people. Robin's family.

Spirals of tubing reached out from under the sheet that concealed the man. The other end led to a steel counter, hanging over the deep sink. Though the tubes were empty, Timmy noticed droplets of a murky fluid inside, remnants of whatever had been flowing through.

On the counter's polished surface was a line of tall glass bottles.

Even from here, Timmy could read the labels: *Embalming.*

"Well," said Robin. "I came here to do it...so..." She took a quivery breath that shook her shoulders. Facing Timmy, she held out the prybar. "Hold this?"

Timmy took the prybar from her hand. He noticed her trembling. "You don't have to do this. We can leave."

"No. We've gone this far, right?"

Timmy nodded.

Robin took another deep breath that sloshed her cheeks. She shivered. "I'm going to do it."

"I'll go with you."

Robin closed her eyes, looking relieved. When she opened them, she offered something that resembled an appreciative smile. "Thank you, Timmy."

He held out his empty hand. Robin smiled again, raised her hand to his, and held it.

Together, they approached the metal slabs. Timmy stared at the sheets to avoid seeing the bare gray feet. Robin made short steps around to the side of the gurney with the little feet, stopping near the top.

And stared.

Timmy was beginning to think she'd decided not to look when her hand lifted.

It gripped the sheet, tugging it down.

Gasping, Robin turned away and buried her face in the nook of Timmy's shoulder. He stared, numb, down at the face of a nightmare. He knew it had to be Carol Clark, though what was left no longer resembled what he remembered. Her once pretty face had been mangled by deep gashes. An eye had been torn out of its socket, leaving an empty hole underneath the tatters of her eyelids. The other was a droopy slit that showed only white inside. Her lips were twisted, teeth bared.

Timmy had to agree her condition supported evidence of an animal attack.

Until he noticed her neck.

Holes.

Pairs of them covered the side of her neck in different positions. The girth of a sharpened pencil tip, the holes spread across her skin like a connect-the-dots puzzle. Spatters of blood connected a few of them together.

Something had bitten her, many times.

But not any animal Timmy had ever seen had teeth like that—a pair, about an inch apart, that could make such perfect spherical indentions.

"What happened to her, Timmy?" Robin's voice was muffled against his chest. He felt his coat flutter from her words. "What kind of animal could do this?"

"I...I don't know."

"Do you think it was an animal, Timmy? Do you?"

Timmy gulped. His stomach felt odd, cold and quivery, as if it were shrinking. "No."

"Let's go, Timmy. I don't want to be in here anymore."

"What about...?" Timmy looked at the other body, covered in white. He noticed a few dark blotches of blood had seeped through the fabric.

"Forget it. I just want to go."

Timmy nodded, though Robin couldn't have seen it. Putting his arm around Robin's shoulders, he started walking. Something hard bumped his thigh. He nearly screamed, but luckily he remembered he was holding the prybar. His sweaty hand clutched so tightly, his knuckles felt stiff.

He wondered what Robin would want to do now. Would she continue to pursue her mission for the truth, or would she let it go?

Does she think an animal did that?

Probably not. But like Timmy, what could she do about it?

Nothing much. We're just kids. Nobody will listen to us.

That wasn't true, he realized. He knew of one person who not only would listen, but would probably believe—Eddie Gein.

Nobody'd listen to him, either.

Feeling defeated, scared, and a tad frustrated, Timmy led Robin toward the far wall. It was hard to move with Robin pressed so tightly against him. But Timmy didn't stop. He didn't look back, either. Once had been enough. That one glimpse of Carol Clark would haunt him for the rest of life.

They were approaching the coffin when Timmy realized they'd forgotten to blow out the lamp.

"Wait," he said.

"What's wrong?" Robin lifted her head. Tears smeared her cheeks in shiny moisture.

"The lamp."

Robin turned. Her hair brushed Timmy's face. "Shit," she said.

"I'll get it. Wait here."

"No. If you're going over there, I'm going too."

"Sure."

They started walking toward the small desk.

A noise drifted through the hopper window—the dry crunching sound a foot might make on gravel.

"Somebody's coming," he said.

Robin started to squeal, but Timmy got his hand over her mouth in time to stifle it. He felt the patter of her warm breaths against his palm. Being shorter than Robin, he had to reach up to make it work. Since he couldn't turn around, Timmy stared at Robin's lovely eyes.

And watched them slide toward the window, growing wider as the footsteps became louder.

They're getting closer!

The footsteps stopped right outside the window. Timmy watched the side of Robin's face. His hand mashed her cheek toward her eye, making a bulge of skin above his thumb. His fingers were wet from her tears. Whenever she breathed on his skin, it tickled, making goosebumps rise.

No other stepping noises came. Maybe whoever it was had left.

Then somebody spoke. "Timmy? Robin? Are you in there?"

Robin's eyes flicked toward Timmy, narrowing with confusion.

Timmy was confused as well.

Because the voice that came from outside the window had sounded like Peter.

-28-

Ed turned off the engine, stuffing the key in his pocket. Before he could say anything, Bernice shouldered her door open and climbed out. Ed followed her. Together, they quietly pushed the doors to the frames without clicking them in place.

The weather was crisp, with a warm tinge mixed in. He wore his coat, but could probably go without it and not be cold. At least the clothes were clean. Though he'd protested it at first, he was glad Bernice drove them to his house so he could change.

Bernice reached into the back of Ed's truck, removing her bag. She carried it with her to the front and set it on the hood. Pulling the bag apart, she dug through the contents. The bitter odor of garlic hit him. His eyes brimmed with tears. Garlic tasted great on food, but on its own, it was hard to enjoy. And the smell was impossible to wash off his fingers. Seemed to cling to his skin for days afterward.

Her hand came out, placing a large, shiny crucifix on the hood. The moonlight made it gleam and twinkle. Then she set two glass bottles beside it. To Ed, they looked like medicine bottles.

"Holy water," said Bernice.

Not medicine, something better.

"Put this on," she said.

She held out a wreath of garlic bulbs.

"You're kidding," he said.

"Do I look like I'm kidding?"

The Vampire of Plainfield

Her grim stare told him she was very serious. He took the garlic wreath and slung it over his head. It hung across his chest like a giant, malodorous necklace.

Bernice pulled one over her head as well. She looked back in the bag. Ed liked that she had a bag of her own, filled with her tools and trinkets.

Like me.

He looked to the back of his truck. His sack lay on its side. Though it was full of his shovels, Bernice's contained fragments of a world Ed didn't know existed. But the more he dwelled on that notion; he realized his also held evidence of a world Bernice didn't know existed.

At least he hoped so.

"And we'll need this," she said. Bernice held up a block-shaped object with both hands. To Ed it looked like a large candy bar, but much thicker. Bernice began unfolding it. Each time she pulled out a section, it made a reedy click. A strap dangled from the front of it, held together by a pointed riser.

A slingshot?

Couldn't be. Seemed too large for that. Bernice clicked other pieces into place—two curved limbs, string dangling between each tip. Soon, the block was transformed into something else. When he noticed the trigger, he realized what it was.

"Was my granddaddy's," Bernice said. "He made it himself."

Not a slingshot, after all. It looked like an ancient crossbow. A pulley mechanism was attached to the top, a string stretching in a U-shape. Bernice's finger slipped through the trigger guard, keeping almost an inch of space between the tip and trigger.

"Arrows?" asked Ed.

"Even better."

Bernice put a short, carved stake on top, blunt end against the band. Holding it below the point, she pushed the stake against the strap, making the string stretch back. There was a click, and the stake stayed in place. She held the flat, wooden stock up to her shoulder, leaning her head to the side. One eye squinted. "It's a damn accurate shot," said Bernice. "But it also has a hair-trigger. Be careful."

She held the improvised weapon out to Ed, keeping the sharp end of the stake pointed toward the tavern. Ed was wary of taking it. She thrust the crossbow at him to make him. Ed reached for it with trembling hands. Before he could take the weapon, Bernice pulled it away from him.

"Now, Ed," she said. "I warned you about the trigger. If you're shaking like a naked baby in the snow, then I don't know if you should be the one to handle it or not."

"I don't know if I want to."

Bernice smirked. "Take the damn thing and be a big boy."

Ed took a deep breath, willing his hands to stop their trembling. It seemed to work. Bernice nodded once, then offered him the weapon again. This time, she didn't pull it away from him. As dinky as the gadget looked, it was surprisingly heavy in his hands. The wood was durable, probably oak. And the mechanics were solid and old. He put it against his shoulder, squinted an eye, and gazed down the riser. It looked like it would hit whatever he aimed it at.

He kept his finger away from the trigger.

"What are you going to use?" he asked, lowering the crossbow.

"Oh, I have these." She held up two stakes, then slipped them into a harness. "And this."

Bernice showed him the curved blade of a scimitar. The long knife reminded Ed of paintings he'd seen of pirates in sword fights. She dropped it into the sheath on the side of the harness, the bending blade pointing behind her. With the weapons dangling like morbid charms, she tied the harness around her waist.

"Ready?" she asked.

"Shouldn't we come back in the daylight?"

"Can't. The full moon, Ed. It'll be at its highest later tonight. Needs to be done now."

Bernice's plan had put them entering the vampire's lair when it would be alert and strong. Plus, they would also have Mary Hogan to handle, and she was another kind of dangerous obstacle he feared they weren't prepared for.

Ed followed Bernice toward the rear of the tavern. Darkness piled down from the overhanging roof, leaving a wide spread of impenetrable blackness. The shadows swallowed Bernice like murky water when she stepped through, as if she'd stepped through a black portal. He was tempted to call out for her, but held it back.

Ed felt his hand holding the modified crossbow start to shake. With his free hand, he gripped his wrist to hold it steady. He took another deep breath, filling his lungs with chilly, night air. Then he slowly let it out.

"Ed, come on," he heard Bernice say in a sharp whisper.

Nodding, Ed entered the shadowy chasm. Dark dropped over him.

"Over here," Bernice whispered.

"Okay," he muttered.

Her voice had come from his right. He shuffled through a thick wall of darkness to the rear of the tavern, coming out next to Mary's car. The front end was busted, windshield split with cracks, a headlight completely obliterated. He wondered when she'd been in an accident.

He looked to his side. He saw the pale curves of Bernice's body. Moonlight twinkled at her thigh from the polished blade of her scimitar.

The ground was uneven, making Ed's movements unbalanced. He kept the crossbow pointed down, just in case he accidentally set it off. Bernice stood at the back wall, waiting for him. As he neared her, he noticed a rectangle shape of paleness above her shoulder. Though it was also dark, it was a bit lighter than the black surrounding it.

Oh, no.

The backdoor had been left open.

"Looks like they're expecting us, Ed."

Ed's heart dropped into his stomach.

So much for the element of surprise Bernice predicted they'd have.

"What do we do?" he asked.

"Nothing's changed," she said, and started up the rickety steps. The wood groaned under her feet as she climbed. A Bernice-sized shape was cut into the soft light of the doorway when she walked inside.

Though Ed sweated profusely under his clothes, he felt cold and shaky. His shirt stuck to him. He put a foot on the lowest step, noticing how badly his knee trembled.

Stop it, Ed.

He needed to quit being so scared. Bernice needed his help, and he needed her help to end what he'd started.

Feeling a little calmer, Ed climbed the steps.

He entered the tavern.

-29-

"Peter, is that you?" Timmy asked.

"Yeah, it's me!"

Timmy couldn't help the laughter that flowed from him. He looked at Robin, saw she was smiling, and laughed with her this time.

"What are you doing up there?" Robin asked.

"I thought I saw you two come over here. Took me a little while to find you."

"Where were you?" Timmy asked. He started walking toward the coffin, with Robin in tow.

"Hiding."

Timmy felt his good mood falter. "Hiding?"

"Yeah. From Eddie."

Timmy remembered Eddie's truck driving by, remembered it stopping for a little while and somebody getting out. Since he and Robin had been hiding, Timmy hadn't been able to see what Eddie had been doing.

Looking for Peter?

Why?

"We're on our way out," said Timmy.

"Good," Peter said. "This place gives me the creeps."

"Hold on," said Robin. She hurried over to the desk. Leaning over, she held back her hair and blew a shot of air into the lamp. The flame died. Darkness fell over them. A wide bar of gray light slashed through the window.

Robin hurried back to Timmy. He let her climb up the coffin first. When she was up there, Timmy climbed up.

Again, he let her go out first. Peter held her hands while she squirmed through the opening. Her kicking legs went out last. This time, Timmy kept his eyes away from between her legs.

Her hands reached through the window. He handed her the prybar. It made a metallic thump when she set it down. Her hands came back in. Grabbing them, he wormed through the tight space.

Cool air brushed his face when his head came out. It made the sweat feel cold on his skin. Robin let go of his hands, and Timmy crawled the rest of the way out. After his feet were clear of the window, Robin squatted and pulled it shut.

Lying on his side next to the stairs to the backdoor, Timmy tried to catch his breath. He looked for Peter, spotting him in a darkened corner between the two buildings. Shadows hid him down to his waist. The pants that showed in the moon's pale light looked filthy. Thick stripes and splatters of stains covered his legs.

Timmy pushed himself up, and waited for Robin. She walked over to him, nodding. "The window seems like it'll hold."

"Good."

Holding hands, they walked toward Peter. They stopped a few steps away from the shadows that smothered half of Peter's body.

"Holding hands?" Peter asked.

Robin gave Timmy a bashful glance, smiling. "Things have changed recently," she said.

"Sure looks like it," said Peter. "Wow, Timmy-boy. Good job."

Timmy rolled his eyes, shook his head. Reunited with Peter for a few minutes and his friend had already started busting his chops.

Then he remembered why they were reuniting.

"Why're you hiding from Eddie?" Timmy asked.

"He's after me. I barely got away."

"Eddie?" Timmy repeated, just to be sure.

"Yes, Eddie. Told you he has the Weirdees."

"What'd he do to you?" Robin asked.

"He got me. Tried to *kill* me."

"What about Dorothy?" Robin asked. "Does he have her too?"

"Yeah, the sicko. You wouldn't believe what he did to *her*. Made her do...stuff. You know? Stuff a kid shouldn't be doing."

"Oh, God," said Robin, her voice thickening. "Crazy bastard."

Timmy couldn't believe it. It wasn't that the shock had made his mind unable to accept what Peter said. The story seemed too impossible to comprehend. No way did this sound like the Eddie Gein Timmy knew. Sure, he was little odd, but it was a goofy kind of peculiarity, nothing ominous about him.

Most of the time, Timmy felt sorry for Eddie.

Then he remembered the head in Eddie's kitchen, the shrunken head in his pocket. He patted his jacket and felt the hard lump of the shrunken head inside.

"If this is true," Timmy said, finding it hard to speak.

"It's true," said Peter, a bit of force in his voice.

"Then we have to tell my dad."

"He's out with the search party," said Robin.

"Search party?" Peter said.

"Yeah," said Timmy. "Half the town's out looking for you and Dorothy."

"Really?" said Peter, sounding impressed. "Wow."

It was like talking to a pair of legs with no upper body. Peter remained partly draped in darkness. Timmy wondered why he wouldn't come any further.

"Maybe we should go back inside the funeral home," said Robin. "Hide out there until morning."

"What?" Timmy said. "Our parents'll kill us."

"Maybe. But Goult will be here in the morning, and we can tell him what happened."

"Everything?" Timmy said.

"We have to. How else will we explain being in there when Peter found us?"

Made sense. But he knew once the shock of the situation had worn off, he would be in a lot of trouble.

Real nice, Timmy. Worry about yourself in a time like this.

Timmy was being selfish, and hated himself for it.

"We have to go now," said Peter. "I can't be here in the morning."

"Why not?" Robin asked.

"Oh, uh...it'll be too late by then. Eddie still has Dorothy."

"We *really* have to find my dad," said Timmy.

"There's no time," Peter said. "Hard telling what Eddie might do to her if he thinks I'm gone for good. I've read enough crime stories to know how these things go. In a panic, he might do something to her to keep her from talking."

"Like what?" Robin asked. "You mean...?"

"I don't know...kill her, probably."

"God," Robin said. She started to cry.

"What should we do?" Timmy asked.

"Go after Eddie," said Peter.

"Are you crazy?" Timmy asked. "If Eddie really is a madman, then that's the last thing we need to do."

"What about Dorothy?" Robin asked. "Have you forgotten about her?"

"Of course not."

"If she's with Ed Gein," Robin said, "then she's not safe. It's like Peter said, he'll probably kill her. We have to save her."

"We need *help* to do that," Timmy said. He wanted to remind her that even though she was a couple years older, she, like Timmy and Peter, was still a kid. Eddie was an adult, and they needed adults' help to stop him.

Stop him? You don't really believe...

Why would Peter lie about this? Sure, Peter told some whoppers from time to time. But would he really make this up?

Timmy gave his friend a quick glance. Though he couldn't see Peter's eyes, he could feel them slithering across him like a snake's tongue. Something wasn't right about this whole situation.

"Timmy," said Robin. "There's no help out there right now. It's just us. We're the only help Dorothy's going to get tonight."

"Right," said Peter.

"And if we wait until tomorrow, like I originally said, then it might be too late."

"It will be," said Peter. "Eddie'll snap. He'll go kill crazy."

Timmy sighed. Though he felt like they were making a big mistake, he nodded. "Let's go after Eddie," he said.

"Thank you," Robin said, leaning in. She gave him a soft kiss on the lips. She pulled away much too soon. "We'll be all right."

"Wow, a kiss too?" said Peter, stepping away from the corner of the building. The shadows slid off his shoulders, his head. His shirt was just as soiled as his pants, coated in what looked like motor oil. It had dried, turning to a heavy crust on the fabric. His face was overly pale, somehow thinner, and streaked in grime. His eyes looked overly bright on his dirty face. "A lot really has changed, huh?"

Timmy watched Robin work to keep the smile going. Peter's appearance had sucked her emotions dry. "Told you so," she said. Gone was the sweet braveness in her voice. Now she sounded how Timmy felt.

Like a frightened child.

"Follow me," said Peter, grinning. "I know where Eddie was going."

-30-

It stank worse inside the tavern than the death-rot inside the caskets after Ed had pried them open. Such heavy darkness filled the room that Ed could've been convinced he'd gone blind.

Walking slowly, the crossbow held at an angle before him, Ed's hip bumped something hard. It made a scooting sound on the floor.

A chair.

Wanting to apologize to Bernice, Ed remained quiet. He didn't want to make more unnecessary racket. He felt two quick tugs on the sleeve of his coat. The dark seemed to shift before him, and move away. He followed the movement, knowing it was Bernice. She wanted him to follow her.

Up ahead, a murky band stretched across a small section of the black. The bar, most likely. Above that, he recognized the mirror, though it looked like mucky water. They were moving toward the front of the tavern, taking small steps. But Bernice had already gotten quite a ways ahead of him.

Ed started to pick up his pace.

A scratching click came from his left, followed by a burst of light. Ed turned, squinting at the guttering flame. It moved through the darkness, thinning when it touched the end of what looked like a cigar. In the match's orange spread, he recognized Mary's face. Eyes closed, her lips were puckered around the cigar. Her heavy cheeks worked as she puffed the cigar to life. It looked as if she were lying atop the bar, on her side. He thought he saw her bare, thick legs bent below her waist, knees pointing at Ed.

The flame shook and died. When the absence of light returned, Ed saw quick flashes each time he blinked. The distorted, glowing dot of the cigar, brightened for a moment with the sound of a heavy breath. Pink streaks of Mary's face appeared for a moment before vanishing when the cherry blot of the cigar dimmed.

"Hello, Eddie-baby," he heard Mary say in that husky voice of hers.

The sweet odor of cigar smoke carried over to Ed. It made him want to fire up his pipe.

"Mary," he said in a casual voice.

"It's good to see you," she said. "Been a while."

"A couple days."

"Too many, you ask me. Been busy digging, I suppose?"

"I have."

"That's a good boy."

"What are you up to, Mary?"

"Been waiting on you," she said. "Thought you might've come sooner, so I made sure I was ready. Was beginning to think you weren't going to show."

"Waiting on me?"

"Yeah. We know why you're here, Eddie-baby."

Ed felt a burst of ice around his heart. They knew he'd come with Bernice to kill the vampire.

"You found her and have come to tell the master," Mary said.

Ed nearly groaned with relief. Mary obviously hadn't seen Bernice, didn't even know she was here. That was good. They still had surprise working in their favor.

"That's right," Ed said.

"But he already knows, and he's very pleased. He wants you to join us, Eddie-baby. Not like them, Eddie, but like me. You and I will be together, protecting our masters during the day and ruling by their side at night. Plainfield will once again become theirs, its citizens will be our slaves."

"I see."

"Do you?" she asked. "I don't think you really do."

He heard her inhale, saw the burning nub of the cigar brighten for a moment. She let out a breath. "Aren't you tired of being the laughingstock of Plainfield, Eddie-baby?"

"I'm not the..."

"You are, and you know it." He heard the bar groan from Mary's body shifting. "Now, have *I* ever ridiculed you, baby?"

"No."

"And I never would, Eddie. We're alike. We're outsiders in our home town. Hasn't it always felt as if you didn't belong here?"

Ed supposed he'd always felt that way. "Well, yeah."

"Me too. But I stayed. And it was so easy for me to rob these goody two-shoes of their devoted husbands. Didn't take much. Just let them have me and do what they wished. They even *paid* me to ruin their good marriages. And now, we can do that together. It starts tonight with the full moon. The master will awaken his bride, and their time will be again. Plainfield, as we know it, will be no more. And Eddie-baby? We'll get to be a part of it; we'll be gods in this drab shithole. Together."

He heard soft squeaking sounds. The kind naked skin might make sliding across wood. Two heavy thuds followed that Ed thought were Mary's feet hitting the floor. The glowing tip of the cigar moved from high to low.

"No more laughing at you behind your back," she said. There were scratchy noises, like footsteps on a dusty floor, moving closer. "No more making you feel stupid. Worthless. You'll be above them, for once in your life, Eddie. Nobody will ever tease you again."

She's coming over here.

Where was Bernice?

Ed looked around, but could only see darkness. She was hidden among it somewhere, but Ed had no clue as to where.

And if Mary had any idea Bernice was with him, she gave no indication.

"Now, do you *see?*" Mary asked. "Or would you like to *feel?*"

The red tip of the cigar seemed dimmer as if it were covered by a wispy cap. Ed heard a tapping sound. The wrapper of ash dropped off. The glow was much brighter in front of Ed.

"Here I am," Mary said.

Ed gulped. "Yep." He quietly moved the crossbow to his left hand, slipping his finger over the trigger.

Mary chuckled softly. "Feel me," she said, "for the first time. You will be able to feel me forever."

"Mary," started Ed, but he stopped when he felt fingers curl around the wrist of his right hand, raising it.

"Take this glove off, baby," Mary said.

The glove was pulled from his hand. He winced as it dragged across his busted blisters. The glove smacked the floor a moment later.

Mary's fingers glided across the bandages fastened around his. "Aw, baby," she said. "Your hand's hurt."

"Yeah," Ed said in a groggy voice.

"From digging so much?"

"Yeah."

He felt the soft pecks of her lips start at the tip of his finger and move down to his wrist. When she stopped, she said, "Better?"

"It helps," he said.

Mary laughed. "I want you to feel me with your *skin*."

His hand was pulled slowly forward. It touched a mound of flesh that felt springy, yet soft. It sunk under his fingers.

Mary released a shuddery sigh. "There you go."

Something hard pressed the palm of his hand as his fingers squeezed.

It's her damn tit!

He'd never felt anything like it. Kneading the plump softness, he enjoyed how it seemed to bobble in his hand. The skin of Mary's tit became slick and warm as Ed played with it.

Fingers gently grabbed his wrist again.

"Now this," said Mary in a scratchy voice. She sounded winded.

Ed's arm was lowered. His finger ran down the jiggly firmness of her stomach, dipped into her navel, and moved through a tuft of fuzzy hair. Ed knew what he was touching and felt himself tremble. His lungs felt too big for his chest, making his breaths turn squeaky.

"It's okay, Eddie," said Mary. "Don't be nervous. Go on..."

She released his wrist, leaving his finger nestled in the bristly hair.

She wants me to stick my finger in her.

"I know you want to," she said, voice quivering. "If you do it, I'll know you're one of us."

Mary shook against his finger when he moved it down a fraction. The tip hovered above the edge of her pubic mound, gently tapping the moist cleft. Any lower he would be inside.

Bernice!

Bernice was probably watching this vulgar display transpire. Unless something had happened to her. He didn't think she'd been harmed, but he couldn't know for sure. But if she was fine, why hadn't she come forward and put a stop to it? Hopefully she hadn't been able to see everything. Maybe Mary's bulk blocked her from seeing much, or the dark was too much for her to decipher what Ed had done.

And what he was about to do.

Ed's finger slipped lower, dipping into a fleshy fold of wet heat.

Moaning, Mary slapped a hand down on Ed's shoulder. Her hand gripped his coat to hold on.

Ed moved his finger around the sopping softness, delving deeper.

Mary made cooing sounds as she shook. "Oh, Eddie...baby, do it."

He moved his finger in as far as it would go. His knuckle bumped the dripping walls of her sex.

"That's it, Eddie," gasped Mary.

"Yeah," said Ed.

Her hand moved down his chest. He felt her fingers move over something hard and round. Something rustled like thin paper.

"Wha...?" said Mary. "Is this...?"

He felt her grab something on his chest, lift it. She sniffed, then gagged. "This is...garlic?" Yanking the foul-smelling necklace, the string snapped at the back of his neck. He heard it rustle when she threw it. Somewhere in the room, it banged when it landed.

He'd forgotten all about the garlic wreath. How had she not noticed it sooner? How had he stopped smelling it?

"You *bastard!*"

Before Ed could say anything, Mary punched the blazing end of the cigar against his neck. Intense heat made sizzling sounds on his skin. As Ed screamed, Mary twisted the cigar, grinding the hot pain deeper into his neck.

Ed's other hand flew up. He meant to push her off, but his arm bumped hers, which caused his finger to yank the trigger of the crossbow.

There was a sound like a knife being stabbed into raw beef.

Mary stumbled away from Ed. His finger slid out of her.

He heard a faint click somewhere in the dark. Light exploded in the room.

Blinded, Ed stumbled back. His ass knocked against a table, tipping it over. The wooden legs shot up, striking the backs of his legs and throwing them into the air. Ed's back crashed through the wood, pounded the concrete floor. The crossbow bounced away from his hand.

Winded and hurt, Ed's head bobbed as he peered down his body. Between his legs sprawled on broken shards of the table, he saw Mary's beefy, naked thighs. Crooked ribbons of blood flowed down their pale shapes. His eyes followed the dark streams up to the jutting tip in her throat. The stake had entered slightly under her chin. Her hands slapped at the hunk of wood as blood coated her fingers. When her mouth opened on a quacking gasp, he saw wood had pushed her tongue aside on its way up.

But even with the stake jabbed up through her like that, she hadn't fallen.

"Ed!"

Ed turned. Bernice, on the opposite side of the room, had her arm extended toward a metal box. Her fingers still pinched on the toggle switch.

That's where she's been. Trying to find a damn light.

He wished she'd found it sooner.

Bernice looked at Mary, face twisting into repulsion. "What did you do!?!"

Ed had no answer for her. His arm had twitched and even against Bernice's warnings, he'd accidentally fired a stake through Mary's throat.

Sitting up, Ed pushed aside broken table portions. He held the crossbow up, saw the strap dangling loosely, and sighed. "Damn," he muttered.

Mary made sloughy, breathing attempts. "...*yoush...sonsh..of-ah...bishhh...*"

Ed looked up. Her massive, crimson-soaked breasts hung heavily, stretching the skin that connected them to her chest. Now those flabs of skin acted as ramps for blood flowing from her throat.

Mary's arms hung stiffly at her sides, hands balled into fists. Her eyes gleamed hatred toward Ed.

"Oh, shit," he said.

Mary shuffled forward.

"Get up, Ed!" shouted Bernice, tugging at the scimitar dangling from her hip. She stepped past the back room door an instant before it shot off its hinges and flew across the room. The door smacked the wall on the opposite side and stayed there, as if an entrance to another room had suddenly appeared.

The vampire emerged from the doorway in a swirling cloud. It was dressed in the same black, old-fashioned suit. Fuzzy, blue hands crossed at its chest, dark claws curled upward—it seemed to float along the carpet of smoke. Its bow-shaped ears flicked this way and that through its thick, coal-black hair. Its nose flaps looked moist as they tittered above its curved jowls that exposed its colossus fangs.

Bernice froze. The color drained from her face. "My God Almighty, it's you."

The vampire's head snapped toward Bernice, hissing when it spotted her. Its eyes burned red. Ed understood the creature somehow recognized Bernice, and wasn't pleased to see her.

Then hands slapped Ed's chest, clutching handfuls of his coat. He was hoisted from the ground, raised high. Looking down, he could see the top of Mary's head below him.

Everybody in Plainfield knew Mary was strong, but he doubted anybody had a true inclination just how much.

Mary spun around and released Ed. He flew the short distance toward the bar, hit the top and slid over the side. His back smashed the shelves on the other side, then he dropped, landing on the floor behind the bar. Tin mugs and glass bottles came down with him, clamoring and shattering when they hit the floor.

Though Ed was riddled with pain, he couldn't stay on the floor, no matter how much he wanted to. Rolling over, he pushed himself up. Then he gripped the lip of the bar, pulling himself to his knees.

His eyes found Bernice. She stood several yards away and hadn't moved.

But the vampire had.

On all fours, its body popped and trembled under the old, black garments. The snout, which moments ago had looked compressed against its dingy, pale-blue face, now seemed to stretch outward into an elongated maw. Sharp teeth flashed under its quivering lips. The three-fingered claws fattened and swelled into paws.

My God, it's changing...

Into something that resembled a beastly, monstrous dog. The black clothes sagged on its emaciated body, showing patches of bristly fur spread across its gray flesh. A tail that looked more like a ribbed worm sprinkled in wooly hair, extended from its rump like some kind of atrocious growth.

The creature stretched its muscles, shook like a dog after a bath, and stepped out of its clothes.

Bernice stood, watching in frozen horror as the vampire-dog stalked toward her. The big balls of garlic looked like a ruffled collar around her neck.

"Bernice! Snap out of..."

A hand clutched Ed's throat, cutting off his voice. Ed moved his eyes up.

Mary, looming over him, was soaked in blood. "Bashtardsh…"

Then Ed was pulled across the bar, and thrown to the floor. Before he could get up, he felt a firm kick on his ass. It knocked him forward. His chin scraped the concrete.

Growls came from somewhere nearby. Bernice screamed.

I have to help her!

Ed looked in time to see Bernice narrowly avoid a vicious bite as the vampire dog lunged. Twirling away, Bernice swung the sword behind her in a blind swipe. The blade glanced off the dog's boney shoulder, leaving a gash that emitted smoke. The vampire howled as if in pain.

Blade must be made of silver.

"*Nuuuh!*" Mary groaned. She turned in Bernice's direction and started toward her. Her legs moved stiffly, as if her first time walking. She made slurping gasps with each breath.

Ed reached for Mary's leg, curling an arm around her ankle.

Mary kept moving, dragging Ed.

"Stop, Mary!" he cried from the floor.

The big woman didn't stop. She walked slow and stilted toward Bernice.

Ed spun on his side. He tried planting the heels of his boots against the floor, but they slid easily across. Twisting around, Ed squatted, hugging her leg. He let out a long grunt, teeth grinding, and pulled the thick leg.

Mary couldn't be stopped.

Beginning to panic, Ed caught sight of the table his back had shattered. Amongst the debris, he spotted the crossbow on its side. He released his insignificant hold of Mary, rolled sideways, and stopped beside the weapon.

He looked up to check on Bernice.

The older woman was running at the dog, the long, bowed knife poised above her head. She unleashed a warrior's cry as she swung down. The creature's head jerked to the right, missed the swooping blade, and snapped its teeth on Bernice's forearm.

Bernice shrieked as the creature's sharp teeth dug into her flesh. It jerked its head viciously from side to side. Ed figured had it not been for the garlic, those teeth might have found her neck.

Bernice's sleeve hung around the beast's snout in shreds as blood pumped and sprayed. The blade canted to the side, her fingers losing their grip. As the scimitar dropped out of her hand, her other hand shot forward, catching it by the handle. Then she swung the weapon back, severing the vampire dog's tail at the halfway point. The halved nub spurted blood in a high chute that spattered the ceiling.

The beastly dog's teeth pulled away from Bernice's arm. Turning a circle, the creature yipped and bit at its blood-spewing nub, as if trying to catch what it was losing.

"Nooosh!" Mary slurped.

Ed took one of the table's legs that had broken off and, with both hands, slammed it on his knee. It snapped in two.

Bernice stepped around the side of the vampire dog, raising the scimitar up in a sacrificial pose. The sharp underside was positioned above its scrawny neck.

As Ed got to his knees, Mary bumped into Bernice's back, hugging her burly arms around Bernice's front. Bernice's breasts were squished under the X-shape of Mary's blood-streaked forearms. Choking on her groans, Bernice dropped the blade. It made a resounding clamor when it hit the hard floor.

Bernice was spun around, Mary now blocking her. But in that quick glimpse, Ed noticed Bernice's face was already turning pink.

Damn woman's going to crush her!

"Mary!" Ed called. "Let her go!"

Mary ignored Ed's shouts and continued to violently cuddle Bernice in her strong arms. At her feet, Bernice's legs kicked the air, her dress fluttering around her knee-high stockings. Below Bernice's shoes, the vampire had dropped onto its side and was licking its spilled blood from the floor.

Ed, remembering how Bernice had loaded the weapon, clicked the shorter chunk of wood in place without any trouble. The wood leg sat a little crooked, and the tip wasn't filed to a point, but it was jagged and sharp and would hurt somebody.

Ed raised the crossbow to his shoulder. He had no time to make a good aim. But with Mary's back to him, he had plenty of space for a target. Unless Mary turned at the last minute, then he'd run the risk of hitting Bernice.

Please, don't move!

Not allowing himself to balk, he squeezed the trigger.

The string snapped back, making his hand jerk. The modified stake was launched. He'd expected it to peg Mary somewhere on her wide back.

But the wood punched into the center of Mary's buttocks, disappearing between the tubby dunes of meat as if swallowed.

Mary unleashed a startled grunt, dropping Bernice on her side. Coughing and gagging, Bernice rolled away from Mary and the vampire dog.

Ed continued to stare at Mary's naked rump. Blood began to drip from the valley of her buttocks. A trickle at first, it quickly escalated to a steady flow. Wobbling, Mary turned around and leered at Ed. Her eyes were wide and white.

"Oh, no," Ed muttered.

Mary lifted a shaky arm, pointing. Her lips pulled back. The teeth were slick with blood. Before Mary could speak, Bernice appeared behind her. The curved blade rose above Mary's shoulder.

Ed heard a quick whistle of cutting air. The blade appeared for a flash of an instant at Mary's neck, then it was gone and Mary's head was spinning away from her neck as the ragged stump left behind pumped thick surges of blood.

The vampire cocked its head into the air and released an earsplitting howl that shook the walls. Glass shattered. The tables and chairs trembled. Ed felt vibrations in the floor underneath him.

The canine-like snout began to retract back into its skull. Its legs stretched, paws extending into sausage link fingers.

Turning to look at Bernice, Ed screamed when he spotted Mary's headless body hobbling toward him, arm still raised, finger still extended. Her chubby foot kicked her detached head aside as she shambled closer.

Ed, hollering hard enough to strain his neck muscles, crab-crawled in reverse. His eyes remained glued to Mary's blood-soaked, naked flesh. Though the uneven neck stub still spouted blood, it wasn't as heavy as before.

Mary made a few more steps before stopping. Her body swayed forward, then stumbled back. It looked as if she were about to go forward again, but suddenly dropped backward.

Mary's body pounded the floor with a heavy, jiggling thud.

Ed stared at Mary's blood-soaked carcass for several seconds. The sound of Bernice's heavy bottomed shoes scuffing across the floor brought his attention to her. She stepped around the side of the vampire. He was mostly back to his normal form, though not entirely. Down on all fours, his head hung low to the floor as his skin crackled and snapped back to shape.

Bernice turned to the vampire, unhurt arm raising her blade.

"It's over, for good," she said in a winded voice.

Ed felt himself smile as she started to bring the scimitar down.

"Nana!"

Bernice froze. Ed froze. Both turned their heads.

Timmy stood between the frames of the backdoor. A horrified grimace split his face.

-31-

"Timmy?" Bernice said, lowering the blade by her side.

Ed saw shame on her face, as if Timmy had walked in on her dancing naked.

"Wha...?" Timmy shook his head. He blinked as if it would make what he was seeing go away. "What are you doing?"

Robin Hicks pushed her way past Timmy, carrying a prybar in one hand. She paused a few steps ahead of the boy. Her eyes scanned the room. First spotting Bernice, they jumped to Ed, then back to Bernice. Then they lowered, and from how her expression dropped away to shock, Ed figured she'd noticed the vampire.

"Oh God..." she said, voice turning shrill. "What is that?"

Now Timmy looked. His eyes rounded.

"Timmy," said Bernice. "I...didn't want you to see this. I figured..." She took a deep breath, swayed slightly. "I figured I could sit you down and explain things one day while we were at the store."

Timmy raised a palsied hand, pointing at the floor. "Is that a...?" He made a sour face, as if tasting something gross. Maybe it was the knowledge he was about to ask his grandmother if she was standing over a wounded vampire that had disgusted him.

Ed assumed so.

"Yes," Bernice said. "It's a vampire."

Robin brought her empty hand to her face, fingers covering her mouth. "My God," she whispered.

Ed stayed sitting on the floor, afraid to move. He wanted to say something that might help Bernice explicate the situation, but he knew anything said couldn't make the queer scene Timmy stumbled upon make any sense.

He checked on the vampire. It had completely changed back to normal. On its hands and knees, it seemed to be waiting for the final swipe of Bernice's blade.

"How did you know to find us here?" Bernice asked.

Timmy stared at the vampire. The color had left his face.

"Timmy?" Bernice said.

Blinking, Timmy shook his head as if waking up. "Huh?"

"How'd you know where we were?"

"We were at Goult's…"

"Why?"

"Robin wanted to see her aunt and uncle…and we were about to leave when Peter came out of nowhere…"

"Peter?" Bernice said. She gave Ed a quick glance, then stepped toward Timmy. "You saw Peter?"

"Yeah…he said…Eddie would be here."

"Timmy, listen to me. You can't believe a word Peter has said to you. He belongs to the vampire now."

"What?"

"The only words that will come out of his mouth are lies. Whatever he told you to get you here, wasn't true."

Robin shook her head. "No. That's not right. Peter said Eddie has Dorothy."

Bernice sighed. "Not true."

"He said we had to come save her!" Robin's voice was near hysterical.

"Robin," said Bernice, "he lied."

"No." She shook her head. "No."

"Dorothy belongs to the vampire as well."

"STOP TALKING!" Robin grabbed a handful of her hair, pulling it, her scalp bulged.

"Robin," said Timmy. "Calm down."

Staring at the floor, Robin's eyes were big and wild. Head twitching, she huffed, lips flapping.

"Timmy?" Bernice asked. "Where's Peter now?"

"Uh..." The boy looked behind him. Facing his grandmother again, he shrugged. His limp arms smacked against his legs. "He was behind us...I don't know where he went."

"He's close," said Bernice. "Probably watching us. Waiting to see what we're going to do next." Bernice held out the scimitar.

Getting onto his knees, Ed prepared to stand.

Then movement caught his eye. He looked past Timmy to the back door.

Dorothy sauntered in, walking sluggish and rigid as if in a trance. In a white Sunday dress, she moved between Robin and Timmy. Fresh blood was spattered across the white ruffles in the front.

Both kids noticed Dorothy at the same time.

"Dorothy?" Robin said in a scared and helpless voice. "What are you doing?"

Robin went to follow her, then looked down. And screamed.

Ed saw it too—being dragged by a paw in Dorothy's hand. Its head slid across the dirty floor, leaving a wide path of smeared blood behind it.

A coyote. Its throat had been torn open.

At first, Ed thought the vampire girl was heading toward him, but she turned in Bernice's direction.

"Dorothy?" Robin shrieked. "What have you done?"

"I told you," said Bernice. "Peter made her..."

"No!" Robin shouted.

"...a vampire."

"You shut up, you old hag!"

"Robin, she's not human anymore!" Bernice stepped back, keeping her hurt arm close to her side. "Look at her. Can't you see that?" She began to lift the scimitar with the other.

Seeing this, Robin screamed. She went to run at Bernice. Timmy grabbed her arm, the one clutching the prybar.

"Stop!" He said, straining to hold her back. "I know you see her! Can't you tell Nana's not lying?"

"Let me go!" Robin shouted.

Bernice, turning sideways, kept her eyes on Robin. "She's one of the undead! The sweet Dorothy we all knew is gone forever."

Dorothy, as if she were oblivious to Bernice and her blade, knelt down in front of the vampire. She slid the coyote's mangled corpse over to the vampire's mouth. Giving her an appreciative nod, it slid its hands under the coyote, lifted the gorged neck to its mouth, and dug in.

The slurping sounds of the vampire's feeding carried over Robin's screams.

"Dorothy!" Robin cried. "Why are you doing this?"

"She's not Dorothy!" Bernice pleaded. "I promise you, Dorothy's gone!"

"It's not true. That's Dorothy!" Robin tried to pull her arm free, but Timmy held on with both hands. "Dorothy! It's me, Robin! Snap out of it!"

"Robin," said Timmy, groaning. "Stop!"

Robin turned to Timmy, and stepped back. Not expecting this, the boy stumbled to the side, hands slipping off Robin's arm. As he went to make another grab, Robin shoved his chest. Timmy stumbled back, hitting the bar, and tumbling to the floor.

As Ed started to get up, Robin ran. By the time he got to his feet, she was halfway to Bernice, who was starting to bring the scimitar down to Dorothy's small neck.

Robin screamed.

Bernice might've succeeded in beheading the little girl, but she stole a fleeting glance behind her. Had she not done that, she wouldn't have twisted slightly so she could see.

And the prybar might've caved in the back of her head, instead of whacking the side of her face. The metal bar made a *thunk* sound when it hit Bernice. Though it hadn't bashed her skull inward, the impact had been hard enough to spin Bernice like a top. Her stomach hit the edge of a table, folding her at the waist. The scimitar flew from her hand, hitting a chair and bouncing off.

Sliding down the table's surface, Bernice made lethargic attempts to hold on but brought the table down with her. The wood clattered and crunched when it hit the floor.

Yelling, Timmy got to his feet as Ed dashed past Robin. He stared down at Bernice. A lump on her temple was oozing blood.

"No," he muttered. Crouching, he put his gloveless hand to her neck, fingers on her pulse. Though it was faint, he felt the thump of her heart.

Looking back at Timmy, he said, "She's okay."

"Thank God," Timmy said.

They shared a relieved look, then turned to Robin. The blonde teenager dropped the prybar. It clamored loudly when it hit the floor. Dropping to her knees, she held out her hands. Dorothy's back was to her, watching the vampire as Robin reached for her shoulder.

"Dorothy?" she said quietly.

Dorothy whipped around, gnashing her fangs. She let out a throaty hiss.

Screaming, Robin scurried back on her knees. Dorothy lunged for her cousin, but Ed jumped in front of Robin, catching Dorothy in his arms. They rolled across the ground. Ed released her during their tussle. Coming to a halt on his stomach, he shoved the floor and got to his knees.

Dorothy was already crouched, arms up and ready to strike again.

Where's the crossbow!?!

Ed spotted it on the floor just out of reach.

Dorothy caught him looking at it. As he wildly crawled toward the weapon, Dorothy sprang forward like a cat going for a rabbit. His fingers tapped the wooden stock, then the girl slammed into him.

His fingers stroked the weapon, barely missing.

Ed's back whammed the floor, knocking the air out of his lungs. Dorothy came down on top of him, scrambling up his midsection, pinning his arms down between her bare, scrawny legs. Though she was frail in size, she felt as big as Mary, crushing him.

She leaned over. Hissed. A putrid stench gusted against his face. Her fangs dripped saliva-thinned blood on his face. Thin shreds of flesh were stuck in her gum line, coyote hair jutted like fuzzy growths.

Gripping his hair, she jerked his head sideways. Briefly, Ed wondered what happened to his hat.

"Watch," she said.

Before his eyes could focus, Robin screamed.

-32-

Crouched by Nana, Timmy saw a blur of movement in the corner of his eye. He looked to the right and saw Dorothy knock Eddie onto his back. She crawled up his chest, spreading her legs. Her knees touched the floor, trapping Eddie's arms.

Timmy's mind was a whirlwind of incomplete thoughts. He tried to lock one down, hoping it was an idea on how to save everybody.

Robin wouldn't be any help. She'd succumbed to a squealing wreck in front of his eyes. Mashing her hair to the sides of her face, she watched as Dorothy forced Eddie's head to turn toward them.

Looking around the floor, Timmy had no idea what he was trying to find. When he spotted the small sword Nana had been using on the floor, he realized that was it. He ran for the blade, leaning over. His hand was near enough to grab the handle.

"I wouldn't do that, Timmy-boy."

Peter!

Sounded as if his voice had come from...above.

Looking up, Timmy spotted Peter hiding in the rafters, arms and legs spread and grasping a beam, a flabby spider in a web of wood girders. Peter smiled, brandishing a mouthful of enlarged teeth. A curved fang hung lower on each side.

"It's time to play," said Peter.

Then Robin screamed.

It was cut short by the surge of wind that threw Timmy aside. He hit the floor and rolled a few times, coming to a stop on his stomach.

Looking up, he saw Peter had managed to knock Robin onto her back and get on top of her in a blink. His crotch wedged between Robin's kicking legs, Peter tore her blouse in a savage swipe to unveil a thick, heavily padded bra. The skirt had fallen back on her legs, showing a lot of tawny skin as they thrashed the air.

"Get away from her!" Timmy yelled.

Peter's head twisted impossibly around. Bulges of skin appeared on the side of his neck like a stack of dough. "Don't worry, buddy. You'll get your turn."

Timmy tingled inside, but also felt a wave of nausea.

"Help me, Timmy!" Robin cried. "Please!"

"Timmy!" Eddie's voice. "Get him...*ah!*"

Dorothy, holding his head by the hair, bashed Eddie's head against the floor. Not hard enough to do any damage, but it was enough to shut him up.

Timmy looked at Peter in time to see him ripping off Robin's bra.

His breath snagged in his throat.

Damn, oh, damn.

Robin's breasts were full and springy, her nipples tiny rigid dots. The fleshy humps looked painted in white cream and jiggled as Peter began tugging at her skirt.

Timmy shook his head. This couldn't be happening. It was wrong and so unreal. Like a nightmare he couldn't escape. He prayed to wake up in his bed, but knew it wouldn't happen.

And Robin...

Timmy couldn't stop staring at her breasts. Their large size surprised him, made him feel hot and squirmy inside. He imagined how they'd feel in his hands as his thumbs poked her turgid nipples, pushing them into the plump skin, and watching them plop back out.

Robin's shrieks hurt Timmy's ears, but did nothing to make him move. He thought of *The Vampire's Graveyard Kiss*, those lurid panels flicking through his mind. The woman was moaning as the vampire took her from behind. The drawings began to change, taking new details.

Now the woman was Robin, and the vampire...was Timmy.

Peter glanced back at Timmy, saw he hadn't moved, and laughed again. "Ready for this?"

Timmy's voice barely registered when he said, "Peter...no..." He doubted anybody other than himself had heard it at all.

Peter, holding Robin down by her throat, used his other hand to reach between her legs.

Don't do it, Peter!

But the warning never made it to Timmy's mouth. And he watched Peter tear Robin's underwear apart. The tattered garment clung to his fingers like webbing. He shook his hand, freeing his fingers of the silky shreds.

It was dark between Robin's thrashing thighs, but Timmy could faintly make out the bushy tuft of hair crowning the curve of flesh. At Goult's, he hadn't been able to see anything past the white band of her underwear.

As he looked at the tattered ribbons between her legs, he spotted a dark slit...

"Well, look at that," said Peter. "She has *hair* there..." He sniffed. "And she smells sweet. Like peaches."

Timmy rolled onto his side, and realized he had an erection. It jutted painfully against the inside of his pants.

"Tell you what," said Peter, talking loudly over Robin's cries. "I'll let you go first, Timmy-boy."

"Me?"

Peter's head moved down, then up. The sharp teeth, inhuman eyes, reptilian bumpy skin, and lashing, snake-like tongue barely registered with Timmy. He knew he should be terrified of the thing his best friend had become. But it hardly seemed to matter in this moment.

"You know what to do," said Peter. "We read about it in Eddie's magazines. And if you can't remember, I'll tell you how. I learned a lot with Dorothy."

With Dorothy? Did he mean…?

Dorothy nodded. "I pretended I didn't like it, but I really did. Can't wait for more."

Robin groaned with a mixture of disgust and grief.

"Come on, Timmy. You know you *want* to. Just stuff your wiener in her. Right here." Peter pointed to the slit that was like a winking eye under a fluff of bristly hair. "You'll *love* it. Feels so soft and tight and warm. After you pop in there, I'll let you taste her blood. And that's even better. Just like Dorothy, I bet Robin's blood'll taste sugary-sweet. The master says the fear is what makes it taste like that." Peter trembled. "Just thinking about it makes me wild."

I have to stop him.

Timmy pushed against the floor, getting to his knees.

"That's it, buddy," said Peter. "Come on."

Timmy saw himself climbing on top of Robin, feeling her hot, naked flesh squirming underneath him. She'd be slick with sweat, feeling as if she'd just come from a hot bath. His skin would slide across hers.

It made Timmy tingle deep inside.

I… have… to stop him.

Timmy got to his feet. Looking down, Timmy saw the front of his pants pointed out like a witch's hat. If he unzipped his pants and freed his penis, he knew it'd feel so much better. Putting it inside of Robin…well that would be amazing.

But Eddie's watching. And Dorothy.

And...

The vampire. Now on its feet, the vampire stood with its arms folded over its midsection. Watching like a proud father at a wedding.

I have to...stop...

Timmy took a wobbly step.

"There you go!" Peter made hooting sounds, just like he did when they used to play cowboys and Indians.

Timmy shambled forward.

The room was no longer a tumult of Robin's screams. From the floor, she now watched Timmy with piteous eyes that twinkled from her tears. Her sobs made the pale mounds of her breasts jitter. Her legs, open and spread around Peter's wide girth, lay on the floor in tawny arcs.

But her eyes...

Her eyes looked heartbroken and betrayed. "Timmy..." she said. "I've always liked you."

Timmy tilted his head, unable to grasp what she'd just said.

Robin took a deep breath, continuing, "Even when I sat with you for your parents, I liked you. I knew it was wrong because you were younger...but you were just so different. You seemed older than what you really were, and more mature than a lot of the boys I know."

"Shut up," said Peter. "Don't screw with his head."

Robin ignored him. "Remember the last time I sat with you? The dress? I wore that for you, Timmy. I wanted you to see me in it. I bought it just for that night. I hoped you just...I don't know, do something. I was afraid to make the first move, because I didn't know what you'd do. But nothing happened, and that was okay with me too. Your mother called mine that night. She told my mom I couldn't sit with you anymore because she felt I was getting to be...inappropriate around you! And she was right, really.

Because that night…I wanted to…I wanted you to touch me…"

"He's going to touch you now, Robin," said Peter. "So, you're going to get your wish."

I can't believe I'm going to do this!

Finding the zipper on his pants, he tugged it down.

Seeing this, Robin closed her eyes. She sucked in her bottom lip as she cried some more. When she opened her eyes again, they were focused intently on Timmy. "Okay, Timmy. I want it too…you can…have me."

Peter howled. "Hear that, Timmy-boy? You can *have* her! Hot damn! Get in there. Show her what you're made of!"

Robin's legs parted even more. Her hands, which had been gripped onto Peter's, lowered to her skirt. She pulled it higher, fully exposing her groin. The small mound of hair was pale on top of the sleek, curved skin.

Timmy reached into the gap of his pants, fingers brushing the stiffness inside. A warm fluttery sensation filled his groin.

Peter's forked tongue slithered over his lips. Two sharp fangs nearly filled the space inside his mouth.

The toes of Timmy's shoe bumped something hard. He looked down at the floor.

A metal bar.

A tizzy of images rushed rapidly through his mind—the talks with Robin, their kissing and holding hands. Her big smile and boisterous laughter. Her confession from moments ago. He remembered Peter. He remembered Peter attacking Robin.

He remembered Nana and Eddie.

He remembered Dorothy, and…the vampire.

The tongue.

The fangs.

It felt as if a curtain opened inside Timmy's head and light spread through the dark alcoves where his morbid temptations lurked.

And now Timmy's penis was shrinking in his hand. He released his dwindling organ and tugged his hand from his fly.

Peter was too occupied by his own perverse laughter to notice Timmy crouching down and picking up the prybar. With the heavy tool, Timmy felt a smidge braver. Those lurid sensations were fading quicker now.

He walked right up to Peter, raising the bar high.

Dorothy yelled for Peter to turn around.

Peter stopped laughing as if a switch had been flicked. He looked up at Timmy. Red glowered deep in the pits of his dull sockets. "You dummy," Peter said.

Timmy swung down with all he had.

And his wrist was caught by a gargantuan hand the size of a catcher's mitt. Three fingers curled around his fist, twisting his wrist awkwardly to the side. A severe burst of pain seized his arm. Fingers locking, the prybar fell from his hand.

As Timmy was spun around, he glimpsed Robin squirming, trying to get up, shouting, "Timmy!"

But Peter kept her down.

Still holding Timmy's wrist, the vampire stretched his arm the wrong way across his chest and pulled him back. His elbow was torqued painfully to the side, his arm slanting away from his shoulder.

"Enough," the vampire said in a voice that reminded Timmy of grinding stones. *"It is near time for my darling to return to me."*

"Aw," said Peter, pouting. "But I was about to have some fun."

The vampire backhanded Peter with the hand not bending Timmy's arm, knocking his head to the side. Peter kept his head down, staring at the floor like a dog chastised by its master.

"*Bring the girl with you. I'll take the boy.*"

"No!" Timmy yelled. "I'm not—"

The vampire pulled Timmy's arm, making him holler. It felt as if the vampire wanted to rip his arm from the socket.

Eddie and Robin yelled for the vampire to release Timmy. Instead, it kept tugging Timmy's arm, the tendons in his shoulder stretching.

"Okay!" Timmy shouted. "Okay!"

The vampire stopped pulling his arm.

"*It's time to begin.*"

Nodding, Peter stuck his arms under Robin and easily lifted her. Robin thrashed and bucked in the cradle of his arms, screaming, as she pounded his shoulders. Peter made a face, as if annoyed by a pesky mosquito buzzing in his face.

Putting his back to the vampire, Peter carried Robin through the open back door. Rapid flapping sounds and a high-pitched squeal like a broken engine came from outside. Then there was a loud gust that threw dirt and debris into the tavern. After that, silence.

The vampire started to follow, forcing Timmy along by his twisted arm.

"Master?" Dorothy said.

Pausing, the vampire turned around to face the little girl. She straddled Eddie, who had given up fighting. He stared off the side, his eyes blank.

"*Yes, child?*"

"What about these two?"

The vampire looked at Ed, then turned and stared where Nana lay on the floor. The upturned table tilted beside her like a wooden ramp. One arm slanted against the lopsided table, the other, mangled arm, was folded over her stomach. Timmy glimpsed the slow rise and fall of her weak breaths.

"Kill them both."

"Yes, master."

"No," Timmy said. "Please, don't hurt them!"

Ignoring Timmy's pleas, the vampire started toward the door. Screaming, Timmy tried to break away from the vampire's powerful hold. It hurt his shoulder, made his elbow pull taut, but he didn't care. He wanted to save his grandmother, his friend.

Timmy was pulled through the doorway. Slapping at the frame, his fingers scraped across the wood paneling, pulling up paint. His fingers slipped off, and he was pulled into the night. The last thing he saw before the vampire took flight, carrying Timmy into the sky by his arm as if he were a chick snatched by hawk, was Dorothy's face dipping toward Eddie.

Her mouth had been open wide, the corners overextending back, fangs slavering.

-33-

Hot saliva dribbled in Ed's eyes. Wincing, he turned away, blinking. His lashes felt gummy, sticky as if glued. With her mouth so close, Ed could smell the awful flavor of her tongue, ghost miscellanies of whatever she'd been feeding on.

"Dorothy," he said. "Don't do this. My blood's not good."

"Smells fine to me," she said. Her tongue slithered over her bottom lip. A thick coating of slobber made her lip shimmer in the light. "Can't wait to taste…"

"But I ate a lot of garlic today."

"Liar." She sniffed. "Though I have no breath, I can smell your blood. It's hoary, insalubrious, but will taste divine as I drink from you. Your soul is blackened, and though yours beats, it is not alive. Mr. Gein, the living dead heart of Plainfield. Your dark soul will taste as fresh as one of virtue."

Ed stared at the little girl. Eyes closed, her lips were slightly parted, relishing the probable taste of his blood. She was a pubescent shell, hiding an olden lifeform behind the costume of a little girl.

"Who are you?" Ed asked.

Opening her eyes, she smiled sweetly, innocently. "Well, I'm just a little girl, Mr. Gein. Can't you tell?"

"Now who's the liar?"

Leaning back her head, she laughed. "You really are very inquisitive, aren't you?"

"Nope. I just know little girls don't talk like that."

"Ah," said Dorothy, looking at him again. Her face was pale except for the dark smudges of her evil eyes. "But you're not the imbecile you pretend to be, are you, Mr. Gein?"

"How do you mean?"

"You sulk around this abysmal town, your head down to avert eye contact, praying to God that nobody will speak to you. And why is that? Because you know you can't correlate with them in a way that suits them. Correct?"

Ed stared, unable to speak.

"Things that...turn *you* on are considered wicked and obscene to the likes of Plainfield." She shook her head, clucking her tongue. "Mr. Gein, how do you think these credulous people would respond if they knew you get a *thrill* out of digging up the dead bodies of their loved ones so you can dress in their skin?"

Ed could hardly breathe, and it had nothing to do with Dorothy's weight on his chest. "How...how do you know that?"

"Oh, Mr. Gein. We know everything about the darker side of the night. There's a whole other realm below the darkness. It's where we get to play. You dwell down there with us. When you're out on one of your graveyard jaunts, we're with you, supporting you as you crack open the caskets to rifle around the sleeping dead inside."

"You're not Dorothy...you're something else."

"Oh, Mr. Gein. Again, you show how perceptive you truly are." Smiling, she shook her head again. "It's not going to give me any great release to kill you. At least, not right away. However, I'm positive once I taste your blood, I'll forget all about my qualms."

Dorothy's face came at Ed, mouth wide. Her throaty hiss shot coyote blood on his face. As her mouth made for his throat, her rump lifted off Ed's stomach.

He thrust his hips, threw his knees high into her back.

Dorothy's snarl changed to confusion before she tumbled upward. Her stomach slid across his face. When her legs came up, Ed reached under the bottom of her dress, clutched her knees and flung her higher.

The little girl with the ancient mind hit the floor above his head, rolling.

Ed flipped onto his stomach, looking up. Dorothy, on all fours, rear turned to Ed, looked back at him. Mouth wide, she roared.

"Oh, shit..." Ed looked around, his head whipping this way and that. He spotted what he was looking for. Laughing wildly, he dove for his hat as Dorothy lunged for him. When her chest pounded the floor where his head had just been, his hand snatched the hat. Landing on his side, Ed rolled away, putting distance between him and Dorothy.

Slamming her fists on the floor, she let out a roar more enraged than the first.

Ed got onto his knees, put on his hat, and tugged it down to his eyebrows. He let out a long, quivery breath, feeling whole, once again.

Now he was ready.

Dorothy hopped onto her feet, legs bent and spread like a grasshopper. She jumped again, springing forward, arms outstretched.

Ed caught her under the arms, fell onto his back, and shoved his knee into her stomach. Dorothy let out a grunt as Ed pushed his knee up, bringing her over his head. Dorothy flipped, crashing onto the debris of the table Ed broke.

A jagged piece of wood the width of a baseball bat burst through her stomach, coated in dark blood. Screaming, Dorothy grabbed the hunk of wood.

Momentarily stunned by the accidental injury he'd caused, Ed watched as Dorothy gripped the spikey tip. Blood had made the wood slippery. Her fingers slid off whenever she tried to grab it.

Dorothy groaned. Ed figured it was partly from pain, but mostly aggravation. Giving up on removing the lodged hunk of wood, Dorothy sat up. The flat end of a table leg jutted from her back.

Ed got to his feet, groaning as well. Pain was his only reason. His body throbbed with each footstep toward Bernice's scimitar. It lay on the floor a few feet from Bernice's head. Crouching, he grabbed the knife. Before standing, he gave Bernice a quick inspection. Though the lump on her head had stopped bleeding, it looked as if a baseball had been inserted under her skin. Dark smudges of bruising ran down her cheek and across her brow.

Beaten, not dead.

With the scimitar clutched in his hand, the curl of blade pointing out, Ed faced Dorothy. Her back to him, she had gotten on her knees while he wasn't looking. He needed to get this over with before her shock wore off.

Ed strolled over to the busted table.

"Where are they heading, Dorothy?" he asked.

Her shoulders lifted, held a moment, then dropped. "You know where they're going."

"To the grave?"

"Again, Mr. Gein, you prove your intelligence. Since the master cannot cross the boundary to where his love rests, he will use one of them, the boy probably, to finish the task you were sent to do."

Just as I figured.

Dorothy turned her head, as if trying to watch him from over her shoulder. On the side of her face Ed could see, he noticed thin crimson tails hanging from her eyes. *Tears?* The dark lines reached her jawline, dripping onto her dress.

She seemed to know what was coming.

And Ed didn't hesitate.

The scimitar's blade bit through Dorothy's neck with a sharp whack. Dorothy's head plopped off, bouncing away from her shoulders as the ragged neck ejaculated gloppy black fluid. The headless body fell forward. Instead of landing flat, the wood protruding from her stomach hit the floor. Dorothy's body rested at an incline, neck spurting.

Other than that, nothing happened. Ed waited for some kind of triumphant response to the death. Frowning, he was disappointed by the lackluster repercussion. In the books and comics, the undead either burst into flames or exploded into clouds of ash, some kind of extravagant demise.

Sighing, Ed used the bottom of Dorothy's grimy dress to wipe the blade. He stood up, twirled the handle in his hand, and sighed again.

What a mess.

The Vampire of Plainfield

Geiner:

*What did Ed say to the cop who arrested him?
"Have a heart!"*

-34-

Ed nearly sped past his own driveway. Stamping the brakes, he jerked the wheel hard to the left and aimed the front of the truck between the trees. The truck bounced hard when it hit the dip between the road and his driveway.

Bernice jumped in the seat. Her head bonked the window.

Wincing, Ed expected her to sit up shouting. She didn't. Bernice was still out cold.

He stomped the gas. The tires scraped the gravel, throwing out a cloud of dust and rock behind them.

Please be all right.

The condition the vampire's maw had left Bernice's arm in was hard to look at. Deep rips in her flesh showed tendon and bone. He wished he knew if Bernice was in danger of turning into a vampire herself. He didn't think so, but Ed's knowledge on vampire lore came from the little Bernice had told him and what he'd read in made-up stories.

All those stories agreed on one thing—if the head vampire was killed, everything would be fine.

Almost everything. As Bernice had said, it was too late for Dorothy and Peter.

Don't have to worry about Dorothy anymore.

He'd taken care of her. He'd hated to do it, but felt no remorse that it had been done. Plus, she knew things about him. After she'd become a vampire, she seemed to know all of Ed's secrets.

Would Bernice know those things?

Ed hoped not. Kill the vampire, and Bernice would be fine.

The summer kitchen came into view, quickly growing in size as they got closer. He slammed both feet on the brake pedal. The wheels locked, but the truck kept sliding, scraping the dirt underneath, and throwing up walls of dust outside the windows.

Ed spotted Bernice's car where she'd parked it earlier. For a terrifying moment, he thought the truck was going to wham into its back end. He managed to maneuver the truck just enough to lightly scrape the car's rear. It made a soft squeak as they went by.

The truck came to a rocky halt.

Ed carried Bernice inside first. The house was dark and quiet. There was no time to light a lamp. Making his way through darkness, Ed entered the living room. He wanted to take her upstairs, but knew his back wouldn't handle it. So he dropped her down in his favorite chair, folding her hands on her lap.

"Sorry Bernice," he said. "Wish I had time to take care of you like you did me, but I don't."

"E...Ed?" Bernice said in a weak and tired voice.

"Bernice?" Ed ran to the side of the chair, crouching.

"Wha...? Ed?"

Shushing her, he pulled the afghan down from the top of the chair. The blanket was one of his favorites. Mama had made it herself. He unfolded it over Bernice, covering her to her shoulders. "Just sit tight. Get some rest."

"My...head..."

"I know," he said. "I know. I'll be back soon as I can."

Bernice's eyes were closed. He just now noticed she wasn't wearing her glasses. She looked odd without them. Her face somehow seemed bigger, though her shut eyes looked much smaller. "Where are you going?" she said, smacking her lips.

Ed stood up. "I'm going to get ready."

-35-

With Dorothy draping his shoulder, Ed slammed the summer kitchen door, throwing the bolt in place to lock it. He turned around, stepping into the room. Carrying the little girl's head by the hair, he underhand tossed it. The head smacked the wall, toppled down, and hit the table. It rocked back and forth, going still on its side. Her pale face, dark splotches for eyes, leered at him. Letting his shoulder sag, her body dropped. She made a sick *thud* when she hit the floor.

The flame in the lantern flickered, filling the room in a dim golden hue. Mary, on her back, was a few feet away. He'd brought her into the summer kitchen minutes ago. *Dragged* her since he didn't have Bernice's help to carry her. It had been rough work, but he'd finally gotten her inside.

Gazing at Mary's large breasts pitched back on her chest, somehow making them look both flatter and larger at the same time, Ed took several deep breaths. They started off rapid, but soon slowed as he took air into his lungs, and slowly let it out.

A warm fog began to drift through his head, muting his thoughts, pacifying his emotions.

Stripping from his clothes, Ed left them where they fell.

Soon, he felt blank, unattached.

The ax whacked off Mary's head in one easy swing.

His secret place, where he allowed himself to go while he worked—a void where Ed's integrity slept as deeply as the dead.

Mary's head was clamped in a vice on Ed's workbench, the bar twisted until each thick side squeezed what remained of her neck. Ed kissed her forehead. Her flesh was cold and tasted slightly rotten.

Sometimes images broke through the mental blinder—

Mary's ankles were bound with rope.

The rope was fed through the pulleys bolted into the ceiling beam, a length left dangling.

Ed gripped the length and pulled. Mary's body lifted off the floor, feet first, as the pulleys whined and the ceiling beam groaned.

Mary's arms rose last, fingers brushing the floor as she swayed.

With Mary suspended shoulders above the floor, the pointed crossbar above the beams was shoved through her feet.

Her body was secured.

—but they were only fractions, flashing glimpses of his incongruous activities.

The dressing knife stabbed into the side of Mary's neck.

The blade slid easily up to her ear, making a perfect incision in the dead, tacky flesh.

The knife carved all the way around her face, to the first incision on the neck.

A hand palmed Mary's face, pressing snug against her nose.

Slipping fingertips in her hair, the hand slowly twisted, as if turning a dial.

Thick, moist crackles came from the other side of her face.

Her face moved.

One by one, fingertips slipped behind the flimsy edges of skin.

Starting at her brow, the fingers pulled.

Her forehead stretched, creases in her skin flattening as the face peeled away from the head. Underneath were bumpy ridges, coated in crimson paste.

The thin sheet of skin wilted like wet newspaper.

The hump of her nose dipped when it popped loose.

The top lip plucked free, sagging low and hiding the teeth.

The bottom began to stretch like gum, the plump skin jiggling above the strong, cleft chin.

It pulled away with a juicy, slashing sound.

Only the cap of hair held it on the head, the face a rumpled curtain over the skull.

Mary's body hung upside down—a colossal tower of flesh and bone.

The knife started at her crotch and ran down to the stub of her neck, making a T from shoulder to shoulder.

The cut was repeated from hip to hip to form an I. Blood-streaked hands parted the skin as if opening drapes. Innards sloughed out like gloppy rain, forming piles on the floor. The organs were ignored as the knife continued to whittle the skin.

Sewing needles fed thread through the flimsy edges of skin, putting the pieces together.

Mary's saggy face watched from the vice, awaiting its turn, as the needles constructed a suit from her hulled skin.

Its turn came, added to the suit by the flabby neck skin, the edges sewed to the top of the chest.

Dorothy's arms came off in quick, vicious strikes of the ax.

Her legs followed.

The arms and legs were gathered, carried to the workbench and dropped on top like logs for a fire.

Her arm was selected first.

The knife made a slit from the wrist to the elbow on both sides.

As if unwrapping a morbid present, the sleeve of skin was torn away. A glove of insipid flesh remained on the hand, but that was okay, only the forearm was needed.

Hands kept peeling and cutting, stripping the bones until the prospects were set aside. Some had hands still attached, a couple were tipped with rigid, elfin feet.

The meat cleaver came next.

Lifting the heavy instrument, a distorted reflection was glimpsed in the glowing blade, the reflection like a vampire himself—deep-socketed eyes, pale tint of skin, and wild oily hair.

Holding the arm by the nub, the cleaver came down. It chopped through the tiny wrist, pounding the table hard enough to rattle it. The hand bounced away and fell off the side of the workbench.

The cleaver chopped the rest, severing pieces that weren't needed.

A file was used to sharpen the tips.

Finished, the hand picked up a bone stake, tapping the filed tip with a finger.

Then the stake was thrown at Mary's hanging body.

The sharp end of the bone punched into what was left of her chest, sinking in deep. There was a meaty squelch of the tip puncturing her heart.

Bare, hairy legs slid into the skin leggings, hiking up the waist.

The upper half of the suit hung behind, attached to the leggings by thread. Like putting on a jacket, arms stuffed into the empty sleeves until the hands poked out the ends.

The skin was pulled together in front.

The suit felt cold and tacky and stiff against the naked flesh. It itched.

Mary's crotch pressed snugly. The sticky touch made him shudder with pleasure.

The front, vest-like section was fringed with tatters of thread. Tying them together squeezed the suit against his body, making leathery sounds when the arms reached over his shoulders to grab the mask.

It was pulled over like a hood. Only a slight adjustment had to be made so it could be seen through.

Mary's hands were pulled over his, fingers flexing as he worked to make them fit inside. Rope was used to tighten the gloves around his wrists.

Bernice's garlic wreath was slung over the head. It draped the chest piece.

Bernice's harness belt was fastened around the waist, covering a trellis of thread that held the two sections together.

The bone stakes were slipped through each leathery loop like bullets in an outlaw's bandolier.

Bernice's scimitar was dropped into the sheath, dangling against the stiff legging covering his left thigh.

The stake was wrenched from Mary's heart, loaded into the crossbow. The chord snapped in place, readying the crossbow to fire.

Ed took a deep breath, relishing the feel of his skin armor.

He was ready to kill.

-36-

Timmy wished he were in his room right now, working on a story. The situation he was in was like something he'd have conceived for one of his characters. Laughing while he put him through unimaginable scenarios and pulling for them to make it through to the end. He could have written this scene—a boy his age that'd just been carried through the sky by a vampire and dropped on the ground deep in the dark woods behind a cemetery.

Had he read at night by his lamp, it probably would have prevented him from sleeping.

Timmy saw his bed, saw himself tucked under his blankets, sleeping. He longed to be there.

If only he hadn't let Robin talk him into leaving home.

Hardly took much convincing to get him out of his room. Besides, she'd have gone to Goult's without him. Come across Peter, and Timmy would have never known.

Maybe that would've been better.

No. He was glad he was with Robin.

Some help I've been.

What if he was in somebody else's story? Maybe an ominously creative writer was sitting at his or her desk right now, allowing Timmy to guide his pencil through the plot. Maybe the writer already had a destination in mind, a happy ending.

Fat chance of that.

This was no story. Hard as it was to accept, this was reality. Timmy wouldn't be able to write himself out of the predicament.

And he felt a hollow space open up in his heart when he realized he'd probably never get to write again.

He wondered what would happen to his stories. Would his parents keep them? Maybe read them from time to time as a way to reconnect with him after he was gone?

I'll be fine.

Something inside told him he was wrong. Whether he lived or died, nothing would ever be the same again.

"*Boy. Time is not plenty. Now, do as I say.*" The vampire offered his hand. "*Take my hand, and I will instruct you on what you must do next…for me.*" Mouth stretching wide, purple lips pulled back over a cavern filled with teeth. The longer ones up front curved to points.

Unlike any vampire he'd ever seen. Sure, all he had to base its undead appearance on were comics, books, and movies. So his experience in vampire facades was limited. And if this creature was truly a vampire, then every rendition that existed up to 1954 had gotten it wrong.

Gulping, Timmy got to his knees. There would be no fighting his way out of this. For one, he'd never been in a fight before and wasn't sure he was any good at it. Another reason, the most crucial one, was he was just a kid, held captive by a pair of monsters.

Sighing, Timmy raised his arm, reaching for the vampire's proffered hand. He knew once his hand voluntarily slid into the vampire's clutch, it would be taken as Timmy's submission to the vampire's hold.

But there was nothing else he could do. By now, the only other people who knew about the vampire were probably dead. And that made him feel helpless and very small.

The Vampire of Plainfield

"*That's a good boy,*" the vampire said. "*Take my hand.*"

Nodding, Timmy unclenched his fist. The vampire went to grab…

Then Timmy knocked its hand away.

As Timmy jumped to his feet, the vampire unleashed an enraged hiss that nearly made Timmy's bladder go loose. Holding back his pee, Timmy ran straight ahead.

Where he was going, Timmy didn't know. He just ran as hard as he could. Pumping his arms, Timmy leaned forward, and pushed himself. He knew under normal circumstances, he could run faster than he was. But he was tired, confused, and fighting shock. Any kind of speed he could garner was a success, and he seemed to be doing all right.

Timmy saw the space between the trees, a wedge of path entering the blackness that filled the woods ahead. If he went that way, the trail should lead him to the cemetery, then he could get to the road.

He thrust himself forward. His shoes pounded the ground, kicking up small clouds of dust at his feet. He was almost to the mouth of the path when Peter stepped out the darkness.

He held Robin in front of him.

Timmy skidded to a halt, arms flapping. He looked behind him and saw the vampire, tall and menacing, under a shaft of moonlight. He hadn't chased after Timmy.

Probably already knew there had been no need to pursue.

Winded, Timmy looked at Peter again.

"Where are you going, Timmy-boy?"

"Peter…" Timmy gulped, panted. "Let us go."

"Can't do that. Besides…" Peter used his finger to pluck Robin's torn sweater open. A tawny, smooth breast was exposed. Her nipple jutted. Peter flicked it with the same finger, making Robin squeak in horror. "…you don't really want to leave, do you?"

Again, that repulsive eagerness returned to Timmy's groin. Despite his wishes, he felt himself getting hard.

"Leave her alone," Timmy said, though the firmness of his voice didn't match his words.

Peter laughed. "Turn around, head on back. We need your help."

"*My* help?"

"Oh yeah," said Peter. "Eddie didn't finish the job. And I volunteered you to finish it for him."

What's he talking about?

"Now," Peter said, "go on. Don't make us chase you, or…"

Peter's finger extended. The fingernail popped free to make room for a growing claw. He made a slow swipe above Robin's nipple. Squirming, Robin moaned, but there was no pleasure in it. When Peter lowered his hand, a straight dark line was on Robin's breast. Thin trickles ran from the wound.

"Son of a bitch," Timmy said.

Peter laughed. "I would say watch your mouth, but you've met my mother." The laughter stopped as quickly as it had started. "Go, Timmy-boy."

Timmy took a few steps back. Peter repeated the movements, going forward. Timmy looked around him. Dark woods to his right and left, a clearing and two vampires, one to his front and back. One of them was his best friend, holding the girl of his dreams hostage in front of him.

His imagination tried to whip up possible strategies that would bring not only him, but Robin, to safety.

There were none.

He couldn't escape.

Peter kept moving forward, and Timmy kept moving backward. A couple times, his feet nearly tangled and brought him down, but he managed to stay upright. Each near fall brought an amusing chuckle from Peter.

That's not Peter.

Like Nana had said about Dorothy—Peter was gone.

Reaching the clearing, Timmy turned around. The tall vampire, smiling, put his hands together as if he was about to clap but decided not to. *"Such potency in a small boy."* Its hand rose to its face, moving a strand of oil-black hair away from its eyes. *"I could almost admire such bravery. Not tonight. In trade for your life, you will assist me."*

The vampire lifted an overly long arm, pointing toward a circle of rods. Timmy hadn't noticed them before now. Assembled like a small enclosure, the rods were close together. Small gaps between each made it hard to see through. Timmy figured at one time, they probably had been touching, but through the years, elements had caused them to shift.

"Break the barrier that prevents me from reaching my essence."

Timmy turned his head from the fence and looked up at the tall creature. Shadows streaked its face, but its red eyes glowed like two blood-filled stars. "I...I don't know how."

"Bring her to me."

"Who?"

The vampire huffed, a low raspy rattle rose in its chest. Timmy recognized it was becoming annoyed with him. Its hand shot toward Timmy's face. He flinched, expecting a hit, but the hand paused under his chin. A finger curved up beside his cheek, its thumb rose along the other one. It felt as if Timmy had slipped his head between mossy clamps.

He felt his head being tilted up.

"You are of the same blood as my destroyer. And though your demise is imminent, it will not be tonight. Do this for me, boy. Or your heart will suffer as mine."

Timmy tried to open his mouth, but the U of the vampire's hand wouldn't allow it. Huffing through his nose, he wanted to pull his face free. Couldn't. The vampire kept Timmy's head poised back, their eyes locked. Timmy gazed into the twin, blazing circles of the vampire's leer.

What did the vampire mean by his heart would ache…?

Robin's painful cry echoed through the night, and Timmy understood what the vampire meant.

"Do we have a deal, boy?"

Timmy strained to say they did. The vampire must have understood since its hold on Timmy's face was suddenly released. Timmy hadn't realized he'd been pulled up to the tips of his toes until he stumbled back.

"Get to work."

"I…" Timmy gave another glance at the fence. "I'm not strong enough…"

But the vampire was already retreating to the dark patches of shadow under the trees. It vanished within the black.

Timmy looked to the right and saw Robin squirming in Peter's hold. His arm reached around Robin's front, cupping a breast in his hand. His finger playfully flicked her nipple. With each touch, Robin whimpered.

Timmy wanted to run over there and rip Peter's hand off. He felt himself begin to take a step toward them, but thankfully, stopped himself. He'd only make it a couple steps before being stopped. Then Peter would hurt Robin again, probably worse this time.

As much as he wanted to be Robin's hero, there was nothing he could do to save her. He felt pathetic. Useless. How he'd felt every day until recently; until the other day, when Robin started making him feel strong and brave. Two weeks ago, he wouldn't have had the courage to sneak out of his bedroom.

Wouldn't have had the guts to *kiss* her.

Robin gave him a strength he'd lacked all his life.

I'm not going to fail her.

Timmy started walking toward the fence. Everything inside the clearing was dead and rotting compared to the rest of the woods. He spotted a small pile of dirt on the far side of what looked like a flattened stump. As he got closer, the stump seemed to change color. No longer dark, it looked soft gray, the color of stone. Standing outside the fence, Timmy realized it actually was stone—a broken gravestone.

Timmy felt tight and squirmy inside.

"Be a good little ghoul," said the vampire, letting out a raspy chuckle.

Timmy glanced over his shoulder. He saw only darkness.

Why doesn't it come over here? Or Peter?

Timmy looked at the fence, lightly stroking a rod with his finger. It felt cold and smooth, like...silver.

That's it!

Timmy nearly laughed.

They're afraid of the silver. In some vampire stories, they didn't cast reflections in mirrors because of the silver backings. Silver weakened a vampire's defenses. He'd even read one story where a silver stake had been used to slay a vampire.

Timmy could just stay right here, the vampires couldn't come near him. Stay here all night, if he had to. Wait until sunrise, then track the vampires back to the lair and kill them while they slept.

Get Dad to help me.

His father wouldn't believe him. If he went home in the morning, his dad was likely to whip his ass a good one and send him to his room before he could even begin to explain what was going on. Wouldn't matter *why* Timmy had been out all night to Dad. If he broke one of the laws of the house, he'd be punished for it, no matter what reason.

No. It's up to me.

He would be safe here. The vampires couldn't touch him.

"Timmy!" Robin's grief-stricken voice cut through the night. "Please, hurry!"

That canceled his plan. One thing he hadn't considered was what would happen to Robin if he didn't do what the vampire wanted.

Your heart will suffer as mine.

They'd kill her.

If there was a way he could get her away from them...

Sighing, Timmy turned around and started following the length of the fence. He reached what looked like a gate. It had been pried open, the frame bent outward, and he noticed scuff marks in the silver.

The gate pulled open easily, and Timmy went inside. The temperature seemed to plummet as he neared the grave. Though no wind blew, Timmy felt cold air swishing all over. His skin hardened with gooseflesh. His teeth clattered. The hair on the back of his neck stood erect. And there seemed to be a cold rock forming inside his head, sending sharp tendrils of fear down his spine.

He'd been terrified before, standing among the vampires, fearing for Robin's life and his own. But as he slowly crouched at the hole of the solitary grave, he felt something inside that made his veins feel as if filled with ice water.

The hole looked partially dug. Dirt made a small pile on the far side of the hole.

What was in there was pure evil, and Timmy somehow knew if it was set free, everything he'd ever cared about would suffer more than his young mind could comprehend.

Robin squealed. Timmy could hear the sniffling hisses of her sobs. He tried not to imagine what Peter was doing to her, but it wasn't hard to figure out.

Messing with her.

Any time Peter noticed Timmy balking, he'd probably mess with Robin to get him moving again. With no other option, Timmy climbed down into the hole. One foot came down on a slope of dirt. The other bumped something hard that clinked softly against the soil.

What?

Crouching, Timmy felt around the soft dirt. A knuckle knocked against something spikey. *"Ow!"* Timmy pulled back his hand and saw his knuckle had been punctured. A dab of blood scurried down his finger.

Ignoring the blood, he reached out again, being more careful this time. His hand found a bar. Felt like wood. He lifted it and was surprised by its weight. Bringing it up to his face, he recognized the round tip of a shovel. A dark stain that might have been blood streaked the underside of the blade. It looked dry, so Timmy knew it hadn't come from his knuckle. Dirt clung to the blemish as if it had been glued on.

About a foot of broken handle jutted from the metal tube above the blade.

He felt slits in the wood, a carved word. Using his thumb, he traced the letters—*GEIN.*

Eddie?

Eddie carved his name in all his tools. He'd once told Timmy it was because he'd loaned out a lot of tools over the years that had never been returned.

And Eddie had been here? Digging?

Was this the job he hadn't finished?

Timmy wondered why the shovel was broken and bloody, but another cry from Robin diverted his thoughts. There was no time to figure it out. He had a job to do, if he wanted Robin to be okay.

Feeling like crying himself, Timmy held the broken shovel handle with his hands, and stabbed the round tip into the ground. He scooped out a clump of dirt, tossing it out of the hole.

He worked fervently, shoveling and tossing the dirt away. Some of it fell back in and he had to scoop it out again, adding more work to the already taxing chore. Sometimes the dirt sprinkled down like a dry rain, coating his head and shoulders in flakes. Bits became tangled in his hair. When he tried to ruffle it out with his hand, his fingers got entwined in his hair. He jerked his hand free, plucking out hair.

But he kept digging until the shovel struck something hard.

Timmy had no way of knowing how long it had taken him, but now that he'd found what he was looking for, he noticed his body was drenched. His eyes burned from sweat and dirt. He used his soiled forearm to wipe his eyes.

Standing, Timmy bent at the waist and used the shovel's tip to scrape away the dirt. A strip of pale flatness appeared between the mounds of dirt. A thin line ran vertically on either side. Timmy scraped away some more dirt and recognized he was uncovering the top of a wooden casket.

My God...

Pushing the mounting fear aside, Timmy kept scraping until he'd uncovered everything. Some thin patches of dirt remained, but there was no mistaking that Timmy was standing on top of a casket. Broad up top, it gradually narrowed as it reached the bottom. At Goult's, he'd accidentally stood on an empty casket. This one wouldn't be empty. Something sinister was inside.

Panting, Timmy leaned against the dirt sidewall.

Robin let out a loud cry. *"No! Stop!"*

Peter's disturbing laughter carried over to where Timmy stood.

He'd stopped working again, and again, Robin had suffered for it.

-37-

Ed didn't use the brake when he whipped the truck onto the dirt road that led to the cemetery. Behind him, the truck's tail swerved this way and that on the loose gravel, the taillights illuminating the dust like a misty inferno behind him. Straining to hold on, he kept it from smashing a tree.

Mary's skin felt tight and itchy against his, trapping his body heat. He felt as if he was inside an oven. Soaked in sweat, the threaded parts pressed tightly against the areas where he was bent. But, overall, the suit felt fine. And he liked how Mary's crotch hugged his groin, holding his testicles in a dry, comforting fold.

Dust swirled in the headlights' glare, making it hard to see beyond the foggy barrier. But he knew the area well. He could spot every rut in the road with his eyes closed. He dodged them with the truck, making the hasty drive as smooth as possible.

The cemetery's entrance appeared up ahead. A damp fog clung like webbing to the tops of the stone pillars, hiding the cemetery's name on the iron signage. Ed stomped the gas and dashed through gateless ingress.

The pathway narrowed here, dipping and rising forward, gravestones undulating on either side. Ed punched the brakes, and brought the truck to a wild stop in front of a crypt. On top, a featureless, weeping woman chiseled from stone hugged herself. Her gown hung limply over her body, covered the front, leaving her arms bare. It was one of Ed's favorite shrines. Though he had no idea what she represented, he loved trying to imagine what she looked like underneath the molded covering. Tonight, he couldn't take time to cherish her blank beauty.

Ed switched off the headlights, killed the engine. He shouldered his door open and hopped out. Mary's skin tooted and squeaked with his movements.

Standing beside his truck, he gave a quick look around the cemetery. From here, he couldn't tell which graves he'd exhumed. Under the fog hovering low to the ground, all of them looked untouched.

Reaching inside the truck, Ed grabbed the crossbow. He kept his finger away from the trigger as he twisted and turned the weapon to get it out. He checked to see if the bone stake was still loaded. It was—the tip patterned in Mary's glutinous blood.

Ed started walking. He'd maybe gone twenty feet when he caught the sound of flapping wings. Looking up, he saw nothing above him but stars. A thin shredding of cloud was sketched across the moon.

Bringing the crossbow up, Ed straightened his index finger next to the trigger guard. Alert, he started walking again. He'd gone a few more feet when the flapping repeated.

Ed spun around, slamming the crossbow against his shoulder. He aimed.

Nothing was behind him. The fog swirled together, reconnecting where Ed parted it when he walked through. Taking deep breaths, Ed walked backward.

Wings flapped at the back of his neck. Something smacked the padding of his armor, sharp things scraped across. He felt the compressions, but not the pain, which meant the suit had done its job.

With an alarmed cry, Ed twirled on his heels. He thrust the crossbow forward.

Nothing there. More curling fingers of fog, thinning and stretching to block his path.

Ed faced the other way. He walked with caution, slowly, one step at a time. Putting the front of his boot down first, rolling his foot to silence his steps. The ground still made scratching sounds, but they were quiet.

The dry flaps returned, filling his ears. He felt something heavy pound his head. Things latched on and pulled at Mary's fire-colored mane. The mask pulled taut against his face as it was being tugged from above. Ed pointed the crossbow toward his head, and quickly thought better of it. If he fired, the stake would probably stab through his skull. Lowering the crossbow, he swung his left arm over his head, swatting at whatever was up there attacking him.

His gloved hand smacked something solid, yet soft. Like punching a sack of dirt, hard but easy to cave in. The assault on his head momentarily broke before coming back even harder. He felt sharp things digging at the skin armor, unable to pierce its resilient texture.

"Get away from me!" Ed shouted at the unseen enemy, flogging his hand blindly above his head.

Unable to accurately defend himself, Ed did the only thing he could think of.

He ran.

Swatting and slapping as if a swarm of bees were chasing him, Ed sprinted up the narrow path between the graves. Mary's skin squeaked and groaned and rattled and popped between each whack of his footsteps. He felt jabs on top of his head, pinchers plucking away at Mary's hair in a desperate dig for his skull.

What the hell's up there? For God's sake, what is it?

The stakes strapped around his waist shook and conked together. Something flat smacked against his leg as he ran. It was on the left side, swaying outward and back in to give his thigh a firm whack.

Bernice's knife!

He swatted above him again, missed, then switched the crossbow to his left hand. He used his right to grab the handle of the knife and yank it free of the sheath. Weight dropped on his head, pushing it forward.

Something had landed on the crown of Mary's hair.

In a wild swing, he flung the blade up before losing his balance. He fell forward. Mary's chest hit the path, then scooted as dust flew up around him. Rolling onto his back, Ed stared between the part of his stitched leggings.

At first, he saw only dust. Then a tattered wing landed on his stomach. The black feathers trembled. Where the triceps should be, a bloody stump pointed at Ed. Recognizing what the wing belonged to, Ed smiled, knowing he'd hurt it.

He sat up, slapping the severed wing aside. He held up the knife and saw the vulture's blood sliding down the tip.

"Got...you, you bastard...bird!"

Behind him came a miserable caw. Ed tried to turn his head, but the stiff skin collar made it difficult. It was awkward moving around, but he managed to scramble his way up to his feet. Then he turned all the way around.

The vulture, balanced atop a lopsided headstone, fluffed its chest and let out another squawk. Its lone wing stretched out and whipped forward. Blood spurted from the hole where its other wing had been. It seemed to be daring Ed to make a move. Even without its wing, it wanted another go at Ed.

Ed huffed through the mask, and stepped forward.

The vulture stretched its back, unleashing a high-pitched, rallying cry. Its wing arched and shook, the feathers quivering.

Ed swung his arm forward, sliced the blade through the vulture's neck, and slipped the knife into his sheath in one quick motion. Then he walked past the headstone as the vulture's head tumbled to the side. Its tube-like neck spurted blood. When its head hit the ground, the vulture's decapitated body leaped from the headstone and ran like a drunkard trying to escape the police. It made a few circles around the headstone, then dropped onto its side. The legs kicked a few times. As if realizing they were no longer on the ground, the legs went still.

Though Mary's mouth remained firm, Ed attempted a smile behind it.

Damn bastard bird.

Ed stepped forward and kicked the bird's carcass. It flew into the air, vanishing inside the mass of fog. He didn't hear it land.

As he entered the dark path in the woods, he patted the top of his head. The vulture's pecking had caused some tiny bald patches, so he combed the hair to cover them.

But other than the missing hair, the suit was in great shape. It should hold up with the vampire, at least for a while.

He took a long, deep breath. It was hard getting air through Mary's open nostrils, but it was enough to help slow his raging heartbeat.

He started down the path, heading toward the isolated grave.

Hopefully, he wasn't too late.

Hopefully, Timmy was all right.

Hopefully, Ed wouldn't mess everything up when he got there.

-38-

The stench was unlike anything Timmy had ever smelled—rot, combined with garlic and death. He wiped his runny eyes, and gazed down. Standing with a foot on either side of the casket, Timmy saw the withered corpse between his legs. He only knew it was a corpse because it had a head—or something that resembled a head, with thin strands of fuzzy white hair. On the gray bulb were two holes, positioned where eyes should be, and two upright slits that might've been nostrils. Another sideways slit might've been a mouth. Timmy counted two, pointy nubs on both sides of the head. Either horns or ears, he couldn't tell which.

From the shoulders down, the body formed a moldy teardrop shape of papery skin and bone. Timmy could make out the bulging, skeletal shapes of wings. The corpse's texture reminded Timmy of the wasp nest he'd found in the woods behind Nana's house.

A blanket of frail webbing sheathed the body from top to bottom. Bits and pieces of dead bugs, worms, and rats, dangled from the fluffy lattice.

And jutting from the right side of its chest was a short shaft of wood.

"*Now, boy, bring her to me! Quickly!*"

Timmy jumped at the vampire's grated voice.

"Her?" he muttered.

Didn't look like a *her*. It looked like a giant bat that might've once been stuffed full of candy and busted open at a birthday party, then left to rot in a field.

And I have to…

He held up his dirty hands, fingers spread. Clumps of dirt rolled down from the indentions of his fingers. He'd have to *carry* the thing out of here. Looking up, he saw the top of the hole a few feet above his head. Not only carry the corpse, he was supposed to climb out of the hole.

Looking at the corpse, Timmy groaned.

He should've known that was the next step.

But he didn't want to. Not only was he afraid to *touch* it, afraid of what it would *feel* like, he worried that he might damage it. He pictured himself picking it up and the thing crumbling in his hands like a model kit that hadn't been properly glued.

I'm dead if that happens.

Probably dead if it didn't happen.

Dead either way.

Robin shrieked—an earsplitting cry that made Timmy cringe.

"You are almost out of time, boy!"

"Okay!" Timmy shouted. "Just…just leave her alone!"

"Timmy!" Robin called, "please…don't let them hurt me anymore…"

Robin's sad and hopeless voice made Timmy's throat tighten. Tears filled his eyes. She sounded awful, and hurt. Begging Timmy to make them stop hurting her. As if it were his fault they had been.

An inkling of an idea sprouted in his mind. He shook his head, trying to knock it away before he could focus on it.

Too late. The idea was there, foolish as it was.

They'd hurt her more.

Maybe not.

Feeling the corner of his mouth twitch from a smile, Timmy squatted. He found the half of Eddie's shovel between the casket and dirt wall. He picked it up, tapping the blade against the casket to knock off the clumps of dirt. He noted the sharp, round tip and the jagged wood. Either could do some serious damage if used correctly.

Then he pulled up his shirt, and slid the shovel between the waistband of his pants. The wood was cold against his skin and made him jerk rigid. Hissing between his gritted teeth, he lowered his shirt over the handle. Hopefully they wouldn't notice it before he was able to attempt his plan.

Timmy slipped one arm behind the shriveled corpse's head, the other behind its legs. He stood up straight, lifting. Surprisingly light, he nearly flung the corpse into the air. He stumbled back a few steps, and caught the corpse before he could drop it. Fuzzy, dry hair brushed his hands, feeling like he'd just walked through a spider's web. The skin of her face felt like old newspaper as it brushed his upper arms.

Timmy was thankful the corpse was so light. If not, he'd have a hard time raising her above his head. Doing so, he still couldn't quite reach the top. He jumped, gave the corpse a shove over the top, and dropped back down into the casket. The wood cracked under his feet.

Now that the hardest part was over, Timmy started to climb. It took a couple tries because the dirt kept piling down, but he managed to reach the top. He threw a leg over the lip of the hole, wiggled his back, and got his knee on the ground. Then he crawled forward and dropped his face to the ground, trembling from the exertion. His heavy breaths stirred the dust in front of him.

Though he was exhausted, he knew he couldn't stay here forever. He pushed against the ground, straightening his back. On his knees, the shovel handle poked his back. The blade mashed and pinched his rump.

He stood up, staring over the pointed tops of the enclosure. The darkness was like a translucent curtain closed over the trees. He saw only hints of their pale trunks in the black.

Bending over, he scooped up the corpse. He walked toward the gate. At the end of autumn, Dad made him rake the leaves and stuff them in a sack. Then he was supposed to carry them to the back for burning. Carrying the corpse was not unlike carrying a sack stuffed full of dead leaves. It even made the same soft, rattling sounds as dry things rubbed together.

He sidled through the gate, staying close to the fence as he walked. "Where are you?" he asked. Timmy halted just inside the clearing, the toe of his shoe barely an inch from the grass. He stood there. The corpse balanced in the folds of his arms as if he was about to carry his bride away to their honeymoon.

The darkness shifted before him, moving this way and that as shadows slithered against more shadows.

The vampire stepped forward...

No...

He floated. How the vampire moved so smoothly, there was no way he was walking. His arms were held out, hands bent at the wrists and its thick fingers pointing at Timmy. *"Give her to me..."*

"No," said Timmy.

The vampire slowed to a stop. A few feet of open space separated them. *"Don't provoke me, boy."*

"Get Robin first, then I'll let you have..." Timmy shook the corpse. "...this."

"You are not the one who bargains. That attribute is mine."

"I'm not going to let you have this, until I know...that Robin's okay."

The vampire leered at Timmy. His blazing eyes cut two red paths through the night. Timmy began to wonder if he was going to speak at all. Then, *"Very well."* His arm reached out, hand motioning. *"Bring her."*

It's working!

Timmy didn't think he'd make it this far. Now he had to figure out what he was going to do next. So far, his plan had only consisted of him demanding they give him Robin. Where he should go from here, Timmy had no idea.

To the fence.

Great plan. But what if they chased him? What if they wanted to fight?

The shovel nudged his back, reminding him it was there. He was glad to have it, though he doubted he'd get the chance to use it.

If this went bad...

Timmy noticed movement behind the vampire, pale blurs moving awkwardly forward.

"Timmy?"

"Robin?"

She made a noise that was either a laugh or a stuttering sob. "It's me." She made short steps closer, her feet shuffling across the ground as if walking a tight line.

"You're okay?" he asked.

"Been better. You?"

"Getting better, now."

Robin's weird movements made more sense when he saw she still had Peter's arm stretched across her chest. His forearm mashed her breasts, rumpling her torn sweater. As she scooted a little closer, Timmy spotted Peter's head behind her shoulder. His eyes also glowed, a soft red, like embers on a dying fire.

Robin's hair draped most of her face in tangled spirals. But he could see her chin and mouth, her plump lips, the dot in the upper corner, which were wet and shiny in the streaks of moonlight.

Timmy began to tremble. She was so close to him now. Any moment and they would be together again. If he could just keep this going his way, Robin would be back with him.

Then we'll run to the fence, get on the other side.

And the vampires couldn't touch them.

"Timmy-boy," said Peter. "You're making a mistake."

"What mistake is that?" Timmy tried to keep his voice steady, but it came out weak and shaky.

"The master made you a generous offer, and you're ruining it. He'll kill you, you know. You could've been one of us, and you blew it!"

"I don't want to be..." The vampire's head jerked in Timmy's direction, causing him to step back. Gulping, he stepped forward. "I don't want to be one of you!"

The vampire held up his hand in front of Peter.

Peter stopped, yanking Robin back. She grunted when her back hit his front. Her breasts popped loose from behind Peter's arm, jiggling and swaying. Timmy couldn't stop staring at them.

The vampire turned, bringing Timmy's eyes away from Robin's lurching breasts. *"Your turn."*

Shaking his head, Timmy said, "No way. I said I want you to let Robin go, and you have to..."

"No. You simply said you wanted to know if Robin was all right. And now you know that she is. That was the deal."

"What? No, I..."

"I have fulfilled my half of the bargain. And now, it is your turn."

"I said..." Timmy stopped talking. The vampire was right. He hadn't told them to let her go. He'd thought it, had the words on his tongue, but never spoke them.

I really did blow it.

He looked at Robin. Her head was turned slightly sideways, face angled toward Peter. Her hair curtained the side of her face. Again, he could see her mouth. Could see how her lips were curled as she breathed heavily.

Then he looked down at the gross thing in his arms. The hollow slits where eyes should be gazed blankly at him.

"New deal," he said.

"Boy, I have grown tired of your bargaining."

"Not a bargain. Just a...trade."

"I'm listening."

"Let Robin go first."

"No."

"Look, I have something you want. You have something—some*one* I want. Let her go. And I'll give you..." He held up his arms to show the vampire what he wanted.

The vampire seemed to consider this for a moment. His large head turned from Timmy to Robin, then back to Timmy. His black hair looked as if it was moving, flowing like a fine, dark lake from the top of his skull down his back. His ears jutted in two narrow points, pushing through the hair and tilting in all directions like radars.

Finally, the vampire nodded. *"Very well. This better not be a hoax."*

"It's not."

And it wasn't. Timmy was ready to be done with this. Though the corpse barely had any weight, his arms were getting tired of holding it up.

The vampire motioned at Peter again.

"But master..." Peter said.

"Now."

Peter closed his mouth. His lips narrowed into a tight line. Timmy could tell his old friend was not happy with the decision. For a moment, he thought he might disobey and not release Robin.

But his arm slowly lowered away from Robin. When it was away from her front, she quickly pulled her sweater over her breasts and held it shut with her hand.

"Come on," he said to Robin.

"Thank you, Timmy."

"And now, mine." The vampire pointed at the corpse. *"Put her down. On this side."*

Looking down, Timmy saw where the two sections of ground met. His toes were just over the line. He kept his eyes on Robin as he slowly squatted. She was walking toward him, moving away from Peter.

Timmy put his hands on the ground, straightening his arms.

Robin passed the vampire, not looking at it.

Timmy gently shook his arms, so the corpse would slide down. It took a few tries before the parched skin peeled away from his sweaty arms. The corpse slipped down to his hands.

Robin was a few steps away from Timmy when he pushed the corpse across the line.

The vampire pushed past Robin, knocking her over. Timmy thought he was making a lunge for him and reached behind his back. He tugged at the shovel, but his shirt was in the way. He couldn't get a hold of it.

Timmy screamed.

The vampire snatched up the corpse and twirled away, its head whipping side to side like a hungry dog daring another animal to try taking its scraps. Hissing, the vampire walked backwards.

Peter followed his master.

"Timmy?"

He looked to where Robin had fallen. She lay on her side. Her skirt had dropped high up her legs. There were some small scratches on her inner thigh, more further down. He glimpsed the fluffy patch of hair between her legs, averting his eyes. Her knee was scratched up. Moaning, Robin rolled onto her back.

"Are you hurt?" he asked, crawling to her.

"Not...not real bad."

"Thank God," he said. Her knee was bleeding, but it should be okay. "Can you walk?"

Nodding, Robin's hair shook. "I think so."

"Good. Let me help you up. We have to get behind the fence. Now."

"Okay."

Timmy reached for her, his hand brushing her thigh. Her skin felt...cold. He hoped she wasn't getting sick from being out in the cool weather, half-stripped.

"Why do you want to go over there?" she asked, bending her arm when he grabbed her elbow.

"They can't hurt us behind the fence. It's made of silver."

"I know," she said.

Timmy, about to grab Robin's hand, stopped. "You do?"

"Uh-huh..." She giggled. "That's why we had to get you over *here*."

Timmy's back felt as if cold little feet scurried up his spine. "What did you say?"

Robin shot stiffly upright, rising like a plank of wood. Her sweater fell low on her shoulders, opening to show him both pale breasts. On the left one was a pair of holes that matched those he saw on Carol Clark's neck. Her hair fell away from her face, revealing a brick-shaped brow that extended over her eyes, which had turned the color of honey. When she smiled, Timmy saw a pair of fangs where her teeth used to be.

A forked tongue ran between her lips.

"Oh my God," he whispered. Then he twirled sideways, the heels of his shoes scratching the dirt. He prepared to run.

Robin snatched his arm, threw him to the ground. He landed on his side, yelling in pain when the shovel jabbed him between his buttocks.

"And thank you, Timmy, for being so predictable."

-39-

Robin's hands caressed his chest, rubbing lower. He felt her fingers wiggling and stroking as her hands traveled down to his waist.

"Stop," he said, swatting at her hands.

Robin cackled like a witch from the old spooky radio show he used to listen to when he was little. Her gruff shrills reverberated through the night. Robin threw a bare leg over his waist, and squatted above his midsection. Reaching between her legs, she tugged the front of his pants.

"What are you...Robin! *No!*"

The button of his pants was plucked off. The zipper lowered with a quick *rip*. Robin moaned as if she were about to taste something delicious. Her hand slid inside his pants. He felt her cold fingers stroking him.

"No..." he said, though without much emphasis.

Leaning over his face, the tips of her hair tickled his nose, cheeks, and mouth. Before, when they'd been this close, he'd been able to feel her breaths. Now he felt nothing. She wasn't breathing.

Her glowing eyes came close to his. "Join us, Timmy."

"Stop."

"Please. I meant what I said. At the tavern? I want you, Timmy."

"Robin...why? How'd this happen?"

"When you were digging…Peter bit me. And the master woke me up."

"I'm sorry," he said. "I didn't want anything to happen to you."

"Don't be sorry. I *asked* him to."

"You…what?"

"When I realized what they really were, I practically begged them to change me. I mean, who wouldn't want to be a vampire? Living forever, never getting old. I thought to myself: 'Why should Dorothy have all the fun?' I wanted to have some fun too. My daddy never lets me have any fun. Now I'll get to have all the fun I could ever want." Robin wrinkled her nose, pursing her lips. "And you know what else? When the master changed me, I suddenly knew a lot more than I did before. I just seem to know *everything*. You can too, Timmy." Her hand tugged on his erection. "You can be with *me*. Doesn't that sound wonderful?"

Being with Robin did sound wonderful—a dream come true. To do so would be a nightmare of unmeasured proportions. If becoming a vampire was anything like it was in the stories, he would have to die first. Then he would awaken as a creature of the night, cursed to feed on the blood of the living. He could never truly die. His soul would never rest.

"How about it, Timmy-boy?"

Robin's lip curled almost to a snarl. Her eyes looked up. "Peter. I told you stay out of this."

"Well, you don't seem to have the charm on Timmy like you thought you did. I mean, I couldn't even get him to boink you earlier, could I?"

"Shut *up*." She said, a growl rising in her throat. She pulled her hand out of his pants.

"Whoaaaa," said Peter. "Already showing your nasty side, huh?" Laughing, Peter looked down at Timmy. He put his hands on his wide hips. "How about it, Timmy? Want to wake up next to *that* every night for an eternity?"

"*Dweeb*," said Robin.

Timmy felt as if he were already dead and trapped in a living hell.

"But Robin did say *some*thing true," Peter added. "It *is* a lot of fun. And just think, having a girl like Robin by your side at all times."

Robin smiled bashfully. "Oh, Peter."

"Come on, Timmy. Join us. *Be* one of us."

Taking rapid breaths, Timmy looked from Peter to Robin. He pressed his lips together, huffing through his nose. Gulped. Said, "Go to hell."

And readied himself for what came next.

Peter sighed.

So did Robin. "Well," Robin said, "if you won't join us. Then you're going to be the first feeding for our master's bride!"

"Robin, don't!" Timmy shouted.

She climbed off his stomach, reached down, grabbed a handful of his hair, and pulled. His scalp exploded with pain as he was dragged along the ground. Crying, Timmy reached up and gripped her arms. He gouged at her skin, trying to get her to let go. Her grip was too strong. Looking down the length of his body, he saw his kicking legs. Beyond his feet, Peter slunk along, head down as if pouting.

When Timmy's scalp felt as if it were about to tear loose, Robin dropped him. Sharp blasts of heat shot down his face from the top of his head. His skin felt as if it had been overstretched. He patted his head, expecting to feel a drooping scalp. His head was intact, but his hair was falling out in clumps.

Crouching, Robin grabbed his shoulders and jerked him to a sitting a position. Then she forced him to turn around. She pulled him against her, holding him in a similar fashion as Peter had held her earlier.

"What is this?" she asked.

Timmy wasn't sure what she was talking about until he felt her hand go under his shirt. "No, Robin, don't…"

The shovel was jerked free of his pants and lowered in front of him. "You were hiding this?"

Timmy gulped.

"What did you plan do with it?" she asked.

"Nuh-nothing."

"Oh, sure."

She threw it down. The blade stabbed into the ground at the pruned, withered feet of the corpse. Timmy's eyes looked past the jagged tip of the handle, following the corpse's feeble torso upward to its head. The vampire was knelt on one knee beside the corpse. He looked at Robin as she squeezed Timmy tighter. Then his hellfire eyes lowered to the jutting shovel. *"I suppose he did not accept the offer."*

"No," said Robin. "The idiot."

"Then it will be better this way, without the boy choosing wisely. My darling will live again, and she will feast tonight."

Understanding that the decrepit thing he pulled from the ground was going to wake up soon and he would be its supper, Timmy squirmed in Robin's hold. She held him captive with zero effort. "Please, Robin," he said. "Don't do this."

"Shut your mouth!" She gave him a firm shake. "You had your chance, and you turned it down. Most don't even get the option once, but you've gotten it twice tonight. From Peter and me. You denied us. So now you will be a gift to our master's bride for her reawakening."

"No, please..." said Timmy in bubbly voice. Tears filled his eyes, making his vision blurry. "Robin, don't..."

"Great. Now he's crying."

"Peter!" Timmy cried. "Please, Peter. Don't let them do this."

"Even if I wanted to help you," said Peter. "You made your decision."

Timmy let the tears flow. His body quaked and jerked as he sobbed. He didn't care how childish it made him look. He didn't want to die. He wanted to see his parents again. He wanted to write again. He wanted to do so much again.

But he wasn't going to get to.

I'm going to die tonight.

"Enough of this pathetic display." The vampire's hand lowered to the jutting shaft in the corpse's chest. *"My darling."* His monstrous hand clutched the shaft. *"Live again!"*

The shaft made a *squelch* sound as it was jerked loose.

A funnel of blue light shot toward the sky with a thundering crash. Timmy was thrown against Robin. She held onto him, and didn't fall.

The blue light stabbed the sky for several seconds before it began to swell around the body. No longer shooting up, the light traced the deformed pattern of the corpse. A high-pitched screech like bad brakes assaulted Timmy's ears. He wanted to use his hands to cover them, but Robin wouldn't allow it. She gave him another hard shake, and Timmy understood she was telling him to be still.

The dwarf-like size of the corpse began to develop into strong features—shoulders shifted and adjusted with a series of cracks, the neck lengthened, and breasts began to swell. The blue light spread across the body, engulfing the budding torso in a dazzling glow. The top of the head began to thrash and flutter like blue fire. The frantic motions made sounds like a hundred lashing whips. The blue light burst into a spray of sparks, revealing a thick mane of raven-black hair. Dense curls slithered like a nest of snakes from the top of a blue, radiant head.

The vampire threw back his head, screeching at the sky. Red droplets that Timmy assumed were tears fell from his eyes.

The sheet of sparkling blue began to shrink, pulling inward to the center of the body. The woman-like shape began to sit up, the light still shrinking. Now she had long, firm arms, pale as snow. Thin purple veins webbed the skin. She held up her hands, flexing fingers tipped with sharp black nails.

The blue light faded to a pale shimmer that reached from her stomach to the hollow of her neck. The exposed skin had changed from dead and papery to a soft smoothness.

A pair of heavy breasts with tiny, erect dots for nipples rose through the blue glitter. A small navel appeared on a flat stomach.

The light seemed to be generating a grotesquely stunning she-creature.

"She's beautiful," Robin said in an astonished voice.

"Yeah," Peter agreed.

Timmy stared at the developing naked flesh—wide hips and a narrow waist with muscular legs and breasts that sat high and full on her chest.

Then he saw her face.

The mouth was void of lips, just a gaping, flat oval lined with canine teeth. Her white eyes slashed downward toward two smaller slits for a nose. Spikes, the size of nail tips, ran up the center of her face. At the nose they reached out on either side.

The vampire clasped its hands together, and held them close to its mouth.

The she-creature's body continued to restructure itself, pieces shifting this way and that, as she rose to her feet. The blue light was under her skin now, coalescing in a variety of patterns through her body. She held out her arms, and tilted back her head. A long, alleviated moan swirled loudly from her lipless maw. Her release shook the ground, rustled the limbs and trees. Timmy felt vibrations through his shoes.

With her arms still held out, the she-creature's head lowered. She looked at the vampire. Something like a smile pulled at the immovable mouth.

Reaching up, the vampire's hands turned so its palms faced up. Fingers extended to take her hand.

The she-creature's arm slowly moved toward the vampire's. "My love," she said in a whispery rattle.

Then a stake punched into her chest above her left breast.

-40-

Silence filled the area as Timmy watched the she-creature look down at herself. Seeing the stake poking from her chest, she emitted a frenzied cry that quickly broke off to a painful moan. Her skin, which had been luscious and pale and smooth, hardened like clay. Cracks ran up and down, right to left, making crooked patterns all over.

Her eyes blinked out.

Then she fell forward, dropping like a statue that had been knocked over.

The vampire caught her in his arms, and gently lowered her to the ground. *"No! This...No!"*

The vampire whipped around, screeching. He caught the stake meant for his head and snapped it easily in half.

"Seize him!" The vampire pointed the stake's busted tip past Timmy. He tried to turn to see what the vampire was pointing at, but was violently thrown aside. He pounded the ground, and quickly rolled onto his front. Looking up, his breath caught in his throat.

What...in God's name...?

About twenty feet away, a horrid woman stepped out from behind a tree. She stood with her weight on one leg, a hip jutting. Her naked skin was pallid in the soft glow of the moon, her hair a mussed bushel.

And very long and...red?

She started walking forward, moving slightly rigid, as if her legs couldn't bend right. She clutched a large object in front of her. The closer she got, Timmy began to make out the wide and narrow end. The moonlight showed a tight string on either side.

A crossbow.

The woman halted in a small of pool light on the forest floor. She put a gray, sharp object into the crossbow, and jacked it in place.

"That you, Eddie?" Peter asked.

"It is," answered the woman in a muffled voice.

That's Eddie?

Sounded like the old goofball Timmy had known for so long. What was he wearing? When Eddie turned slightly sideways, Timmy saw breasts. Though they looked a bit flat and crumpled, they were big, like four of Robin's compressed into one. The pinky-sized nipples looked almost black in the night. Timmy scanned the slender frame, stopping on the rump protruding like a smooth hill. Roughly-stitched lines made dark, crooked paths from the thigh, vanishing into the twin gorges.

It's a suit!

Like the one Eddie had been wearing the day he told Timmy about the cannibal tribes he'd been reading about. They used the skin of their fallen tribesmen as body armor.

The face looked familiar, Timmy realized. A lot like Mary Hogan, though flatter and lacking emotion.

Before Timmy could give it another thought, Robin and Peter pounced. Eddie quickly ducked Robin's dive, and spun around as Peter's teeth gnashed. The sharp fangs hit Eddie's shoulder and slid off. No harm had been done. Momentarily stunned, Peter raised a hand to his mouth, as if checking that his fangs were still there.

"Timmy!" Eddie called. "Go for their hearts or cut off their heads!"

Eddie threw something that had been at his hip. It gleamed as it spun, end over end, through the dark.

A long blade stabbed into the ground in front of him.

Seeing this, Peter screeched and charged at Timmy, moving so swiftly that Timmy missed the majority of his travels when he blinked. Timmy made a grab for the protruding knife's handle.

His hand gripped...

Then Peter slammed into him. In a tangle of arms and legs, Timmy and Peter rolled across the ground. Timmy's back stopped them when it whammed a tree. A cry exploded from Timmy's mouth. A tingling ache moved down his back and into his legs before the pain crippled him.

Neither of them moved for several moments. With each inhale, Timmy's back stung him with hot pain. He wanted to push Peter off him, but moving felt like too much work. His arms wouldn't act right.

Why wasn't Peter doing anything? Was he hurt too?

As if to show Timmy he was wrong, Peter began to move. Not a lot, just a little twitch here and there for a bit. His arm lifted up and down, as if working the feeling back into it. Then Peter began to squirm his way out of Timmy's draping arms. Lying on his side, Timmy held up his hands, about to swing the knife Eddie had thrown him. His right was empty. Checking his left, he saw there wasn't a weapon there, either.

He groaned.

He was certain he'd grabbed the knife. He thought he'd just gotten the blade raised before Peter...

"Tim...Timmy?" Peter said in a choked voice.

Timmy moved his eyes to look at Peter.

But he saw the knife first. It stuck out from the center of his chest at angle, the sharp side slanted toward his heart.

It looked as if when Peter hit Timmy, the knife had stuck in deep, but not entirely through the heart.

It just nicked it...

But Peter was hurting. He lay on his back, arms splayed out, one knee pointed up, and the other leg stretched limply sideways.

Timmy turned onto his stomach with a wince. Using his elbows, he slowly dragged himself to where Peter lay. He gave another glance at the knife, noting the blood that had spattered its shiny surface looked like oil. From this position, he saw the blade had done more than nick Peter's heart. It had sliced into it.

Just not enough to...kill him.

"I'm..." Peter coughed up a wad of black phlegm. "Sorry, Timmy. I..." He blinked. The evil glow in his eyes sputtered like a dying bulb.

"Sorry?" Timmy said.

Peter attempted a nod, but only got his chin to move. "Yeah...so sorry...for not ripping out your throat sooner."

Timmy spotted Peter's sharp fingernails lurch. His beefy hand clasped Timmy's throat, shutting off his air. Timmy made quacking coughs as he tried to breathe. Slapping at Peter's hand, he couldn't get it to let go. He felt the points of Peter's nails digging into his skin.

Timmy dropped his hands away from Peter's and gripped the handle of the knife. Using all his weight, he threw himself on top of Peter. There was a deep crunch when the knife pushed into Peter's heart. The tip of the handle jabbed Timmy's midsection and sent hot, painful blasts through his insides. He slid sideways, landing on Peter's arm. He stayed there, as if they were cuddling lovers watching the pretty full moon in the sky.

The hot pain seizing his gut reminded him of how it felt to be kicked in the nuts. He couldn't move, so he was forced to watch up close as Peter's skin crackled and faded. The glowing light in his sockets faded to black.

When Peter looked like a sculpted replica of ash, Timmy began to cry.

-41-

Robin Hicks made a grab at Ed. Instead of snatching a chunk of armor, her fist closed on a bulb of garlic. Hissing, Robin snatched back her smoking hand. She held it close to her bare chest, shaking her charred fingers.

"That *hurt*!" she cried.

"Good," said Ed.

Robin's mouth widened. Screaming, she ran at him, but suddenly stopped. Looking past Ed, her eyes widened. "No!"

Though Ed knew he shouldn't have, he glanced over his shoulder. Before Robin jumped onto his back, he glimpsed Timmy straddling Peter and ramming Bernice's knife deep into the fat boy's chest.

Ed was smiling behind the tight mask when Robin's weight pounded his back. He let out a *"Nuh"* and stumbled forward. He couldn't feel the touch of Robin's naked skin on his back, but felt her thrashing weight as if he wore a thick coat while she tried to ride him. Her arms went under his chin and squeezed his throat.

Ed went down on one knee, dropping the crossbow. The landing jolted the trigger apparatus and launched the stake. It whacked his forearm, stabbing into Mary's flesh. He felt a quick stinging pain from the tip scraping him. If it weren't for the suit, the stake probably would've stabbed all the way through his arm. Now it dangled loosely from Mary's skin.

Robin squeezed harder, pressing the neck piece against his throat. Though it was too stiff for her to accurately strangle him, it was enough to make it even harder to breath.

Gotta get this crazy whore off me!

Ed made his rump buck, as if he truly were a mule.

A horse's ass is more like it!

He gave another hard buck.

Shrieking and thrusting on Ed's back, Robin held on. She even hooted, as if enjoying the ride. "That's it, baby!" Robin shrieked. "Make me bounce!"

And Ed did. On all fours, he crawled in circles, throwing his ass into the air. Robin stayed on his back, her arm bent over his throat. He thought he felt her swatting his ass as he made his way around. He pictured her on him, one arm high in the air, her breasts jiggling and swaying.

"Get 'er up!" Robin squeaked. "Whoo! Yeah!"

This time, he was certain she'd smacked his ass like a horse. Humiliation aside, Robin's crude gesture gave him an idea. He flung himself high into the air, like a horse about to make a heroic charge.

Since Robin was only holding on by the one arm, his sudden springing thrust threw her off his back. Spinning, Ed plucked the stake from his forearm, and threw himself toward Robin as her back hit the ground. The hit jolted her, made her breasts shake. Her eyes pinched shut, mouth dropped open to let out a quick grunt. He spotted the fangs, and knew she was definitely one of the vampire's minions.

Then he slammed the bone stake above the mound of her left breast. It punched in deep. Ed put a hand flat on the stake, then put the flat of his other hand on it and pushed the stake in deeper. As the stake plunged, Robin groaned as if straining to lift something heavy. Her skin became parched and colorless as Ed pushed the stake.

Her arms quavered stiffly. Her legs kicked. Her feet dug through the ground.

When the stake could go no deeper, Ed sat back. He looked down at the dead girl. She looked like something he'd find inside a casket. Her hair was like an old doll's, her skin the color of driftwood and the texture of seaweed.

He pushed himself up. Standing, he tried to catch his breath. The limited air holes made it difficult. He felt a tad light-headed. He turned around, walked over to the crossbow, bent down, and picked it up.

Timmy was standing beside him when he straightened. The boy's face was pale, but not because he'd been changed. He looked famished and appalled, gaping at what was left of Robin.

"You going to be okay?" Ed asked.

Timmy blinked. "Yeah."

"Did you like her?"

Another blink. "No. I loved her."

Nodding, Ed's suit squeaked. "I understand."

"Do you? Because I don't."

Ed sighed. "Honestly...I don't, either." He put his hand on Timmy's shoulder. The boy jerked as if waking from a bad dream. Ed figured he was, in a sense that was hard to explain.

Timmy looked at Ed, his head moving slowly down, then up. "That's really you under there?"

"It's really me."

Timmy nodded. "Yeah, sure."

"We're not done."

"I know."

Together, they turned and looked to where the bride had been put back down by Ed's stake. The vampire, on his knees, had his back to them. Leaning over the bride's shriveled carcass, he yanked the stake from her and quickly put it back in.

It did this over and over, oblivious to Ed's and Timmy's silent approach.

Watching the vampire's desperate, unsuccessful tries to revive its bride, made Ed sad. He felt a tinge of pity for the creature.

"You know it won't work," Ed said.

The vampire stabbed the bone stake back into the bride's chest. Instead of trying again, it let its hand hang by its side. *"I know."*

"She can't be awakened again until the next full moon."

"I know this as well."

"How do you know that, Eddie?" Timmy asked.

"Bernice told me."

"Nana?"

"I see the boy has no knowledge of his birthright."

"Not yet," Ed said. "But he will."

The vampire's shroud of hair moved in a nod. *"He and I will meet again."*

"No," said Ed. "It ends here."

"Does it?"

"Yes."

The vampire released a throaty chuckle that reminded Ed of stones rubbing together. *"A vampire defeated by a ghoul. Never would I have imagined such drivel."*

"You know one thing my worthless father taught me at a young age, something that I've grown to base my whole life around?"

"Yes?"

"Sometimes, shit happens."

The vampire chuckled again. *"That it does, Ghoul. That...it...does."*

Ed felt something hard slam into him. The crossbow went flying away from Ed's hand as his body went flying in another direction. The vampire's blue face shot toward his, shrouded inside the blurry darkness of its flapping hair. Cheeks trembling around its opened maw, shaking like the sails on a boat under heavy wind, its body pressed against his, its large hand gripped his throat, the talons stabbing through Mary's flesh to prick his own.

They weren't on the ground. Ed realized this from how everything zipped by on both sides of him before coming to a juddering halt when Ed's back banged against something sturdy that clanged like metal.

Not metal...silver.

He was against the silver enclosure. As he started to wonder how the vampire was able to step inside the clearing, smoke began swirling from the cuffs of its tattered sleeves. Ed heard sizzling sounds as more thick plumes rose from the vampire's wing-shaped collar. Gelatinous fluid oozed down the vampire's face.

It still can't be in here. It just doesn't care what happens to itself!

Clawing at Ed's throat, the vampire said, *"Before I go...I will see you die, Ghoul!"* Gooey chunks sloughed down its face, showing pieces of skull underneath.

Its melting fingers ripped the throat piece of Mary's skin away to expose Ed's neck. Then its claws peeled back, tearing off as if held on by liquid wax.

"I do not want your blood! I want your life!"

The vampire's chin cracked and crunched as it seemed to lower to the bottom of its throat. Smoke swirled from its cavernous mouth. A sulfur-like stench drifted out. Its jowls stretched until they ripped to unveil massive, glassine fangs.

It's going to bite my head clean off!

And there was nothing Ed could do to stop it. Pinned against the fence, he wasn't strong enough to fight the vampire off.

Roaring, the vampire came in for the bite.

Ed closed his eyes, primed for the pain.

-42-

The bite never came.

Or maybe it had been so quick, he hadn't noticed.

All he saw was darkness. But maybe that was all there was after you died—an empty void of dark.

But was there still pain? Ed hurt all over, and it felt as if he was being slowly crushed underneath a mighty weight.

Maybe there was pain where he'd gone. Mama had warned him since he was little, he would wind up in hell if he didn't repent.

I never repented. Never even prayed.

Maybe some weak, halfhearted prayers when he felt really desperate. Nothing major, unless he was asking for something.

So maybe there was pain where he'd gone. A lot of pain.

"Eddie?"

Timmy was here too? Poor kid. What'd he do to be sentenced to eternity in a blank abyss of pain?

Had the vampire dispatched Ed and then gone for the boy?

Seemed possible, though not likely.

Ed cracked an eye open.

Through thin layers of smoke, the vampire's teeth filled Ed's vision. Ed screamed. He squirmed and thrashed. He felt himself move.

Also felt hardness under his back. The ground.

Opening his other eye, Ed turned and looked. It *was* the ground. He was on it. Squirming and kicking, Ed tried to wiggle his way loose. Hands gripped his arm, and pulled. He was being held down. The vampire was holding on, not allowing him to get up.

"Help!" Ed cried.

"I am, if you'll let me!"

Timmy?

Ed eased off on his struggles, letting his tugged arm guide him. He moved to the right, then left, wiggled his hips. His chest came free. The pull on his arm stopped. A moment later, he felt his shoulders being pushed.

Don't push me back in!

He wasn't being pushed back toward the vampire. He was being pushed *up.*

Ed leaned forward. He sat there, arms limp, legs stretched and crushed under the vampire's sizzling body. Sticking up from the right side of its back was the blade of his broken shovel. A lot of smoke clung to its pointed tip, growing thicker as it poured from where the wood was imbedded in the vampire's coat.

And the shovel seemed to be growing.

Hollering, Ed kicked. The vampire tumbled sideways off his legs. Stabbed through its chest was the jagged tip of the handle.

Ed pulled his legs to his chest. Mary's skin showed restrain, as if it wanted to jerk Ed's legs straight. It made popping sounds while he hugged his knees.

"What the hell...?" he muttered.

"I killed it."

Ed looked up at Timmy. It was easy to do now, without the neck piece. Flaps of Mary's skin dangled under his jawline. "You?"

Timmy nodded. He showed no hint of pride for what he'd done. "Yeah."

"With my shovel?"

Another nod. "Yeah. Got him from behind. He was about to bite you, Eddie. So I..." Timmy's lips quivered. He took a deep, trembling breath. The boy was about to cry. "I stopped him."

"Thank you."

Timmy nodded. "Yeah, well...it had to be done."

"Thank you...again."

"Yeah. It's hard to look at you with...that stuff on you."

Ed reached up, and gripped Mary's hair. It felt as if it might rip his face off as he pulled the mask back. Finally, it came free with a sticky pop. He let it hang behind his back, where it was stitched on. "Better?" he asked, winded. He took a deep breath. Though it smelled like old feet cooking over a fire of shit, he smiled.

"Not really."

Ed looked down at his suit. "Can't take this stuff off." He patted the stomach appliance.

"Why not?"

"Not wearing anything under it."

At first, Timmy frowned. Then his shoulders jerked. Ed thought he was about to let out his cry, but the boy began to laugh.

Ed joined him.

And it felt good.

-43-

Timmy helped Ed load the bodies in the back of his truck. Then, working as a team, they reburied the bride. Finished with that, they walked through the cemetery, and filled in all the graves Ed had dug up for the vampire. Ed demanded that Timmy be careful while he worked, since he was down to three shovels. With the others broken, his supply was very limited.

Timmy promised he would be.

It didn't take nearly as long with the both of them working as it would have had Ed been alone. He was glad to have Timmy's help.

There was no reason why they recovered the graves, but somehow both seemed to know it needed to be done.

After that, they drove over to the church and filled those in as well. Neither of them spoke while they worked. Ed didn't explain anything, and Timmy never asked any questions.

Their final stop was the small graveyard back in the woods, the site of where this macabre ordeal began. There, they returned the vampire to its grave. Before filling in the dirt, Ed shoved his hand into the vampire's chest and pulled out its heart.

"Why'd you do that?" Timmy asked.

"So nobody can make this mistake again."

Timmy was quiet for a moment, then nodded. "What are you going to do with it?"

"Keep it."

"Then take this too," said Timmy, tugging something out of his pocket. He tossed it.

The small object smacked Ed's chest. Bringing his arm up, he opened his hand. The shrunken head he'd given to Timmy landed in his palm. "You…don't want it?"

Shaking his head, Timmy looked at Ed. The boy's eyes were grim. "I don't want anything that'll remind of this night."

Frowning, Ed dropped the head in the grave. It bounced off the vampire's chin, rolled, and came to a stop against the stake. He understood why Timmy would want to bury the trinket, just as the boy probably wanted to bury the memory. But Ed still felt sad that Timmy gave it back. It had been a present, for luck.

Brought the boy no luck at all.

He thought he remembered Bernice telling him something about shrunken heads welcoming evil. If that was true, then he'd doomed Timmy from the start by giving it to him.

"Let's get started," Ed said.

Neither spoke while they piled the dirt back in.

Together, they dug three fresh holes where Ed had found the original corpses. Ed made Timmy wait in the truck while he handled the task of burying Peter and Robin by himself. Before putting them in the ground, he laid the kids on their backs. Then he put the blade of his shovel to their necks, and stomped it down with his boot.

Their heads tumbled away from their necks.

Just as he'd found the others, he put the bodies in the ground, placing their heads between their legs. He gave each body an equal amount of garlic from Bernice's wreath. When he finished, a vacant string dangled around his neck.

The Vampire of Plainfield

By the time they reached Ed's house, the dark sky was cracking with sunlight.

Neither of them washed up, but Ed did excuse himself to peel off Mary's flesh. He put on some clothes, and though they weren't clean, they felt much lighter on him. His skin was able to breathe again.

In the living room, they waited for Bernice to wake up.

And she did before the sun had fully burned away the night. Since he didn't have an icebox, Ed soaked rags in cold creek water, letting Bernice press them against the hardened lump jutting from her temple. Though she was battered, she seemed okay.

Ed sat in silence while Bernice explained everything to Timmy. She went into every detail, leaving nothing out, sharing much more than what she'd told Ed before.

The boy barely reacted to any of the information, and Ed could tell this bothered Bernice. It bothered Ed, as well. He figured the boy was having trouble absorbing everything he'd witnessed, and what he'd been told. Too much all at once. Plus, the boy had survived hell.

And he was...just a boy.

Ed thought Timmy was handling everything just fine. He'd be okay. So long as his parents didn't ring his neck for being gone all night.

Timmy left with Bernice shortly after nine in the morning.

Ed entered the kitchen, found a paper bag, and put the vampire's heart inside. Then he rolled the bag up, tossing it into a box on his way out of the kitchen.

He went to his bedroom and collapsed on the bed.

Ed was asleep within seconds.

-44-

Ed strained to open the window in the living room. Grunting, he tugged at the base until it popped loose. The window flew up, banging inside the frame. The night's mild air drifted inside. It smelled fresh, like springtime. Crickets chirped, frogs croaked. Together, they made a calming melody that Ed enjoyed.

He took a deep whiff, and sighed. Already, the stuffiness of the room began to thin.

Walking over to his favorite chair, Ed sat down, letting his body relax. His achy muscles tingled with relief. He felt cozy and tired in the soft cushions hugging him like fluffy arms.

Moaning, Ed kicked off his boots.

It'd been a long day.

He'd tilled the ground for Bernice's garden. They'd spent the rest of the day making hills and planting seed. It had taken till suppertime for them to finish. At least Bernice had fed him afterward.

He wished Timmy could have been there, but the boy was still grounded.

"Better grounded than dead," Bernice had said.

Her idea that they should go along with Tom Worden's wild animal theory had paid off. She'd convinced Timmy to go home and say he and Robin were attacked by some kind of monster. He wouldn't be lying to his parents, but she knew nobody would believe him. They'd assume he was in shock, and had mistaken some kind of animal for a monster.

Neither Ed nor Bernice had expected somebody would actually shoot a bear a few days later. Since there had been no other disappearances, the bear was blamed for the deaths of Dorothy Clark's parents and the missing kids.

But that didn't explain the mutilated cattle, and the disappearing dogs. Or the strange footprints that kept popping up in the fields strewn with the body parts of dead cattle.

Worden believed they had wolves coming in from the deeper parts of the woods, looking for food. Now the farmers watched their livestock around the clock, rifles ready to fire.

People figured Mary Hogan had run off with some scoundrel she'd met at the tavern. Ed doubted Tom Worden was looking too deeply into it, because of the relationship he'd had with Mary. Probably, most of the men in town were glad she was gone. The women, too.

When Timmy came home from the hospital, and was able to sleep in his own bed again, Tom and Barbara Worden informed him it was all he'd be doing for a month. Didn't matter what he'd been through, he'd lived to see his punishment, so he would get it. He bet Timmy was somewhat relieved to be prisoned to his room for a while. It gave the boy plenty of time to fiddle around with his stories.

And Ed doubted Timmy was in any kind of hurry to see Ed, maybe not ever again. Bernice also acted as if things had changed between them. Ed thought the vampire ordeal would have brought them all closer together, but instead, the aftermath put up some kind of invisible barrier between them all. He hated it. But he also figured he deserved it. He'd been the one who caused everybody so much pain, so maybe he was being punished for it.

Ed grabbed his pipe and book from the end table beside the chair. He checked the bowl to make sure it had tobacco in it, then lighted it. He took several puffs before putting the pipe back on the table.

He found the page in the book he'd dog-eared, then folded it back. He didn't like that the page now had a crease in the upper corner, but it couldn't be avoided. This was another book he'd ordered from the back of a crime magazine. Written by Henry Cartwright, the book was thick as the bible and covered a wide array of monster information. Ed thought it might be a good idea to read something that offered insight on monsters of all sorts. The mailman delivered it yesterday, and he was already almost finished.

Maybe when he was done with the book, he'd venture out to a cemetery. Just to look around. He hadn't dug up anything in almost a month.

The idea sounded just fine to Ed.

As he began to read, a high-pitched, raucous howl resonated from somewhere in the distance. Ed jumped to his feet, dropping the book. It stayed open to his page when it hit the floor. Looking down, he stared at the artist's illustration of a large wolf, walking on its hind legs. A small child was clamped in its mouth, arms and legs dangling.

The chapter's heading said—*Werewolves!*

He looked back to the window.

Another howl tore through the night, and made Ed flinch.

He walked on legs that felt frail and puny to the window. Bending over, he put his hands flat on the sill and leaned out. The crickets and frogs had gone quiet. The howl had sent them into hiding.

Ed twisted his neck so he could look up at the sky. His mouth went dry as a handful of sand. His back felt cold and tight.

The moon was full.

He heard the howl again and shoved away from the windowsill. The back of his head bonked the bottom of the window, but he ignored the pain and stumbled back. Though the howl had sounded as if it had come from the hills, he stared at the open window as if a wolf might lunge through.

He looked down at his opened book, at the scary drawing of the child-eating wolf.

It can't be.

But living in Plainfield, Wisconsin, Ed had heard plenty of wolves howling at night. Tom Worden hadn't sounded out of his mind when he suggested wolves had come in to find more food. Things like that happened every so often.

But no wolf Ed had ever heard sounded as menacing and...evil as this one.

Ed returned to the window, and pulled it down. Then he closed the curtains.

He picked up his book on the way back to his chair, then sat down.

And began to read.

Somehow, he knew he would need to learn as much as he could about werewolves.

About the Author

Kristopher Rufty is the author of several books, including *Jagger, The Skin Show, Proud Parents, The Lurkers*, and *Bigfoot Beach*. He has also written and directed the independent horror films *Psycho Holocaust* and *Rags*. But what he's best at is being married to his high school sweetheart and the father of three amazing children. Together, they reside in North Carolina with their giant dog and numerous cats.

For more about Kristopher Rufty, please visit his Website www.lastkristontheleft.blogspot.com

He can be found on Facebook and Twitter as well.

Enjoy this book?

Try other books by

Sinister Grin Press

Jackpot by Shane McKenzie, David Bernstein, Adam Cesare and Kristopher Rufty

Jagger by Kristopher Rufty

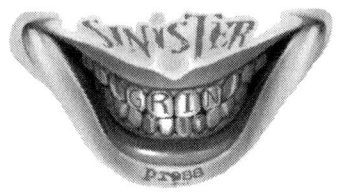

Coming Soon

Fort by **Mark Allen Gunnells**

Relic of Death by **David Bernstein**

Gardens of Babylon by **Sara Brooke**

Find these and other horrific books at sinistergrinpress.com

Made in the USA
San Bernardino, CA
02 January 2016